The Killing

BOOK 1
PARTS 1–6

David Hewson

Based on the BAFTA
Award-Winning TV Series
Written by Søren Sveistrup

W F HOWES LTD

This large print edition published in 2012 by
W F Howes Ltd
Unit 4, Rearsby Business Park, Gaddesby Lane,
Rearsby, Leicester LE7 4YH

1 3 5 7 9 10 8 6 4 2

First published in the United Kingdom in 2012
by Macmillan

Based on Søren Sveistrup's *Forbrydelsen* (*The Killing*) – an
original Danish Broadcasting Corporation TV series co-written
by Torleif Hoppe, Michael W. Horsten and Per Daumiller

The right of David Hewson to be identified as
the author of this work has been asserted by him
in accordance with the Copyright, Designs and
Patents Act, 1988.

A CIP catalogue record for this book is available
from the British Library

ISBN 978 1 47120 606 1

Typeset by Palimpsest Book Production Limited,
Falkirk, Stirlingshire
Printed and bound in Great Britain
by MPG Books Ltd, Bodmin, Cornwall

MIX
Paper from
responsible sources
FSC
www.fsc.org
FSC® C018575

Non nobis solum nati sumus.
We are not born for ourselves alone.

Cicero, *De Officiis* (Book I, sec. 22)

PRINCIPAL CHARACTERS

Copenhagen Police
Sarah Lund – *Vicekriminalkommissær, Homicide*
Jan Meyer – *Vicekriminalkommissær, Homicide*
Hans Buchard – *Chief Inspector, Homicide*
Lennart Brix – *Deputy/Acting Chief, Homicide*
Svendsen – *Detective, Homicide*
Jansen – *Forensic Officer*
Bülow – *Investigations Officer*

Birk Larsen family
Theis Birk Larsen – *father*
Pernille Birk Larsen – *mother*
Nanna Birk Larsen – *Theis and Pernille's daughter*
Anton Birk Larsen – *Theis and Pernille's son*
Emil Birk Larsen – *Theis and Pernille's son*
Lotte Holst – *Pernille's younger sister*

Rådhus (City Hall) politicians and employees
Troels Hartmann – *leader of the Liberal Group and Mayor of Education*
Rie Skovgaard – *Hartmann's political adviser*
Morten Weber – *Hartmann's campaign manager*
Poul Bremer – *Lord Mayor of Copenhagen*

Kirsten Eller – *Leader of the Centre Group*
Jens Holck – *Leader of the Moderate Group*
Mai Juhl – *Leader of the Environment Party Group*
Knud Padde – *chair of the Liberal Group*
Henrik Bigum – *committee member of the Liberal Group*
Olav Christensen – *a civil servant in the Education Department*
Gert Stokke – *a civil servant heading Holck's Environment Department*

Frederiksholm High School
Oliver Schandorff – *a pupil, Nanna's former boyfriend*
Jeppe Hald – *a pupil*
Lisa Rasmussen – *a pupil*
Rektor Koch – *the headmistress*
Rahman Al Kemal – *a teacher, popularly known as Rama*
Henning Kofoed – *a teacher*

Others
Hanne Meyer – *Jan Meyer's wife*
Carsten – *Lund's former husband*
Bengt Rosling – *a criminal psychologist, Lund's current boyfriend*
Mark – *Lund's son*
Vagn Skærbæk – *Birk Larsen family friend and long-term employee*
Leon Frevert – *taxi driver and part-time Birk Larsen employee*
Amir El' Namen – *son of an Indian restaurant owner, Nanna's childhood friend*
John Lynge – *a driver for Troels Hartmann*

CHAPTER 1

Friday, 31st October

Through the dark wood where the dead trees give no shelter Nanna Birk Larsen runs.

Nineteen, breathless, shivering in her skimpy torn slip, bare feet stumbling in the clinging mud.

Cruel roots snag her ankles, snarling branches tear her pale and flailing arms. She falls, she clambers, she struggles out of vile dank gullies, trying to still her chattering teeth, to think, to hope, to hide.

There is a bright monocular eye that follows, like a hunter after a wounded deer. It moves in a slow approaching zigzag, marching through the Pinseskoven wasteland, through the Pentecost Forest.

Bare silver trunks rise from barren soil like limbs of ancient corpses frozen in their final throes.

Another fall, the worst. The ground beneath her vanishes and with it her legs. Hands windmilling, crying out in pain and despair, the girl crashes into the filthy, ice-cold ditch, collides with rocks and logs, paddles through sharp and cutting gravel, feels her head and hands, her elbows, her knees, graze the hard invisible terrain that lurks below.

The chill water, the fear, his presence not so far away . . .

She staggers, gasping, out of the mire, clambers up the bank, splays her naked, torn and bleeding feet against the swampy ground to gain some purchase from the sludge between her toes.

At the ridge ahead she finds a tree. Some last few leaves of autumn brush against her face. The trunk is larger than its peers and as her arms fall round it she thinks of Theis her father, a giant of a man, silent, morose, a staunch and stoic bulwark against the world outside.

She grips the tree, clutches at it as once she clutched him. His strength with hers, hers with his. Nothing more was ever needed, ever would be.

From the limitless sky falls a low-pitched whine. The bright, all-seeing lights of a jet escaping the bounds of gravity, fleeing Kastrup, fleeing Denmark. Its fugitive presence dazzles and blinds. In the unforgiving brilliance Nanna Birk Larsen's fingers stray to her face. Feel the wound running from her left eye to her cheek, vicious, open, bleeding.

She can smell him, feel him. On her. In her.

Through all the pain, amidst the fear, rises a hot and sudden flame of fury.

You're Theis Birk Larsen's daughter.

They all said that when she gave them reason.

You're Nanna Birk Larsen, Theis's child, Pernille's

too, and you shall escape the monster in the night, chasing through the Pentecost Forest on the fringes of the city where, a few long miles away, lies that warm safe place called home.

She stands and grips the trunk as once she gripped her father, arms round the splintering silver bark, shiny slip stained with dirt and blood, shivering, quiet, convincing herself salvation lies ahead, beyond the dark wood and the dead trees that give no shelter.

A white beam ranges over her again. It is not the flood of illumination falling from the belly of a plane that flies above this wasteland like a vast mechanical angel idly looking for a stray lost soul to save.

Run, Nanna, run, a voice cries.

Run, Nanna, run, she thinks.

There is one torchlight on her now, the single blazing eye. And it is here.

CHAPTER 2

Monday, 3rd November

'Around the back,' the cop said. 'Some homeless guy found her.'

Seven thirty in the morning. Still dark with the rain coming down in straight and icy lines. Vicekriminalkommissær Sarah Lund stood in the lee of the dirty brick building near the docks, watching the uniform men lay out the Don't Cross lines.

The last crime scene she'd ever see in Copenhagen. It had to be a murder. A woman too.

'The building's empty. We're checking the block of flats opposite.'

'How old is she?' Lund asked.

The cop, a man she barely knew, shrugged his shoulders then wiped the rain from his face with his arm.

'Why'd you ask?'

A nightmare she wanted to say. One that woke her at six thirty that morning, screaming bolt upright in an empty bed. When she got up Bengt, kind, thoughtful, calm Bengt, was padding round the place finishing the packing. Mark, her son, lay

4

fast asleep in front of the TV in his room, didn't even stir when, very quietly, she peeked in. That night the three of them would catch the flight to Stockholm. A new life in another country. Corners turned. Bridges burned.

Sarah Lund was thirty-eight, a serious woman, staring endlessly at the world around her, never once herself. She was starting her final day in the Copenhagen police. Women like her didn't have nightmares, terrors in the dark, fleeting glimpses of a frightened young face that might, once upon a time, have been hers.

They were fantasies for others.

'No need for an answer,' the cop said, scowling at her silence as he lifted up the tape and walked her to the sliding metal door. 'I'll tell you something. I've never seen one like this.'

He passed her a pair of blue forensic gloves, watched as she put them on, then put his shoulder to the rusting metal. It opened squealing like a tortured cat.

'I'll be with you in a minute,' he said.

She didn't wait, just walked ahead the way she always did, alone, staring, this way then that, bright eyes wide open, always looking.

For some reason he rolled the sliding door shut the moment she was inside, so rapidly the cat squealed an octave higher than before. Then fell silent with the metallic clatter of the heavy iron slamming out the grey day behind.

★　★　★

Ahead lay a central corridor and a chamber like a meat store hung with hooks at intervals along the rafters. A single set of bulbs in the ceiling.

The concrete floor was damp and shining. Something moved in the shadows at the end, swinging slowly like a gigantic pendulum.

There was the clatter of an unseen switch and then the place was as dark as the bedroom that morning when a savage unwanted dream shook her awake.

'Lights!' Lund called.

Her voice echoed round the black and empty belly of the building.

'Lights, please.'

Not a sound. She was an experienced cop, remembered everything she was supposed to carry, except for the gun which always seemed an afterthought.

She had the torch though, safe in her right pocket, took it out and held it the way cops did: right hand upright, wrist cocked back, beam ahead, searching, peering into places others didn't look.

The light and Lund went hunting. Blankets, discarded clothes, two crushed Coke cans, an empty packet of condoms.

Three steps and then she stopped. By the right wall, visible at the point it met the floor was a puddle of liquid, scarlet and sticky, two horizontal lines along the peeling plaster, the way blood smeared when a body was dragged along the floor.

Lund reached into her pocket, took out the packet of nicotine gum, popped a piece in her mouth.

It wasn't just Copenhagen getting left behind. Tobacco was on the hit list too.

She bent down and placed a blue gloved finger in the sticky puddle, lifted it to her nose and sniffed.

Three more steps and she came upon a woodman's axe, the handle clean and shiny as if it had been bought from a store the day before. She placed two fingers in the pool of red liquid that ran around the blade, tested it, sniffed and thought.

She'd never learn to like the taste of Nicotinell. Lund walked on.

The thing ahead was getting clearer. It swung from side to side. An industrial tarpaulin so smeared with red it looked like the shroud of a slaughtered beast.

What lay inside had a familiar, human shape.

Lund changed the position of the torch, held it close to her waist, beam upwards, checking the fabric, looking for something to grip.

The material came away in one swift movement and what lay beneath swung slowly in the beam. The frozen face the light caught was male, mouth open in a perpetual O. Black hair, pink flesh, a monstrous plastic penis erect and winking. And over its head a vivid blue Viking helmet with silver horns and gold braids running down.

Lund cocked her head and, for their sake, smiled.

Tied to the chest of the sex toy was a notice: *Thanks boss, for seven great years. The boys.*

Laughter from the shadows.

The boys.

7

A good prank. Though they might have got real blood.

The Politigården was a grey labyrinth on reclaimed land near the waterfront. Bleak and square on the outside, the interior of the police headquarters opened up to a round courtyard. Classical pillars stood in a shadowy arcade around the edge. Inside spiral staircases led to winding corridors lined with striated black marble running round the perfect circle like calcified veins. It had taken her three months to find her way around this dark and maze-like complex. Even now, sometimes, she had to think hard to work out where she was.

Homicide was on the second floor, north-east. She was in Buchard's room, wearing the Viking helmet, listening to their jokes, opening their presents, smiling, keeping quiet beneath the cardboard horns and the golden braids.

Then she thanked them and went to her office, began to clear her belongings. No time for fuss. She smiled at the photo of Mark she kept in a frame on the desk. Three years before, back when he was nine, long before he came home with the ridiculous earring. Before – just – the divorce. Then along came Bengt to tempt her to Sweden and a life across the bleak, cold waters of the Øresund.

Young Mark, unsmiling then as now. That would change in Sweden. Along with everything else.

Lund swept the rest of the desk, her three-month supply of Nicotinell, the pens, the pencil sharpener in the shape of a London bus, into a flimsy card-board box then placed the photo of Mark on top.

The door opened and a man walked in.

She looked, she judged, the way she always did. A cigarette hung from the corner of his mouth. His hair was short, his face severe. Big eyes, big ears. Clothes cheap and a little too young for a man who wasn't far off her own age. He was carrying a box much like hers. She could see a map of Copenhagen, a kid's basketball net for the wall, a toy police car and a pair of headphones.

'I'm looking for Lund's office,' he said, staring at the Viking helmet perched on the new pair of skis they'd given her at breakfast.

'That's me.'

'Jan Meyer. Is that uniform around here?'

'I'm going to Sweden.'

Lund picked up her belongings and the two of them did a little dance around each other as she struggled to the door.

'For the love of God . . . why?' Meyer asked.

She put down the box, swept back her long brown wayward hair, tried to think if there was anything left that mattered.

He took out the basketball net, looked at the wall.

'My sister did something like that,' Meyer said.

'Like what?'

'Couldn't keep her life in one piece here so she moved to Bornholm with a guy.' Meyer stuck the net above the filing cabinets. 'Nice guy. Didn't work.'

Lund got sick of her hair, pulled an elastic band from her pocket and tied it in a ponytail.

'Why not?'

'Too remote. They went mad listening to cows fart all day long.' He took out a pewter beer tankard and turned it in his hands. 'Where are you going?'

'Sigtuna.'

Meyer stood stock still and stared at her in silence.

'It's very remote too,' Lund added.

He took a long draw on his cigarette and pulled a small child's football out of the box. Then he put the toy police car on the desk and started running it up and down. When the wheels moved the blue light burst into life and a tiny siren wailed.

He was still playing with it when Buchard walked in, a piece of paper in his hand.

'You've met,' the chief said. It wasn't a question.

The bespectacled uncle figure she'd sat next to at breakfast had vanished.

'We had the pleasure—' Lund began.

'This just came in.' Buchard handed her the report slip. 'If you're too busy clearing up . . .'

'I've got time,' Lund told him. 'All day . . .'

'Good,' Buchard said. 'Why not take Meyer with you?'

The man with the box stubbed out his cigarette and shrugged.

'He's unpacking,' Lund said.

Meyer let go of the car, picked up the football and bounced it in his hand.

He grinned. Looked different, more human, more rounded that way.

'Never too busy for work.'

'A good start,' Buchard said. There was an edge to his voice. 'I'd like that, Meyer, and so would you.'

Window down, looking round from the passenger seat, Lund scanned the Kalvebod Fælled. Thirteen kilometres south of the city, near the water. It was a bright clear morning after a couple of days of rain. Probably wouldn't stay fine for long. Flat marshland, yellow grass and ditches, stretched to the horizon, with a bare dark wood to the right. Faint smell of sea, closer stink of dank decaying vegetation. Moisture in the air, not far from freezing. A hard cold winter stirring.

'You can't carry a gun? You can't make arrests? What about parking tickets?'

An early morning dog walker had found some girl's clothes on wasteland near a patch of silver birch woodland known as the Pinseskoven. The Pentecost Forest.

'You've got to be Swedish to arrest people. It's a . . .' Lund wished she'd never answered his questions. 'It's how it works.'

Meyer shoved a handful of potato crisps into his mouth then balled the bag into the footwell. He drove like a teenager, too fast, with little thought for others.

'What does your boy think?'

She got out, didn't check to see him follow.

There was a plain-clothes detective by the find, a uniform man wandering through the hummocks of grass, kicking at the dying clumps. This was all they had: a flowery cotton top, the kind a teenager might wear. A card for a video rental store. Both inside plastic evidence bags. The top had blood-stains on it.

Lund turned three hundred and sixty degrees, her large and lustrous eyes looking for something the way they always did.

'Who comes here?' she asked the uniform man.

'During the day nursery school kids on nature trips. At night hookers from the city.'

'Some place to turn a trick,' Meyer said. 'Where's the romance these days? I ask you.'

Lund was still going round slowly on her heels.

'When was this stuff left here?'

'Yesterday. Not Friday. There was a school trip then. They'd have seen it.'

'No calls? No hospital reports?'

'Nothing.'

'No idea who she is?'

He showed her the bag with the top.

'Size eight,' the detective said. 'That's all we know.'

It looked cheap, the flowers so garish and child-like they might be ironic. A teenager's joke: childish and sexy too.

Lund got the second bag and examined the video rental card.

It had a name: Theis Birk Larsen.

12

'We found that near the track,' the cop added. 'The top here. Maybe they had a fight and he threw her out of the car. And then . . .'

'And then,' Meyer said, 'she found her shoes and coat and purse and pack of condoms and walked all the way home to watch TV.'

Lund found she couldn't stop looking at the woods.

'You want me to talk to this Birk Larsen guy?' the uniform asked.

'Do that,' she said and glanced at her watch.

Eight hours and it was over. Copenhagen and the life that went before.

Meyer came round and she found herself swamped in smoke.

'We can talk to him, Lund. Leaving a hooker out here. Beating her up. My kind of customer.'

'Well it's not our kind of work.'

The cigarette went into the nearest ditch.

'I know. I just . . .' A pack of gum came out of his pocket. This man seemed to live on crisps and sweets and cigarettes. 'I just want to have a little talk with him.'

'About what? There's no case. The hooker never complained.'

Meyer leaned forward and spoke to her the way a teacher might address a child.

'I'm good at talking.'

He had prominent, almost comical ears and a good day's stubble. He'd do well undercover, she thought. And maybe had. She remembered the

way Buchard spoke to him. Street thug. Cop.
Meyer could play either.

'I said . . .'

'You should see me, Lund. Truly. Before you go.
My gift to the Swedes.'

He took the card from her fingers. Read it.

'Theis Birk Larsen.'

Sarah Lund turned one more circle and took in
the yellow grass, the ditches and the woods.

'I'll drive,' she said.

Pernille perched above his big chest laughing
like a child.

Half-dressed on the kitchen floor in the middle
of a working morning. That was Theis's idea, like
most things.

'Get dressed,' she ordered and rolled off him,
rose to her feet. 'Go to work, you beast.'

He grinned like the tearaway teenager she still
remembered. Then climbed back into his bright-
red bib overalls. Forty-four, ginger hair turning
grey, mutton-chop sideburns reaching down to his
broad chin, face ready to switch from hot to cold
then back to its usual immobile in an instant.

Pernille was one year younger, a busy woman,
still in shape after three children, enough to catch
his eye as easily as she had twenty years before
when they first met.

She watched him clamber into his heavy uniform
then looked around the little apartment.

Nanna had been in her belly when they moved

14

to Vesterbro. In her belly when they married. Here, in this bright, colourful room, pot plants in the window, photographs on the wall, full of the mess of family life, they raised her. From squawking baby to beautiful teen, joined, after too long an interval, by Emil and Anton, now seven and six.

Their quarters stood above the busy depot of the Birk Larsen transport company. The place downstairs was more ordered than the cramped rooms in which they lived, five of them, forever in each other's way. A jumbled mess of mementoes, drawings, toys and clutter.

Pernille looked at the herbs on the window, the way the green light shone through them.

Full of life.

'Nanna's going to need an apartment soon,' she said, straightening her long chestnut hair. 'We can put down a deposit, can't we?'

He grunted with laughter.

'You choose your moments. She can choose hers. Let Nanna finish school first.'

'Theis . . .'

She wound herself back into his burly arms, looked into his face. Some people were scared of Theis Birk Larsen. Not her.

'Maybe it won't be needed,' he said.

His rough face creased in a crafty, teasing grin.

'Why?'

'Secret.'

'Tell me!' Pernille cried and punched his chest with her clenched fist.

15

'Then it wouldn't be a secret.'

He walked down the stairs into the depot. She followed.

Trucks and men, pallets and shrink-wrapped goods, inventory lists and timetables.

The floorboards always creaked. Maybe she'd cried out. They'd heard. She could see it in their grinning faces. Vagn Skærbæk, Theis's oldest friend, who pre-dated even her, tipped an imaginary hat.

'Tell me!' she ordered, taking his old black leather coat from the hook.

Birk Larsen put on the jacket, pulled out the familiar black woollen cap, set it on his head. Red on the inside, black on the out. He seemed to live inside this uniform. It made him look like a truculent red-chested bull seal, happy with his territory, ready to fight off all intruders.

A glance at the clipboard, a tick against a destination, then he called Vagn Skærbæk to the nearest van. Scarlet too, and like the uniforms it had the name Birk Larsen on the side. Like the red Christiania tricycle with the box on it that Skærbæk kept running eighteen years after they bought it to ferry Nanna round the city.

Birk Larsen. Patriarch of a modest, happy dynasty. King of his small quarter in Vesterbro.

One clap of his giant hands, barked orders. Then he left.

Pernille Birk Larsen stood there till the men went back to work. There was a tax return to finish. Money to be paid and that was never welcome.

Money to be hidden too. No one gave the government everything if they could help it.

We need no more secrets, Theis, she thought.

Beneath Absalon's golden statue, beneath the bell-tower turret and castellated roofline, against the red-brick, turreted fortress that was the Rådhus, Copenhagen City Hall, stood three posters.

Kirsten Eller, Troels Hartmann, Poul Bremer. Smiling as only politicians can.

Eller, the woman, thin lips tight together in something close to a smirk. The Centre Party, forever stuck in a philosophical no man's land, hoping to cling to one side or the other then catch the crumbs that slip from the master's table.

Below her Poul Bremer beamed out at the city he owned. Lord Mayor of Copenhagen for twelve years, a plump and comfortable statesman, close to the Parliamentarians who held the purse strings, attuned to the fickle opinions of his shiftless party troops, familiar with the scattered network of backers and supporters who followed his every word. Black jacket, white shirt, subtle grey silk tie, businesslike black spectacles, Bremer at sixty-five wore the friendly disposition of everyone's favourite uncle, the generous bringer of gifts and favours, the clever relative with all the secrets, all the knowledge.

Then Troels Hartmann.

The young one. The handsome one. The politician women looked at and secretly admired.

He wore the Liberal colours. Blue suit, blue shirt,

17

open at the neck. Hartmann, forty-two, boyish with his Nordic good looks, though in his clear cobalt eyes a hint of pain escaped the photographer's lens. A good man, the picture said. A new generation vigorously chasing out the old, bringing with it fresh ideas, the promise of change. Part way there since, thanks to the voting system, he ran with energy and vision the city's Education Department. Mayor already, if only of its schools and colleges.

Three politicians about to fight each other for the crown of Copenhagen, the capital city, a sprawling metropolis where more than a fifth of Denmark's five and a half million natives lived and worked, bickered and fought. Young and old, Danish-born and recent, sometimes half-welcome, immigrant. Honest and diligent, idle and corrupt. A city like any other.

Eller the outsider whose only chance was to cut the best deal she could. Hartmann young, idealistic. Naive his foes would say, bravely hoping to knock Poul Bremer, the grandee of city politics, from the perch the old man called his own.

In the chill November afternoon their faces beamed at the camera, for the press, for the people in the street. Past the smoke-stained ornamental windows of the red-brick castle called the Rådhus, in the galleried corridors and cell-like chambers where politicians gathered to whisper and plot, life was different.

Behind the fixed and artificial smiles a war was under way.

★   ★   ★

Shining wood. Long slender leaded windows. Leather furniture. Gilt and mosaics and paintings. The smell of polished mahogany.

Posters of Hartmann stood everywhere, leaning against walls, ready to go out to the city. On the desk, in a wooden frame, a portrait of his wife on her hospital bed, placid, brave and beautiful a month before she died. Next to it a photograph of John F. Kennedy and a doe-eyed Jackie in the White House. A band played in the background admiring them. She was smiling in a beautiful silk evening dress. Kennedy was talking to her, saying something private in her ear.

The White House, days before Dallas.

In his private office Troels Hartmann looked at the photos, then the desk calendar.

Monday morning. Three of the longest weeks of his political life ahead. The first of an endless succession of meetings.

Hartmann's two closest aides sat on the other side of the desk, laptops before them, going through the day's agenda. Morten Weber, campaign manager, friend since college. Committed, quiet, solitary, intense. Forty-four, unruly curly hair beneath a growing bald patch, a kind, intense and neglected face, roving eyes behind cheap gold-rimmed glasses. Never knew what he looked like or cared. For the last week he'd seemed to live in the same shabby creased jacket that didn't match his trousers. Happiest in the minutiae of committee paper and cutting deals in smoke-filled rooms.

Sometimes he'd roll his office chair away from the table, propel himself into a quiet corner, take out his needle and insulin, pull his shirt from his waistband and jab a shot into his flabby white belly. Then slide back into the argument, tucking himself back in without losing a single thread.

Rie Skovgaard, the political adviser, always pretended not to notice.

Hartmann's mind wandered from Weber's tally of the appointments. He found himself torn from the world of politics for a moment. Thirty-two, angular, intense face, attractive more than beautiful. Combative, strident, always elegant. Today she wore a tightly cut green suit. Expensive. Her dark hair she seemed to take from that photo on Hartmann's desk. Jackie Kennedy around 1963, long and curving into her slender neck, seemingly casual though not a strand was ever out of place.

The 'presidential-funeral cut' Weber called it, but only behind her back. Rie Skovgaard hadn't looked that way when she arrived.

Morten Weber was the son of a schoolteacher from Aarhus. Skovgaard came with better connections. Her father was an influential backbench MP. Before she moved to the Liberals she was an account executive with the Copenhagen office of a New York-based advertising agency. Now she pitched him, his image, his ideas, much the way she once sold life insurance and supermarket chains.

An unlikely team, awkward sometimes. Did she

20

envy Weber? The fact that he preceded her by two decades, working his way up the Liberal Party secretariat, the backroom man while Hartmann's handsome smile and fetching ways brought in the publicity and votes?

Rie Skovgaard was a newcomer, scenting opportunity, bored by ideology.

'The debate this lunchtime. We need posters at the school,' she said in a calm, clear professional voice. 'We need—'

'It's done,' Weber replied, waving his fingers at the computer.

It was a dull day. Rain and cloud. The office gave out onto the front of the Palace Hotel. At night its blue neon sign cast an odd light on the room.

'I sent a car out there first thing.'

She folded her skinny arms.

'You think of everything, Morten.'

'I need to.'

'What's that supposed to mean?'

'Bremer.' Weber muttered the name as if it were an expletive. 'He didn't own this city by accident.'

Hartmann came back to the conversation.

'He won't own it for much longer.'

'Did you see the latest poll numbers?' Skovgaard asked.

'They look good,' Hartmann answered with a nod. 'Better than we hoped for.'

Morten Weber shook his head.

'Bremer's seen them too. He won't sit on his comfy arse and let his kingdom slip through his fingers.

This debate at lunchtime, Troels. It's a school. Home ground. The media will be there.'

'Talk education,' Skovgaard cut in. 'We've asked for extra funds to put in more computers. Better access to the net. Bremer blocked the allocation. Now absenteeism's up twenty per cent. We can throw that at him . . .'

'Blocked it personally?' Hartmann asked. 'You know that?'

A subtle, teasing smile.

'I managed to get hold of some confidential minutes.'

Like a guilty schoolgirl Skovgaard waved her delicate hands over the documents in front of her.

'It's there in black and white. I can leak this if I have to. I'm finding lots we can throw at him.'

'Can we avoid this kind of crap, please?' Weber asked with an ill-disguised peevishness. 'People expect better of us.'

'People expect us to lose, Morten,' Skovgaard replied straight away. 'I'm trying to change that.'

'Rie . . .'

'We'll get there,' Hartmann interrupted. 'And we'll do it properly. I had a meeting with Kirsten Eller over breakfast. I think they want to play.'

The two of them went silent. Then Skovgaard asked, 'They're interested in an alliance?'

'With Kirsten Eller?' Weber grumbled. 'Jesus. Talk about a deal with the devil . . .'

Hartmann leaned back in his chair, closed his eyes, felt happier than he had in days.

'These are different times, Morten. Poul Bremer's starting to lose support. If Kirsten throws her not inconsiderable weight behind us . . .'

'We've got a coalition that holds the majority,' Skovgaard added brightly.

'We need to think this through,' Weber said.

His phone rang. He walked to the window to take the call.

Troels Hartmann skimmed the papers she'd prepared for him, a briefing for the debate.

Skovgaard moved her chair next to his so they could read them together.

'You don't need my help, do you? You came up with these ideas. We're just reminding you what you think.'

'I need reminding. I lost my watch! A good watch. A . . .'

Skovgaard nudged him. The silver Rolex was in her hand, held discreetly beneath the table so no one else could see.

She opened his fingers and pressed it into his palm.

'I found it under my bed. I can't imagine how it got there. Can you?'

Hartmann slipped the Rolex onto his wrist.

Weber came back from the window, phone in hand, looking worried.

'It's the mayor's secretary. Bremer wants to see you.'

'About what?'

'I don't know. He wants to see you now.'

'Fifteen minutes,' Hartmann said, checking the time. 'I'm not at his beck and call.'

Weber looked puzzled.

'You told me you'd lost your watch.'

'Fifteen minutes,' Hartmann repeated.

The hallways ran everywhere, long and gleaming, frescoes of battles and ceremonies above them, grand figures in armour staring down at the figures beetling along beneath.

'You don't look happy,' Hartmann said as they walked to the Lord Mayor's quarters.

'Happy? I'm your campaign manager. We're three weeks from an election. You're forming alliances without even telling me. What do you want? A song, a dance and a joke?'

'You think Bremer knows? About Kirsten Eller?'

'Poul Bremer can hear you mumbling in your sleep. Besides, if you're Kirsten Eller trying to cut a deal . . . do you only offer it to one side?'

Hartmann stood outside the council chamber door.

'Leave this to me, Morten. I'll find out.'

Poul Bremer was in shirtsleeves standing on the podium by the ceremonial chair he'd occupied these past twelve years. Jovial on the phone.

Hartmann walked ahead and picked up the book on the table by the mike. A biography of Cicero. And listened, as he was meant to.

'Yes, yes. Hear me out.' That deep and generous laugh, Bremer's breathy blessing on those he

24

favoured. 'You'll be in the government next. A minister. I predict it and I'm never wrong.' A glance at his visitor. 'Sorry . . . I must go.'

Bremer took the deputy's seat. Not the Lord Mayor's.

'You've read the book, Troels?'

'No. Sorry.'

'Take it. An instructive gift. It reminds us the one thing we learn from history is . . . we learn nothing from history.' He had the voice and manner of a genial schoolmaster, honed across the years. 'Cicero was a fine man. Would have gone far if he'd bided his time.'

'It looks heavy going.'

'Come and sit with me.' Bremer beckoned to the seat beside him. The Lord Mayor's. The throne. 'Try it for size. It doesn't belong to anyone. Not even me, whatever you think.'

Hartmann went along with the joke. Fell onto the hard polished wood. Smelled the mahogany, the scent of power. Looked around the chamber with its semicircle of empty councillors' seats, flat-screen monitors and voting buttons in front of them.

'It's just a chair, Troels,' Bremer said, grinning at him.

He always spoke and moved like a younger man. That was part of the image.

'Rome liked Cicero, appreciated his ideas. Ideas make pretty rhetoric. Not much more. Caesar was a dictator but a rogue the Romans knew and loved.

25

Cicero was impatient. Pushy. An upstart. You know what happened to him?'

'He went into TV?'

'Very funny. They slaughtered him. Put his hands and head on show in the Forum for everyone to laugh at. We serve an ungrateful bunch of bastards sometimes.'

'You wanted to see me?'

'I saw the polls. Did you?'

'I did.'

'You'll make a fine Lord Mayor. You'll run this city well.' Bremer smoothed down the sleeves of his black silk jacket, pulled out the cuffs of his smart white shirt, took off his glasses and checked they were clean, ran a hand through his silver hair. 'Just not this time around.'

Hartmann sighed and looked at his silver Rolex.

'I retire in four years. What's the hurry?'

'I believe it's called an election. Third Tuesday in November. Every four years.'

'I've an offer for you. A seat around my table. Running more than schools. There are seven mayors. Lord Mayor and six for the departments. You'll get any of the six you want. You'll learn how this city runs. When the time comes you'll be ready for the job and I'll happily hand it on.'

Bremer turned that swift smile on him.

'I guarantee no one will stand against you. But you can't have it now. You're not ready.'

'That's not your decision, is it?'

The smile was gone.

'I'm just trying to be friendly. There's no need for us to be enemies . . .'

Hartmann got up to leave. Poul Bremer strode in front, stopped him with an outstretched hand. He was a burly man, still fit. There were stories about how he'd strong-arm for support when he was young. No one knew whether they were true. No one had the courage to ask.

'Troels.'

'You've outstayed your welcome,' Hartmann said curtly. 'Go quietly. With dignity. Maybe I could find you a job somewhere.'

The suave old man stared at him, amused.

'Does one tiny promise from the Centre Party inspire such confidence? Oh please. They're the house pets. That fat bitch Eller will suck the cock of anyone then let you piss on her. So long as she gets a subcommittee after. Still . . .' He straightened his gold cufflinks.

'They know their place. A wise politician does.'

Bremer picked up the book, held it out to him and said, 'Read about Cicero. You might learn something. No one wants to end up torn to pieces for the public to gloat over. It's best these transitions are managed. Quietly. Efficiently. With some—'

'You're going to lose,' Hartmann cut in.

The old man chuckled.

'Poor Troels. You look so impressive on the posters. But in the flesh . . .'

He reached out and touched the collar of Hartmann's silk suit.

27

'What's under here, I wonder? Do you even know yourself?'

Meyer was out before she'd time to kill the engine, flashing his ID at a woman packing the boot of an estate car.

Red.

Everything here seemed a vivid shade of scarlet. The workmen in their bib overalls. The vans. Even a shiny Christiania trike with a box on the front for taking kids to school, bringing back the shopping, riding a lazy dog around town.

All the same colour, all with the name Birk Larsen on them.

Lund walked over, half-listening to Meyer, mostly looking around.

Two sliding doors opened to a depot-cum-garage. Beyond the crates and cases and machinery she could see an office behind glass windows in the corner, stairs at the back with a sign that read 'Private'. This was Birk Larsen's home address. He had to live above the job.

'Where's Theis Birk Larsen?' Meyer asked.

'My husband's working. And I'm going to the accountants.'

A woman in her forties, smart, good-looking with chestnut hair just a touch better tended than Lund's own. She wore a fawn gaberdine coat and a harassed, preoccupied air. Kids, Lund thought. She owned the badge. And she didn't like the police. Who did?

'You live here?' Lund asked.

'Yes.'

'Is he upstairs?'

The woman walked back into the garage.

'Is this about the vans again? We're a transport company. We get in the way.'

'It's not about the vans,' Lund said as she followed a couple of steps behind. More scarlet and uniforms. Hefty men heaving around crates, checking clipboards, looking her up and down. 'We just want to know what he did at the weekend.'

'We went to the seaside. With our two boys. Friday to Sunday. Took a cottage. Why?'

Tarpaulins and ropes. Wooden chests and commercial pallets. Lund wondered what she'd meet as a not-quite-cop in Sweden. She'd never really asked herself that question. Bengt wanted to go. She wanted to follow.

'Maybe he came back to town on business?' Meyer said.

The woman picked up an accounts ledger. She was getting sick of this.

'But he didn't. First weekend off we've had in two years. Why would he?'

Untidy office. Papers everywhere. Big companies didn't work this way. They had systems. Organization. Money.

Lund walked outside and looked in the woman's boot. Papers and folders. Kids' toys. A small football, much like the one Meyer had left in the office. A battered Nintendo. She wandered back into the office.

'What did he do when you got home?' Meyer was saying.

'We went to bed.'

'You're sure.'

She laughed at him.

'I'm sure.'

While they talked Lund strolled around the office, looking at the mess, searching for something personal in all the bills and receipts and invoices.

'I don't know what you think he did . . . and I don't care either,' the woman was saying. 'We were at the seaside. Then we came home. That's it.'

Meyer sniffed, looked in Lund's direction.

'Maybe we'll come back another time.'

Then he went outside, lit a cigarette, leaned against one of the scarlet trucks and stared at the starkly pallid sky.

At the back of the office, behind some rickety, old-fashioned filing trays, was a set of photographs. A beautiful teenage girl smiling with her arms round two young boys. The same girl close up, bubbly blonde hair, bright eyes, a little too much make-up. Trying to look older than she was.

Lund took out her packet of nicotine gum and popped a piece in her mouth.

'You've got a daughter?' she asked, still looking at the girl, the fetching smile. Both photos, alone, too old, and with the young boys when she played big sister.

The mother was walking out of the office. She stopped. Turned, looked at her and said, her

30

voice quiet and small, 'Yes. And two boys. Six and seven.'

'Does she borrow her dad's video rental card sometimes?'

The Birk Larsen woman was changing as Lund watched. Face falling, getting older. Mouth open. Eyelids twitching as if they had a life of their own.

'Maybe. Why?'

'Was she here last night?'

Meyer was back inside, listening.

The woman put down the papers. She looked troubled now, and scared.

'Nanna spent the weekend at a friend's house. Lisa. I thought . . .' Her hand went up to her chestnut hair for no real reason. 'I thought she might phone us. But she hasn't.'

Lund couldn't take her eyes off the photographs, the face there, happy, staring out at the camera without a care.

'I think you should ring her now.'

Frederiksholm High School in the city centre. Where the money was. Not Vesterbro. Morning break. Lisa Rasmussen phoned again.

'This is Nanna. I'm doing my homework. Leave me a message. Bye!'

Lisa Rasmussen took a deep breath and said, 'Nanna. Please call me.'

Stupid, she thought. Third time that morning she'd left the same message. Now she was sitting in school, listening to Rama the teacher talk about citizenship and the coming election. No one knew where Nanna was. No one had seen her since the Halloween party downstairs in the school hall the previous Friday.

'Today,' Rama said, 'you'll have the opportunity to decide who to vote for.'

There was a photo on the whiteboard. The semicircle of seats in the Rådhus. Three politicians, one good-looking, an old man, a smug fat-faced woman. She couldn't care less.

Out came the phone again and she typed one more message. *Nanna, where the hell are you?*

'We're lucky to live in a country where we have the right to vote,' the teacher went on. 'To decide our own future. To control our destiny.'

He was thirty or so, from the Middle East somewhere, not that it showed in his voice. Some of the girls fancied him. Tall and handsome. Nice body, cool smart clothes. Always helpful. Always had time for them.

Lisa didn't like foreigners much. Even when they smiled and looked good.

'So let's hear the questions you've prepared for the debate,' Rama said.

Class full, the rest of them seemed interested.

'Lisa.' He had to pick her. 'Your three questions. Are they on your phone?'

'No.'

She sounded like a petulant kid and knew it. Rama cocked his head and waited.

'I can't remember them. I can't . . .'

32

The door opened and Rektor Koch walked in. Scary Koch, the stocky middle-aged woman who used to teach German before she rose to run the school.

'Excuse me,' Koch said. 'Is Nanna Birk Larsen here?'

No answer.

Koch walked to the front of the class.

'Has anyone seen Nanna today?'

Nothing. She walked over to talk to the teacher. Lisa Rasmussen knew what was coming next.

One minute later Lisa was outside with the pair of them, Koch glaring at her with those fierce black eyes and asking, 'Where's Nanna? The police are looking for her.'

'I haven't seen Nanna since Friday. Why ask me?'

Koch gave her that 'you're lying' look.

'Her mother told the police she spent the weekend at your house.'

Lisa Rasmussen laughed. People used to think she and Nanna were sisters sometimes. Same height, same clothes, blonde hair too though Nanna's looked better. And Lisa was always heavier around the middle.

'What? She didn't stay with me.'

'You don't know where she is?' Rama asked a little more gently.

'No! How could I?'

'If she calls tell her to ring home,' Koch said. 'It's important.' She glanced at Rama. 'They need your classroom for the debate. Be out of there by eleven.'

33

When she was gone Rama turned, took Lisa Rasmussen's arm and said, 'If you've any idea where she is you must say so.'

'You're not supposed to touch me.'

'I'm sorry.' He took his hand away. 'If you know—'

'I don't know anything,' Lisa said. 'Leave me alone.'

Lund and Meyer were upstairs in the Birk Larsen flat. It was as cluttered as the office but in a pleasant way. Photos, paintings, plants and flowers. Vases and mementoes from holidays. *Decorated*, Lund thought. She never got round to that herself. The woman she now knew to be Pernille Birk Larsen worked at being a mother. Seemed good at it. As far as Lund could judge.

'She's not at school,' Lund said.

Pernille still wore her raincoat as if none of this was happening.

'She must be at Lisa's. They're friends. Lisa rents a flat with a couple of boys. Nanna's always there.'

'Lisa's at school. She says Nanna never stayed with her.'

Pernille's mouth hung half open. Her eyes were wide and blank. On the kitchen wall Lund saw the same two photos from the office: Nanna with the boys, Nanna on her own looking beautiful and too old for nineteen. Fixed to a cork-board alongside a timetable for school sports events. The easy, casual air of domesticity hung around this place. Like the smell of a dog, unnoticed by the owner, apparent to a stranger from the outset.

34

'What's happened to her? Where is she?' Pernille asked.

'Probably nothing. We'll do our best to find her.'

Lund walked into the tiny hall and phoned headquarters.

Meyer took Pernille out of earshot and began asking about photos.

Through to Buchard, Lund said, 'I need everyone we can spare on this.' The old man didn't even ask a question, just listened. 'Tell them we're looking for nineteen-year-old Nanna Birk Larsen. Missing since Friday. Send someone here for the photos.'

'And you?'

'We're going to her school.'

Hartmann and Rie Skovgaard had an empty classroom to prepare. She went through the numbers about the education allocation again. He paced round nervously. Finally she closed the laptop, came and checked his clothes. No tie, blue shirt. He looked good. But still she fiddled with his collar, came close enough so he had to hold her.

Hartmann's hands slipped round her back. He pulled Skovgaard to him, kissed her. A sudden passion. Unexpected. She wanted to laugh. He wanted more.

'Move in with me,' he said and pushed her against the desk. She fell on it, giggling, wrapped her long legs round him.

'Aren't you too busy?'

'Not for you.'

'After the election.'

His face changed. The politician returned.

'Why the big secret?'

'Because I've got a job to do, Troels. And so have you. We want no complications.' Her voice fell a tone. Smart eyes flashing. 'And we don't want Morten jealous.'

'Morten's the most experienced political aide we have. He knows what he's doing.'

'So I don't?'

'I didn't say that. I don't want to talk about Morten . . .'

Her hands were on his jacket again.

'Let's deal with this when you've won, shall we?'

Hartmann was reaching for her again.

The door opened. Rektor Koch was there. She looked embarrassed.

'The Lord Mayor's arrived,' she said. A confidential smile. 'If you're ready.'

Hartmann buttoned his jacket and walked out into the corridor.

Poul Bremer was beaming beneath a poster of a half-naked pop singer. Skovgaard left them alone and went to check out the room.

'I hope the Centre Party likes your ideas, Troels. A lot of them are good. Very like your father's.'

'Is that so?'

'They have his vigorous energy. His optimism.'

'Conviction,' Hartmann said. 'They came from

what he believed. Not what he thought might win a few votes.'

Bremer nodded at that.

'It's a shame he was never quite good enough to see them through.'

'I'll think of him. When I've got your job.'

'I believe you will. One day.' Bremer pulled out a handkerchief and cleaned his spectacles. 'You're more robust than he was. Your father was always . . . How should I put it?' The glasses went back on, those icy eyes looked him up and down. 'Fragile. Like porcelain.'

Bremer held up his right hand. A big fist. A fighter's, in spite of all outward appearances.

'He was always going to snap.'

The click of his strong fingers was so loud it seemed to echo off the peeling walls.

'If I hadn't broken him he'd have broken himself. Believe me. It was a kindness in a way. It's best not to allow one's delusions to linger too long.'

'Let's get to this debate,' Hartmann said. 'It's time . . .'

When they turned to go Rektor Koch was walking towards them. She looked worried. With her was a woman in a blue cagoule, an odd black and white patterned sweater visible beneath it, hair swept back from her face like a teenager too busy to think about boyfriends.

A woman who thought nothing of her own appearance. Which was odd since she was striking and attractive.

Now she was looking straight ahead, at them, nowhere else. She had very large and staring eyes.

Somehow Hartmann wasn't surprised when she pulled out a police ID card. It read: *Vicekriminalkommissær Sarah Lund.*

Bremer had retreated to the back of the corridor the moment he saw the cop approaching.

'You have to cancel the debate,' Lund said.

'Why?'

'There's a missing girl. I need to talk to people here. People in her class. Teachers. I need . . .'

Rektor Koch was ushering them into a side room, out of the corridor. Bremer stayed where he was.

Hartmann listened to the cop.

'You want me to cancel a debate because a pupil's skipping school?'

'It's important I talk to everyone,' Lund insisted.

'Everyone?'

'Everyone I want to talk to.'

She didn't move. Didn't stop looking at him. Nothing else.

'We could put back the debate an hour,' Hartmann suggested.

'Not for me,' Bremer cut in. 'I have appointments. This was your invitation, Troels. If you can't make it . . .'

Hartmann took a step towards Sarah Lund and said, 'How serious is it?'

'I hope nothing's happened.'

'I asked how serious it was.'

'That's what I'm trying to find out,' Lund replied

then put her hands on her hips and waited for an answer. 'So . . .'

She looked round, checking the rooms.

'That's agreed then,' Lund added.

Bremer took out his phone, checked some messages.

'Call my secretary. I'll try to fit you in. Oh!' A sudden flash of geniality. 'I've got good news for your inner-city schools. It seems absenteeism is up by twenty per cent.' He laughed. 'We can't have that, can we? So I've allocated funds for extra facilities. More computers. Children love those things. That'll fix it.'

Hartmann stared at him, speechless.

Bremer shrugged.

'I would have told you in there. But now . . . We'll put out a release straight away. Good news. I trust you'll welcome it.'

A long moment of silence.

'You're happy, I see,' Bremer said, then, with a wave, walked off.

Half past three in the afternoon. They were still in the room where the debate was supposed to happen, getting nowhere. Nanna had been to the Halloween party in the school hall the previous Friday, dressed in a black witch's hat and garish blue wig. No one had seen her since.

Now it was the teacher's turn.

'What's Nanna like?'

They all called him Rama. He stood out and not

just because of his dark, striking Middle Eastern looks. He was one of Troels Hartmann's role models, part of an initiative to bring immigrant groups more closely into the fabric of the community. An articulate, intelligent, convincing man.

'Nanna's a clever kid,' he said. 'Always full of energy. Always wanting to do something.'

'I saw the photo. She looks older than nineteen.'

He nodded.

'They all want that, don't they? Desperate to grow up. Or to feel they have. Nanna's top of her class in most things. Bright kid. Doesn't stop her wanting what the rest do.'

'Which is?'

The teacher looked at her.

'They're teenagers. Are you serious?'

'What happened at the party?'

'Fancy dress. A band. Ghosts and pumpkins.'

'Does she have a boyfriend?'

'Ask Lisa.'

'I'm asking you.'

He looked uncomfortable.

'It's best a teacher stays out of these things.'

Lund went outside, stopped the first girl she found, sat her down, talked to her until she got an answer.

Then she went back to the teacher.

'Oliver Schandorff. Is he here?'

'No.'

'Did you know Oliver was her boyfriend?'

'I told you. It's best we keep some distance.'

She waited.

'I'm their teacher. Not their guardian. Not a parent either.'

Lund looked at her watch. The interviews had run on for more than three hours and this was all they had. All anyone had. Meyer, out in the woods and fields near the airport with a search team, hadn't found a thing.

'Shit.'

'I'm sorry,' the teacher said.

'Not you.'

Me, she thought. She could surely have got this out of Pernille in a few minutes if she'd tried. Why was it the best questions only came when she had something – people, evidence, crimes – in front of her?

Two hundred and thirty-five three-storey terraced houses made up the place called Humleby, a tiny estate four streets from Birk Larsen's home. The colour of slate and gunmetal, they were built in the nineteenth century for workers at the nearby ship-yard. Then the Carlsberg brewery expanded and the houses fell into the hands of men who made beer. They came onto the market slowly, sought after even if some needed much expensive restoration. Theis Birk Larsen had bought the cheapest he could find. Squatters had been in before, leaving behind their junk, mattresses and cheap furniture. It needed clearing, a lot of repair work. He'd do most of it himself, quietly, without telling Pernille, not until it was close to time to move in and escape the tiny apartment above the garage.

Vagn Skærbæk was helping. The two had known each other since they were teens, gone through a lot together, including a few appearances in court. To Birk Larsen he'd become almost a younger brother, uncle to the kids, steady employee in the transport company. Reliable, trustworthy, kind to Anton and Emil. A solitary man who seemed to have no life of his own once he took off the scarlet uniform.

'Pernille's looking for you,' Skærbæk said coming off the phone.

'Pernille's not going to know about this place. I told you. Not a word until I say.'

'She's phoning round, asking where you are.'

There was scaffolding on the outside, sheeting against the rotting windows. Birk Larsen was paying his own men to carry in new floorboards, guttering and piping, making them promise to keep quiet about the place when Pernille was around.

'The boys can have their own rooms,' he said, looking at the grey stone house. 'You see that top window?'

Skærbæk nodded.

'Nanna gets that whole floor, a staircase of her own and some privacy. Pernille a new kitchen. And me . . .' He laughed. 'Some peace and quiet.'

'This is going to cost a fortune, Theis.'

Birk Larsen stuffed his hands into the pockets of his red bib overall.

'I'll manage.'

'Maybe I can help.'

'Meaning?'

Skærbæk was a slight and fidgety man. He stood there shuffling from foot to foot even more than usual.

'I know where there's thirty B&O TVs going cheap. All we've got to—'

'You're in debt? That's it?'

'Listen. I've got buyers for half of them . . . We can share . . .'

Birk Larsen pulled a wad of notes out of his pocket, ripped off a few.

'All I need is to borrow a forklift . . .'

'Here you go.' He folded the money in Skærbæk's hand. 'Forget the TVs. We're not teenagers any more, Vagn. I've got a family. A business.' Skærbæk kept hold of the money. 'You're part of both. Always will be.'

Skærbæk stared at the cash. Birk Larsen wished he'd lose that stupid silver neck chain.

'How'd the boys feel if they had to visit their Uncle Vagn in jail?'

'You don't have to do this . . .' Skærbæk started.

Theis Birk Larsen wasn't listening. Pernille was riding towards him on the Christiania trike, so quickly the shiny scarlet box on the front bumped up and down over the cobblestones.

He forgot all about the secret house, about building work and where the money might come from.

She looked terrible.

Pernille got off, came straight up to him, took the collars of his black leather coat.

'Nanna's missing.' She was breathless, pale, scared. 'The police found your video rental card out near the airport. They found . . .'

Her hand went to her mouth. Tears started in her eyes.

'Found what?'

'Her top. The pink one with the flowers.'

'Lots of kids wear tops like that. Don't they?'

She gave him a sharp look.

'And the video card?'

'Did they talk to Lisa?'

Vagn Skærbæk was listening. She looked at him and said, 'Please, Vagn.'

'You want any help?'

Birk Larsen stared at him. He went away.

'What about that bastard kid?'

'She isn't seeing Oliver any more.'

There was a touch of red anger in his cheeks.

'Did they talk to him?'

A deep breath then she said, 'I don't know.'

He had his keys out, called to Skærbæk, 'Take Pernille home. And the trike.'

A thought.

'Why didn't you drive?'

'They wouldn't let me use the car. They said I couldn't move it.'

Theis Birk Larsen took his wife in his broad arms, held her, kissed her once, touched her cheek, looked her in the eye and said, 'Nanna's fine. I'll find her. Go home and wait for us.'

Then he climbed into the van and left.

'I'll drop you off at Gran's. You've got your key?'

The weather was closing in, the day ending in mist and drizzle. Lund was driving out to Østerbro, her twelve-year-old son, Mark, in the passenger seat.

'You mean we're not going to Sweden after all?'

'I've got something to do first.'

'Me too.'

Lund looked at her son. But in truth all she was seeing in her head was the flat yellow grass, a teenager's bloodstained top. And the photograph of Nanna Birk Larsen, smiling like an older sister proud of her little brothers. Looking too grown-up with all that make-up.

She hadn't a clue what Mark was talking about.

'I told you, Mum. Magnus's birthday party.'

'Mark. Our flight's tonight. We decided this ages ago.'

He grunted and turned to stare out of the rain-streaked window.

'You look like a moose with the mumps,' she said.

Lund laughed. He didn't.

'You'll love it in Sweden. It's a great school. I'll have more time for you. We can—'

'He's not my father.'

Lund's phone started ringing. She looked at the number and began fumbling the headset into her ear.

'Of course he's not. He's found you a hockey club.'

'I've got one.'

'You must be sick of being the youngest at FCK.'

Silence.

'Aren't you?'

'It's called KSF.'

'Yes,' she said to the phone.

'KSF,' Mark repeated.

'I'm on my way.'

Mark began to speak very slowly.

'K . . . S . . . F . . .'

'Yes.'

'You get it wrong every time.'

'Yes.'

It wasn't far now which pleased her on two counts. She wanted to see Meyer. And Mark was . . . in the way.

'Not long now and then we go to the airport,' she said. 'You do have your key, don't you?'

Beneath a sullen monochrome sky a single line of twenty blue-clad officers moved slowly across the yellow grass, prodding the mud and clumps of vegetation with red and white sticks, search dogs snuffling at the damp earth.

Lund watched them for a moment then went into the wood. There a second team was working through the lichened trees, examining the ground, putting down markers, following another set of dogs.

Meyer was in a police jacket, soaked to the skin.

'How clear's the trail?' she asked.

'Clear enough. The dogs followed her from where we found the top.' He looked at his notes and gestured to a thicket ten metres away. 'We also got some blonde hair caught on a bush.'

'Where does it lead?'

'Here,' Meyer said, gesturing with the map in his hand. 'Where we're standing.' Another look at his notes. 'She was running. Zigzagging through the woods. This was where she stopped.'

Lund came and peered over his shoulder.

'What do we have close by?'

'A logging road. Maybe she was picked up there.'

'What about her mobile phone?'

'Switched off since Friday night.' He didn't like these obvious questions. 'Listen, Lund. We've gone over her route with a fine-tooth comb. Twice. She isn't here. We're wasting time.'

She turned and walked away, looked back to the marshland and yellow grass.

'Hello?' Meyer said with that dry sarcasm she was starting to recognize. 'Am I invisible?'

Lund came back and said, 'Spread out. Go over it all again.'

'Did you hear a word I said?'

The local intercom on one of the search team's jackets squawked her name.

'We've found something,' a voice said.

'Where?'

'In the trees.'

'What is it?'

47

A pause. It was getting dark. Then, 'It looks like a grave.'

The same sluggish twilight crept over the city, damp and dreary, wan and cold. In his campaign office, beneath the coral-coloured petals of the artichoke lamps, Hartmann listened to Morten Weber's answers. Poul Bremer wouldn't return to the school for another debate. Running the city was more important than begging for votes.

'Doesn't that suit him?' Hartmann said.

Rie Skovgaard placed a cup of coffee on his desk.

'Bremer's office announced the new allocation of funds while we were at the school. He was ready to come out with it whatever happened.'

'He knew about the twenty per cent. How's that possible, Morten?' Hartmann asked.

Weber seemed thrown by the question.

'Why ask me? Maybe he did his own survey. Makes sense. Promising money for education always wins you Brownie points.'

'And he got the same results? He knew.'

Weber shrugged.

'You shouldn't have cancelled,' Skovgaard said.

Hartmann's mobile rang.

'A young girl's missing. I had no choice.'

'It's Therese,' said the voice on the line.

Hartmann glanced at Rie Skovgaard.

'This isn't a good time. I'll ring you back.'

'Don't hang up, Troels. You're not too busy for this. We have to meet.'

48

'That wouldn't be a good idea.'

'Someone's trying to dig up dirt on you.'

Hartmann took a deep breath.

'Who?'

'A reporter rang me. I don't want to talk about this over the phone.'

'We've got a fundraiser here at five. Get here then. I can come out for a while.'

'Five it is.'

'Therese . . .'

'Take care, Troels.'

Weber and Skovgaard were watching him.

'Something we need to hear?' Skovgaard asked.

Theis Birk Larsen went to the student house in Nørrebro where Lisa Rasmussen lived with Oliver Schandorff and some other kids from the school, pretending they were grown-ups, screwing around, drinking, smoking dope, acting the fool.

Lisa was outside wheeling away her bike. He took hold of the handlebars.

'Where's Nanna?'

The girl was dressed like a teenage tart, the way they all did, Nanna if he let her. She wouldn't look him in the eye.

'I told them. I don't know.'

His big fist didn't move.

'Where's that bastard Schandorff?'

Still staring at the wall.

'Not here. Not since Friday.'

He bent down and put his whiskery face in hers.

49

'Where is he?'

Finally she met his eyes. She looked as if she'd been crying.

'He said his parents were away for the weekend. He was staying there I think. After the Halloween party . . .'

Birk Larsen didn't wait to hear more.

On the way he called Pernille.

'I just talked to Lisa,' he said. 'I'm going to get her.'

He could hear the relief in her single brief sigh.

'It's that rich punk again. His parents went away. He's probably . . .'

He didn't want to say it, think it.

'You're sure she's there? Lisa said so?'

The evening traffic was heavy. The house was out on one of the new developments, south, near the airport.

'I'm sure. Don't worry.'

She was crying. He could see her tears. He wished he could touch them, brush them away with his fat, rough fingers. Pernille was beautiful and precious. Like Nanna, Emil and Anton. They all deserved better than he'd given them and soon they'd get it.

'Won't be long, sweetheart. I promise.'

When Lund was back among the bare dark trees Buchard called.

'The helicopter. Three forensic units. I hope you've found something?'

'A grave.'

'You left me out of the loop.'

'I tried. You were in a meeting.'

'I was at your leaving party. People don't say goodbye over breakfast . . .'

'Hang on a minute.'

Meyer was walking towards her through the wood. In his arms was a plastic forensic sheet. Something beneath. A body.

'Have you found something?' Buchard demanded.

Meyer put the sheet on the ground, opened it and showed her a dead fox. Stiff and dry, caked with earth. It had a cub scout kerchief around its neck along with the wire noose that had strangled it.

'We can put out a call for any kids nearby,' Meyer said, lifting the fox by its back legs. 'Animal cruelty's a shocking thing.'

'No,' Lund told Buchard. 'Not yet.'

'Pack up, come home and give me a full report. Maybe there's time for a beer before you catch your plane.'

Meyer was watching her, the stiff dead animal beneath his arm. Its eyes were black and glazed, its fur streaked with mud.

'Meet my new friend Foxy,' he said with a quick sharp grin. 'You'll like him.'

One more reception among so many. Part of the political calendar. A chance to meet, to negotiate, to forge alliances, confirm enmities.

The food came from an oil corporation, the drink

from a transport magnate. A string quartet played Vivaldi. Morten Weber talked policy while Rie Skovgaard spoke spin.

Hartmann smiled and chatted, shook hands, made small talk. Then when his phone rang he excused himself and walked back to his office.

Therese Kruse was waiting for him. A couple of years younger than him. Married to a boring banker. A serious, well-connected, attractive woman, tougher than she looked.

'You're doing well in the polls. People in government are noticing.'

'So they should. We worked for this.'

'True.'

'Did you get the reporter's name?'

She handed him a piece of paper. *Erik Salin.*

'Never heard of him,' Hartmann said.

'I made some enquiries. He used to work as a private investigator. Now he's a freelance selling dirt for the highest fee. Newspapers. Magazines. Websites. Anyone who pays.'

He pocketed the note.

'And?'

'Salin wanted to know if you paid your hotel bills with your own credit card or the office's. If you buy lots of presents. Stuff like that. I didn't say anything, naturally . . .'

Hartmann took a sip of wine.

'He wanted to know about us,' she added.

'What did you say?'

'I laughed off the whole idea, of course. After

all . . .' The smile was brief and bitter. 'It's not as if it was anything important. Was it?'

'We agreed it was best, Therese. I'm sorry. I couldn't . . .'

He stopped.

'Couldn't what, Troels? Take the risk?'

'What did he know?'

'About us? Nothing. He was guessing.' The caustic smile again. 'Perhaps he thinks if he asks enough women he's bound to strike gold. I think he's got something else though. I don't know how.'

Hartmann glanced at the door, made sure they were alone.

'Such as what?'

'He seems to have seen your diary. He was checking dates. He knew where you'd been and when.'

Hartmann looked at the name again, wondered if he'd heard it somewhere.

'No one sees my diary outside this office.'

She shrugged. Got up. The door opened. Rie Skovgaard looked at the pair of them.

With that stiff suspicious smile she said, 'Troels. I didn't know you had company. There are people in reception you need to meet.'

The two women stared at each other. Thinking. Judging. No need for words.

'I'm coming,' Troels Hartmann said.

Oliver Schandorff was a skinny kid of nineteen with a head of curly ginger hair and a sour

53

unsmiling face. He was puffing on his third smoke of the day when Theis Birk Larsen burst through the front door.

Schandorff leapt out of his chair and retreated as the big and angry man marched towards him.

'Call her now,' Birk Larsen bellowed. 'She's leaving.'

'Hello!' Schandorff cried, skipping into the hall. 'There's a bell here. Private house.'

'Don't mess with me, sonny. I want Nanna.'

'Nanna isn't here.'

Birk Larsen began marching round the ground floor, opening doors, yelling her name.

Schandorff followed, at a safe distance.

'Mr Birk Larsen. I'm telling you. She isn't here.'

Birk Larsen went back to the hall. There were clothes on a chair by the sofa. A pink T-shirt. A bra. Jeans.

He swore at Schandorff and made for the stairs.

The kid lost it, raced in front, punched Birk Larsen's chest, yelled, 'Do you mind? Do you—'

The big man picked him up by his T-shirt, carried the kid back down to the hall, launched him against the front door, balled a massive fist in his face.

Oliver Schandorff went quiet.

Birk Larsen thought better of it. Strode up the open-plan stairs two at a time. The place was vast, the kind of mansion he could never dream of owning, however hard he worked, however many scarlet trucks he ran.

There was deafening rock music coming from a

54

bedroom on the left. The place stank of stale dope and sex.

A double bed with crumpled sheets, crumpled duvet. Curly blonde hair poked out from beneath the pillows. Face down, naked feet out of the bottom. Stoned. Drunk. Both, or worse.

He glowered back at Schandorff who was following him, hands in pockets, smirking in a way that made Theis Birk Larsen want to punch him out on the spot.

Instead he walked to the bed, wondering how to play this, pulled back the duvet and said gently, 'Nanna. You need to come home. It doesn't matter what happened. We're going now . . .'

The naked woman stared up at him, her hard face a mix of fright and fury. Blonde too. Same shade. Twenty-five if she was a day.

'I did tell you,' Schandorff said. 'Nanna was never here. If I could help . . .'

Theis Birk Larsen walked outside wondering what to do. What to tell Pernille. Where to go next? He didn't like the police but maybe it was time to talk to them. He wanted to know something, find something. Or make it happen.

There was a sound overhead. A helicopter, the word POLITI underneath.

He hadn't thought much about the location when he came here. Nanna was in Oliver Schandorff's house. There was nothing more to know. Now he realized he wasn't far from the marshland east of the airport.

Pernille said that was the place where it all began.

Lund was back on the flat ground of the Kalvebod Fælled where they found the bloodstained top, looking at the map.

'Let's go home,' Meyer said, lighting one more cigarette.

Her phone rang.

'Are you coming to Sweden or what?' Bengt Rosling asked.

She had to think for a moment before saying, 'Shortly.'

'How about a house-warming party on Saturday? We could invite Lasse, Missan, Bosse and Janne.'

Lund was scanning the fading horizon, wishing she could slow time a little and hold back dusk.

'And my parents,' Bengt added. 'And your mother.'

Lund took one more look at the map, one more sweep of the marsh and the woods.

'Your mother's going to fix up the guest room,' Bengt said.

Three young kids walked past pushing bikes. They were carrying fishing rods.

Mark never went fishing. No one to take him.

'That would be nice,' she said, gesturing at Meyer to get his attention.

'I don't want her sleeping on the sofa,' Bengt said.

Lund wasn't listening by then. The phone hung in her fingers by the side of her blue cagoule.

'What's over there?' she asked Meyer.

56

'More woods,' he said. 'And a canal.'

'You did look in the water?'

He grimaced. Meyer was the kind of man who could look angry in his sleep.

'The girl ran the other way!'

Lund went back to the phone.

'We're going to miss the flight.'

'What?'

'You catch it. I'll come tomorrow with Mark.'

Meyer stood there, arms crossed, pushing crisps into his mouth between puffs on his cigarette.

'Do we have trained divers among the forensic teams? And gear?' Lund asked.

'We've got enough men here to start a small war. How about Sweden? Let's face it. That's the only way you'll get there.'

The two of them drove over to the canal. Walked up and down. There were tyre marks by a low metal bridge. Going off the edge of the muddy bank towards nothing but black water.

The bleak terrain mirrored Theis Birk Larsen's state of mind: a maze of baffling dead ends and pointless turnings. A labyrinth without an exit.

He drove and drove, into the dying grey sunset, away from it, finding nothing. Even the drone of the helicopter had disappeared. Pernille was with him every aching second, her shrill scared voice chanting through the phone clamped to his left ear.

'Where is she?'

How many times had she asked that? How many times had he?

'I'm looking.'

'Where?'

The Kalvebod Fælled he wanted to say. The place Anton came on a school nature trip once, and talked about bugs and eels for the best part of a day before forgetting the whole damned thing.

There were lights ahead. One of them was blue.

'Everywhere.'

The narrow lane stood above the slender canal, built from the earth that created it. Lund stared at the tracks, the lifting truck, the chain. The car emerging from the sullen water.

Look, think, imagine.

Someone parked on the lane, front wheels turned towards the water at the top of the slope. Then got out, pushed it. Gravity did the rest.

Meyer was next to her, watching as the car rose against the sky. Water poured from all four doors. The paint was black, the colour of the canal, but very shiny as if it was cleaned yesterday.

Ford hatchback. Brand new.

'Look up the registration,' Lund said the moment the number plate was clear.

The truck was parked on the bank, long crane arm extending over the canal. It turned the vehicle away from the water, dangled it over the grassy lane. Then three officers guided the Ford slowly down to the ground until it sat there, unremarkable except for the torrents of foul-smelling liquid gushing from beneath each door.

Meyer was off the phone. The two of them walked over and looked through the windows. Empty.

The divider was down on the boot hiding anything inside.

He walked to the back and tried the rear door. Locked.

'I'll get a crowbar,' Meyer said.

There were lights behind. Lund turned and looked. Not car lights. A van, she thought. It looked red in the beams of the police vehicles.

Birk Larsen was still on the phone when he reached the line of Don't Cross tape. So close he couldn't count the blue lights beyond it. They'd set up high portable floodlights, the kind they used at sports events.

His head didn't feel right. His heart was beating so hard it banged against his ribs.

'Hang on a second,' he said and didn't hear her reply.

Got out. Walked on.

'Where are you?' Pernille asked.

'On the marshes in Vestamager.'

A pause then she asked, 'Are the police still out there?'

Two cops came up and tried to stop him. Birk Larsen brushed them aside with a sweep of his huge arm, kept walking towards a low metal bridge across the narrow canal.

59

'I'll sort this out. I told you.'

'Theis.'

More cops now. They swarmed on him like angry bees as he kept walking forwards, batting away their clutching hands, phone locked to his head.

He could still hear her voice above the commotion.

'What's there, Theis? *What's there?*'

A sound ahead.

Water rushing.

Water rushing. It cascaded out of the rear compartment after Meyer levered it open. Gallons and gallons pouring onto the muddy ground.

The smell was worse.

Lund popped another Nicotinell in her mouth and waited.

After the water a pair of naked legs fell onto the shiny rear bumper. She shone her torch there. Naked ankles bound tightly with plastic fasteners.

Then movement. A snaking dark shape wound its way round and round the dead pale limbs, clinging to the skin, slithering down to the feet, over the bumper onto the ground.

One of the uniform cops started to puke into the yellow grass.

'What's the noise?' Lund asked, taking a step towards the car.

Meyer nodded at the retching man.

'Not him,' she said.

It was a loud coarse voice and it was furious.

Lund watched the last of the water drain from the rear, two more eels sliding their way to freedom, then walked forward and put her head inside. The blonde hair didn't look the way it had in the photos any more.

But the face . . .

The angry voice was bawling a name.

'Oh Christ,' Meyer said. 'The father's here.'

Theis Birk Larsen was a big strong man. It was a long time since he'd fought with cops. Some things you always remembered. Two swift punches, a roar and he was moving forward again, towards the black bridge.

Beyond that point he could see a car on the road next to a recovery truck. Busy shapes swarming there.

The phone was back to his ear.

'Theis!' Pernille cried.

'I'll talk to them.'

The cops he'd shaken off were at his back again. More this time. Too many.

A woman had left the car on the road and was walking steadily towards him. Beneath the harsh floodlights he saw she had a serious face, long brown hair, and shining, sad and interested eyes.

'For God's sake Theis . . .' Pernille whined.

They had him now, six cops, maybe seven. Had everything but his free arm with the phone.

Birk Larsen stopped struggling. Said again, as

61

calmly as he could, 'I'm Nanna's father. I want to know what's going on.'

The woman stepped over one more line of red and white police tape.

She didn't say a thing, kept walking steadily towards him, staring into his face, chewing gum.

A voice, detached, not his at all, said meekly, 'Is that my daughter?'

'You can't stay here.'

Pernille was in his ear, his head, all in a single question, 'Theis?'

The woman stood in front of him.

'Is it Nanna down there?' Birk Larsen asked once more.

She was silent.

'Is it?'

The woman just nodded.

The roar was born deep in his belly, rose through him, burst into the damp night air. So loud and full of uncomprehending grief and fury it might have carried all the way to Copenhagen on its own.

But the phone was there. No need. As he struggled, screamed to see her, Pernille was with him shrieking, crying too.

Mother and father. Lost dead child.

Then all the fury, all the power, died. Theis Birk Larsen was a weeping, fractured man, feeble and distraught, held upright by the arms that seconds before had fought his boundless strength.

'I want to see my daughter,' he begged.

'You can't,' she said. 'I'm sorry.'

A tinny howling sound came from the man's right hand. Lund stepped forward, opened his fingers. Those of a labourer. Strong and scarred, the skin leathery and old.

He didn't protest as she took the phone from him, looked at the name on the screen.

'Pernille. This is Lund. Someone will be with you soon.'

Then she pocketed the phone, nodded to the officers to take Birk Larsen away, went back to the drowned Ford, shiny and black, by the lifting truck.

Forensics were swarming there already. All the set procedures were in place. Officers in protective clothing. She didn't need to see any more.

Black car. Bright and shiny. Meyer was right. It was so very new and clean.

Lund found him smoking by the crane truck, shaking his head.

'We've got an owner,' he said. 'You won't believe this.'

Lund stood beside him, waited.

'The car belongs to Troels Hartmann's campaign office,' Jan Meyer said.

'Hartmann the politician?'

With a single finger Meyer flicked his cigarette out towards the canal.

'The Mayor of Education. Poster boy. Yeah. Him.'

CHAPTER 3

Tuesday, 4th November

Buchard arrived just after midnight. Then came the duty pathologist and his team. A huddle of forensic officers measuring tyre tracks, taking endless photographs, cordoning off the soaking muddy ground.

They trudged through the soaking rain leaving till last the bloodied, bruised corpse of a young girl still in her ragged slip, wrists and ankles tied with black plastic fasteners, dumped in the back of a shiny black Ford.

Lund talked to them all. She was officer in charge. No thoughts for Mark or Bengt or Sweden.

More camera flashes around the perimeter of the car. Then finally the team moved towards the open boot, starting to record details of the small, still body and its wounds, the dead face, the staring blank light-blue eyes.

Buchard asked, as he always did, about time of death. She told him what the pathologist said: no idea. Nothing had been reported over the weekend. It would take some time to establish.

The old man scowled.

'What a godforsaken place . . .'

'We don't know she died here. He didn't want her found. A day or two more, rain like this . . .' She glanced at the activity around the car. They'd move her soon. Someone needed to think about the family. 'The tyre tracks would have gone.'

Buchard waited.

'He knew this place,' Lund said. 'He knew what he was doing.'

'Cause of death?'

'They don't know yet. She was assaulted. Violent blows to the head. Signs of rape.'

'And this car? It belongs to Hartmann's team?'

'It's the best lead we have.'

Bengt Rosling rang. Lund walked away to take the call.

'What happened?' he asked.

'We found a girl. I'll tell you later. I'm sorry I didn't make it.'

Bengt was a criminal psychologist. That was how they met. Through a drug murder in Christiania. The victim was one of his patients.

'What about Mark?' he asked.

'He's with my mother.'

'I mean tomorrow. He's supposed to be starting Swedish lessons at school. In Sigtuna.'

'Oh. Right.'

'I'll tell them he'll be there on Wednesday.'

'We'll book another flight. I'll let you know the time.'

Buchard came over and asked, 'Is the girl connected to Hartmann?'

'I'll check.'

'If a candidate's involved report back to me.'

'I can't do this, Buchard.'

A horn was sounding. It was Meyer, cigarette in mouth, calling her.

'Use him,' she said.

The chief came close.

'This shouldn't be Meyer's first case. Don't ask. I'll call the Stockholm police and clear it.'

'No,' she insisted. 'It's not possible.'

Lund walked away, back towards Meyer and the car.

'You found this kid.' Buchard hurried behind her, talking to the back of her shiny wet blue cagoule. 'Would Meyer have done that? All he dug up was a dead fox in the woods.'

She stopped, turned, glared at him.

He looked like an old grizzled pug dog, had the same importunate eyes sometimes.

'Just one more day, Sarah.'

Silence.

'Do you want Meyer to talk to the parents?'

'I hate you. You know that?'

Buchard laughed and clapped his fat little hands.

'I'll work through the night,' Lund said. 'In the morning it's down to you.'

The morgue was deserted. One echoing antiseptic corridor after another.

Still in the black leather jacket and woollen hat, the scarlet cotton overalls, Theis Birk Larsen clumped across the clean tiles towards the single door at the end.

An anteroom.

Pernille there in her fawn gaberdine coat, turning to look at him, wide-eyed, face full of questions. He stopped two paces from her, no idea what to say or do. Felt shapeless words rise to his mouth then stay there, unfinished and uncertain, afraid to breach the cold dry air.

A big man, powerful, forbidding sometimes, silent, his gleaming eyes now pools of tears.

Ashamed when that broke her, made Pernille come to him, place her gentle arms around his shoulders.

She held him, damp face against his bristled cheek. Together they stood, together they clung to one another in close silence. Together they walked into the white room of brilliant tiles and medical cabinets, of taps and sinks and shining concave silver tables, of surgical implements, all the tools that codified death.

The cops led the way, the woman with the staring eyes, the surly, big-eared man. Walking towards a clean white sheet then stopping, half-looking at them in expectation, waiting. From the corner came a man in a surgeon's suit, blue mob cap, blue bib, blue gloves. There'd been doctors like this when Nanna was born. Theis Birk Larsen saw this picture clear in his head. The same colours, the same harsh chemical smells.

Without a word, without a glance, the man was beside them, lifting the white cotton.

Pernille edged forward, eyes widening.

All the while the woman cop watched, every gesture, every breath and move.

Birk Larsen removed his black hat, embarrassed that he still wore it. Looked at the bloodless, bruised face on the table, the dirty stained hair, the lifeless grey eyes.

Images filled his memory. Pictures, sounds, a touch, a word. A baby's cry, a much-rued argument. A hot afternoon by the beach. A freezing morning in winter, out on a sledge. Nanna tiny in the red Christiania trike Vagn fixed and painted, stencilling the logo *Birk Larsen* on the side.

Nanna older, climbing into it when she was sixteen, seventeen, laughing at how small it seemed.

Distant moments never to be recovered, unspoken promises never to be made. All the small pieces that once seemed so humdrum now shrieked . . .

See! You never noticed. And now I'm gone.

Now I'm gone.

Pernille turned, walked back to the anteroom, the gait of an old woman, broken and in pain.

'Is this Nanna?' the woman asked.

He glared at her. A stupid question and she didn't seem a stupid woman.

No, Birk Larsen wanted to say. *It was.*

Instead he nodded, nothing more.

★   ★   ★

68

Four of them face to face across a plastic table.

Plain facts.

Birk Larsen, his wife and their two young sons left for the seaside on Friday, returned Sunday evening. Nanna was supposed to be staying with friends.

'What sort of mood was she in?' Lund asked.

'Happy,' Birk Larsen said. 'She dressed up.'

'As what?'

'A witch.'

The mother sat there, mouth open, lost somewhere. Then she stared at Lund and asked, 'What happened?'

Lund didn't answer. Nor Meyer.

'Will someone talk to me! What happened?'

In the cold empty room her shrill voice bounced off the bare white walls.

Meyer lit a cigarette.

'The car was driven into the water,' he said.

'Was she interested in politics?' Lund asked.

Birk Larsen shook his head.

'Did she talk to anyone who was?'

'No.'

'At the Rådhus maybe?' Meyer wondered.

He scowled at the lack of an answer, got up and walked to the back of the room, making a call.

'Boyfriends . . . ?'

'Not lately.'

'How did she die?' Pernille asked.

'We don't know yet.'

'Did she suffer?'

Lund hesitated and said, 'We're not sure what happened. We're trying to understand. So you haven't talked to her since Friday? No calls? No contact? Nothing out of the ordinary?'

Narrow eyes, a bitter scowl, a note of sarcasm as he snarled, 'The ordinary?'

'Things you'd expect. It could be anything unusual. A little thing.'

'I got cross with her,' Pernille said. 'Is that ordinary? She was being too noisy. I shouted at her for running around with her brothers.'

She watched Lund.

'I was doing the accounts. I was busy . . .'

Birk Larsen wound his big arm round her.

'She just wanted to play with them. Just . . .'

More tears, Pernille shook beneath his grip.

'Just what?'

'Just wanted to play.'

'I'll have someone take you home now,' Lund said. 'We need to seal off Nanna's room. It's important no one goes in there.'

Lund and Meyer walked them to the door where the uniformed men with the car were waiting.

'If you think of anything . . .' Lund said and handed Birk Larsen a card.

The stocky father looked at it.

'How much do you know?'

'It's too early to say.'

'But you'll find him?'

'We'll do everything we can.'

Birk Larsen didn't move. There was a grim, hard set on his face when he asked again, more slowly, 'But you will find him?'

'Yes,' Meyer snapped. 'We will.'

The father stared hard at him then left for the car.

Lund watched them go.

'They just lost their daughter. And you're yelling at them?'

'I didn't yell.'

'It sounded like—'

'This is yelling!' Meyer bawled.

His voice was so loud the pathologist put his head round the corner.

Then, more quietly, Meyer said, 'I didn't yell.'

His bleak and watchful eyes caught her.

'He hates us, Lund. You saw that.'

'We're police. Lots of people hate us.'

'Picked his moment, didn't he?'

Half past two in the morning. Hartmann was there when they got to the Rådhus. Rie Skovgaard, the slick attractive woman they'd seen at the school, sat on his left. Hartmann's awkward fidgety middle-aged campaign manager, Morten Weber, was on the other side.

'Thanks for coming in,' Lund said.

'We didn't,' Hartmann answered. 'We just stayed. There's an election coming. We work late. Did you find the girl?'

'Yes.' Meyer stared at the politician in the blue shirt, blue trousers. 'She was in your rental car.'

71

Lund wrote out the number, placed it on the table.

'Who was the last person to drive it?'

Hartmann sat rigid in his leather seat.

'Our car?'

Meyer pushed the note closer to him.

'That's what we said. Can we have a little action now?'

'I'll check,' Morten Weber said. 'It'll take a while.'

'Why?' Meyer wanted to know.

'We've lots of cars,' Weber said. 'Thirty drivers. It's the middle of the night. We still have people working. Let me make some calls.'

He left the table and went off into a corner with his phone.

'What do they do, these cars?' Lund asked.

'Deliver campaign material,' Skovgaard said. 'Put up posters. That kind of thing.'

'When did you send a car to the school in Frederiksholm?'

'Probably Friday I guess . . .'

Meyer snapped, put his hands palm down on the table, leaned over and said, 'Guessing isn't much good. The girl's dead. We need to know—'

'We've nothing to hide,' Hartmann broke in. 'We want to help. It's past two in the morning. We can't pull answers out of a hat.'

'Was Nanna Birk Larsen connected to your political work?'

'No,' said Skovgaard straight away. 'She's not on any of our lists.'

72

'That was quick,' Meyer said.

'I thought you wanted quick.' Weber returned.

'The campaign secretary's in Oslo right now.'

'Screw Oslo!' Meyer cried. 'This is a murder case. Get some answers.'

Weber sat down, raised an eyebrow at him, looked at Lund.

Checking the hierarchy, Lund thought. Smart man.

'So I asked the security desk. The keys were collected by Rikke Nielsen on Friday.'

'Who's she?' Lund asked.

'Rikke's in charge of our team of volunteers.' Weber shrugged. 'Anyone can volunteer. We use temps when there aren't enough.'

He glanced at Meyer who was now pacing the room, hands in pockets, like a cockerel pushing for a fight.

'You've phoned her?' Meyer demanded.

'Her phone's off. She's probably organizing the posters.'

Meyer nodded sarcastically.

'Probably?'

'Yes. Like I said. Thirty drivers to coordinate. It's a lot of work.'

'Stop!' Meyer was back at the table again. 'There's a dead girl and you're sitting here as if it's beneath you.'

'Meyer,' Lund said.

'I want answers,' he barked.

'Meyer!'

Loud enough. He stopped.

'Call headquarters,' she ordered. 'Give Buchard an update. Tell him we're going to interview the volunteers.'

He didn't move.

'It's past Buchard's bedtime . . .'

She locked eyes with him.

'Just do it.'

He went off to the window.

'Do you have any idea where this woman is now?' Lund asked.

Weber looked at a piece of paper. He highlighted something with a green marker.

'My best bet.'

Skovgaard took it, checked the names, then handed it on.

'The press,' she said. 'There's no need for them to know.'

Lund shook her head, puzzled.

'A young girl's been murdered. We can't keep this secret.'

'No,' Hartmann said. 'If it was our car we need to issue a statement. It's important no one can accuse us of hiding anything.'

'I don't want you making details public,' Lund insisted. 'You talk to no one but me.'

Skovgaard stood up, arms waving.

'There's an election going on. We can't afford to wait.'

Lund turned to Hartmann.

74

'The information we just gave you was confidential. If you choose to make it public and jeopardize a murder inquiry that's your choice. You can live with the consequences. And there will be consequences, Hartmann. That I promise.'

Weber coughed. Skovgaard went quiet. Meyer looked pleased.

'Rie,' Hartmann said. 'I think we can wait a while. Provided . . .'

The briefest, pleading smile.

'Provided what?' Meyer asked.

'Provided you tell us when you decide to go public. So we can work together. Make sure everything's right.'

He folded his arms. The shirt was the blue of the campaign poster above his head. Everything here was coordinated. Planned.

Lund took out her personal card, crossed out her name, wrote Meyer's there instead.

'Tomorrow morning ring Jan Meyer on this number,' she said. 'He'll update you.'

'You're not on the case?' Hartmann asked.

'No,' Lund said. 'He is.'

Weber left with the cops. Skovgaard stayed with him, still smarting.

'What the hell is this, Troels?'

'Search me.'

'If we agree to hide things the press could crucify us. They love the words cover-up. It gives them a hard-on.'

75

'We're not covering up. We're doing what the police asked us.'

'They won't care.'

Hartmann put on his jacket, thinking, looked at her.

'She didn't leave us much choice. They'd crucify us for screwing up a murder inquiry too. Lund knew that. It's nothing to do with us. Forget about it.'

Sharp eyes wide open, mouth agape.

'A girl's found dead in one of our cars? It's nothing to do with us?'

'Nothing. If you want something to worry about, take a look round this place.'

He pointed to the main office beyond the door. Eight, ten full-time staff working there during the day.

'Meaning what?'

'Meaning are we secure? The computers? Emails? Our reports?'

A caustic look.

'You're not getting paranoid about Bremer, are you?'

'How did he come up with that trick about the school funding? How did he know about the twenty per cent?'

Hartmann thought about the conversation with Bremer, what the mayor said about his late father.

'That cunning old bastard's up to something.'

She came to him with his coat, helped him on with it, zipped it up against the cold night.

'Such as?'

Hartmann told her a little about why Therese Kruse came to see him. About the reporter asking questions. He left out the personal details.

'Some of that had to come from in here. Had to.'

She wasn't happy.

'Why didn't you tell me?'

'I'm telling you now.'

He walked into the big office. Desks and computers. Filing cabinets, voicemail. All the private details of the campaign lived inside this room, deep in the heart of the Rådhus, locked securely every night.

'Go home,' she said. 'I'll take a look around.'

Hartmann came over, took her shoulders, kissed her tenderly.

'I could help.'

'Go home,' she repeated. 'You've got to cut the deal with Kirsten Eller first thing. I want you wide awake for that.'

He looked out of the window into the square.

'They said she was nineteen. Just a kid.'

'It's not our fault, is it?'

Troels Hartmann stared at the blue hotel sign and the yellow lights in the square.

'No,' he said. 'It isn't.'

'Why did you say we'd find him?' Lund asked.

They were in her unmarked car, Meyer at the wheel.

'You won't pull a trick like that on me again,' he said. 'In front of those clowns. Of all the people . . .'

His anger was so open and puerile it was almost amusing.

'I won't need to. I'll be gone. Why did you say that? To the father.'

'Because we will.' A pause. 'I will.'

'You don't make promises,' she threw at him. 'Read the book. Page one.'

'I've got my own book.'

'So I noticed.'

Meyer turned on the radio. A deafening, all-night rock station. Lund leaned forward, switched it off.

She checked the address.

'Turn here.'

A statue of a figure on horseback, sword raised. A grand illuminated building. A multi-storey parking garage. The place Hartmann's campaign team assembled before going out to plaster the city with his posters, leaflets, badges, hats and T-shirts.

The cars were on the second level. Identical black Fords, just like the one they'd pulled from the canal. Lund and Meyer walked round, looking at the same photo of Troels Hartmann plastered to the windows. One back door was open. Three hours earlier, in a vehicle identical to this, she'd seen the scarred half-naked corpse of Nanna Birk Larsen frozen in death in a torn, stained slip. Here there were boxes and boxes of leaflets, and the same photo of Hartmann. That uncertain boyish smile, some pain behind his open, honest eyes.

A blonde woman walked round from the back,

looked at her uncertainly. Lund showed her ID, asked, 'Rikke Nielsen?'

She seemed exhausted. Nervous too when Meyer came from the other side of the car, folded his arms, sat in the open boot and watched her.

'I need the name of a driver from the weekend,' Lund said.

'Why?'

'The number plate is . . .' Lund fumbled for her notebook.

'XU 24 919,' Meyer said unprompted. He got up, came close to the Nielsen woman. 'Black Ford like this one. We'd like to know who drove it last.'

Then he smiled, in a way he probably thought pleasant.

There were men carrying placards of Hartmann's beaming face to cars down the line.

'This is quite an organization you've got. You must keep a logbook.'

'Of course.'

'Can we see it? Please.'

She nodded, walked off. Meyer winked at Lund. The Nielsen woman came back. 'That was XU . . . ?'

'XU 24 919.'

Lund left him, watched the men with the placards and posters. It was cold in the parking garage. But not so cold.

One of the volunteers was a lanky figure in a worn and dirty anorak. He had the hood pulled up around his face. Put the posters in the back of the car. Turned. Grey sweatshirt. Face in shadow. Trying to hide.

Meyer's strained nice-guy act was wearing thin.

'I'm staying very calm here,' she heard him say behind her. 'So you stay calm too. I don't want to hear any more "ifs" or "buts" or "let me ask Mr Weber". Just give me the name of the damned driver.'

He was getting loud. The men stuffing the cars with Hartmann posters could hear. They were glancing at Rikke Nielsen. But not the one in the hood.

Lund turned to tell Meyer to cut the volume. When she looked again the figure in the grey sweatshirt and anorak wasn't there.

A black Ford in the line burst into life, roared out of the parking spot, back door open, scattering the smiling face of Troels Hartmann everywhere.

'Meyer!'

The driver had to get past her to reach the ramp.

Lund walked into the centre of the lane, stood there, stared through the oncoming windscreen.

Man in his late thirties, forties maybe. Stubbled, angry face, afraid, determined.

'For Christ's sake,' Meyer screamed and flew at her, caught her shoulder with one hand, dragged Lund out of the way.

Still accelerating the Ford raced past them, no more than a metre away.

Lund watched it, barely conscious she was in Meyer's arms and he was peering at her, breathless. Furious probably. She had that effect sometimes. The car turned the corner, headed up towards the roof. Meyer let go, set off for the ramp, arms pumping, handgun out, yelling. Lund went the other way, racing for the stairs, taking the concrete steps three at a time, up, up.

One floor, two. Three and there were no more. The roof was black and gleaming in the night rain. Ahead lay the grand baroque dome of the Marble Church softly lit against the city skyline. The car was parked by the far wall, headlamps blazing.

No gun. Still she walked towards it, trying to see.

'Police!' she called.

'Lund!'

Meyer emerged from the ramp exit, panting, coughing, barely able to speak.

There was a sound from the far side. A door opening and closing on a floor below. Lund dashed over to look, Meyer followed. A second set of stairs ran down the building. He'd come here to lose them. Managed it too.

They watched a figure reach the ground floor then flee into the night and the vast dark city.

Meyer in his fury leapt up like an animal, swearing, shrieking so loud she covered her ears.

They slept in their clothes, wrapped in each other, his grief in hers, hers in his.

Waking. Theis Birk Larsen unwound his arms without disturbing her, sat by the bed, quietly got up.

Washed his face, ate some bread, sipped coffee as the boys and Pernille slept. Then went down to face the men.

Twelve on that shift. Vagn Skærbæk, pale-faced, damp-eyed, among them. Vagn. Part of the family. The first person he'd called at two that morning, holding a conversation Birk Larsen could scarcely recall so punctuated was it by tears and cries and fury.

Vagn was a good man for hard times. Times Birk Larsen thought would never come again. He had a family. A rock to lean on, as he was a rock to them.

Sometimes the rock shifted on unseen sand.

He went into the office, took his black coat off the hook, put it on carefully, as he'd done for years. Then went out and stood before them, the boss as always, laying down the orders for the day.

Most of these men had worked for him for years. They knew his family, watched the kids grow. Brought them birthday presents. Read their home-work. Wiped their tears sometimes when he or Pernille weren't there.

A couple were close to crying. Only Skærbæk could look him in the face.

Birk Larsen tried to speak but stood there saying nothing.

Work.

There was a clipboard. A list of jobs that defined the way the hours would pass. He took it, walked into the office. Went looking for something to do.

A long moment's silence. Vagn Skærbæk called to the men by the vans, 'Let's get a move on, huh? I'm not your babysitter.'

Then he came and sat opposite Birk Larsen. A small, insignificant man. Stronger than his puny frame suggested. Face not much changed from when they were in their teens. Dark hair, blank eyes, cheap silver chain round his neck.

'You do what you need to, Theis. I'll deal with the rest.'

Birk Larsen lit a cigarette, looked at the office walls. Photos everywhere. Pernille. Nanna. The boys.

'Some reporters called. I hung up on them. If they call back you give those bastards to me.'

Slowly the depot came to life. Cardboard cases moved beyond the window. Pallets got shifted. Vans went out into the street.

'Theis, I don't know what to say.' Same woollen hat, same red bib overall. Big brother, little brother. 'I want to help. Tell me . . .'

Birk Larsen looked at him, said nothing.

'Do they have a clue who did it?'

Birk Larsen shook his head, drew on his cigarette, tried to think about the schedule, nothing else.

'Let me know if there's anything . . .' Skærbæk began.

'The delivery on Sturlasgade,' Birk Larsen said, the first words he uttered that morning.

The man with him waited.

'I promised them a cherry-picker.'

'It's done,' Vagn Skærbæk told him.

Meyer waved a mugshot at the plain-clothes team in the briefing room. It was of an unremarkable man in a black T-shirt holding up a prison number. Balding, bruised, stubbly face, droopy grey hippie moustache. The long slash of what looked like an old knife wound scarring his right cheek. Staring at the camera, looking bored.

'His name is John Lynge from Nørrebro. He's not at home. He's a known criminal and we . . .' He pinned the photo to the noticeboard. '. . . are going to put this bastard in jail. Talk to neighbours. People he worked with. Bars. Pawnshops. Dope dealers. Anyone who knows him. He's forty-three. Sad, solitary bastard . . .'

Lund listened from the adjoining office, sipping at a coffee in between talking to her son. She'd caught three hours' sleep in a spare room. Didn't feel too bad.

'He's got no plan,' Meyer announced as if this were a given. 'No bolt-hole. Sometime he's going to come up for air. And then . . .'

Meyer clapped his hands together so loudly the noise sounded like a gunshot.

Lund stifled a laugh.

'You're not getting out of Swedish lessons,' she told Mark down the phone. 'How can you? We're going to live there. Bengt can explain to the teacher why you're late. You won't be in trouble.'

Meyer held up a new photo of Nanna. Still pretty. No make-up, no forced sexy smile. Not trying too hard.

'We need to know everything about her. Text messages, voice-mails, emails. Anything that connects her to Lynge.'

Mark was getting sulky.

'We'll fly out tonight,' Lund said. 'I'll let you know when I've booked the plane.'

'Let's move,' Meyer cried and did the handclap again.

Then, when the team had left, he came through and said, 'Buchard wants a word before you go.'

The old man had Lynge's mugshot in front of him on the desk that was once hers. Meyer was going through what he'd learned from the files.

'Thirteen years ago he was caught flashing children in a playground. One year later he raped a girl. Fourteen.'

The chief listened. Lund stood in the door with her cold cup of coffee. She didn't like the look on Buchard's face.

'Six years after that he was put in a psychiatric prison. Released eighteen months ago.'

All this Meyer recited from memory, from a single look at the case records. Impressive, she thought. In a way.

'So why's he out?' Buchard asked.

Meyer shrugged.

'Because he was deemed no longer dangerous?' Lund suggested.

'They always say that.'

'Not always, Meyer,' Buchard said. 'Sarah?'

'We have to talk to him.'

Meyer threw up his hands in mock glee.

'That's the understatement of the year.'

He was playing with the toy police car. Running it to make the blue light flash and the siren wail. Just like a kid.

Buchard said, 'Cut that out. I'd like to talk to her alone.'

Meyer put the car back on the desk with exaggerated care.

'If it's about the case . . .'

Something in Buchard's face stopped him. Meyer raised his palms and walked out.

The moment the door was closed Lund picked up her bag and said, 'We've been through this. You know the answer.'

'Things change.'

'Chief! We don't have anywhere to live. Bengt's waiting for me in Sweden. Mark starts school tomorrow.'

She went for the door.

Buchard said, 'I came from the lab. The girl was still alive when she went into the canal. It takes twenty minutes for a car like that to fill up. Add to that the time it takes to drown.'

He was pulling out a file of photos.

'It's not my case,' Lund said, messing with her bag, rearranging the things she'd rearranged once before.

'She was raped repeatedly. In the vagina. In the anus. He wore a condom and took his time.'

Lund watched him read this from the file and said, 'Mark's so excited about moving. No!'

'She was abused like this for hours. All weekend probably. The bruises indicate she was held somewhere else before the woods.'

Lund got her coat.

'And then there's this,' Buchard said, holding up a small plastic evidence bag.

Lund looked, couldn't help it.

'Meyer showed it to the mother. She says she's never seen it before.'

Buchard cleared his throat.

'The girl was clutching it in her right hand when she died. My guess is he made her wear it. She ripped it from her throat when she was drowning. I can't think of any other explanation.'

Lund stood by the window, looking out at the bleak courtyard in front of the prison cells.

'This isn't the usual, Sarah. You know that. Rape a kid then kill her to shut her up.' She couldn't avoid those beady bright eyes. 'Do you think we'd even know she was dead if we'd left it all to . . .' He nodded at the door. 'Our new friend Meyer?'

'I'm not—'

'I talked to Stockholm. They've agreed you can report there when the case is closed.'

Then he walked away, left the photos, the files, the small clear evidence bag on the table. Walked out and left Lund on her own.

She thought about Mark and Bengt. About Sweden and a new civilian job in Stockholm. But mostly about Nanna Birk Larsen, a broken body in the back of a black Ford car dumped in a dank canal.

Lund picked up the bag, held it to the light.

It was a pendant on a gold chain. Cheap glass. Tacky. Different.

A black heart.

Meyer came back in from the corridor. He looked red-faced. Buchard must have told him.

'This is outrageous.'

'Couldn't agree more. We do things my way until the end of the week. If the case is still alive then you can have it.'

'Fine.'

It didn't look fine.

'We go by my rules. We treat people with respect, whether we like them or not. In the car you won't smoke, you won't drive at more than thirty miles an hour . . .'

'May I fart?'

'No. And I don't want cheese crisps or hot dogs everywhere either.'

'Any particular kind of underwear you prefer?'

She thought for a moment.

'How about clean?'

★ ★ ★

A school was a world in miniature, riven with gossip and rumour. When the teacher called Rama arrived that grey morning he felt the news flitting through the corridors like a mischievous ghost.

Then Rektor Koch told him, 'I can do it if you wish.'

'My pupil,' he said. 'My class.'

Five minutes later he walked into the room, no books in his hand, no smile on his face. Looked at them, all of them, not children, not adults. Oliver Schandorff with his wild ginger hair, his dope eyes, his sour face. Lisa Rasmussen, Nanna's best friend, though never so pretty or smart.

What did you say except the obvious? What did you offer but the banal?

His dark face morose, Rama said, 'It's just been announced . . .' He stopped, closed his eyes, heard the words' harshness even before he spoke them. 'The police say Nanna's dead.'

A quick communal intake of breath. Tears and moans and whispers.

'There'll be no more lessons today. You're free to go home. Or stay. The teachers will be here all day. We'll have counsellors available.'

A hand went up at the back. Someone asked the inevitable.

What happened?

The man they knew as Rama thought of his own family's journey, the difficult, perilous land they'd left behind. He was only a child then. But still he could sense from them how safe this city seemed by comparison.

'I don't know.'

Another hand.

'Was she murdered?'

Lisa Rasmussen's fingers flew to her face, a cry of grief and pain escaped them.

'You've all got questions I know. Me too. There are no . . .' A teacher was never lost for words. A teacher was always honest. 'Sometimes there are no quick answers. We have to wait for them.'

He thought of what Koch had told him. Went straight to Lisa, put an arm round her bent back, tried to meet her eyes.

'They need your help,' he said. 'Lisa?'

No answer.

'The police want to see you.'

She buried her face in her arms.

'You and Oliver.'

Rama looked up. He was there a minute ago. But now the seat was empty.

Lund showed Lisa Rasmussen a photo of the black Ford estate.

'You've seen this car?'

Lisa nodded.

'Maybe. One like it.'

'When?'

She thought and said, 'Friday. Before the party. I think they were dropping off some stuff.'

Lund held up the mugshot of John Lynge.

'And him?'

The girl stared at the bald man with the staring eyes, the grey moustache and scarred cheek, the police number in front of him.

'Did he do it?'

'Just tell me if you've seen him.'

Lisa peered at the photo and said, 'I don't think so. What did he do to Nanna?'

'Maybe he's been in the school. Or somewhere you and Nanna went together.'

A long moment, then she shook her head.

'No. I haven't seen him before.'

Lund put the photo away.

'Do you have any idea why Nanna said she was staying with you?'

'No.' The tears were back. She looked fifteen again. 'I thought maybe she'd gone off with someone.'

'Who?'

'I don't know.'

'Lisa—'

'I don't know!'

Another tack. They talked about the party.

'How was she?' Lund asked.

'Happy.'

'In a good mood?'

'Happy.'

'And . . . ?'

'And she left. I thought it was a bit early. But—'

'Why did she leave early?'

'She didn't say.'

'Did she leave with someone?'

'I didn't . . .'

Her voice trailed off into silence.

Lund bent down and tried to catch her eyes.

'I didn't see! Why do you keep asking me questions? What am I supposed to know?'

Lund let the outburst die down, bit into a piece of Nicotinell.

'Nanna was your best friend, wasn't she? I thought you'd want to help.'

'I don't know anything.'

The pile of photos was sorted carefully. Nothing physical. Nothing disturbing. Lund took out the last shot and showed it to her.

'Do you recognize this necklace?'

Black heart on a gold chain.

Lisa shook her head.

'Looks old,' she said.

'You never saw Nanna wear it?'

'No.'

'Are you sure . . .'

'I'm sure, I'm sure, I'm sure, I'm sure!' the girl screamed. 'I saw her at the party. I hugged her. I didn't know it was the last time . . .'

Lisa Rasmussen stared at the table, not at the photographs, never at Lund.

'I didn't know,' she said again.

'I checked,' Rie Skovgaard said. 'Lynge isn't a party member. He was a temp from an agency we used a couple of times. Could have been working for anyone.'

92

They were outside the campaign office, in the corridor, speaking in whispers. Hartmann looked as if he'd hardly slept.

'That's good,' he said.

'Only if people know. If we don't say something and the press get hold of this . . .'

'What?'

'They'll say we hired a killer and covered for him. If Kirsten Eller hears we can kiss goodbye to your alliance. We've got to issue a statement. Make the position clear immediately.'

Hartmann hesitated.

'I'm supposed to be your adviser, Troels. I'm telling you. We're standing on the precipice here. You don't wait until you're falling . . .'

'Fine, fine. Do it. But let the police know first.'

'Eller and the party?'

'Leave them to me.'

By midday the school was empty. Lund and Meyer were comparing notes in a deserted corridor, next to the lockers. On one side was a set of government health warnings about drugs and drink and sex. On the other a line of posters for movies and rock music.

Meyer had been busy. He had three witnesses who saw Lynge delivering campaign material to the school just after midday.

'And in the evening?'

'The car was here then too. Maybe he heard about the party and returned.'

93

'Are we certain this was the car?'

Meyer slapped some photos in her hand and grinned.

'They took pictures for the school website. Party time. Look in the background in the exterior shots. It was the car.'

His phone rang. While he talked she ran through the pictures. Behind kids in ghoulish costumes, masks and wigs, hideous monster outfits, was the black outline of the Ford.

Meyer was getting mad.

'I told you before that's out of the question,' he barked into the phone.

An angry Jan Meyer. That was something new. She looked at more photos. They didn't have Halloween like this when Lund was nineteen. Even if they had . . .

She wondered what her mother would have said.

'I'm not telling you again,' Meyer shouted. 'The answer's no.'

He stared at the phone. Swore.

'I don't believe it. She hung up on me.'

'What's going on?'

'Hartmann's issuing a press statement. Trying to get his scrawny arse off the . . .'

Lund slapped the photos in his arms.

'We're going to the Rådhus. You drive.'

Birk Larsen went out to the job in a daze, got there only to be appalled by his own lack of consideration, came straight home, sat with Pernille in the kitchen, not talking just waiting, for what neither knew.

Then Lotte arrived, her sister. Eleven years younger, as close to Nanna as she was to Pernille. Birk Larsen sat mute and lethargic in the corner, watched them hug and cry, envying their open emotions.

'What about the boys?' Lotte asked.

'We haven't told them yet,' Pernille said. 'Theis?'

'What?'

It was the first word he'd spoken in an hour.

Lotte sat at the table and sobbed. Pernille checked the school timetable, on the cork-board with the family photos.

'We'll pick up the boys after art. It ends at two.'

'Yes.'

Lotte was in pieces.

'What was she doing there? Nanna'd never get into a stranger's car.'

More black coffee. It stopped him wanting to scream.

Pernille moved photos around the cork-board for no good reason.

'We need to . . .' She sniffed, took two long breaths. 'We need to think about the boys.'

She was crying again but didn't want to show it.

Birk Larsen longed to do something. To be out of this place so badly. Knew that unspoken thought was a kind of betrayal too.

'We've got to tell them,' he said.

★   ★   ★

95

Lund walked into the Liberal Party office. It smelled of sweat and polished wood and old leather. Skovgaard, Hartmann's too-elegant too-confident political adviser, was on the phone talking about the press release.

'I want to see him,' Lund said when Skovgaard came off the phone.

'He's in a meeting.'

Lund said, 'Oh.'

Watched her go back to the computer, typing standing up, the way busy people did.

'Your statement's going out?' she asked.

Still typing.

'Can't wait any longer.'

'It has to.'

Skovgaard glanced at the door behind her, said very slowly, as if talking to an idiot, 'We can't.'

Lund walked over, pushed Skovgaard away when she flew at her, screaming, opened the door.

Troels Hartmann looked bemused. So did the woman next to him.

Kirsten Eller. The plump woman from the election posters.

She wasn't smiling. She didn't like to be disturbed.

'Sorry,' Lund said to the man in the pressed blue shirt. 'But we have to talk.'

One minute later by the window, Kirsten Eller out of earshot on the sofa.

Hartmann said, 'If the media think I'm lying . . .'

96

'This is a murder case. The details are confidential. You can't jeopardize our chances . . .'

'What about my chances?'

He was an unusual man. Blessed with a politician's charisma. An aura of blithe candour. He managed to say that without any obvious shame.

Her phone rang, she snatched it out of her bag, sighed when she saw the number, answered anyway.

'Bengt. Can I call you back?'

The sound of hammering. Distant.

'I'm at the house. The carpenters are here. What kind of wood do we want for the sauna?'

Lund closed her eyes. Hartmann wasn't walking away. That was something.

'What kind usually goes in saunas?'

'Pine.'

'Pine is fine. That sounds good.'

'But it depends on . . .'

'Not now. I'll phone you later.'

End of call.

Hartmann was walking back to the woman waiting patiently on his sofa.

Lund took his arm, looked into his eyes. There was something there . . .

'We're very close to catching him. Don't get in our way.'

'How close? Today?'

'I hope so.'

Hartmann hesitated.

'OK,' he said. 'I'll wait for that. So long as it is today.'

97

'Thanks,' she said.

'Polar pine.'

Lund stopped.

'Polar pine. It's better for saunas than ordinary. Has less resin.'

'Oh.'

Meyer was at the door, back from hunting round the corridors.

Time to go.

Kirsten Eller was smiling when Hartmann came back.

'Bad news, Troels?'

'Not at all. It's no bother.'

She watched him.

'Really? You looked worried.'

'I said it's nothing.'

'If I'm to divorce Bremer this must be a marriage. Not a fickle affair.'

'Of course,' he said, nodding vigorously.

'Requiring frankness in all things.'

Hartmann smiled at her.

'There's no bad news, Kirsten. Can we get down to business?'

Just after two Pernille and Theis Birk Larsen waited on the grey pavement by the fountain, watched the kids come running from the playground, wrapped in warm coats, hats and gloves, backpacks on, brightly coloured kites waving in their hands.

Tuesday. They always made something.

Emil, seven, with his short fair hair, Anton six, ginger as his father once was. The boys came stumbling, trying to make their kites catch on the chill winter breeze.

Emil's was red, Anton's yellow.

'Why's Dad with you?' Emil asked straight out.

Into the grey street, watching the traffic. Cross the road carefully. Small hands in theirs.

Anton wanted to know if they could go and fly the kites in the park. Sulked when his mother said no.

The sky loomed dark and heavy. They packed the boys' things in the boot.

A call. Vagn Stærbæk anxious in Birk Larsen's ear.

'Don't come home yet,' he said.

'Why not?'

'The police are searching her room. Some photographers have arrived.'

Birk Larsen blinked, watched Pernille fasten the boys into their safety seats, buckles checked, a kiss on the forehead.

Not anger, he thought. Not now.

'How long will they be?'

'No idea. Should I get rid of them?'

Birk Larsen couldn't think of a thing to say.

'The boys, Theis. You don't want them to see this.'

'No. Call me when they're gone.'

So they got in the car and he said, 'Let's fly those kites. Let's do that.'

Two small cheers, fists punching the air in the back. Pernille looked at him.

No words needed. She knew.

Meyer was driving the way he usually did.

'Did Poster Boy get your vote then?'

'Meaning?'

'You smiled at him, Lund.'

'I smile at lots of people.'

'He kept looking at your jumper.'

She still wore the black and white sweater from the Faroes. It was warm and comfy. Bought it on the holiday just after the divorce, with Mark, trying to ease him through the shock. She liked them so much she got some more. Different colours. Different patterns. There was a mail order place . . .

'Last time I saw my granny she was wearing one like that,' Meyer said.

'That's nice.'

'Not really. She was in a box. I hate funerals. They seem so . . .' He slammed the horn as a cyclist got in the way. 'Final.'

'You made that up,' she said and he didn't answer.

The Faroe Islands were green and peaceful. A quiet, sleepy world away from the grimy urban landscape of Copenhagen.

'I'm sure he couldn't be stealing a glance at your tits. I mean . . .'

She didn't listen, let him ramble on. Get it out of his system.

In the green world of the Faroes nothing much

happened. People got by. Seasons came and went. Cows farted. Just like Sigtuna.

'Where are we going, Meyer?'

'Lynge hasn't been in his apartment since last night. He's got a sister. She runs a hair salon in Christianshavn. He went to see her this morning. Turned ugly.'

Meyer grinned at her.

'Some men are like that.'

Lynge's sister was a good-looking woman with long straight hair and a mournful face.

'Where is he?' Meyer asked.

'Haven't a clue. He's my brother. I didn't pick him.'

Lynge was waiting down a side street when she opened up that morning. Forced his way in. Bad timing. All she had was five thousand kroner in the till. He took it, trashed the place a little. The sister was mopping up shampoo and conditioner from the floor as she spoke.

Lund walked round, leaving the questions to Meyer.

'Where do you think he's gone?'

'I don't know him any more. He's sick.'

'We know that.'

'No.' She tapped the side of her head. 'Not just there. He's sick. Ill. He needs to be in hospital.' She stopped mopping. 'I've never seen him that bad. It was just money. Don't put him back in jail. Not again. He'd get even crazier.'

101

'Does he have anywhere to go? A girlfriend?'

'No one wants to know him. Not after what he did.' She hesitated. 'There was a woman.'

'What woman?' Lund asked.

'A prison visitor. A volunteer.' The sister frowned. 'You know the kind. Christian. Never gives up. She contacted me a few weeks back. Begged me to get back in touch with him. Said it would help.'

They waited.

'It wouldn't help. I know him. Besides . . .'She looked around the little salon. 'I've got a life. A right to that. Haven't I?'

Meyer picked up a hairbrush, played with it.

'You've got a name for this woman?'

'Sorry. She came from one of the prison charities I think.'

The sister looked at Lund.

'He killed that girl on the TV, didn't he? I knew it was going to happen. They shouldn't have let him out. He was so scared.'

'When I get hold of him he will be,' Meyer murmured.

The woman didn't say anything.

'What?' Lund asked.

'This morning. He looked really scared. I mean . . . I don't know.'

'We need to find him. We need to talk.'

She started mopping again.

'Good luck,' the sister said.

Outside. Steady rain.

'Take my car. Get someone onto the prison visitor,' she told Meyer. 'Then call me.'

'Where are you going?'

Lund hailed a cab and was gone.

Mathilde Villadsen was seventy-six, half-blind, living in an old apartment block with her cat Samson and her second-best friend the radio. It was playing music from the Fifties, the decade she thought of as hers.

Then the swing band got interrupted by the news.

'The police have imposed a news blackout . . .' the reader began.

'Samson?'

It was time to feed him. The tin was open. The food was in the dish.

'. . . over the case of Nanna Birk Larsen who was found dead on Monday.'

She walked to the kitchen sink, turned off the radio. It was cold in the draughty flat. She wore what she did for most of the winter: a long blue woollen cardigan, a thick scarf round her wrinkled neck. The price of heating was terrible. She was a Fifties girl. A little hardship was a cross she could bear.

'Samson?'

The cat was mewing outside the flap into the corridor. In her old, loose slippers she shuffled to the front door, undid the chain.

It was dark in the stairwell. The kids were always knocking out the lights. Mathilde Villadsen sighed, got down on her painful knees, wished the cat wouldn't play these games.

In the gloom, feeling the cold stone through her stockings, she scrambled across the hall calling, 'Samson, Samson. Naughty cat, *naughty* cat . . .'

Then she bumped into something. Struggling to see, she felt with her fingers. Dirty leather, denim trousers above it.

Glanced up. A bald head, a scarred face in the flickering flame of a cigarette lighter, close to the cat's whiskers as it sat in the arms of a man above her.

He looked unhappy. Frightened.

'My cat . . .' she started to say.

The lighter got closer to Samson's face. Samson mewed and tried to scramble free from his strong arms.

In a low hard voice he said, 'Don't squawk. Get inside.'

There was a wedding dress on the mannequin, white satin covered in embroidered cotton flowers. Lund's mother, Vibeke, made them for a local shop. Not so much for money, more for something to do. Widowhood didn't suit her. Not a lot did.

'What does Bengt say about all this?'

She was a stiff-backed woman, always smart, always serious, with a brisk, sometimes caustic manner and a judgemental eye.

'I'm going to call him.'

Vibeke stood back and considered the dress. Put

104

a stitch in the breast, another in the arm. Lund thought she liked the idea of women getting married. It narrowed their options. Tied them down the way God meant.

'So you haven't even told him you're not coming?'

'No time.'

Her mother uttered that short brief sigh Lund had known since childhood. Even so she remained amazed how much distaste and disapproval could be compressed into a single breath.

'I hope you don't chase this one away too.'

'I just said I would call!'

'Carsten . . .'

'Carsten hit me!'

The look, long and cold.

'Once. That's all. He was your husband. The father of your child.'

'He—'

'The way you behave. This obsession with your work. A man needs to know he's wanted. Loved. If you don't give them that . . .'

'He hit me.'

With great care Vibeke placed the needle in the shiny satin fabric at the neckline.

'Do you ever wonder if you asked for it?'

'I didn't ask for it. No one ever does.'

Lund's mobile rang. It was Meyer: 'I talked to the prison.'

'And?'

'He had three visitors in all. One's dead. One's moved. One's not answering her phone.'

'Come and get me,' Lund said and gave him the address in Østerbro. 'Twenty minutes.'

'Blue light taxi's on the way. I hope you tip well.'

The police people had left their marks and trails all over the apartment. Numbers and arrows. Puffs of dust where they'd looked for prints.

Anton, always the most inquisitive, stood outside her room and asked, 'What's that on Nanna's door?'

'Get away from there!' Theis Birk Larsen barked at him. 'Come to the table.'

The table.

Pernille and Nanna made it one empty distant summer three years before when there was nothing else to do but watch the rain. Cheap timber from the DIY store. Photos and school reports glued then lacquered onto the top. The Birk Larsen family frozen in time. Nanna turned sixteen, growing quickly. Anton and Emil so tiny. Faces captured in the place that was the heart of their small home. Smiling mostly.

Now the boys were six and seven, bright-eyed wondering. Curious, perhaps a little afraid.

Pernille sat down, looked at them, touched their knees, their hands, their cheeks and said, 'There's something we have to tell you.'

Birk Larsen stood behind. Until she turned to him. Then, slowly, he came and sat by her side.

'Something's happened to us,' Pernille told them.

The boys shuffled, glanced at one another.

'What?' Emil, the elder, though in a way the slower, asked.

Beyond the window the traffic rumbled. There were voices in the street. It was always like this. For Theis Birk Larsen it always would be.

Together. A family. Complete.

His great chest heaved. Strong, scarred fingers ran through greying ginger hair. He felt old, impotent, stupid.

'Boys,' he said finally. 'Nanna's dead.'

Pernille waited.

'She's not coming back,' he added.

Six and seven, bright eyes glittering beneath the lamp where they all ate supper. Static faces staring at them from the tabletop.

Emil said, 'Why's that, Dad?'

Thinking.

Struggling.

'There was a time we saw a big tree out in Deer Park. Remember?'

Anton looked at Emil. Then both nodded.

'Lightning struck it. Tore off a big . . .'

Was this real, he asked himself? Or imagined? Or a lie to let children sleep when the darkness came?

'Tore off a big branch. Well . . .'

It didn't matter, Birk Larsen thought. Lies could work too, as well as the truth. Better sometimes. Beautiful lies might let you sleep. Ugly truths never.

'You could say lightning's struck us now. It took Nanna away.'

They listened in silence.

'But just like the tree in Deer Park keeps growing we do too.'

A good lie. It heartened him a little.

He squeezed Pernille's hand beneath the table and said, 'We have to.'

'Where's Nanna?' asked Anton, younger, quicker.

'Someone's taking care of her,' Pernille said. 'In a few days everyone will go to church. Then we say goodbye.'

The boy's smooth brow furrowed.

'She won't *ever* come back?'

Mother and father, their eyes briefly locked. These were children. Precious, still trapped in their own world, no need to escape it.

'No,' said Pernille. 'An angel came and took her to heaven.'

Another good lie.

Six and seven, bright eyes glittering. Not a part of this nightmare. Not . . .

'How did she die?'

Anton. Had to be.

The words fled them. Pernille walked to the cork-board, stared at photos, the timetables, the plans they'd all made.

'How did she die, Dad?'

'I don't know.'

'Dad.'

'It just . . . happens sometimes.'

The boys fell quiet. He held their hands.

Wondered: have they ever seen me cry before? How long before they see it again?

'It just happens.'

Lund and Meyer walked up the stairs, rang the bell, waited. The hallway was dark. Broken bulbs. It stank of cat piss.

'So you've moved in with your mother instead of that Norwegian?'

'Bengt's Swedish.'

'You can tell the difference?'

There was no answer from the address they had. Junk mail was piled up at the foot of the door.

Lund walked to the next apartment along. There was a light behind the frosted glass. The nameplate said Villadsen.

Meyer's radio squawked. It was too loud. She glared at him and banged on the door.

Nothing.

Lund knocked again. Meyer stood to one side, fists on hips, silent. She almost laughed. Like most of the men in homicide he wore his 9-millimetre Glock handgun on his waistband in a holster. It made him look like a cartoon cowboy.

'What's wrong?'

'Nothing.' She tried not to smile. 'Nothing at all.'

'At least I've got a gun. Where's . . . ?'

There was a rattle. The door opened just a couple of inches on the chain. An elderly woman's face, not clear in the darkness.

109

'I'm Vicekriminalkommissær Sarah Lund from the police,' Lund said, showing her ID. 'We need to speak to your neighbour, Geertsen.'

'She's away.'

Old people and strangers. Fear and suspicion.

'Do you know where?'

'Abroad.'

The woman moved as if to close the door. Lund put a hand out to stop her.

'Did you see anything unusual around the block today?'

'No.'

There was a sound from behind her in the apartment. The woman's eyes wouldn't leave Lund's.

'Do you have a visitor?' Meyer asked.

'It's just my cat,' she said then quickly slammed the door.

One minute later, back in her squad car, Lund on the radio, Meyer by her side. He was getting twitchy.

'I need back-up. The suspect may be at this location.'

'We'll send a car,' control replied.

They could see the apartment window from the street.

Meyer said, 'The lights are out. He knows we're here.'

'They're on their way.'

He took out the Glock and checked it.

'We can't wait. A man like that. An old woman. We're going in.'

Lund shook her head.

'To do what?'

'Whatever we can. You heard the sister. He's a lunatic. I'm not waiting till the old bird's dead.'

Lund leaned over the seat, looked him in the eye, said, 'We're staying here.'

'No.'

'Meyer! There's two of us. We can't cover the exits . . .'

'Where's your gun?'

She was getting sick of this.

'I don't have one.'

It was the look she saw the day before when they talked about Sweden. Utter amazement.

'What?' Meyer asked.

'We're going nowhere. We'll wait.'

A long moment. Meyer nodding.

'You can wait if you want,' he said then leapt out of the car.

Across the city, in a campaign car speeding through the night, Troels Hartmann took the last call he wanted. A news agency. Official this time. A journalist with a name he recalled.

The reporter said, 'We know about the car, Hartmann. Nanna Birk Larsen was found in one of yours. You kept it quiet. Why is that exactly?'

In the apartment above the depot, while Pernille quietly wept, Theis Birk Larsen sat with Anton and Emil, one on each huge knee, telling more stories

111

about angels and forests, watching their faces, hating his lies.

Sarah Lund bit on another piece of Nicotinell, thought about Jan Meyer, thought about the dead girl who came out of the water.

Then she pulled open the glove compartment by the wheel, sorted through the packs of gum, the dead lighter, the tissues, the tampons and took out her gun.

Halfway up the dark dank staircase she heard the sound of breaking glass.

Lund ran the rest of the way, took hold of Meyer's arm as he smashed at the panel in the door with the grip of his gun.

'What do you think you're doing?'

'What does it look like?'

'I told you to wait.'

He broke more glass, opened up the hole with his elbow, put a hand through, looked at her and winked.

'You go left,' Meyer said. 'I go right.'

Hand through, searching. There was the sound of an old key turning an old lock. Then the door moved. Inside was as black as the night they'd just left. Meyer scuttled through and was gone in a stride. She went to the wall, edged forward, the Glock an unfamiliar shape in her right hand.

The place stank of mothballs and liniment, cat and washing.

Three steps and she bumped into a sideboard, nudged something with her arm, just managed to catch it before the thing fell to the floor. Lund could just see what she'd touched: a porcelain figurine, a country milkmaid grinning beneath her burden of buckets. Placed it back without a sound. Moved forward, stepped on something, heard a tinny mechanical voice break the silence.

'Your weight is fifty-seven point two kilograms.'

She got off the scales wondering what Meyer was saying to himself.

'Fifty-seven point two kilograms,' the thing said again.

There was a pained sigh from somewhere ahead. Then footsteps. A silhouette. Meyer, trudging in front of her, gun out.

No other sound. Three more steps. A door on the right, ajar. Laboured, arrhythmic breathing. She pocketed the weapon, walked through, fumbled her fingers against the wall, found a light switch. Turned it on.

In the dim yellow bulb of a single wall-light the old woman struggled, trussed like a farmyard bird, wrists and ankles, a cloth rag round her mouth.

Lund got down, put a hand to her shoulder, pulled off the gag.

A long high wail of terror and pain burst from the old woman's lips.

Meyer was close by, cursing.

'Where is he?' Lund asked. 'Mrs Villadsen?'

'What did she say?' Meyer snapped.

The woman was panting, gasping for breath. Terrified.

'What did she say?'

Lund looked at him. Listened. He got the message. Went back out in the dark apartment, feet tapping on the tiles.

She waited.

You take the left. I'll take the right.

Did that still apply? Yes, she guessed. Meyer was a little like her in some ways. There was one plan and one plan only. You stuck with it until something changed. He didn't like working with someone else either.

She undid the woman's ankles and wrists, told her to stay there, stay still.

A pair of scrawny hands clawed at her.

'Don't leave me.'

'I'll be right back. We're here. You're safe.'

'Don't leave me.'

'It's fine. Don't worry.'

Still the wrinkled fingers clutched at her.

'I need my cane.'

'Where is it?'

She gasped, thought, said, 'In the hallway.'

'OK.' Voice calm, steady. Which was how Lund felt. 'Stay here.'

She got to the door, bore left.

Kitchen smells. Drains, food. The cat. Another old lamp, frilly shade, faded yellow. A chair, a small desk. Striped curtains running to the floor. Gently moving as if the window behind was open.

In November.

114

Lund folded her arms, thought, moved forward, gently pushed the fabric aside.

The pain bit at her arm like a wasp sting, rapid and savage.

There was a figure coming from behind the stripes, silhouetted against the faint lights behind the window. His right arm was flailing, right and left, up and down.

Another flash of agony.

Lund yelled, 'Get back! Police! Get back.'

Fumbling like a fool for her gun.

The wall stopped her. He lunged forward. And now the light caught him. In his hand she saw a box cutter, short blade, sharp. Threatening.

He swore, slashed at her, so close she could feel the air move past her cheek.

A furious, insane face, mouth opening, yellow teeth grinning. He roared. One more cutting, sweeping slash . . .

Her fingers tightened on the gun butt. She raised it, pointed the barrel dead in his face.

John Lynge's eyes narrowed. He was sweating. Looked sick. Looked mad.

'Calm down, John. I won't hurt you.' No sound from Meyer. She knew what he'd be doing.

Lynge retreated a step. Her eyes were getting used to this light. She saw his shoulders, his arms.

Kept the gun straight on him.

'I didn't do anything!'

Frightened, she thought. That was good.

'I didn't say you did, John.'

Keep using the name. Keep turning down the heat.

He started rocking backwards, forwards, sobbing, hands to his face.

The blade was still there. Did he know that?

'You don't believe me,' Lynge grunted.

'I'm listening. Put down the knife.'

He flashed the box cutter at her. Didn't flinch at the gun.

'You're not putting me back in jail!'

Crazy voice. A man in agony.

'We're just talking, John. Let's do that. OK? The school . . .'

Stiff and furious, shaking, close to the edge, Lynge bellowed, 'I felt sick. I went to the hospital. I got back. The car was gone. Maybe, maybe . . .'

'Maybe what?'

'Maybe I dropped the keys when I was throwing up. I don't know.'

'What keys?'

'The car keys! You're not listening.'

He was getting madder all the time.

'You were sick. I hear you, John.'

He moved a step to the left. She could see him in the orange light from the street.

'You felt ill and you left the car. Put down the knife. Let's talk.'

'I'm not going back to that place. They'll know—'

'You won't—'

'John!'

A hard male voice from the hallway. Lund took

a deep breath. Looked. Meyer was there. Gun up. Pointed straight at John Lynge's head. Ready.

'Drop the knife,' he said in a slow threatening tone.

'I have this, Meyer,' she said. 'It's under control . . .'

Lynge was running already. Meyer after him. Two dark shapes crossing the floor.

A scream and shattering glass. A tumult of bitter curses. Then a hideous crash outside. The sickening sound of flesh and bone on pavement.

'Meyer?' she said.

There was a figure at the window.

Lund walked to it.

'Meyer?' she said again.

John Lynge was unconscious, strapped to a trolley, tubes and apparatus everywhere, getting rushed down a hospital corridor. It was ten in the evening. Lund asked, for the third time, 'When can I speak to him?'

The surgeon didn't break his pace, just stared at her then said, 'Are you serious?'

'Is he going to live?' she asked when they got to the operating theatre doors.

Lund stopped, repeated the question at twice the volume.

No answer. Then John Lynge was gone.

'We've got prints,' Meyer told her. 'Forensics have got his boots.'

'And nothing to match them with. He says he went to the hospital!'

'Puh!'

'Have you ever heard someone say that, Meyer? Not I was screwing my girlfriend. I was in a bar. But I went to hospital?'

Nothing.

'He told me he left the keys at the school. When he came back the car was gone.'

'He was lying!'

Meyer looked at her and shook his head.

'He cut you, Lund. He'd have cut you again.' He came close. 'Cut your face to ribbons. Doesn't that bother you?'

'It doesn't mean he killed Nanna Birk Larsen. Check the hospital records.'

'Oh come on. Do you really think—'

'If he's got an alibi I want to know. Find out.'

She shouted that last order. Which wasn't like her. This man had got under her skin.

Lund took off her jacket, checked the sleeve of her black and white jumper. The thing was ruined. Lynge's blade had slashed a cut through the wool, opened up a flesh wound across the top of her arm just below the shoulder.

'You should get that seen—'

'Yes! I should. What about the old lady?'

'I called while you were yelling at the doctors. She's going to stay with some relatives.'

Lund nodded. Calm now. The cut hurt, not that she was going to show it.

'Go and get some sleep,' she told him. 'Tell them to let me know if his condition changes.'

118

He folded his arms, didn't move.

'What?' Lund asked.

'I'm not going anywhere until I see you talk to a nurse.'

The TV debate was over. A draw at best, Hartmann thought.

Outside, in the huddle waiting for their cars, he took Rie Skovgaard to one side, asked, 'Have you heard from Lund?'

'No.'

'Did you call her?'

'I can't get through.'

It was raining. There was no sign of their driver.

'We can't afford to wait any longer. Put a statement together.'

'Finally . . .'

'Give it to the reporter who phoned. He's legit. Tell him it's an exclusive. Win us some breathing space . . .'

Bremer strode up, jacket over shoulder, glanced at the rain, stepped back beneath the shelter of the roof.

'Crisis meeting?'

The two of them went quiet.

'I thought you were a little rusty tonight,' Poul Bremer said. 'If you don't mind my saying so.'

'Really?'

No points scored on either side. No balls dropped. But the way Bremer smiled throughout gave Hartmann pause. Every issue, every question he forced round to the question of character. Hartmann's lack of experience, of proven trust.

The old bastard knew something. He was waiting for the right moment to say it.

'Rusty,' Bremer repeated. 'You'll need to do better than that.'

'Still three weeks to the election,' Skovgaard said. 'Lots of time—'

'Pacing yourself. A wise move from what I hear. Goodnight!'

Hartmann watched him go.

'One day I will tear that old dinosaur apart,' he muttered.

'You really have to work on your temper,' Skovgaard said.

He turned his icy gaze on her.

'Do I?'

'Yes. It's good to come across as passionate. Energetic. Committed. But not bad-tempered, Troels. People don't like it.'

'Thank you. I'll try to remember that.'

'Bremer's looking for weak points. Don't hand him one on a plate. Your temper leaves you vulnerable. He's not the only one who's noticed.'

She didn't quite meet his eye.

'I need you to work on this.'

Skovgaard held up her phone.

'Ritzau news agency have heard about the car too. The story's out there.'

The black saloon came and parked in front of them. The Rådhus driver got out and opened the doors.

'I told you we needed to get this out early,' she said. 'Now we're racing round trying to clean up something we should have killed at birth.'

'Bremer's behind this.'

'Someone in the police more likely. How would he know?'

'Twelve years on that burnished throne. Maybe the Politigården works for him too.'

A long limousine ran past. Bremer wound down the window, grinned at them, waved like a king hailing his subjects.

'He's got someone,' Hartmann muttered. 'We need to know who it is.'

Ten minutes later the car pulled into the Rådhus. A crowd of reporters and cameramen flocked around them.

'Say what we agreed,' Skovgaard said. 'Be calm, be authoritative. Don't get mad. Don't go off script.'

'Whose script?' he said, and then they were in the middle of the mob, hands clawing at the doors to get them open.

The rain was heavy and constant. Hartmann pushed through the crowd to the steps of the building. Listening to the questions. Thinking about them.

'Hartmann? What's your connection to Nanna Birk Larsen?'

'Where were you on Friday?'

'What do you have to hide?'

A sea of hostile voices. When he got to the doors

121

he stopped, watched the voice recorders come up ready to capture every word.

What he said would be on the radio in minutes. Captured for ever, repeated in newspapers, replayed on the web.

He waited till they listened then said, in as calm and statesmanlike a manner as he could manage, 'A young woman was found dead in a car that my office rented. That's all I can tell you. The police specifically asked us not to comment. But let me say something—'

'When did you hear?' a woman shouted.

'Let me say . . . No one in the party or the organization is involved in this case. That's as much as I can—'

'Do you deny withholding information for the sake of the election?'

Hartmann looked. He was a stocky bald man of about thirty-five, cigarette in smirking mouth.

'What?'

The hack pushed his way nearer.

'This isn't a tough one, Hartmann,' the reporter bawled through the forest of voice recorders. 'Do you deny you deliberately deceived the public to win some votes. Is this what we can expect of the Liberal Party?'

He didn't stop to think about it. Was through the crowd so quickly Skovgaard couldn't stop him, had the man by the collar.

The smirk never left the bald hack's face.

'Yes,' Hartmann said close up. 'I deny that.' A

pause. He let go, brushed the man's collar as if this were a joke. 'It's nothing to do with politics. This girl . . .'

He was off script. He was drowning.

'Troels?' Skovgaard said.

'The girl . . .'

Cameras flashed. A spiky crown of voice recorders bristled around him.

The hack he'd so nearly punched pulled out a card and thrust it into Hartmann's fingers. Not thinking he took it.

'Troels?'

Drowning.

She had his arm, quietly pulled him away, through the door, into the vestibule, through the inner courtyard and the gleaming silence of the Rådhus until they found safety behind its fortress walls.

Hartmann felt the paper in his hand. Looked.

It was a business card.

Just a mobile number. And a name.

Erik Salin.

All evening she'd sat in the dark front room watching TV, switching from news channel to news channel.

Now it was the main bulletin.

'Troels Hartmann is cooperating with the police in solving the murder,' the story said. 'He denies any connection to the girl or the crime.'

She'd seen his posters everywhere. Striking, handsome, more like an actor than a politician. He always looked sad too, she thought.

A noise from behind. She didn't turn.

He came and slumped by her side on the carpet.

'The car belonged to that politician,' Pernille said. 'They're looking for a driver.'

He had his head in his hands. Said nothing.

'Why don't they tell us what's going on, Theis? It's as if we don't matter.'

'They'll tell us when they've got something to say.'

His lethargy infuriated her.

'They know more than we do. Don't you care?'

'Stop this!'

'Don't you care?'

The TV was the brightest thing in the room.

'How could Nanna know this driver? Someone in politics? How—?'

'I don't know!'

There was a gulf between them. A chasm that was new. His big and clumsy hand went out to touch her. Pernille shrank back.

'Listen,' he said. 'I think it's best we go away for a few days. Maybe rent the cottage from last weekend.'

In the semi-darkness, their faces lit by the news about their daughter, Pernille looked at him, astonished.

'The police are here all the time,' he said. 'The boys keep seeing Nanna in the papers. On that damned thing. The kids talk to them at school.'

She started crying. His hand went to her damp face. This time she didn't shrink from him.

'And you,' he said. 'Watching it. Reliving it. Every minute of the day—'

'You want me to run away from Vesterbro when my daughter needs a funeral?'

They hadn't even used that word yet. Hadn't faced the thought.

Birk Larsen ground his big hands together. Squeezed his narrow eyes tight shut.

'Tomorrow we'll talk to the minister,' she said. 'We'll arrange everything. That's what we'll do.'

Silence in the wan kitchen light. The big man head in hands.

Pernille Birk Larsen picked up the remote, found another channel.

Watched it.

Carefully, trying not to make it hurt more, Lund took off the sweater from the Faroes. Looked at the bloody gash. Wondered if the jumper could be mended. Not by her. But . . .

The wedding dress was still on the mannequin, needles and thread in the sleeves and collars.

They were the only things her mother ever made. It was like a one-woman campaign to marry off the female population of the world.

She left the jumper by the sewing box anyway. Her mother came yawning, grumbling out of her room.

'Do you know what time it is?'

'Yes.'

Vibeke glowered at the table.

125

'Please don't throw your clothes everywhere. No wonder Mark's such a messy boy.'

She saw the cut, naturally. Came, bent down, looked.

'What happened?'

'Nothing.'

'There's a cut on your arm.'

Meat stew and potatoes on the cooker. The gravy had congealed. The potato was dry. Lund spooned some of each onto a plate and shoved it in the microwave.

'A cat scratched me.'

'Don't tell me a cat did that.'

'It was a stray cat.'

They looked at each other. A kind of truce was called. On this anyway.

'Why do you insist on going to work?' Vibeke asked. 'Now you can have a proper life?'

The microwave beeped. The food was lukewarm. Enough. She was hungry. Lund sat down, picked up a fork, began to eat.

'I told you this morning. It's just till Friday. If it's a problem we can stay in a hotel.'

Her mother came to the table, a glass of water in her hand.

'Why should it be a problem? Why . . . ?'

Her mouth full, Lund said, 'I'm sorry. I'm tired. Let's not argue.'

'We never argue. You always walk away.'

Lund smiled, picked up another forkful of meat and potato. She'd been eating this since she was a child. Nothing special. Sustenance. It never changed.

'It's delicious,' she said. 'I mean it.'

Her mother watched her.

'Bengt asked if you'd come to the house-warming party on Saturday. We're fixing up the spare room.'

She was watching the food, following how much got eaten, what got left.

'Bengt called here,' Vibeke said. 'This afternoon. He was wondering where you were.'

Lund's head fell. She swore.

'You didn't say I was here till Friday, did you?'

'Of course I did! Am I supposed to lie?'

Lund pushed away the food, got a beer from the fridge, went into her bedroom and called.

Bengt Rosling didn't get angry. Ever. It was beyond him. Or beneath. She never quite knew.

They spoke about parties and polar pine, made small talk, acted as if nothing had happened. Nothing was wrong.

He didn't know she was watching the news on her computer as they talked. She kept the sound low. It was all about Hartmann.

Come Friday she'd be in Sweden. With Mark, with her mother too for a little while. The new life would start. The past would slip away. Copenhagen and Carsten. The Vicekriminalkommissær's badge.

She felt better for speaking to him, put down the phone happy. Remembered straight away what she'd forgotten to say.

127

Before she could call back it rang.

Bengt, she knew. So she picked it up and, with a deliberate effort, found herself saying, 'I love you.'

'Wow! That just made my day.'

Meyer. The sound of him driving. She could picture the car going too fast through the black rain. Cheese crisps on the passenger seat. Chewing gum and tobacco.

'What do you want?'

'You told me to call about the hospital!' He was playing hurt. 'Lynge went in on Friday.'

'For how long?'

'He was there till seven the next morning. The idiot's a heroin addict. He screwed up his methadone or something.'

Troels Hartmann was on TV. Almost swinging a punch at a mouthy reporter.

He'd lost it over a simple question: Do you deny withholding information for the sake of the election?

She'd thought Hartmann a calm and reasonable man.

'Could Lynge have sneaked out?'

A noisy, chomping pause.

'Not a chance. They had him in a public ward. Medicated. Was there all night.'

'Will you leave those crisps alone? If they're all over the car . . .'

'I haven't had anything to eat all day.'

'Did you find Nanna's bike?'

'No.'

'What about her mobile phone?'

That was in Hartmann's car too. Which seemed odd.

'The lab got it working,' Meyer said. 'Her last call was on Friday. Maybe made from school. They're not sure.'

'OK. We go back there in the morning.'

'No, Lund. You're not coming.'

He was still eating crisps. She could hear him crunching them in that frantic way he had, as if there'd never be another packet in the world.

'Why not?'

'I ran into Buchard. Hartmann wants a meeting. It's about you.'

She thought about that.

'Get some sleep. Write your report.'

'Thank you. Sleep tight too, sweetheart.'

'Ha, ha.'

'Lund? Think about it. Hartmann didn't call you asking for that meeting. He called Buchard. Or maybe someone above Buchard. Or maybe . . .' The crunching could drive her crazy. 'Someone above him. We've got politicians on our backs now. My bet is every last one of them's calling upstairs trying to dump shit on our heads. Sleep on that.'

In the tiny bedroom, listening to her mother trawl around the kitchen tidying things, sweeping things, Sarah Lund followed the news on her computer. Watched Troels Hartmann carefully, second by second.

CHAPTER 4

Wednesday, 5th November

Hartmann arrived at headquarters just after nine, came straight to Lund's office. Sat in the bright winter sun streaming through the narrow window opposite her and Buchard. The sharp, severe Rie Skovgaard was next to him, following every word.

'I could have avoided all this shit last night,' he said. 'If I'd done the right thing and put out a statement straight away. Before you people leaked.'

This was politics, a world Lund had managed to avoid before the Birk Larsen case. She felt out of her depth. But interested.

The chief bent forward, caught Hartmann's eye, said, 'There was no leak from here. I guarantee it.'

'Has the driver confessed?' Hartmann asked.

Lund shook her head.

'No, and he won't. He's innocent.'

The face from the poster, handsome, thoughtful, benevolent, was gone. Now Troels Hartmann was getting mad.

'Wait a minute. Yesterday you said—'

'Yesterday I said he was a suspect. He was. He isn't now. That's the way it works. That's why we asked you to keep quiet.'

'But you're still saying someone used our car?'

'They did.'

'Maybe it was stolen,' Buchard added.

'Stolen?' He didn't seem happy with that idea. 'When are you making this public?'

'Not yet,' Lund said. 'We need to wait.'

'Wait for what?' Skovgaard wanted to know.

Lund shrugged.

'The driver was injured. We'll talk to him today. See what he has to say—'

'If our car was stolen,' Skovgaard said, 'the press must be told. The damage this is doing . . .'

Lund folded her arms, looked straight at Hartmann, not the woman.

'It could help us if the man we're looking for thinks we suspect someone else.'

'We can't keep playing this game,' Hartmann said. 'Rie can draft a release.' He turned to Buchard. 'You'll see a copy. It's going out. As soon as . . .'

Lund pulled her chair across the office, sat straight in front of him.

'I would really appreciate it if you waited.'

'I can't help that.'

'The damage this could do us . . .'

Hartmann's eyes lit up.

'What about the damage to me? It's done already. It's getting worse. Buchard . . .'

The chief nodded.

131

'You'll see a copy,' Hartmann promised. 'If you find an error tell us. I don't want to hear about anything else.'

'I appreciate that.'

'That's it.' Hartmann got to his feet. 'We're done here. Goodbye.'

Lund wasn't done at all. She got up and went into the corridor. Caught up with Hartmann and the Skovgaard woman as they walked towards the spiral stairs.

'Hartmann! Hartmann!'

He stopped. No smile.

'If you'll just listen to me—'

'The press are behaving as if I'm a suspect.' Hartmann stabbed his chest with a finger. 'As if I killed that kid.'

'On TV you said you'd cooperate.'

'We have cooperated,' Skovgaard said. 'Look where it got us.'

Lund stood in front of Hartmann, bright eyes shining, insistent.

'I need your help.'

Skovgaard said, 'We have to go.'

'Lund?'

Svendsen, one of the homicide team, came out of the incident room, beckoned to her.

'Your visitors are here.'

She touched Troels Hartmann's arm.

'Just a minute, please. We haven't finished. One minute. Spare me that.'

Two figures at the end of the long corridor. A giant of a man, grizzled features, long sideburns, black leather jacket. A woman in a fawn gaberdine raincoat, chestnut hair, an attractive face that looked lost and afraid. He held a black hat in his fidgeting hands. Waiting, in anticipation of something they didn't want to see. She stared at the shining black marble walls and clung on to his arm.

Lund strode towards them, businesslike, animated. Spoke briefly then they walked down the corridor, past Hartmann and Rie Skovgaard who stood to one side.

No words spoken. No words needed.

Briefly the woman turned and stared then walked on.

'We're late,' Skovgaard told him. 'Troels. We have to go.'

Lund watched. Hartmann was trapped by the sight of them.

'Troels?'

Hartmann said, 'Was that . . . ?'

Lund nodded, looked at him, waited.

'Will it make a difference?'

'Yes.'

'You know that?' Skovgaard snarled.

'I know that if you put out a statement we've lost an opportunity. An advantage maybe.'

Lund sighed, shrugged.

'We've got so few. I'll fight to keep any I can.'

'OK.' He didn't look at Skovgaard glaring at him stony-eyed. 'Only till tomorrow. Then . . . Lund . . .'

She listened.

'Tomorrow,' Hartmann said, 'we make our position clear. Whatever you say.'

In Lund's room, coffee sitting on the desk, untouched, Theis and Pernille Birk Larsen listening.

'We've got a preliminary medical examiner's report,' Lund said. 'But he's not quite finished. A funeral—'

'We need to get away,' Birk Larsen broke in. 'We're going to the seaside this afternoon. All these damned reporters. The boys.' He looked into her face. 'You people coming round the apartment all the time. You can do what you like when we're not there.'

'If that's what you want.'

'What are they doing to her?' Pernille asked.

'Some more tests. I don't know exactly.' A lie, one she always used. 'We'll let you know when her body can be released.'

The mother was somewhere else, Lund thought. Lost in her memories. Or imagination.

The father again.

'Where will Nanna go?'

'Normally to a funeral director. It's your choice.'

Pernille woke.

'What happened to her?' She sniffed. 'What did he do?'

Lund opened her hands.

'I have to wait for the full report. I understand you want to know. It's . . .'

134

Theis Birk Larsen looked ready to put his big hands over his ears.

There was a knock at the door. An officer from the team. Said sorry, started asking for documents from her desk.

So many, and they said so little. Lund helped him. Got involved. Got lost for a moment. Never noticed the door was open.

But Pernille Birk Larsen did, and saw a chink, a brief shocking glimpse of the room beyond. The case office.

Photos on the wall. A pair of ankles bound with black plastic. Bruised legs on a silver table. A dead face, Nanna's, covered in wounds, eyes closed, lips purple and swollen. A bloodied eye. A broken nail. The slip with a stab mark. A top ripped and torn.

Arrows pointed to details, to bloodstains and slashes. Circles marked stains, notes described lesions.

Her body, side on, hands tied, legs bound. Lying on a table still as could be.

Pernille rises.

Breath pumping, heart racing, Theis beside her, walking to the door.

One noise: a pencil falling as she passes.

The spell broke. Lund looked, fury rising, dragged the officer with her, pushed him through, cried, 'Shut the door!'

She turned back to them.

'I'm sorry,' she said.

They stood in silence. The big man and his wife. Beyond tears, she thought. Beyond feeling.

'I'm sorry,' Lund said again and wanted to scream.

He was clutching the desk with one hand, his wife's fingers with the other.

'I think we should go now,' Theis Birk Larsen said.

They walked down the corridor like two ghosts lost in limbo, hand in hand, not noticing where they were going.

'Phone me any time,' Lund called after them, wishing there was something else to say.

Rektor Koch was too busy for the police.

'I need this school back to normal,' she said. 'We have a memorial service coming. I'll make a speech.'

'This isn't about what you need,' Lund told her.

They were in the corridor outside Nanna's class. Kids coming and going. Oliver Schandorff, Lund saw, hanging round, trying to eavesdrop.

'You can't possibly think the school's involved.'

Meyer came to the argument like a nail to a magnet.

'You know what? If you let us do our job maybe we can answer that.'

He gave her his best filthy look. When she left he said, 'Lynge arrived at noon and was told to leave his posters in the basement. Someone saw him hanging round the gym too.'

'Why?'

'No idea. Maybe he was feeling lazy. Or sick. Or liked seeing girls playing netball.'

'Maybe he lost the car keys there.'

Meyer shrugged.

'Who had PE afterwards?' Lund asked.

'No one. The next class was on Monday. No one reported any keys found. Surprise, surprise.'

They walked down the corridor towards the entrance hall.

'What do we have on the girl?'

Meyer went through his notes.

'Top pupil. Good marks. Popular. Good-looking. The teachers rated her. The boys wanted to sleep with her.'

'Did she let them?'

'Only Oliver Schandorff and she broke up with him six months ago.'

'Drugs?'

'Nothing. Didn't drink usually either. I got a photo from the party. No one saw her after nine thirty.'

Lund looked at the print in Meyer's fingers. Nanna in a shiny blue wig and a black witch's hat, Lisa Rasmussen next to her. Both smiling, Lisa like a teenager, Nanna more . . .

'She looks a very . . . grown-up kid,' Meyer noted.

'Meaning?'

'Meaning . . . she looks a very grown-up kid. Specially next to her friend.'

He turned up another photo. Nanna and Lisa again, maybe a moment before or after. Lisa with her arm round Nanna who was grinning, mouth open this time.

137

Lund looked at the wig and the hat.

'She went to all this trouble for a costume and left early?'

'Yes. Funny, huh?'

Lund looked down the corridor, looked at the lockers and the posters on the walls.

Meyer rattled his notebook at her.

'Got some answers?' she asked him.

'Got questions, Lund. That's a start.'

They took Lisa Rasmussen into an empty classroom.

Lund's first question.

'You never told us Oliver and Nanna fought on the dance floor. Why not?'

The teenage pout, then, 'It wasn't important.'

Meyer squinted at her.

'Your best friend got raped and murdered and that wasn't important?'

She wasn't going to cry. Today was hostile-to-cops day.

'We were dancing. Oliver came over. It wasn't a big drama.'

Lund smiled at her.

'Oliver threw a chair.'

Nothing.

'Was Nanna drunk?'

In a rising, nasal petulant voice she said, 'Nooooo.'

'You were,' Meyer said.

A roll of the shoulders.

'A bit. So what?'

138

'Why'd they break up?' he asked.

'I dunno.'

He leaned across the table, said very slowly, 'Why . . . did . . . they . . .'

'She told me he was immature! Just a kid.'

'But you still thought she was with him?'

'I couldn't find her.'

Lund took over.

'What was the argument about?'

'Oliver wanted to talk to her. She didn't want to talk to him.'

'And then she left. Where was Oliver then?'

'Behind the bar. It was his turn.'

'You're sure?'

'I saw him.'

Meyer pushed a piece of paper over the table, looking at Lisa Rasmussen all the time.

'This is the bar schedule,' Lund said. 'His name's not on it. No one else remembered him working that night.'

She didn't look at the schedule. Just bit her lip like a little kid.

'What was she wearing?' Meyer asked.

A moment to think about it.

'A witch's hat with a buckle. A blue wig. She had a broom. Made out of twigs. Kind of this tatty party dress . . .'

'It's cold out there, Lisa,' Meyer broke in. 'Didn't you think it was odd she had so little on?'

'She had a jacket in the classroom, I guess.'

'Then she'd have gone upstairs,' said Lund.

139

'But no.' Meyer came in like a shot. 'She went downstairs. Lisa told us earlier.' He looked at her. 'Downstairs right?'

'Downstairs,' the girl muttered.

'Then how'd she get her jacket?' Lund demanded.

'Yeah.' Meyer was on her now. 'How?'

'I don't know she had a jacket. There were people. Lots of . . .'

Lisa Rasmussen stopped, face red, looking guilty.

Meyer peered at her.

'I thought you weren't going to cry today, Lisa. Why's it so hard suddenly?'

'You don't know when she left or whether Oliver followed her,' Lund said.

'We know you're lying to us!' Meyer yelled. 'Did Oliver find the car keys? Did he screw her in the car to prove what a man he was? Did you watch for fun?'

Lund intervened, put an arm round the girl. Floods of tears now.

'It's important you tell us what you know,' she said.

In the squeaky frightened voice of a child Lisa Rasmussen whimpered, 'I don't know anything. Leave me alone.'

Meyer's phone rang.

'You need to tell us . . .' Lund began.

'No she doesn't,' Meyer said and got his jacket.

There was a warren of rooms making up the school's basement floor. They'd had Svendsen

140

going through each in turn, grumbling about being on his own.

He found the broom of twigs with some plastic bags in an area set aside for storing pushbikes.

Lund looked.

Metal doors in rows. Cell-like chambers beyond them.

The blue wig was in one of the plastic bags.

'What about her bike?'

'I'm on my own,' Svendsen said for the fourth time that morning.

'Seal off the area. Get a full forensic team down here,' Lund ordered.

Weber was at his computer. Seemed to live there more with each passing day.

'Seen the new polls?' he asked.

'It's tomorrow's polls that matter,' Hartmann said. 'When they see there's an alliance . . .'

Morten Weber scowled.

'Until Kirsten Eller's name's on a piece of paper let's not count chickens.'

'I talked to them last night. It's done, Morten. Stop worrying.'

Skovgaard came off the phone. She didn't look happy either.

'You two seem close for a change,' Hartmann said. 'What have I done wrong now?'

'Eller's people think you're being evasive,' Skovgaard said. 'So do some of our own.'

'Tell them . . . tell them the car was stolen.'

Weber's phone rang.

'Why not tell them the truth?' he said before answering it. 'We're assisting the police.'

'The police have got their own agenda,' Skovgaard said. 'They don't give a damn about us.'

Hartmann bristled. The Lund woman intrigued him. He was willing to give her a chance.

'I'm not going to milk this, Rie. I'm not that kind of politician.'

Skovgaard said, 'You make me want to scream sometimes. Carry on like this and you won't be a politician at all.'

'That was Kirsten Eller.' Weber put down the phone. 'She wants to see you. Straight away.' Weber looked at Hartmann over his glasses. 'I thought you had this fixed, Troels?'

'What does she want?'

'Wouldn't tell a minion like me, would she? Pretty obvious, isn't it?'

Hartmann didn't speak.

'She wants some wriggle room,' Skovgaard said.

Both of them looked at him as if he should have known this.

'Who wouldn't?' Weber asked.

Hartmann got up.

'I'll deal with Kirsten Eller.'

Fifteen minutes later, Hartmann was alone in a meeting room in the Centre Party offices. Eller didn't smile.

'I underestimated the feelings in the group,' she said.

'How?'

'This mess with the police. It makes people talk about you. Bremer's backers smell your blood.'

'The car was stolen. The driver's innocent.'

'Why does no one know this, Troels?'

'Because the police asked us to wait. It was the right thing to do. What difference does it make?'

'A big difference. You could have warned me.'

'No. I couldn't. The police asked me to keep quiet.'

'Bremer phoned me this morning. He's offering to build ten thousand flats, social housing, minimal rents.'

'You know him. It'll come to nothing.'

'I'm sorry, Troels. There won't be an alliance. I can't. In the circumstances . . .'

Hartmann floundered for a reply, found his temper rising.

'Bremer's stringing you along. He just wants you to dither until it's too late for us to cut the deal. Then he'll drop you like a stone. You won't get the flats. You'll be lucky to get a mayor's seat.'

'It's the group's decision. There's nothing I can do.'

He was tempted to shout. To yell at her for being so stupid but he didn't.

'Unless, of course, you've got a better offer,' Eller said.

★　　★　　★

143

Bremer was in his media studio getting ready for a TV slot. Lights and cameras. A make-up woman. Hangers on.

Fighting to restrain his fury, Troels Hartmann barged in, walked over, looked down at the laughing figure in the white shirt, powder on his cheeks, said, 'You ruthless bastard.'

Bremer smiled and shook his grey head.

'I'm sorry.'

'You heard.'

The make-up woman stopped padding at him with a brush. Stayed. Listened.

'Bad timing for me, Troels,' Bremer said with a genial sigh. 'You too, I think. Later . . .'

'I want an explanation.'

They went to the window, a semblance of privacy. Hartmann couldn't help himself, was started before he got there.

'First you steal our plan. Then you double it and propose an unrealistic number of flats you know you'll never build.'

'Ah,' Bremer said, with a wave of his hand. 'You spoke to Kirsten. A terrible blabbermouth. I did warn you.'

'Then you exploit the death of a young girl and time it to aggravate the situation . . . precisely when we're trying to help the police and the parents.'

Bremer's face fell. He barged into Hartmann, wagged a finger in his face.

'Who do you think you're talking to? Am I

144

supposed to time my proposals according to whatever mess you've got yourself into? Grow up, boy. You had nothing to do with the car yet still you chose not to announce it. I thought Rie Skovgaard had more sense than that.'

'What I do is my business.'

The Lord Mayor laughed.

'You're an infant, Troels. I'd no idea it was this bad. A clumsy alliance with Kirsten's clowns . . . what were you thinking?'

'Don't go lower than you are, Bremer. It's hard I know . . .'

'Oh dear. This is like dealing with your father all over again. The desperation. The paranoia. How very sad.'

'I'm telling you—'

'No!'

Poul Bremer's voice boomed round the studio, loud enough to silence everyone, Hartmann too.

'No,' he repeated, more quietly. 'You tell me nothing, Troels. Go find me a real man to fight. Not a tailor's dummy in a flash suit.'

The church was plain and cold, the priest much the same. They sat as he listed the options. For prayers, for music, for flowers. For everything except the thing they needed most: understanding.

It was like a shopping list.

'Can we have "A Spotless Rose is Growing"?' Pernille asked as she and Theis held the hymn book between them.

The minister wore a brown jacket and grey polo sweater. He peered over the page and said, 'That's number hundred and seventeen. A lovely hymn. One of my favourites.'

'I want it to be beautiful in here with plenty of flowers,' she added.

'That's up to you. I can give you the name of some florists.'

'She loves flowers.'

Next to her on the hard bench Theis Birk Larsen stared at the stone floor.

'Blue irises. And roses.'

'Is there anything else?' Birk Larsen asked.

The minister checked his notes.

'Nothing. Just the eulogy, but I suggest you write down some things. Do it at home. When you have the time.'

He checked his watch.

'You mustn't mention what happened to her,' Pernille told him.

'Only Nanna as you remember her. Of course.'

A long silence. Then she said, 'Nanna was always happy. Always.'

He scribbled a note.

'That's a good thing for me to say.'

Birk Larsen got up. The priest did too. Shook his hand.

Pernille looked around the cold dark building. Tried to imagine a coffin there, saw the stiff, cold body inside.

'If you need to talk to someone,' the minister

said, like a doctor offering an appointment. There was a look of studied, practised sympathy in his eyes. 'Remember that all is well with her. Nanna's with God now.'

The man nodded as if these were the wisest, most fitting words he could find.

'With God,' he repeated.

They walked to the door in silence.

She stopped after two steps, turned, looked at the priest in the brown jacket and dark trousers.

'What good does that do me?'

He was taking back a chair. The notepad was in his pocket, like a carpenter's measuring book. Probably working out the bill in his head.

'What good?' she cried.

'Sweetheart,' Birk Larsen said, trying to take her fingers.

She shook him free.

'I want to know!' Pernille roared at the man on the steps, frozen on the way to the altar, trapped by her fury. 'What good does that do me? You with your sanctimonious words . . .'

He didn't recoil. He found a kind of courage. Came back, faced her.

'Sometimes life's meaningless. Without pity. It's a terrible thing to lose one's daughter. Faith helps to give you hope. Strength.'

Her breath was short, her heart pounding.

'To know that life isn't without meaning—'

'Don't give me this shit!' Pernille Birk Larsen

screeched. 'I don't give a damn if she's with God. Do you understand?'

Her hands clutched at her breast. Her voice began to break. The man stayed where he was in front of the altar. Theis Birk Larsen froze, buried his face in his hands.

'Do you understand?' Pernille wailed. 'She's supposed to be with . . .' In the dark cold church a bird flapped somewhere, dry wings rustling in the eaves. '. . . with me.'

Lund was chewing Nicotinell. She looked at the ginger-haired kid, Oliver Schandorff. Screwed-up face, twitching fingers, seated in an empty classroom, nervous as hell.

'You left school early yesterday, Oliver. You weren't in class on Monday.'

'I felt ill.'

'Idleness isn't a disease,' Meyer said.

Schandorff scowled, looked ten years old.

'You've got an absence rate of seventeen per cent,' Lund added, looking at the records.

'Class lout,' Meyer chipped in with a wicked grin. 'Rich kid. Dumb, forgiving parents. I know you.'

'Look,' Schandorff cried. 'I had an argument with Nanna. That's all.'

Lund and Meyer exchanged glances.

'Lisa told you?' Meyer said. 'What else did she say?'

'I didn't do anything. I'd never hurt Nanna.'

'Why did she dump you?' Lund asked.

He shrugged.

'One of those things. Like I care.'

Meyer leaned forward, sniffed Schandorff 's expensive sky-blue sweater.

'Guess she didn't like you doing dope either.'

Schandorff ran his hand across his mouth.

'Arrested for speed four months ago. Again two months later.' Meyer sniffed again. 'I'd say you're into some kind of I dunno . . .'

He looked at the kid, puzzled, as if seeing something. Leaned forward, a couple of inches from his face, Schandorff recoiling, scared.

'Wait,' Meyer said urgently, peering into his eyes. 'What's that?'

'What?'

'There's something. A tiny speck . . . I dunno. At the back of your eyes.'

Meyer reached out with a probing finger. Schandorff was at the back of his seat, couldn't go any further.

'Oh,' Meyer said, with a sigh of relief. Retreated. 'It's nothing. Just your brain . . .'

'Fuck you,' Oliver Schandorff muttered.

'Did you hand some of that shit to Nanna?' Meyer roared. 'Did you say . . . hey, let's turn on . . . oh and it's better with your pants down by the way.'

The ginger head went forward.

'Nanna didn't like it much.'

'Which?' Lund asked. 'The dope or the . . . ?'

'Either.'

149

'So you got punchy with her?' Meyer had his chin on his hands. A pose that said: going nowhere. 'On the dance floor. Threw a chair around. Yelled at her.'

'I was drunk!'

'Oh.' Meyer brightened. 'That's OK then. So after nine thirty what did you do?'

'I worked behind the bar.'

Lund pushed the sheet across the table.

'You're not on the schedule.'

'I worked behind the bar.'

Meyer again.

'Who saw you?'

'Lots of people.'

'Lisa?'

'She saw me.'

'No, she didn't,' Lund said.

'I was walking round. Collecting glasses . . .'

'Listen, brainiac.' Meyer was loud again, in a different way. Cold and threatening. 'Nobody saw you after nine thirty.'

Got up, pulled a chair next to Schandorff, sat so close they touched. Put an arm round his shoulder. Squeezed.

Lund took a deep breath.

'What did you do, Oliver? Tell your uncle Jan. Before he gets cross. We both know you won't like it if that happens.'

'Nothing . . .'

'Did you follow her outside?' Another squeeze. 'Hang around the basement?'

Schandorff wriggled out of his grip.

Meyer winked at him.

'Nanna had someone else, didn't she? You knew that. You were jealous as hell. I mean really.' Meyer nodded. 'Think about it. School rich kid. She was yours. How could some pretty chick from a dump like Vesterbro screw you around?'

Schandorff was up shouting, running his hands through his wild ginger hair.

'I told you what happened.'

His voice was a couple of tones higher. Young again in an instant.

'The car keys . . .' Meyer began.

'What . . . ?'

'You knew the car was there.'

'What are you talking about?'

'Nanna didn't want you. So you raped her. Dumped her out in the canal. On your way home—'

'Shut up!'

Meyer waited. Lund watched.

'I loved her.'

'Oliver!' Meyer was beaming. 'You just said you didn't give a shit. You loved her but she thought you were a jerk. So you did the thing any no-good little dope-smoking shit would. You raped her. You tied her up. Stuck her in the boot of that black car . . .'

Back on the seat, ginger head shaking side to side.

'Stuck her in there so no one could hear her scream then pushed her into the canal.'

Meyer slammed his fist so hard on the table the

pens, the notebooks jumped. Oliver Schandorff was a crumpled heap on the chair, silent, shaking.

Lund waited. After a while she said very calmly, 'Oliver. If you've got something to tell us it would be best to say it now.'

'Let's take him down the station,' Meyer cut in, reaching for his phone. 'Oliver and me need a quiet chat alone in a cell.'

The classroom door opened and two people walked in. A middle-aged man in an expensive-looking suit. A woman behind him looking worried.

'I'm Oliver's father,' the man said. 'I want a word with my son.'

'We're police officers,' Lund said. 'You're inter-rupting our interview. Get out.'

The man didn't move. The woman was watching him, expecting something.

'Have you charged him with anything?'

Meyer waved a hand in his face and said, 'Hello? Did you hear . . . ?'

A wallet. A business card waved in their faces. Erik Schandorff. Big-shot lawyer from a big-shot firm.

'Don't talk to me like that,' Erik Schandorff said.

'Oliver's helping—' Lund began.

'Dad?'

The cry of a frightened kid. No one could mistake that.

'I want to talk to him,' the father said.

Outside in the corridor, Meyer hissing and cursing beneath his breath, Lund watched through the window.

Father and son, Oliver head down, moving side to side.

Lifted it and then the father struck him full force across the face with the back of his hand.

'Happy families,' Meyer murmured, lighting a cigarette. 'Now if I'd done that . . .'

One minute later, rich lawyer, rich kid, quiet wife walking out. Not a word.

'See you soon, Oliver!' Meyer called as they left.

Lund leaned back against the wall, folded her arms, closed her eyes.

He was watching her when she opened them.

'I know what you're thinking, Lund. That it's vaguely possible I was a bit hard on him. But if that idiot hadn't walked in . . .'

'Fine.'

'No really. I knew what I was doing. I was in control. All the time. Honest . . .'

'Meyer,' she said, coming up to him, peering up into his wide-open, staring eyes. 'I said it was fine. Check downstairs again. Contact forensics. If Oliver drove the car they should know. Time the journey from here to the woods.'

She pulled the car keys out of her bag.

'Anything else?'

'You'll think of something.'

'And you, Lund?'

'Me?'

'Going to catch a movie or what?'

She nodded, left him, smiling when he couldn't see.

*   *   *

153

There were flowers on the sideboard, on the small iron mantel above the fire. Flowers by the sink still wrapped in their paper, bouquets on the floor.

Some were blue irises. Some roses.

Pernille stood washing dishes, staring out of the window.

A woman from the forensic department sat with the boys at the table Pernille and Nanna made, smiling at them. Cotton sticks in her hand.

She looked no more than twenty-two or so. No older than Nanna when she went out for the night.

'Is this really necessary?' Theis Birk Larsen asked.

'We need DNA,' said the woman in the blue uniform. 'For comparisons.'

Downstairs the car was packed. Suitcases with clothes. Boxes with kids' things. Vagn Skærbæk helped as he always did.

He had new toys. Cars. Cheap and tinny but Vagn was bad with money and Pernille lacked the heart to scold him. The men in the depot were like everyone else. Like Theis. Like her. Desperate to do something, lost for what that might be.

'OK?' the woman asked and didn't wait for an answer. Leaned over the table, got Anton first, then asked Emil to open his mouth.

Pernille watched from the sink, dishes in her hand.

They were back in Nanna's bedroom. Two men in blue walking round, putting up more stickers, making notes.

Lotte her sister, younger, prettier, still single, did most of the packing. Now she came and hugged each of them in turn.

'Take some flowers if you want,' Theis said.

Lotte looked at him and shook her head.

'Boys,' Theis said. 'Let's go see Uncle Vagn. Help him finish up downstairs.'

Pernille promised she'd be there soon and watched them go.

Soon.

She left the sink when he was gone. Looked around the untidy room.

In this small warm place an unexpected miracle had emerged between them. The magic that was family. Shared lives. Shared love.

Now men in blue tramped through Nanna's little bedroom, opening drawers they opened yesterday, talking in low tones, going quiet when they thought she could hear.

The boys rushed back up, snatched kites, snatched more toys. Showed her the tinny cars Vagn bought.

'Watch those sharp edges,' she said. 'Watch . . .'

They were gone, not listening, one of the men from the bedroom following, taking some of Nanna's books to the car in his blue gloved hands.

The cop who was left was old with a beard and a sad face. He looked uncomfortable. Couldn't meet her eyes. Grey head down looking at Nanna's bookcase once more.

She picked up her bag, ready to go.

The apartment was so full of the scent of flowers it made her head hurt.

Here we lived. Here we sat around the table, thinking this small, private bliss would never end.

And now we flee, we scuttle away in ignorance and fear as if the fault were our own.

Home. Covered in forensic stickers and their boot marks. Fingerprint dust on walls that still bore Nanna's pretty face.

The bag went back on the old worn carpet. Pernille walked into her room, watched the man working. Sifting through the pieces of her daughter's brief lost life.

She sat on the bed, waited until he had the courage to look at her.

'I won't be long. I'm sorry . . .'

'What happened out in the woods?' she asked and thought: *I will not move, I will not leave until he speaks.*

A father. She could see it in his face. He understood. He knew.

'I'm not the one to talk to. Sorry.' He fiddled with the drawer of Nanna's desk. 'I'm working. You have to leave.'

Pernille stayed on the sheets of Nanna's tidy, made-up bed.

'I need . . .' His eyes were closed. She saw his pain, knew he saw hers too. 'I need to know what happened. I'm her mother . . .'

The desk again. He was doing nothing and both knew it.

156

'What happened to my daughter?'

'I'm not allowed—'

'There were photos. In your office. I saw . . .' Words, she thought. The right ones now. 'I see them in my head at night and I know . . . it can't be worse than anything I imagine. Not worse.'

He stopped, head bowed.

'It can't be worse. But . . .' She tapped her chestnut hair, her skull. Her voice was weak and faint, she made it so. 'In my head I see . . .'

The cop bent stiffly over the desk, didn't move.

'I'm her mother. Do I have to beg?'

No answer.

'Every day she dies in my head. Over and over and each time worse. We need to bury . . .'

He was shaking.

'I need to know,' she said again.

Then watched as he sighed.

Then, finally, listened.

Theis Birk Larsen looked round the depot. Helped Vagn Skærbæk move a cabinet to a truck. Watched as the boys played with their little tin cars. Checked their things in the back of the car: a family reduced to a set of luggage, ready to go.

'Any news, Theis?'

Birk Larsen lit a cigarette, shook his head.

Anton and Emil ran up, clinging to Skærbæk's red cotton legs. Begging for ice-cream money. Making him laugh.

'Do I look like a piggybank?' he said, taking out some coins. They scattered on the floor.

The old joke he always used with them: *no beer now, boys.*

'Who was this driver they caught?' Skærbæk asked. 'The paper didn't even print a name—'

'I don't know. They tell us nothing. Why would they?'

Birk Larsen stared around the depot trying to think the way he used to: of jobs and inventories, bills to be paid, invoices to be collected. Nothing worked. It was as if Nanna's death had locked them in a never-ending present, a frozen point in time with no escape. No prospect of release.

'We're just little people,' he murmured.

'No you're not.'

Vagn Skærbæk stood by him, ignoring the boys tugging at his overalls again.

'Thanks for running things,' Birk Larsen said. 'I don't know what . . .'

Too many words. He patted Skærbæk on the arm.

'You saved my skin, Theis.' Skærbæk's face was hard with anger. The silver chain glittered round his neck. 'I don't forget. That bastard's going to get what's coming to him. You just tell me if you want something done.'

'Like what?'

'When he gets a piddling sentence. And they let him out on parole. You tell me Theis . . . I want to . . .'

'Help?' Birk Larsen shook his head.

'If that's what you want . . .'

'She's dead.'

Poor Vagn. Dumb Vagn. Loyal as a guard dog. No brighter either.

'Dead.' One cruel, short word. 'Don't you understand?'

Still the flame was lit and with it a sudden burst of rage. Theis Birk Larsen hammered his massive fist on a cabinet, set it shaking on its feet.

'Where the hell's Pernille?'

Upstairs in the kitchen, surrounded by the flowers, choking in their scent.

The cop was on the phone. And worried.

'Pernille?'

He'd come up the stairs to look for her.

'We're not going.'

He rocked on his big feet the way he always did before an argument. Not that they had many, and those few he always won.

'I told the boys. The place is booked—'

'We're not going.'

'It's arranged!'

It wasn't that she lost. More that she never fought. That was over now. Lots of other things too. Things she hadn't recognized yet. But would.

'Nanna wasn't dead when the car hit the water.'

Her voice was flat and calm, her face too.

'What?'

'She wasn't dead. She was in the boot of the car. Trapped there. Drowning.'

Pernille walked into Nanna's bedroom.

Clothes. Belongings. Scattered round, pleading to be tidied. A mother's job . . .

She began to move the books, the clothes from one place to another, bright eyes shining, tears beginning to form.

Then she stopped, folded her arms.

'We're leaving now,' Theis Birk Larsen said, standing in the doorway. 'That's that.'

He was next to the fish tank Nanna wanted. Pernille found herself captivated by the swimming golden shapes trapped inside it. Peering out, unable to comprehend anything beyond the glass.

'No,' she said. 'We're staying here. I want to watch them find him. I want to see his face.'

Round and round they swam, puzzled by their own reflections, thinking nothing, going nowhere.

'They have to find him, Theis. They will.'

A moment pivoted between them. One that had never come before.

He fiddled with his woollen hat.

'We're staying here,' Pernille Birk Larsen repeated. 'I'll get the boys. You bring the cases.'

Lynge was awake. A bandage round his head, drips in his arm. Fresh cuts and grazes covered the old scar on his cheek. Traces of blood still caked his grey moustache.

'John?' Lund said.

Movement. Breathing. Eyes half open. She'd no

idea if he could hear this. Any more than the impatient doctor she'd bullied to let her in there.

'I'm sorry this happened. Do you understand?'

The man's eyebrows flickered.

'I know you didn't harm the girl.'

He was connected to a machine with flashing numbers and graphs.

'I really need your help, John. I need to know what happened at the school. Who you met. Where you lost your keys.'

His eyes moved. Turned towards her.

'You parked your car. You took the posters inside. You went to the gym. Is that when you felt sick?'

Lynge coughed, choked on something.

A noise, a word.

'What? John?'

Another sound. An eye flicked wide open. A look there. Fear and pain.

'Basement.'

'You went there to deliver the posters. Is that where you lost the keys?'

'The kid got angry. Said I wasn't supposed to go near there.'

'John.' She got up, got close to his mouth, had to hear this. 'Who got angry? What kid?'

That wheezing sound again. She could smell him.

'Were there bikes there? Bikes?'

'The next one.'

Lund tried to picture that dank warren.

'The next room?'

'The boiler.'

161

A sound. The door opened. The doctor was back and he didn't look pleased.

'Who did you meet in the boiler room? John?'

Lund took out the photos from her bag. School portraits. Pointed to Oliver Schandorff, said, 'Did you see him? This one. Please. Look.'

The wheeze again. Then, 'No.'

'Are you sure? Take a good look.'

The doctor was with them, arms waving, saying, 'OK. That's it. You've got to stop. Leave now—'

'One minute,' Lund said, not budging. 'Just . . .'

She pushed him back, held the school photo over the sick man in the bed.

'I'm pointing my finger, John. One by one. Nod when I get to him. OK?'

One by one, kid by kid.

When she stopped on a tall dark-haired student, pleasant-looking, ordinary, John Lynge nodded.

'You saw him in the boiler room . . . ?'

'That's enough,' the doctor told her, grabbing her arm.

'John?'

The eye opened, caught her. His head moved, the slightest of nods.

Lund rose, threw the doctor's hand off her.

Said, 'Yes, it is.'

Meyer was smoking in the school playground when he answered her call.

'I need you to go back to the basement again,' Lund said.

A pause.

'Please tell me that was a joke.' He looked at the forensic men. He was hungry. So were they. And Svendsen was starting to get on his nerves.

'Go back down there.'

'Forensics are packing up. We've looked everywhere. How's Lynge?'

'He'll be out in a week. Is there a boiler room?'

'They keep it locked. No one can get in there except the janitor.'

'I'm on my way.'

He could hear the sound of traffic. The black rain-soaked streets were empty. She'd be with him in a matter of minutes.

Meyer started walking back down the grimy concrete stairs.

'It's bad to talk and drive, you know.'

'Are you in there yet?'

'We've got the janitor here.'

'I need to know what's inside.'

'All right, all right.'

He told the janitor to open the door.

'Are you in?'

'Yes! Just keep your pants on, will you?'

'What can you see?'

A pause. Then Meyer said, 'I can see the boiler. That's a surprise.'

Then, 'Just a bunch of old junk. Tables, chairs and books.' He cleared his throat. 'OK, Lund. So the kids could maybe get in here. But there's nothing to see.'

'Are you sure?'

'Hang on.'

'Did you hear me?'

Meyer made a disgusting noise down the phone. 'You're breaking up on me, Lund.'

Then muttered, 'For God's sake . . .'

Slammed the phone into his pocket, walked ahead, shining the beam of the torch one side, the other side. Up, down.

He'd thought about this earlier. The janitor said the boiler took an oil feed from a tank outside. No one had to go in there except for maintenance once a week. Every Friday afternoon.

There was a second door at the end. No handle. Looked as if it hadn't been used in years.

Meyer took out a handkerchief, edged the metal open. Peeked in, moved the torch around.

Kids had been here. At his feet the remains of a couple of joints were stamped into the ground. Beer cans. And . . .

Meyer whistled. The sleeve of a condom packet, foil torn, empty.

Noises behind. Something happening out in the main basement. Didn't care.

Pulled out his phone, dialled her number. Didn't wait before he said, 'I think you'd better get here. Lund . . . ?'

Deep in the concrete bowels of the school, there was no signal.

'Really . . .' Meyer whispered.

'Really?'

The sound made him jump. A torch beam in his face. Then on the ground.

'You must have been speeding. Admit it, Lund. You're as bad as me.'

She didn't answer. Just looked at the same thing that he did. A grubby mattress on the floor.

Bloodstains in the corner.

Bloodstains on the peeling grey wall.

Prints were appearing on the peeling plaster of the room in the school basement. Officers in white bunny suits tagging, drawing, taking photos. Lund on the phone to her mother's, telling Mark to do his homework, practise his Swedish.

'I could be here all night. Gran will help you.'

She'd gone back to the school hall to go through the flowers and photos on a small shrine set up for Nanna by the lockers.

'That's good,' Lund said. 'Bye.'

A picture there. Two girls dressed as angels. Nanna, maybe thirteen. Lisa Rasmussen.

A pair of red candles in front of it. A single flame flickering in the cold breeze running down the corridor.

'Who lit the candle?' Lund asked.

Meyer had been here five minutes before her. He looked young and guilty for a moment.

'I don't know. Does it matter?'

'You shouldn't interfere with things, Meyer.'

'Who said . . . ?'

She waved at him.

'Forget it.'

'Shouldn't we go and look in the basement?'

Lund straightened a photo of Nanna. Looked at the dead girl.

She held up a hand. Meyer shook his head, baffled.

'Your lighter. I'm giving up. Remember?'

'Oh.'

He threw her the silver Zippo. It looked expensive. She looked at the photos and the flowers, wished there was more she could offer than this. Knew that had to come. Then she lit the other candle and watched the tiny yellow flame flutter.

A small offering. Pathetic.

'We should look at the basement,' she said and followed him down.

Jansen, a ginger-haired officer from forensics, stood by the portable floodlights. Listed what they had so far. Blood on the mattress, the table, the floor. Some spots that could turn out to be semen. Hair.

A witch's hat. Nanna's it looked like.

And fingerprints. Lots of fingerprints.

'Access?' Meyer asked.

'There's the door from the basement,' Jansen said. 'And one from the school. Just needs a key for either.'

'A . . .'

'A different key,' he said.

Everything was visible under the bright floodlights. On the low table stood empty bottles of

166

Coke and vodka, a Chianti flask. Plates of food. And pills. Red, green, orange. All the colour of children's sweets.

'Joints,' Meyer said. 'Amphetamine. Coke.'

Thirty minutes later Rektor Koch arrived at the school. They kept her out of the location. Too many people in bunny suits. Too much to see.

In a classroom upstairs Lund asked, 'What did you use that room for?'

'Storing tables and chairs.' Koch had brought her dog. A small brown terrier. Cuddled it for comfort. 'Books and the like. Nothing . . .'

'Nothing what?'

'Nothing special. I didn't know the pupils had access. They weren't supposed to have.'

Meyer walked in and said, 'Well they did. They had their own private party there. Right under your nose.'

'What did you find?'

Lund didn't answer. She said, 'The party was planned by the student council. Is that right?'

'It should have been locked,' Koch insisted. She held the dog more tightly. 'Is that where Nanna was?'

Lund took out her stack of school photos, pointed to the kid John Lynge had identified. Jeppe Hald. Nice-looking. Clean tidy black hair. Scholarly glasses.

'Tell me about him.'

Koch smiled.

'Jeppe's wonderful. President of the student

167

council. Star pupil. We're proud of him. Fine parents . . .'

'Where does wonderboy live?' Meyer asked.

'He shares a flat with Oliver.'

Meyer said, 'Is Oliver a good pupil too?'

The smile again, less warm.

'They come from good families. The law. Both of them. I'm sure they'll follow their fathers into the same profession. Be a credit—'

'Better than being the offspring of some sweaty removals man from Vesterbro?' Meyer snapped.

The smile never cracked.

'I didn't say that. We're not prejudiced here. Against anyone.'

'So long as they pay the fees.'

Rector Koch glared at him.

'Oops,' Meyer said. 'I think I just got detention.'

'Thank you,' Lund told her and got him out of the room.

Jeppe Hald strode up and down the window of the office, watching the blue lights flash outside, listening to the occasional wail of sirens.

Lund and Meyer walked briskly in, threw their folders on the table.

Tall and skinny. Thick glasses. Harry Potter's taller geeky brother. Or that was the act.

'Why am I here?'

'Just routine,' Lund said pleasantly. 'Please sit down.'

'But I've got a physics essay to do.'

The two cops looked at each other. Meyer buried his head in his hands and pretended to weep.

While Hald was taking a chair Lund said, 'You met a man in the basement on Friday night. He was delivering election campaign material.'

Hald looked around at the empty chairs.

Meyer leaned forward, grinned cheerily.

'We tried to call your daddy but he was out getting fitted for a wig. The man in the basement?'

'I met him.'

'Why didn't you say so?'

Silence.

Lund said, 'You knew we were looking for a driver.'

'How was I to know he was a driver?'

Meyer raised his hands to his mouth, kissed his fingertips like a chef tasting the perfect dish.

'Superb. You do Shakespeare too?'

'Shakespeare?'

'First,' Meyer roared, 'we kill all the fucking lawyers.'

Jeppe Hald went white.

Lund scowled at Meyer.

'Shakespeare never said fucking. Don't teach the boy wrong. Jeppe. Jeppe!'

'What?'

'The driver lost his car keys. Did you happen to see them?'

'I'm here because of some missing keys?'

'What were you doing in the basement?' Lund asked.

169

'Fetching . . . fetching things for the bar.'

Meyer started picking at his nails. Hand closed to a fist.

'We found a room,' he said. 'Someone had a party. Do you know anything about that?'

Hald hesitated. Almost said no. Instead, 'I think the organizers had a room where they kept beer and soft drinks. Is that the one?'

'The one with beer and soft drinks, blood and drugs and condoms?' Meyer replied, still looking at his nails. 'That's the one.'

'I wouldn't know.'

Lund said nothing for a long while. Nor Meyer. They looked at their papers. Jeppe Hald sat at the table, barely moving, barely breathing.

Then she showed him a photo.

'Nanna's hat. We found it there. Did she go in that room?'

Shake of head. A shrug. No idea.

Meyer breathed a sigh so long it seemed to last a minute.

'I came down for the last beer about nine o'clock. I didn't see anyone.'

Slowly Meyer's head fell to his arms, and he lay there staring at the kid in the chair through half-closed eyes.

'You're sure you didn't go back later?' Lund asked.

A moment, a pause to be convincing. Then, 'I'm very sure.'

'No one saw you after nine thirty. What did you do?'

'Er . . .'

'Think, Jeppe,' Meyer said stifling a yawn. 'Think before you answer.'

Hald bristled. Looked more confident.

'The disco ball blew the fuses. I'd used the last one. So I went to buy more. I had to cycle a long way to get them.'

'We'll check,' Meyer muttered not looking up from his arms.

'When I got back Oliver was asleep in a class-room. He'd had too much to drink. I walked him home.' Folded his arms, looked the model pupil. 'We were there just before midnight. I put him to bed. Had to.'

'That's early!' Lund said brightly.

'I was going hunting the next morning.'

'Hunting!' Lund said, impressed.

Meyer grumbled something obscene into his sleeves.

'On the Sonderris estate. Our hunting club was holding a big event. I spent the night there.'

'I'm going to take up hunting in a minute,' Meyer muttered.

Lund scribbled on her pad.

'I'd really like to help,' Hald pleaded.

In a high-pitched squeal Meyer whined, 'I'd really like to help.'

'But that's all I know.'

Lund smiled at him. Said, 'Fine.' Wrote some more on her pad. 'Well . . .'

She closed her pad, shrugged. Jeppe Hald smiled back at her.

171

'That's it,' Lund said. 'Unless . . .'

She prodded the near-comatose Meyer.

'You want to ask something?'

Head straight up, face in the kid's.

'You won't object if I take a blood sample?' Meyer said very loudly. 'And fingerprints?'

He touched Hald's hand. The kid recoiled.

'I'll be as gentle as I can.'

Meyer waggled his big right ear at Jeppe Hald, listening, hearing nothing.

'Otherwise,' Lund added, 'I'm going to arrest you and we'll take them anyway.'

Jeppe Hald, the smart kid, star pupil, head boy, said in a young and petulant trembling voice, 'I'm not saying any more. I want to see my lawyer.'

Lund nodded.

'A lawyer. That's fine. Meyer?'

'Sure.' He took hold of Hald's arm. 'First you get your phone call, wonderboy. Then let me introduce you to the concept of a cell.'

Thirty minutes later. Meyer had people working the phones.

'I checked up on Oliver,' he told Lund. 'On Saturday he worked in a cafe. Met some woman. Went out and got drunk and took her to his parents' house. The two of them hung out there till Monday.'

One of the cadets came back with a package. Meyer groaned with delight.

'You're an angel.'

He stripped the thing from its wrapping. Lund watched. Big hot dog in a roll. Crispy fried onions. Remoulade sauce. Sliced cucumber pickles on the top.

Lund said, 'You sent a boy out to the *pølsevogn* and you didn't tell me?'

'I thought you only ate Swedish sausage.'

She stood there with her hands on her hips, big eyes boring into him. He took another quick bite of his food. Grimaced.

'Bastard,' Lund said. 'Where's the motive?'

'I was hungry.'

Silence.

'Oh. Right. Jeppe and Oliver. They're lying. Find the lie first. The motive won't be far away. Meyer Handbook of Detection. Page thirty-two.'

Lund still looked angry about the food and the sausage crack. The first mostly.

'I'll talk to Ginger and give you a call,' Meyer said.

'He'll just scream for a lawyer like Jeppe.'

'No,' Meyer insisted. 'Can't demand that unless we arrest him. If I just talk to him as a witness . . . I know the law. Mostly I abide by it. Also . . .'

'No.'

'You're a very negative woman sometimes. Just because I didn't get you a hot dog . . .'

'I want mouth swabs. I want blood samples.' A quick decision. 'Let's arrest them now.'

Meyer looked torn.

'Much as I adore that idea the lawyers won't be

here for hours. We'll be sitting around on our hands until they turn up.'

'No. We search the flat. Check their emails. Phone records. Find the woman Schandorff says he spent the weekend with.'

He was eating and cursing between mouthfuls.

'Anything else?'

That tone of voice again. He had others. She'd heard them. Not often. But they were there.

'Why are you so angry, Meyer?'

The rest of the sausage disappeared while he thought about this.

'Because,' he said, 'I have feelings.'

Silence.

'Anything else?' he asked again.

'No.'

She thought about it.

'Yes.' Lund came and stabbed a finger in his chest. 'Next time you send a cadet out to the *pølsevogn*, get one for me.'

Lund decided to check with Buchard first. The chief was flicking through the morgue photos of the girl. Bloody eye, crouched, foetal corpse, lesions and wounds. Bruising. A violent, prolonged assault.

'What do you have on the boys?' he asked. 'Physical evidence from the room?'

'Nothing until the results come in. The DNA people are giving us priority.'

Buchard flicked through more photos.

174

'You do realize who the parents are?'

Lund frowned.

'Why should we care about that?'

He was in a foul mood for some reason.

'We've caused enough trouble as it is. We need to tread carefully.'

Meyer stuck his head through the door and announced, 'Hartmann wants a meeting.'

'About what?' she wanted to know.

'He wouldn't say. It sounded important.'

'Hartmann can wait,' Lund said. 'We're going to the flat.'

When she made for the door Buchard took her arm.

'What were we just saying? Troels Hartmann might be the next Lord Mayor of Copenhagen. We don't piss off people in the Rådhus without a reason.'

'We've got a suspect's flat to search . . .'

'I can do that,' Meyer cut in. 'Don't worry. I'll keep you posted.'

Buchard nodded.

'Good. That's settled.'

The chief walked out.

'Give Hartmann a ring,' Meyer said, following him down the winding corridor. 'It was you he asked for.'

Lund waited at the counter feeling awkward and uncomfortable. She didn't go out much, even with Bengt. After the last few days this touristy

175

restaurant in Nyhavn seemed too ordinary. Too warm and human.

Hartmann was five minutes late, making excuses. While they waited for a table he asked, 'How are the girl's parents?'

Was that the politician, she wondered? Or the man?

'Is that why you asked me here? To talk about the parents?'

'You really don't do small talk, do you?'

'Not in the middle of a case. One like this.'

'I've got a press conference tomorrow. I want to say the right things.'

'Right for who?'

'For you. For me. Mostly for them.'

Men like this did sincerity so well. It was hard to see any cracks.

'Say what you like,' she told him.

'There've been so many surprises. Will there be any more?'

Without a blink.

'Not that I know of.'

'Can I say you know there's no connection between the crime and us?'

She nodded.

'I suppose so.' She watched him. 'If you think that's true.'

The waitress called. He'd booked a table.

'Is that all?'

Lund got ready to go.

He put his hand to her arm, very gently.

'I'm sorry. I know I made things difficult. There's an election going on. Some odd things have been happening.' Hartmann looked angry for a second. 'I never expected any of this.' He looked at her. 'Are you hungry?'

A plate of food went past. Meatballs and pasta. It looked a lot better than the hot dog Meyer never got her.

'I'll have some of that,' Lund said. Then, 'Just a minute.'

She went to the lobby, called her mother's. Got the loudest, friendliest greeting in months, then found out why. Bengt had arrived from Sweden, would be in Copenhagen for one night only.

'You must talk,' Vibeke crooned then handed the call over.

Don't need this now, Lund thought, listening to him talk about Mark's progress with his Swedish, the Sigtuna hockey shirt he'd found, the perfect wood for the perfect sauna.

She nodded all the while, seeing little in her head but a small and grubby room in the basement of a school, a mattress stained with blood, a table of drink and dope, a discarded witch's hat and a shiny blue wig.

'When will you be home?' Bengt asked.

Back to the awkward present.

'Soon,' she promised. 'Soon.'

A pause.

'When?'

He never pressed her. Never sounded upset or

angry or cold. His pleasant, pacific nature was one of the things she loved. Or maybe it just made life easier.

'When I'm done. I'm sorry this came up. Truly. Let's talk later. I've got to go.'

Back at the table she got stuck into the food. They talked again about press releases. About cooperation. Close up Hartmann interested her. There was a frail naivety to him that was absent from the face on the posters. He was a widower. She'd checked that in the press cuttings library already, at the same time she had checked on Jan Meyer. Hartmann's wife died from cancer two years before. The loss had affected him. At one point it threatened to bring his political career – the only job he'd ever had – to a premature end.

She found he was staring at her, uncharacteristically shorn of the right words.

'What is it?'

'You've got . . .' His hand waved in her direction. 'You've got food on your face.'

Lund grabbed a napkin, wiped her mouth. Ate some more just as greedily.

It was a pleasant cafe. The kind of place couples went. Or men with their mistresses. If someone had walked in at that moment, seen her with this man . . .

'We're agreed then?' he concluded.

'You tell your story. We'll tell ours. Such as it is.'

'What about your life?' He smiled. 'I'm sorry. I don't know why I asked that. It's none of my business.'

'It's good. I'm going to Sweden with my son. My boyfriend lives outside Stockholm. I've got a job there. Civilian with the police.'

She took a quick gulp of wine, wished there was more food.

'Everything will be fine,' Lund insisted.

'How old's your son?'

'Twelve. And you?'

'I'm a bit older than that.'

'I meant . . .'

'I know, I know. We didn't get that far. My wife died. Mostly . . .' He shrugged, looked a little ashamed. 'I spend my time working. I've met someone though. Hopefully it's not too late.'

'The woman from your office,' she said and it wasn't a question. 'Rie Skovgaard.'

Hartmann cocked his head and looked at her.

'Can you see into my pockets too?'

He'd barely touched his food or drink. Hartmann looked as if he could stay there all night. Talking, talking.

'My boyfriend's over from Sweden,' Lund said. 'I have to go. Here . . .'

She took out some money for the bill.

'No, no, no.' He waved it away quickly. 'You were my guest.'

'So long as you pay. Not the taxpayer.'

'I'll pay, Sarah,' Hartmann said, waving a credit card.

'Thank you, Troels. Goodnight.'

★   ★   ★

179

Bengt went straight to sleep the way he always did. Lund got out of bed, pulled on a sweatshirt, went to the window, sat in the cane chair, called Meyer.

'What did you find out?' she whispered.

'Not much.'

Meyer was talking in a hushed tone too. It sounded odd.

'There's got to be something.'

'Forensics have taken a computer and samples.'

The dinner with Hartmann still intrigued her.

'Was there anything in Nanna's room that suggests she was going out to meet someone?'

'Can't this wait until tomorrow? I'm beat.'

'She must have had a date.'

'Yes, Lund. With Oliver. But you won't let me talk to him.' Noises behind his quiet voice. Movement. A baby crying. 'There. Look. You've woken the whole house.'

She went out into the dining room, turned on a light, sat at the table.

'Do the parents remember anything new?'

'I'll ask them tomorrow. OK?' A grunt. 'Some idiot on the team told the mother the girl had drowned in the boot. She's going mad.'

Lund swore.

'You don't need to do that. I'll talk to them.'

'Can I go now?'

'Yes,' Lund said. 'Of course.'

She walked past Mark's room. He was still fast asleep. Bengt was awake but didn't want to show it. Everyone here was fine, Lund thought. They didn't need her at all.

Thursday, 6th November

The morning was dull and damp with drizzle. They ate breakfast together then Lund drove Bengt to the station. Talked about the weekend. Who they'd see in Sweden. What they'd do.

He listened in silence. Then she said, 'The house-warming party . . .'

'Forget about the party. I've cancelled it.'

She wondered: was that a stray note of displeasure in his voice? It was hard to tell. Anger was so foreign to him.

'Let's wait until your case is over, Sarah. Then . . .'

'I don't need to wait. I told you. We're coming Saturday, whatever.'

He gazed out of the window at the traffic and the morning travellers.

'I'm not inviting lots of people for you to call again and say you're not coming.'

That was sharp. Unmistakable.

'Of course I'll turn up! I'm looking forward to seeing your parents. And . . .' His little refrain of Swedish names from the other day came back to her. 'Ole and Missan and Janne and Panne and Hasse and Basse and Lasse . . .'

He was laughing. She could still get that out of him.

181

'It's Bosse, not Basse.'

'Sorry. Still learning.'

'Well. If you're sure . . .'

'I'm sure! It's a promise.'

She dropped him at Central Station then drove on to Vesterbro.

Lund sat on Nanna's bed trying to remember what it was like to be a teenager. The room was small and bright, messy and chaotic. Bags from inexpensive clothing companies, scribbled notes from class, books and magazines, make-up and jewellery . . .

A reflection of Nanna Birk Larsen's personality, her life.

She went through the diary, found nothing. Nothing in the school notebooks, the photos on the cork-board above her small desk.

Lund thought of herself at this age, an awkward, morose child. Her room was more untidy than this. But different somehow. It existed for her, an inward expression of her solitary, introverted nature. Here, she thought, Nanna had created a place for preparation. A private dressing room from which she would emerge to enchant the world outside, entrance it with her beauty, her clothes, her sparkling and obvious intelligence.

All the things the teenage Sarah Lund lacked this girl possessed in abundance. A loving mother too.

And now she was dead.

There was a path from this room to Nanna's

shocking end in the canal at the Kalvebod Fælled. There were reasons, and reasons left traces.

She looked in the wardrobe, sifted through the clothes. A few had scissored labels, bought from a budget store perhaps. A few didn't. And . . .

Lund fought again to recall herself at this age. What did she wear? Much the same as now. Jeans, shirts, jumpers. Practical clothes for a practical life, not the attention of others. It was natural for an attractive teenager to dress to be seen. Lund herself was the exception. Yet the clothes she found sifting through Nanna's coat hangers seemed too good, too adult, too . . . knowing.

Then she brushed the hangers to one side, looked at the back where a small mountain of shoes stood, pair upon discarded pair.

Behind them something glittered. Lund reached in, felt Nanna's clothes fluttering against her cheeks like the wings of gigantic moths, retrieved what was there.

A pair of shiny brown cowboy boots decorated with coloured motifs, glitter, studs, tiny mirrors.

They shouted money.

No. They screamed it.

'My wife's here,' said a brusque male voice behind her.

Lund jumped, banged her head on the hanger rail.

It was Theis Birk Larsen.

He watched her rub her hair.

'Be careful what you tell her.'

★   ★   ★

183

Seated round the table, frozen faces captured in the surface.

'I'm sorry you were told,' Lund said.

The day had brightened. The flowers were fading. But still the place smelled of their sweet scent.

'The officer shouldn't have done that. He's been transferred so you won't see him again.'

Theis Birk Larsen, head down, eyes dead, muttered, 'Well, that's something.'

'It's nothing,' Pernille said. 'I want to know the truth. I want to know what happened. I'm her mother.'

Lund checked her notes.

'No one saw Nanna after the party. She was probably driven away in the stolen car. The one we found her in.'

Lund looked out of the window, looked back at her.

'She was raped.'

Pernille waited.

'She was beaten.'

Pernille waited.

'We think she fought back. That may be why he hit her.'

Nothing more.

'In the woods?' Pernille asked.

'In the woods. We think so.' Lund hesitated. 'But maybe she was held captive somewhere else first. We just don't know.'

The big man went to the sink, placed his fists

knuckles down on the draining board, gazed out at the wan grey sky.

'She told us she'd be at Lisa's,' Pernille said. 'Nanna didn't lie to me.'

'Maybe she didn't.' A pause. 'Do you have no idea?' A glance at the shape at the window, the hunched back clad in black leather. 'Did you remember anything else?'

'If something was wrong Nanna would have told me,' Pernille insisted. 'She'd have told me. We're . . . We were . . .'

Words proved a struggle.

'Close.'

'When did she stop seeing Oliver Schandorff?'

'Is he involved?'

A long, broad shadow fell across the table. Theis Birk Larsen turning to listen.

'I'm just gathering information.'

'Six months ago or so,' Pernille said. 'Oliver was a kind of boyfriend.'

'Was she upset when it ended?'

'No. He was.'

Lund watched her.

'She wouldn't talk to Oliver on the phone. Nanna . . .' She leant forward, tried to hold Lund's wide and ranging eyes. 'If something was wrong she always told me. Didn't she, Theis?'

The silent man stood at the window, a giant figure in his scarlet bib overalls and leather jacket.

Lund's phone rang.

Meyer had something.

'OK. I'll come straight away.'

They stared at her, expectant.

'I have to go now.'

'What was that?' he asked in a low, brutal voice.

'Just a call. I saw a pair of boots in Nanna's room. They look expensive. Did you give them to her?'

'Expensive boots?' he grunted.

'Yes.'

Pernille said, 'Why do you ask?'

A shrug.

'I ask lots of questions. Maybe too many. I put my nose in where it's not wanted.' A pause. 'That's what I do.'

'We didn't buy her expensive boots,' Pernille said.

Interview room. The lawyer was brisk and bald and built like a hockey player. When Lund walked in he was yelling at a bored-looking Meyer who sat on the table edge, chin on fist, smiling childishly.

'You've ignored all my client's rights. You questioned him without a lawyer present . . .'

'Not my fault you wanted a lie-in. What's the big deal? I took him on a tour. Bought him breakfast. I'll change his stinking nappy if you want . . .'

'Come with me, Meyer . . .'

'There will be consequences,' the lawyer bellowed as Lund took him into the next room.

Meyer sat down, looked at her.

'They put Oliver Schandorff in the last free cell we had. So I drove Jeppe round a bit and dropped him off here at five.'

Wondering how bad this might turn out, Lund asked, 'Did you question him?'

'Have you seen his emails? Plenty. And he rang Nanna fifty-six times in one week. If you ask . . .'

'Did you question him without a lawyer present?'

'The lawyer said he would be here at seven. He didn't turn up till nine.' Meyer tried to look the picture of reasonableness. 'Like I said, I couldn't throw the little jerk into a cell. We just had breakfast together.' A small boy's gesture of guilt. 'It would have been rude if I hadn't talked to him, Lund.'

Buchard came through the door. Blue shirt. Grey face.

'We didn't have anywhere to hold the suspect last night,' Lund said straight off. 'The lawyer was two hours late. Meyer bought him breakfast.'

'He wasn't very hungry,' Meyer broke in, 'but it seemed the polite thing to do.'

'Maybe the kid thought he was being interrogated but . . .'

Lund left it at that. Buchard was unimpressed.

'Perhaps Meyer could explain this to me himself.'

'What Lund said,' Meyer told him.

'Write that in a report. Bring it to my office. I'll put it in your file with all the others.' A studied pause. 'After the hearing.'

When the chief left Lund got to her desk, started on the photos and the messages.

Meyer brightened.

'I thought that went pretty well. Didn't you?'

The press conference was packed. Cameras. Microphones everywhere. Troels Hartmann wore a tie this time, black. That morning he went to the barber that Rie Skovgaard chose, sat in the chair as she ordered the cut she wanted: short and severe, mournful.

Then the script.

'It's been a turbulent time. But I've been working closely with the police. The car was stolen. No staff were ever implicated. Our thoughts and sympathies go out to the girl's parents. Our priority all along was to help the police. Nothing more.'

'Is the driver a suspect?' a woman asked.

'The driver came from an agency. He's been cleared.'

A sea of voices, the loudest shouting, 'Is this the position of the police?'

Hartmann looked and saw the bald head and beaming smirk of Erik Salin.

'I don't speak for the Politigården. But I've discussed this with them. They're happy I make it clear our involvement was an unfortunate coincidence. We've nothing to do with this case. Speak to them if you want any more.'

Still the questions rained down on him.

A politician picked the ones he answered. Carefully. Hartmann listened to the clamour, thought of Bremer, waited in silence until the right question came along.

'Will you form an alliance with the Centre Party?'

A puzzled expression, bemused but knowing.

'You know,' he said, 'the world of local politics is rarely as dramatic as you people would have your readers believe. Thank you.'

He rose to leave.

The woman reporter was on her feet.

'You're forming an alliance?'

Nothing.

The political editor from one of the dailies pounced.

'Is Bremer wooing her too?'

There was the flash of a camera in his face. Stick to the script, Rie Skovgaard said.

'He is.' The room went silent, every eye upon him. 'Personally though, I think he's a bit old for her. Now . . .'

Sudden, raucous laughter.

A delicate balance, one that fell in his favour. The hacks hated Bremer as much as he did. At least that's what they said in their cups.

Troels Hartmann retreated to his office next door.

There Rie Skovgaard fussed over him. Adjusted his tie, his jacket. Looked girlish and pleased.

One short ticking-off for the departure from the script at the end. But that worked. So she was happy.

189

'I'm fine,' Hartmann said, retreating from her hands. 'Fine.'

'Troels. You've got a bunch of meetings ahead. Then a school visit. The cameras will be there. They'll want you.'

He stepped back to the window like a sullen child.

She played the same game. A pout. A practised one. She'd had her hair done before him. Black and sleek. Fitted dress hugging her slender body.

Weber rushed in brandishing papers. The draft of the alliance speech. He wanted it cleared with Eller.

'We'll read it in the car . . .'

'Take Morten with you,' Skovgaard said. 'Then the two of you can talk. Go over the points . . .'

Weber shook his head.

'There's nothing new. You don't need me. I've work here—'

'I'll hold the fort while you're gone,' she insisted. 'Go.' She waved at them. 'Go.' A smile. 'And talk.'

Sometimes they played chess together. He usually won. Because she let him? Hartmann wondered that sometimes.

'Go, boys!' Rie Skovgaard shouted like a scolding mother, waving her thin hands, flashing her rings.

'On Saturday night,' Meyer said, 'Jeppe Hald called Schandorff several times.'

'What about the woman Oliver was with?'

'Divorcee out for some fun. She said he was miserable and worried about something.'

Lund scowled at him.

'That's it?'

'No.'

That petulant ring to his voice was back. The smoking ban she'd imposed in the office was getting to him.

'What about the prints from the boiler room?'

'Half the school was down there.'

'What about DNA?'

'Still waiting. Ready?'

She looked through the glass door at the interview room across the passage. Oliver Schandorff, head down at the table.

'I want to be in there,' Meyer said. 'We're supposed to be working on this together.'

This was true.

'OK. You can come in. But leave the questions to me.'

He jumped to his feet. A short salute and click of the heels.

The moment they were through the door Schandorff, scruffy in a green polo shirt, pointed at Meyer.

'I'm not talking to him.'

'No,' Lund announced. 'You're talking to me.' Pause. 'Good morning, Oliver. How are you?'

'I feel like shit.'

She held out her hand. The kid took it. Then the bald lawyer they'd seen earlier did the same. Lund sat next to them. Meyer perched at the end of the room, on a stool in the light from the window.

191

'All we want to do,' Lund said, 'is ask you a few questions. Then you can go home.' No response. 'Nanna told her parents she would be at Lisa's. Was she meeting you?'

'No. I told you.'

'Do you know who she met?'

'No.'

From her folder Lund pulled a couple of photos of the fancy leather boots from Nanna's wardrobe.

'Did you give her these?'

He looked as if he'd never seen them.

'No.'

Meyer leaned back in his chair at the window, let loose a long yawn.

Lund ignored him.

'Why were you so angry that you threw a chair?'

The bald lawyer beamed and said, 'My client reserves the right not to answer.'

Lund ignored the man.

'I'm trying to help you, Oliver. Tell us the truth and you're gone from here. Hide behind this man and I promise—'

'She said she'd found someone else!'

'That's enough,' the lawyer said. 'We're going.'

Lund's eyes never left the ginger-haired kid.

'Did she say who?'

The lawyer was on his feet.

'My client's had a rough night—'

'Did she say anything else?'

'I said,' the lawyer cut in. 'No more questions.'

Schandorff shook his head.

'All I did was ask her if she'd come to the basement and talk to me. But she wouldn't—'

'Oliver!' the lawyer barked.

'Kid,' Meyer cut in. Schandorff glanced at him. 'He's not your dad. He won't hit you. I won't let him.'

'She wouldn't come with me.'

Lund nodded.

'So what did you do?'

'I called her a bunch of names. That was the last I saw of her.'

She picked up her papers.

'Thanks. That's all.'

Outside the room. Thinking.

'Nanna had a date. She had expensive boots no one knew about.'

'Oliver could have bought them,' Meyer said. 'He's lying. Maybe she was going on a date with him.'

'It feels wrong.'

'It feels wrong,' he muttered, reaching for a cigarette.

'Don't smoke in here,' she ordered. 'I told you that already.'

'I'll tell you what's wrong, Lund. You. You've been here so long you're part of the furniture. You think no one can ever replace you. That's what's wrong. You.'

Then he lit the cigarette anyway. Blew smoke in the air. Coughed. Said, 'My office. Mine.'

Svendsen stuck his head through the door.

'Forensics called. The samples from the boiler room were contaminated. There won't be any DNA profiles today.'

Lund said nothing. Looked at the photos on her desk. The boots.

'OK,' Meyer told him. 'We'll go back to the boys' flat.'

Svendsen sighed.

'We were there all night.'

'We didn't look hard enough.'

They left. Lund kept staring at the boots. The phone rang. It was the medical examiner. Wanting to see her.

Pernille waited on her own in the apartment with the flowers, the police tags and Nanna's clothes.

By midday she was ready to go crazy. So she drove to the school, saw an embarrassed Rektor Koch, then the charming, quiet, sad-eyed teacher Rama.

Learnt one thing only: the police held Oliver Schandorff and Jeppe Hald overnight.

Then she waited in an empty office, listening to the young voices outside in the corridor, dreaming she could hear Nanna's bright tones among them. Waited until Lisa Rasmussen came crying, running, throwing herself into the wide open arms of Pernille's gaberdine raincoat, shaking with emotion, sobbing like a little child.

Her hair was blonde like Nanna's. Pernille kissed

it and knew she shouldn't. These two were friends. Sisters almost sometimes. These two were . . .

Pernille let go, smiled, stopped trying to rationalize something that was beyond comprehension. A child was a brief and blissful interlude of responsibility, not a thing to be owned. She'd no idea what Nanna did outside the little apartment above the garage. Didn't ask. Struggled not to think about it.

But Lisa knew. This short, slightly tubby girl trying so hard to be as pretty and clever as Nanna, and never quite succeeding.

Lisa dried her eyes, stood in front of her. Looking awkward. As if she'd like to go.

'There are things . . .' Pernille said. 'I don't understand.'

Silence. The little blonde girl shifted on her feet.

'Was Nanna upset by something?'

Lisa shook her head.

'What about Oliver? Was he involved?'

'No.'

A petulant teenage note in the denial.

'So why do the police keep asking about him, Lisa? Why?'

Her hands fidgeted behind her back, she leaned against the desk, said with a pout, 'I don't know.'

Pernille thought of the policewoman, Lund. Her quiet persistent manner. Her large and shining eyes that never seemed to stop looking.

'But you went to the party together. Did she say anything? Did she seem . . .' Words. Simple ones.

Simple questions. Lund's way. 'Did she seem different?'

'No. She didn't say anything. She was just . . . Nanna.'

Don't get angry, Pernille thought. Don't say what you think . . . You're a lying little cow and it's written all over your plain fat face.

'Why did she say she was staying with you?'

The girl shook her head, like a bad actress in a bad play.

'I don't know.'

'But you're friends,' Pernille said, wondering . . . is this too much? Do I look hard? Do I look crazy?

Said anyway, 'You're friends. She would have told you her plans.' Voice getting louder, chestnut hair waving. 'She would have told you if there was something.'

'Pernille. She didn't. Honestly.'

Shake the child. Scream at it. Yell until she says . . . What?

'Was she angry?' Pernille asked. 'With me?'

'I don't know.'

'You have to tell me!' she cried, voice beginning to shatter. 'It's important.'

Lisa didn't move, grew calmer and more sullen with every angry rising note she heard.

'She . . . didn't . . . say . . . anything.'

Hands on the girl's shoulders, staring into those defiant stupid eyes.

'Tell me!'

'There's nothing to tell,' Lisa said in a voice flat

196

and devoid of emotion. 'She wasn't angry with you. She really wasn't.'

'Then what happened?' Pernille snarled.

Shake the child. Slap her cheek.

'What happened?'

Lisa stood defiant. A look in her eyes that said: do it then. Hit me now. It won't make a difference. Nanna's still gone.

Pernille sniffed, wiped her nose, walked out into the corridor. Stopped at the flowers and photos by the lockers. Nanna's shrine. Sat down among them. The third day. Petals falling. Notes slipped from their fastenings. Everything fading into a lost grey distance beyond her vision.

She picked up the nearest piece of paper. A childish scrawl.

It read, 'We will never forget you.'

But you will, she thought. You all will. Even Lund after a while. Even Theis if he can manage it, placing his boundless, shapeless love in the boys, in Anton and Emil. Hoping their young faces will obliterate Nanna's memory, supplant it with enough devotion to hide the pain.

Figures flitted quickly past lugging satchels, carrying papers, chatting in low tones.

She watched and listened. In these plain grey corridors her daughter once walked. Still did in a way, in Pernille's imagination, which made the hurt more keen. Grief should be an absence, a void, not the physical thing she now felt. Nanna was lost to her. Stolen. Till the thief and the deed became clear her death would mark them all, like the tumour of some cruel disease.

They were locked in the present, no way out. She got to her feet, walked up the steps, stumbled, fell.

A hand reached out. She saw a face, dark and kind.

'Are you all right?'

The teacher, Rama, again.

She took his arm, grabbed the handrail, got to her feet.

They all said that and never wanted the answer.

'No,' she murmured. 'I'm not.'

She wondered what Nanna thought of this handsome, intelligent man. Whether she liked him. What they talked about.

'Did Lisa say anything?' Rama asked.

'A little.'

'If I can—'

'Help?'

They all said that too. Reached for the same words. Perhaps he meant it. Perhaps it was one more trite sentiment, spoken automatically like a prayer.

Pernille Birk Larsen walked out of the school wondering if Theis was right. She was being stupid. The police were looking. Lund ought to know her job.

The woman from the estate agency gazed up at the scaffolding, the sheeted windows, the piles of material stacked by the door.

'It's got to be sold quickly. I want it gone.'

Theis Birk Larsen was in his black jacket, his hat, his rigger boots and red overalls. Work outfit, though work, the thing that seemed so important, now escaped him. The business was in Vagn Skærbæk's hands. Vagn could do the job. There was no choice.

'Of course,' she agreed.

'I'll take what I paid. I just want rid of it.'

'I understand.'

He kicked the scaffolding.

'The materials are included.'

Children played in the street. Kicked footballs. Laughs and shouts.

He watched them, envious.

'It's a lovely house,' the woman said. 'Why not wait a few months?'

'No. It has to be now. Is that a problem?'

She hesitated.

'Not really. You saw the survey?'

She pulled out a sheaf of documents. Birk Larsen hated paper. That was Pernille's job.

'The survey shows dry rot.'

He blinked, felt sick and powerless.

'The insurance must cover that.'

She didn't look at him, shook her head.

'No. It doesn't. Sorry.'

A breeze struck up. The sheets flapped in the wind. Two kids on bikes rode by trailing kites from their hands.

'But . . .'

She pointed a manicured fingernail at the contract.

'It says there. No cover for dry rot. I'm sorry.' A deep and awkward breath. 'If you sell now you'll lose a lot of money. In this condition . . .'

He stared at the place, thought of all the lost dreams. The boys in their rooms. Nanna peering out of the top window now covered in black sheeting.

'Sell the damned thing,' Theis Birk Larsen said.

Troels Hartmann was on his hands and knees, painting with the toddlers in the kindergarten.

Morten Weber came to crouch beside him.

'Troels,' he said. 'I hate to interrupt your fun but the photographers have left. You've other places to go.'

Hartmann drew a childish yellow chicken on the paper, got squeals of delight from the kids around him.

Smiled.

'Are they fun too, Morten?'

'They're necessary.'

Hartmann pointed a finger at the young faces on the floor.

'These are the voters of tomorrow.'

'Well, let's come back tomorrow then. I'm more interested in anyone who's got a vote today.'

'They made us a cake.'

Weber frowned.

'A cake?'

200

Two minutes later they sat alone at a table away from the teachers and the kids.

'Try the cake, Morten.'

'Sorry. Can't.'

'The diabetes is a front. You wouldn't touch it anyway. You're so self-righteous.'

They were close enough for a crack like that, he thought.

'What about this reporter?' Hartmann asked.

'You mean Erik Salin?'

'He's on my tail, Morten. Why? Who is he? How did he know about the car?'

'He's a sleazeball looking to make a bit of money. Take it as a compliment. He wouldn't waste the time if you weren't in with a chance.'

'How did he know about the car?'

Weber squirmed.

'You think someone in the office leaked it, don't you?' Weber asked.

'Do you?'

'It had crossed my mind. But I can't imagine who.'

Hartmann pushed away the cake and his plastic cup of orange juice, listened to the kids giggling over their paintings.

'I've every confidence in our team,' Weber said a touch pompously. 'All of them. Haven't you?'

Hartmann was about to answer when his phone rang.

He listened, looked at Weber.

'We've got to go.'

★   ★   ★

Striding through the long echoing halls, around the central courtyard, Hartmann was livid.

'Where the hell is she?'

'She's going to call in a minute.'

Rie Skovgaard met him at the front door, was struggling to keep up as he marched towards their office, Weber following on behind, silent, listening.

'Eller says Poul Bremer made her a better offer. She's not taken it yet. She wants to know our reaction.'

'Our reaction is she can choke on it.'

Skovgaard sighed.

'This is politics.'

'No it's not. It's a beauty contest. And we're not playing.'

'Listen to her. Hear what she has to say. We could compromise on a few things . . .'

She stopped Hartmann outside the office door.

'Troels. You have to calm down.'

He cast his eyes around the inside of the Rådhus. Sometimes it looked like a jail. A very comfortable prison.

Skovgaard's phone rang.

'Hi, Kirsten. Just a second. We'll be with you soon.'

Call ended, she looked at Hartmann and said, 'Be polite. Keep cool.'

He was walking already. She lost it. Slapped him on the shoulder, yelled, 'Hey!'

Her voice was hard and shrill.

'Shut up and listen to me for once, will you?

If we have Eller on our side we win. If we don't we're one more tiny minority begging for crumbs at Poul Bremer's table. Troels . . .'

Leaving again. Her hand gripped his blue lapels, dragged him back into the shadows.

'Do you understand what I'm saying? You can't get a majority on your own. You don't have the support.' She calmed down a little. 'Nothing can change that now. It's a fact.'

Hartmann held out his hand for the phone.

'Be calm,' she said and gave it him.

Hartmann called Eller. Small talk, then, 'I heard about you and Bremer. Well, that's the way it goes. There's no point in getting upset about it.'

He closed his eyes and listened. Talk of doors remaining open, offers that weren't quite final. The insistent, expectant tone never changed.

'I guess there won't be an alliance, after all,' Hartmann said. 'We should have coffee sometime. Take care. Bye.'

Skovgaard was white with fury. Weber was gone.

'There. How calm was that?'

The medical examiner was a long-winded man with a tanned face and a white beard. All the way to the morgue he talked about making cider.

'They've got good apples in Sweden. I'll give you the recipe.'

'That's lovely.'

They walked in, both pulled on gloves, and went to the table.

'This is an unusual case,' he said, lifting the white sheet.

She looked at Nanna Birk Larsen's body. Cleaned up now and showing the post-mortem marks.

'The blood in her hair clotted long before she hit the water. There's bruising on the arms and legs and down her right side.'

Lund looked. Thought she'd seen enough.

'Come here,' he ordered, pointing to the right thigh.

'We've been through this.'

The leg was covered in cuts.

'Abrasions?'

'No. Feel her skin.'

Lund did. It felt like skin.

'There's redness around the wounds,' he pointed out. 'When a body's been in the water that disappears. But it comes back after a few days.'

Lund shook her head.

'They're sores,' he said. 'She was kept on a rough surface. Maybe a concrete floor.'

'The school basement has a concrete floor.'

She touched the lesions. Thought about the hidden room with the bloody mattress and the drugs.

'How long was she like this?'

'Fifteen to twenty hours.'

Lund struggled with this information, tried to picture what it meant.

'Are you sure?'

'I'm sure. There was a series of rapes with several

204

hours between them. But no DNA we can find so far. He must have used a condom. There's nothing under her nails or anywhere else.'

'Because of the water?'

He nodded.

'That's what I thought. But she was in the boot of the car. Look at her hands.'

He lifted up each one.

'Someone cut her nails.'

He let the hands fall back onto the white sheet. Lund picked up each in turn, took a close look.

'There are traces of ether in her liver and lungs,' he said, reading from a report. 'So she was drugged. Perhaps several times. This was all planned. He knew what he was doing. I wouldn't . . .'

He paused, as if unsure of himself.

'This isn't my field but I wouldn't be surprised if you found he'd done this before. There's a . . . method to it.'

Lund took the report from him.

'Does that help?'

She shrugged.

'Well,' he said. 'I'll send you anything else that comes along. Oh . . .' He smiled. 'And that recipe for cider.'

Lund went back to her office. Buchard was arguing with the bald lawyer outside the door. Struggling to keep hold of Oliver Schandorff and Jeppe Hald. The lawyer would be going in front of a judge to get them freed soon. From the look on

Buchard's face the chief didn't have much hope of winning that particular argument.

Eller closed the door behind her. Sat down, placed her broad hands on her broad hips and said, 'That was some trick you played I must say.'

'No trick, Kirsten.'

'I hope not.'

He waited.

'I said no to Bremer. Don't think that was an easy decision. It's not a word he likes to hear.'

'I can imagine.'

'It wasn't much of a choice really. We're natural partners. He's just . . .' She smiled. 'The bastard who pulls all the strings.'

Still he said nothing.

'I hope you can live up to our expectations,' Eller added. 'My neck's on the line.'

'Your group . . . ?'

'. . . will do as I say. Now . . . shall we get down to business?'

Five minutes later, around the table in a meeting next to the campaign office, the negotiations began. Policies and appointments. Funding and media strategies. Rie Skovgaard took notes and made suggestions.

Hartmann and Eller cut the deal.

Meyer was back from searching the student flat again.

'Did you release those kids?' he asked.

'Yes.'

'We'll have to bring them back in.'

Lund scanned through some of the photos on the desk. Nanna's wounds. The boots.

'I don't think they did it,' she said.

'I'm sure they did.'

He had a memory card reader with him. Meyer placed it on her desk and plugged the cable into the PC.

'Take a look at this.'

The computer recognized what it was being given, fired up a window.

Shaky video came on the screen. The Halloween party. Kids in costume. Drinking beer. Screaming. Acting the way kids did when they knew no one was watching.

Lund watched. There was Jeppe Hald, bright, quiet Jeppe, star pupil, head boy. Screaming at the lens, drunk or doped or both.

Lisa Rasmussen in a short tight dress, sashaying, much the same.

'Where'd you get this?'

'Jeppe Hald's room. He recorded it on his mobile phone then saved it on a memory card.' Meyer looked at her. 'So he could watch it on his computer.'

Lund nodded.

'I don't think he's as bright as that school says,' Meyer added.

'Stop!'

Meyer froze the frame.

Nanna in her black witch's hat. Nanna alive and breathing. Beautiful, so beautiful. So . . . *old*.

She didn't look drunk. She wasn't screaming. She looked . . . bemused. Like an adult suddenly surrounded by a bunch of infants.

'Play,' Lund said.

Meyer set it running slowly. The picture panned from Nanna to Oliver Schandorff, wild hair, wild eyes. Schandorff staring hungrily at Nanna as he swigged at a can of beer.

'We didn't have parties like that at my school,' Meyer said. 'Yours?'

'They wouldn't have invited me.'

'I bet. Here we go.' Meyer let out a long sad sigh and sat down next to her. 'Show time.'

The picture changed. Somewhere else. Somewhere darker. A few lights. Drinks on the table. The place in the basement. Had to be.

Something moving in the background, getting bigger as the lens approached.

Lund leaned forward, looked at this carefully, felt her heart begin to race.

There was a sound. Panting, gasping. Oliver Schandorff naked, ginger head swaying as he writhed over the figure beneath him, naked too, legs splayed and not moving.

The contrast between him and the girl was striking. Schandorff all manic energy and desperation. She . . .

Drunk? Unconscious?

Couldn't tell. But not right.

208

Closer.

Schandorff's hands came and grabbed her legs, made her grip him. Her fingers rose as if to beat him off. He was like a madman, pushed them down, grunted, screaming.

Lund watched.

The lens shifted behind them, to Schandorff's back. Her legs had locked round him. Sex the teenage way. As if a clock somewhere was running, saying, 'Do it now and do it quickly, or you'll never get the chance again.'

More grunts, more savage thrusts.

Closer. The black witch's hat they saw earlier, down over the eyes, over the face. Blonde hair. The hat moves . . .

'Shit,' Lund said.

Something had happened. The camera was off the couple. They heard him, sneaking up on them. Curses and swift movements. The girl just visible, scuttling to cover herself. Blonde hair, witch's hat, bare breasts. Not much more.

'I think I'll bring them in again,' Meyer said.

On the steps of the City Hall Troels Hartmann and Kirsten Eller stood next to one another, blinking in the bright lights of the cameras, smiling, shaking hands.

Waiting for Meyer, Lund watched it all on the news channel on her computer. Then went back to the video. The school.

One segment she'd skipped through earlier.

Nanna in her party dress. Hat on. Beaming into Jeppe Hald's phone. Raising a glass of what looked like Coke. Smiling. Sober. So elegant and natural. Not a kid at all. Not like the others.

And a few minutes later . . .

Naked in the basement, Oliver Schandorff thrusting at her like an animal.

'Be right, Meyer,' she whispered.

The caretaker was letting Lund into the school when Meyer called.

'I've got them both.'

'Don't question them yet.'

A pause.

'The last time I checked we had the same stripes.'

'I need to see something first.'

A long sigh.

'Don't worry, Lund. You'll get the credit.'

Her footsteps echoed down dark and empty corridors.

'Wait twenty minutes,' she said and cut the call.

The flowers on Nanna's shrine beside the lockers looked dead, the candles burned to stumps. Lund walked down the cold stairs to the basement, shining her torch, fumbling for light switches she couldn't find.

Past the Don't Cross tape. Into the hidden room. Lines and markers everywhere. Empty bottles circled, dusty with print powder.

She looked at the bloodstained mattress. There was one single large stain at the foot, then a line

210

of red on the piping at the edge. Not so much blood. And it wasn't smeared.

Meyer didn't wait, didn't see why he should. He had Oliver Schandorff in Lund's office, seated in front of the computer, forced to watch the video. The pumpkin head. The drunken kids. The dope. The booze.

On his own now, free to act as he pleased, Meyer was more relaxed. He sat next to the kid, watched him as he stared at the PC, ginger hair everywhere, face screwed up with fear and pain.

'You've got two choices, Oliver,' he said in a flat, calm voice. 'Either you confess now . . .'

Nanna. In her witch's hat. Smiling. Happy. Beautiful.

'Or we watch the rest. And wait for your lawyer to come in the morning. If he can be bothered to get out of bed.'

The phone was moving, from the hall down the stairs. Into the basement. Towards the hidden room.

Two figures naked in the distance, beneath a single bulb, wrestling.

Schandorff couldn't take his eyes off the screen.

'I've got all night,' Meyer told him. 'But I know you two did it and so do you. So let's get this over with, shall we?'

Silence.

Meyer felt the faint stirrings of anger, tried to quell it.

'Oliver? *Oliver?*'

★　　★　　★

211

Lund took out the photos she'd brought. Close-ups of Nanna's body. Details of the sores, the lesions on her back.

The power was off for some reason so she checked them in the light of her torch. Held them up as she looked at the mattress, the spots of blood on the floor.

Took out a photo of Nanna's hands. Clipped fingernails.

Ran her torch around the room.

Checked the inventory.

No sign of scissors.

Took out her phone, looked at the screen. No signal in this underground tomb.

Oliver Schandorff sat rigid in front of the screen. Two bodies coupling. His own ginger hair bobbing up and down. He grabs her legs, makes her grip him. He pushes away her hands as they reach to claw at him.

The lens is up close behind. His back, his body pumping at her in a crazy, frenetic rhythm. Then confusion. Picture moving everywhere as he pulls himself away, confronts the intruder sneaking up on them.

Lips downturned like a naughty child, face full of shame and anger, Schandorff sat in the homicide office refusing to speak.

'Maybe Jeppe will talk first,' Meyer said.

There was Hald on the screen. Drunk. Out of control.

'You know he might be next door.' Meyer tapped Schandorff on the arm. 'Could be saying it was all you. Just you. Wouldn't be nice, would it?'

Meyer's hand went to his shoulder.

'He's not your friend, Oliver. Think about it. I know I yelled at you, son. I'm sorry. It's just . . .'

Schandorff sat there like a rock.

'Those pictures of Nanna after we got her out of the water.' Meyer watched him. 'I can't get them out of my head. Don't make me show them to you. Best for both of us if I don't do that.'

Lund wasn't ready to go outside and find a signal. More to do here. She pulled out a pair of forensic gloves and picked up a broken beer glass sitting in a ring of chalk.

Shone the torch on it.

Lipstick along the edge. Bright orange. Gaudy.

Got the photo of Nanna from the school set, shot at the party.

Nanna in her witch's hat, the only thing about her that seemed young.

Reached into the ashtray. Sifted through the cigarette ends and joint butts. Pulled out a rolled-up wad of tin foil. Pulled it open with her gloved fingers. Not dope. An earring.

In the light she saw three fake diamonds on a silver setting.

Back to the photos. Nanna and the other kids. Lisa Rasmussen.

It was four days now since they pulled Nanna

Birk Larsen's body out of the chill canal by the airport. In all that time they'd scarcely worked without a lead. Chasing shadows running from them. A puzzle promising answers. Yet . . .

This case was like none she'd ever worked. It had layers and texture. Mysteries. Riddles. Investigations were never black and white. But never had she met one quite so grey and insubstantial.

Lund stared at the photo, Nanna and Lisa, smiling, happy.

Then there was a sound above her. Footsteps in the dark.

'Maybe it wasn't your idea,' Meyer said. 'Jeppe thought of it and you came along for the ride.'

He leaned over, tried to get Schandorff's attention.

'Oliver?'

Nothing. Just a miserable face locked on the computer.

'That would make a difference. If you told us. So what's it to be?'

Meyer leaned back in his chair, put his arms behind his head.

'Do we sit here all night and go through some more pictures? Or get it over with?'

Nothing.

'Fine.' There was an edge in Meyer's voice and he regretted that. 'I'm feeling hungry. Don't have money for two—'

'It's not her, you moron,' Schandorff snarled.

Meyer blinked.

That petulant, tortured teenage voice again. But finally Oliver Schandorff looked at him.

'The girl in the boiler room. It's not Nanna.'

Upstairs in the corridor, in front of Nanna's shrine. A stump of candle flickered in the dark.

Lund checked her phone. There was a signal.

Heard something, footsteps close to the door. Didn't think of hiding. Turned her torch towards the source.

'Lisa?'

The girl stood frozen in the bright white light, a glass vase with some roses in her hand.

'How did you get in?' Lund asked.

Lisa placed the flowers on the shrine.

'They were getting old. People forget.'

'How did you get in?'

'The gym door's open. The lock doesn't work. Everyone knows that.'

She brushed back her long blonde hair, looked at the photos and the flowers.

'When did you get to know Nanna?'

'At primary school. In our last year. Nanna picked Frederiksholm so I did too.' She moved the roses around. 'I didn't think I'd get in. Nanna's clever. Her dad had to find the money. My dad's got the money. But me . . . I'm stupid.'

'When did you fall out?'

Lisa didn't look at her.

215

'We didn't fall out.'

'We've got Nanna's phone. You never called her, texted her lately.'

Nothing.

'Nanna called you.'

'It wasn't an argument. Not really.'

'About Oliver?'

Straight away, 'I don't remember.'

'I think it was about Oliver. Nanna didn't care for him. You're in love with him, right?'

Lisa laughed.

'You ask some weird questions.'

'So you went to the boiler room.'

'Can I go now?'

Lund pulled out the earring.

'You forgot something.'

The girl stared at the evidence bag, swore, turned to go.

'We could waste a lot of time looking for the dress,' Lund said to her back. 'Or you could just tell me.'

Lisa Rasmussen stopped, hugged herself in her skimpy red coat.

'This is important,' Lund said. 'Was Nanna in the room? Or were you and the boys alone?'

Caught between being a kid and an adult.

'I was angry with her! OK?'

Lund folded her arms, waited.

'Nanna made all the decisions. She treated me like I was a child. I was drunk. Then that creep Jeppe came in and started filming us. Oliver got

216

mad. I tried to stop Jeppe. I tripped over some bottles.'

She rolled up her sleeve. Plasters and scratch marks. Long wounds, maybe stitches.

'Cut myself.'

'What happened?'

'Oliver took me to the hospital. We were there all night.'

She sat on a windowsill, plain young face lit by the street lamps.

'He was still mad about Nanna. I thought maybe I could . . .'

She rolled down her sleeve, hugged herself again.

'Stupid. Nanna was right.'

'Where was Nanna?'

'I don't know.'

'Lisa . . .'

'I don't know!' she yelled. 'Maybe half past nine . . . she came to the hall, put her hat on me. Gave me a hug. And said goodbye.'

She looked Lund in the face.

'That was it. She left.'

Lund nodded.

'Does my dad have to know? He'll kill me.'

Hartmann and Rie Skovgaard listened to the radio on the way to the reception. The news was calling the election already. The alliance had altered the game. A change to the long-established political system wasn't far off.

The Birk Larsen case seemed behind them.

217

Ahead lay the hard work of the campaign. Meetings and press conferences. Shaking hands, winning votes.

And private conclaves of the inner circle of Danish politics, in the glittering rooms where right and left and centre gathered to spar gently with smiles and deft promises, trade polite insults, deliver discreet warnings disguised as advice.

Late that evening, exhausted, wishing for nothing more than to take Rie Skovgaard home to bed, Hartmann found himself faced with her father. A long-standing parliamentarian for the Liberal Party. Kim Skovgaard was a burly, genial man with clout. Not unlike Poul Bremer, who chatted amiably with his foes across the room.

The Lord Mayor's raucous laughter boomed over the gathering.

'I didn't realize Bremer was on your party list,' Hartmann said.

'Keep your friends close and your enemies closer,' Kim Skovgaard answered with a knowing grin. 'In the end we're all fighting for the same thing. A better life. We just disagree about the means.'

Hartmann smiled.

'Are you still implicated in the case?' Skovgaard asked.

'You mean the girl's murder?'

'Are there others?'

'We were never implicated. It was a coincidence. You'll hear no more of that.'

Skovgaard raised his glass.

'Good. It would have been hard to back you with those kind of headlines.'

'Dad . . .' his daughter intervened. 'Not now.'

He carried on.

'The Prime Minister . . . and a few others are wondering if you're on top of everything.'

'The campaign's under control. We'll win.' A smile. Lost amidst a sea of others. 'Excuse me . . .'

He walked through to the next room, took Poul Bremer's arm, asked for a word. The two of them strode to an empty space near the fireplace.

'So you won Madam Eller in the end, Troels,' Bremer said. 'Congratulations. I hope the price wasn't too high.'

'I know what you're up to.'

Bremer blinked behind his owlish glasses, shook his head.

'If I catch you playing any more games . . .' Hartmann came close, spoke in a gruff, determined whisper. 'I will take you to court. Do you understand?'

'Not a bit of it,' Bremer replied. 'I don't know what the hell you're talking about.'

'Fine,' Hartmann said, made to go. 'You heard.'

'Troels! Come back here.'

Bremer strolled to his side, peering into his face.

'I've always liked you. Ever since you were a novice here, struggling to make your first speech. Today . . .'

Hartmann tried to judge him, to sift sincerity from the histrionics, and failed.

219

'Today you defeated me. That doesn't happen often. When it does . . . I don't like it. Nor do I like it when in a fit of paranoia you accuse me of things of which I'm ignorant.'

Hartmann stood there, trying not to feel like a scolded schoolboy.

Bremer's big hand came up, thumb and forefinger rubbing together.

'If I'd wanted to crush you, don't you think I would have done it long ago?'

He patted Hartmann's shoulder.

'Think about that.' His smile turned to a scowl. 'You've ruined my mood, Troels. I'm going now. I hope you feel guilty. '

Bremer looked at him.

'Guilty. Yes. That's the word.'

They released Schandorff and Hald. Lund got Lisa Rasmussen to sign a statement, made sure she'd be taken safely home in a car.

On the way out she asked her again, 'You really don't know who she was going to meet?'

The girl looked exhausted. Relieved too. This secret had weighed upon her.

'Nanna was happy. I saw that. As if she was looking forward to something. Something special.'

When she was gone Meyer marched in brandishing papers.

'I'm charging them with perjury. Wasting police time.'

'Is that worth it?'

'Why didn't you call and tell me, Lund? Why haven't you said a word to me? I feel like a fool.'

She held up her phone.

'Basement. No signal. I tried.'

'No you didn't.'

He sounded like one of the petulant kids.

'You're in your own little world. Lundland. Nothing else in it.'

'OK. I'm sorry about that.'

'And I mustn't smoke. Or eat or yell at suspects.'

'Don't worry. I'll be gone soon.'

The pack of cigarettes came out. He brandished one, lit it, blew the smoke at her.

She sighed.

'We don't have a damned thing,' Meyer grumbled.

'Not true.'

'Are you serious?'

She found her voice rising. Must have been the cigarette. She wanted one so badly.

'We have plenty. If only you'd listen.'

He folded his arms, said, 'I'm listening now.'

Five minutes later with Buchard, pug-faced and serious.

She went through the papers, the photos she'd assembled, patiently, one by one.

'We know things about whoever did this. We know he drugged her with ether. He held her captive somewhere and abused her for fifteen to twenty hours. Afterwards . . .'

More shots of the body. Arms, hands, feet, thighs.

'He bathed her. Cut her fingernails. Then drove

221

her to the woods where he knew they wouldn't be disturbed.'

Pictures of the track through the Pentecost Forest. Hair on the dead trees.

'There he played a game. He toyed with her. He let her run away and then caught her. Maybe . . .' She'd been thinking about this for a while. 'Maybe more than once.'

'Hide and seek,' Meyer said, and drew on his cigarette.

'We found designer boots in Nanna's closet,' Lund went on. 'Her parents didn't know about them.'

She passed round the photograph: brown leather and glittering metal.

'Nanna couldn't have bought them. Too expensive. The necklace . . .'

The black heart on a cheap gilt chain.

'We still don't know who this came from. Maybe a gift from whoever gave her the boots. Except it's cheap. And old.'

Lund placed in front of them the photo of Nanna and Lisa at the Halloween party, Lisa looking drunk, a teenager. Nanna elegant and smiling, wearing the black witch's hat as if it was an unwanted joke.

'This is the most important thing. Nanna had a secret rendezvous. She changed out of her clothes and left her costume at school. She was going to meet someone. Even her best friend had no idea who.'

Buchard groaned.

'You're not going to tell me it was a teacher, are you?'

Lund looked at him, said nothing.

'Right,' Meyer said. 'Tomorrow we start all over again.'

'Listen to me!' Buchard ordered. 'The schools fall under the remit of Troels Hartmann. He has to know what we're doing.'

'Fine.' Lund nodded. 'I'll call him tomorrow.'

'And I need you to stay on a little longer,' Buchard added.

Meyer closed his eyes, blew some smoke at the ceiling.

'I'm here till Saturday. Mark starts school on Monday. I've done all I—'

'With all respect,' Meyer cut in. 'I don't think she should stay. I know the ropes. And . . .' He frowned. 'Let's be honest. There hasn't exactly been much teamwork between the two of us. I think Lund should stick to her plan.'

Then he got up and left.

She was looking at the photos. Nanna in the witch's hat. Apart from the kids around her.

Buchard peered at her.

'Meyer's had nothing to eat,' she said. 'It makes him tetchy. No . . .' She waved a finger, corrected herself. 'Tetchier.'

'The school . . .'

'We have to look. We have to look very hard.'

CHAPTER 5

Friday, 7th November

Lund was pulling on her black and white sweater, juggling a piece of toast when her mother said, 'I thought we were leaving tonight?'

'No. We'll go tomorrow afternoon.'

'Tomorrow afternoon? That's when the guests are arriving.'

'It'll be fine.'

'I can't stay in Sweden long. There are things to do.' She looked at the dress. 'There's a wedding on the way.'

'There's always a wedding on the way. We were hoping you'd be with us for a week. Meet Bengt's family.'

A grim laugh.

'You mean take your son to school while you go to work?'

'Never mind.' Lund gulped at her mug, pulled a face. 'It was just an idea. Do we have any hot coffee?'

She went to the percolator. No.

'Is this the kind of mother I've brought you up

to be?' Vibeke asked, shaking her head. 'You haven't even talked to Mark while you've been here. Do you have any idea—?'

'It's been a busy week. I thought you might have noticed.'

Quickly, without a mirror, thinking about Nanna and the school all the time, she took an elastic band from her jeans and tied her long brown hair into a rough ponytail.

'He's twelve years old—'

'I know how old he is.'

'You know nothing about him! Or his life.'

'I have to go.'

'Do you even know he's got a girlfriend?'

Lund stopped. Struggled for a moment.

'Mark's like me,' she said. 'Very independent. We're not in each other's faces all the time. And yes . . . I do know about his girlfriend. Thank you.'

'I'm off,' said a voice behind that made her jump.

Mark, in a blue jacket, ready for school.

She followed him down the stairs.

A dull dry day. He had his scooter with him, started pushing it away the moment they were in the street.

'Mark! You haven't had breakfast.'

He slowed down, got off the thing.

'Not hungry.'

'I'm sorry about this week. I'll make it up to you. I promise.'

He got back on the scooter. She struggled to keep up.

225

'Gran said you had a girlfriend.'

Mark stopped, didn't look her in the eye.

Lund smiled.

'That's nice.'

She tried not to let the earring get to her. He'd got his ear pierced without even asking, by some stupid kid at school.

'What's her name?'

'It's not important.'

'You can invite her to Sweden.'

'I'm going to be late for school.'

'Mark? I'm interested in what goes on in your life.'

'She just broke up with me.'

Twelve years old and such pain on his young face.

'And you don't give a shit. You're only interested in dead people.'

Lund stood on the pavement. Seeing the boy he was at four or five. At eight. Ten. Struggling to separate that child from the surly, sad kid who stared at her now looking . . .

What?

Disappointed.

That was the word.

Mark turned his back on her, pushed himself down the street.

Hartmann came in at nine. Lund took him into her room.

'You told me we were off the hook?'

'I didn't say that . . .'

226

'You never mentioned a teacher.'

'It's one line of inquiry.'

'Into what exactly?'

Meyer stuck his head through the door, said, 'Are we going?'

Hartmann didn't move.

'What have you come up with now?'

Lund shook her head.

'I can't say.'

'These are my schools and my teachers. You will tell me.'

'When I can—'

'No. No!'

He was getting mad. She'd seen this temper before. On TV when he flew at the reporter. Now she had it in her face.

'I need to know who it is! Christ! I have to take precautions.'

'It's not possible—'

'You've made a fool of me once, Lund. It's not happening again.'

'I'm sorry. I can't put your election above a murder inquiry. It wouldn't be right . . .'

He looked livid.

'Don't you understand the damage you'll do? To teachers? To the pupils? To the parents? You spread suspicion like a farmer spreads shit. And you don't give a damn—'

'Don't you dare say that!' she yelled back at him.

Hartmann fell quiet, surprised by the sudden volume.

'Don't ever say that,' Lund repeated more quietly. 'I'm not a politician, Hartmann. I'm a police officer. I don't have time to think about all the consequences. I just have to . . . to . . .'

'What?' he demanded when she never finished the sentence.

'Keep looking.' She dragged her bag onto her shoulder. 'We'll be discreet. We won't start any rumours. We've no interest or desire to damage any innocent party. We just want to find out who killed that girl. OK?'

His sudden rage had fled. These outbursts, she thought, were sharp and unexpected, as much unwanted by Troels Hartmann as they were to those who heard them.

'Fine,' he said, nodding. He looked at her. 'Will you let me help?'

She said nothing.

'I want to, Lund. I'll ask the office to get copies of the personnel files. For the teachers. All the staff.'

'Send them to my office. I'll have someone look through them.'

'I want to help. Believe me.'

His phone went. The mask of the politician, unemotional, distanced, impassive, came upon him again in an instant. Lund left him to his call.

There was a smiling woman in the winding corridor of black marble, fair-haired, carrying a supermarket bag.

She asked Lund, 'Is Jan Meyer here?'

'In a moment.'

Lund went back to checking through the messages on her phone.

'I'm Hanne Meyer,' the woman said. 'I've got something for him.'

A wife. Lund remembered the call the other night. *Now you've woken the whole house.* A baby crying. Meyer had a life beyond the police station. The idea astonished her.

'Sarah Lund,' she said, and shook her hand. 'I work with him.'

'So this is what you look like!'

She was very pretty, with a scarf round her neck and a peasant dress beneath her brown wool coat.

'I've heard a lot about you.'

'I can imagine.'

'Ah.' She gave Lund a knowing look. 'He means well. It doesn't always comes across.' A pause. 'And he thinks you're . . . amazing.'

Lund blinked.

'Amazing?'

'He's to take two of these every hour,' Hanne Meyer said, giving her a bottle of pills. 'If that doesn't help you have to try the bananas.'

She pulled a couple out of her bag, passed them to the wide-eyed Lund.

'Whatever he tells you, Jan must *not* have coffee, cheese or crisps.' She tut-tutted. 'They upset his stomach.'

The woman clapped her hands: all done.

'New jobs are always difficult. Let's hope it works out this time.'

Meyer came round the corner. Old green anorak, sailor's jumper, embarrassed expression on his face.

'What the . . . ?'

'Hi, darling!' Hanne Meyer called cheerily.

Beaming, oblivious to all else, Meyer walked up, kissed her on the lips.

'What the hell are you doing here?'

She indicated the bananas and the pills in Lund's hands.

'You left them in the car.'

'Ah . . .'

Meyer shrugged.

She stroked his stubble, said, 'Take care. Have a good day, you two.'

He watched her every inch of the way, smiling, entranced.

When she was out of his sight his face dropped, turned dead serious.

Meyer took the fruit and the pills from Lund and tucked a banana in each pocket like a gun. Retrieved one, aimed it down the corridor, went, 'Kapow.'

'Amazing,' Lund said.

'What?'

'Nothing. Let's go.'

The campaign team was in place for the morning briefing. Eight workers, Rie Skovgaard running things. Hartmann left the Birk Larsen case till last.

'The press might get hold of something,' he

finished. 'But it'll only be guesswork. We're sending the personnel files to Lund. Let's not get distracted. We've got more important work to do.'

'Wait, wait, wait.' Skovgaard waved at them to stay seated. 'You're saying they think it's a teacher.'

Hartmann packed his papers into his briefcase.

'That's one theory.'

'You know what that means, Troels? We're back in the story again. The press will involve you anyway.'

'It's a police matter . . .'

'You're Mayor of Education. If it's a teacher they'll hold you accountable.'

She never gave up. Never would.

He sat down again, looked at her and asked, 'What are you suggesting?'

'That we act first! Let's read those files before Lund gets them. Check we didn't screw up.'

'How could we have screwed up?'

'I don't know. I just don't want any surprises. Besides . . . Imagine if we passed on some information that helped them find the man. We'd pick up some credit instead of the blame.'

Hartmann gazed at her.

'Troels,' she added, 'if it's a choice between losing votes and winning them it's not much of a choice at all.'

'Fine. Do it.'

When the team left she gave Hartmann his schedule for the day, went through it line by line, minute by minute. The last event was a photo opportunity about social integration. Bringing foreign groups into the community. About role models, the immigrants Hartmann's team had picked to front the initiative.

'Shall we have dinner afterwards?' she asked.

'Sure,' Hartmann said without a thought.

'You can make time for me?'

'Sure.'

'Troels!'

'Oh.'

There was so little time for anything. Hartmann took her in his arms, liked the way her face brightened then. He was about to kiss her when there was a knock on the door. One of the City Hall employees. A young man. He looked embarrassed at walking in on them.

'You asked about some files? The schools?'

'I'll leave this to you,' Hartmann said and left.

Skovgaard sat the civil servant in front of her, listed the ones she wanted. Staff records for Frederiksholm High. Contracts. Assessments. Any complaints.

He listened, said nothing.

'Is this a problem?'

'The city records are for your use as an official? Not for . . . politics? I'm sorry. I have to ask.'

'No,' Skovgaard said. 'You don't.'

'But . . .'

'Hartmann wants this done. Hartmann's the Mayor of Education. So . . .'

He still didn't budge.

'What's your name?'

'Olav Christensen.'

'Is this a problem, Olav? If it is say so. You've seen the polls, haven't you? You know Troels Hartmann's the next Lord Mayor?'

A thin, sarcastic smile.

'It's not my job to dabble in politics.'

'No. It's your job to do what you're asked. So get on with it before I find someone else.'

In a small storeroom off the library, surrounded by books about English, about physics, about art, Lund and Meyer began talking to teachers one by one. About Nanna, about Lisa Rasmussen, Oliver Schandorff and Jeppe Hald. But mostly about themselves. What they did the previous weekend, a question Meyer asked while Lund watched, thinking, listening. Hunting for a flaw.

He ate a banana. Drank two bottles of water, smoked constantly. Consumed two packs of cheese crisps, against her orders. Looked at her between the endless procession of teachers. Said little. Didn't need to.

There was nothing in these ordinary, decent, dedicated people. They were teachers. Nothing more. Or so it seemed.

Pernille Birk Larsen sat in the chilly kitchen, hands on the table they both made. Stared at Nanna's bedroom door, the marks there, the arrows.

Knew now this had to be done.

Heard him downstairs, talking to the men. Low gruff voice. The boss.

Walked into her room. So much gone. Nanna's books and diaries. The photos and notes had disappeared from the cork-board on the wall. The place stank from their chemicals, so strongly it overcame the waning fragrance of flowers. Their pens and brushes and markers stained the walls.

She fought to remember *before*.

Her daughter here, so full of life and energy.

Pernille sat on the bed, thinking.

This had to be done. *This had to be done.*

She went to the small wardrobe, looked in.

The smell of Nanna lingered. A perfume, gentle and exotic. More sophisticated than Pernille recalled.

That lingering thought afflicted her again . . . *You never really knew her.*

'But I did,' she said out loud. 'I do.'

That morning the medical examiner's office called. The body was to be released. A service was needed. A funeral. The last scene in the bleak extended ceremony of a violent and premature death.

In the bedroom, deep in the fragrances of the wardrobe, Pernille fought to remember the last time she chose Nanna's clothes. Even as a child at primary school, seven or eight, she made that decision for herself. So bright, so pretty, so self-confident . . .

Later she'd walk round the house choosing her

own. Take things from Pernille's drawers. From Lotte's when she stayed there.

Nothing constrained Nanna. She was her own person. Had been from the moment she could speak.

And now a mother had to choose the last thing her child would wear. A robe for a coffin. A gown for fire and ashes.

Her fingers reached out and fluttered through the flimsy fabrics. Through flowery prints and shirts, through shifts and jeans. They fell upon a long white dress, seersucker, Indian, brown buttons down the front. Cheap in a late summer sale since no one would want it for the cold winter.

No one except Nanna, who would wear these bright things rain or shine. Who never felt the cold. Never cried much. Never complained.

Nanna . . .

Pernille clutched the soft material to her face.

Looked at the floral smock next to it. Wished she could face anything in the world but this.

Theis Birk Larsen sat in the office with the estate agent, looking at numbers and plans. The name Humleby sounded like a curse to him now. A black and vicious joke that life had waited to play.

'You stand to lose a lot,' the woman said. 'The rot. The condition . . .'

'How much?'

'I don't know exactly.'

Pernille was walking towards them, wide-eyed,

chestnut hair unkempt, face blank and pale and miserable. In her hands were two dresses: one white, one flowery.

'Maybe as much as half a million,' the estate agent said. 'Or you could go ahead and renovate it. Takes time but then you might . . .'

He was looking out through the glass door. Not listening.

The woman stopped. Saw. Got to her feet, embarrassed. Made the noises they both knew now. Hurried words, stuttering condolences. Then fled from the office.

Pernille watched her go, watched her husband snatch a cigarette from the pack on the desk, light it anxiously.

'Is there a problem, Theis?'

'No. It was about selling the house. It's in hand.'

He rifled through the papers.

She held up the dresses.

'I need to know.'

She lifted the white one then the flowered one, as if this were the prelude to an evening. One of the social occasions they never went to. A dinner. A dance.

'Which one?'

He looked for a second, no more.

'The white is nice.'

Sucked on his cigarette, stared at the desk.

'The white?'

'The white,' he said again.

★ ★ ★

Rama, the teacher they saw earlier in the week, was halfway through the list. Same questions. Same uninformative answers. The man was thirty-five. Had worked at the school for seven years.

They asked everyone: what did you make of Nanna?

'Outgoing, happy, clever . . .' Rama said.

Meyer rolled one of his pills onto the table, stared at it.

'You two had a good relationship?' Lund asked.

'Definitely. She was a very clever girl. Hard-working. Mature.'

'Did you see her outside school?'

'No. I don't socialize with pupils. I'm too busy.'

Meyer glugged down his tablet, lobbed the empty water bottle into a waste bin.

'My wife's pregnant,' Rama added. 'Almost due. She works here too. Part-time now. Finishing up.'

'That's nice,' Lund said.

Meyer broke in, asked, 'Did you see Nanna at the party?'

'No. I did the first shift. I left at eight.'

Lund said, 'That's all, thanks. Can you send in the next person?'

She laughed.

'I sound like a teacher.'

Meyer stared at the empty yellow skins on the table.

'Did you eat my bananas?' he demanded.

'One.'

He got up, went to the window cursing, lit a cigarette.

The teacher still sat there.

'There's one thing a while back. A few months ago Nanna wrote an essay. For a mock exam.'

Lund waited.

'She wrote a short story.'

'Why's this important?' Lund asked.

'Maybe it isn't.' Rama looked at her. 'It was about a secret affair. Between a married man and a young girl. It was very . . .'

The teacher was searching for the right word.

'It was very explicit. She wrote it as a piece of fiction. It bothered me.'

Meyer came back to the table, looked at him, asked, 'Why?'

'I read a lot of essays. It sounded to me as if she was talking about herself. Talking about something she'd done.'

'Explicit?' Lund asked.

'They had meetings. They had sex.'

'Why didn't you mention this before?'

He squirmed.

'I don't know if it's important or not.'

'We need to read it,' Meyer said.

'It should be in the storeroom with the others. It was a mock exam. We keep them.'

They waited.

'I can help you look if you like,' Rama said.

★　★　★

238

The officer from the education department returned with a pile of blue folders underneath his arm. Skovgaard thanked him. Smiled.

'What do they say?'

'Model school. Private. Not cheap.' He flicked through some folders. 'The teachers seem well qualified and enthusiastic. The grades are good.'

She stared at the pile of documents.

'No complaints?'

'Nothing I can see. But I don't know what you're looking for.' He waited for a response. 'If I did—'

'It's just routine. We want to know everything's in order.'

Olav Christensen seemed pliable, willing to help, even though she'd leaned on him earlier.

'Everything to do with Troels is usually in order,' he said. 'I wish . . .' he nodded back towards Poul Bremer's office, 'it was the same everywhere. Maybe soon.'

She wondered why he'd suddenly turned helpful. Held up a folder. Said thanks.

Ninety minutes Lund and Meyer spent going through the filing cabinets. The teacher had to leave them to take a class. Then Rektor Koch walked in, scowled at Meyer's cigarette, said, 'Have you found it yet?'

'It's not here,' he said.

'It has to be here,' Koch insisted.

'It's . . . not . . . here. We've been through everything.'

239

Lund brought over a file box.

'This was open when we came to it.'

Koch checked the names on the label, people who'd used it and when.

'One of our teachers is a linguist. He's writing a paper on trends in language. Word usage. I gave him permission to go through anything he needed.'

'Name?' Meyer demanded.

There was a pause, an uneasy look on the woman's face.

'Henning Kofoed. I find it hard to believe he wouldn't put it back. He's usually very meticulous. A highly intelligent . . .'

'Why haven't we spoken to him?' Lund broke in.

'He wasn't one of Nanna's teachers. He only works in the mornings. He's . . .'

Lund picked up her phone, her notepad and her bag.

'We need his address,' she said.

Hard wood and wicker seats. Candles. Gold crosses. Dim lights. A crucifix.

Pernille and Theis Birk Larsen sat next to each other in silence. She clutched the white dress. Freshly washed, freshly pressed, it smelled of flowers and summer.

On the leaded windows above them the winter rain hammered in a constant rattle.

After a while a man emerged. Black suit, white beard, a kindly face, a fixed professional smile. He took the dress, complimented them on the choice. Said, 'Ten minutes.' Then left.

It seemed much longer. They moved from seat to seat, stared at the walls. He took out his black woollen hat, turned it in his fingers. She saw, and tried not to watch.

Then the undertaker returned. The door was half open. A pale gentle light beyond. He beckoned them through.

Afterwards, in the red van driving slowly on the shining city road, Pernille said, 'She looked beautiful.'

Theis Birk Larsen stared through the windscreen, out into the grey rain.

Her hand strayed out, touched the bristle of his sideburn, the rough familiar warmth of his cheek.

He smiled.

'We've got to pick up the Thermos flasks,' she said. 'We can borrow two from Lotte.'

He tapped at a light on the dashboard.

'I need some screen wash.'

A small filling station. Cars and vans. Men and women. The ordinary life, the mundane passage, the daily routine. All this swam around them as if nothing had happened. Nothing changed or broken or lost.

He didn't reach for the pump. Didn't do anything except march into the shop, race to the toilet.

There, in this anonymous place, door locked, in his black coat and woollen cap, Theis Birk Larsen crouched over the basin, sobbing, shaking, bawling like a child.

Twenty minutes she waited. No one approached. No one spoke. Then he came out pink-eyed, red-cheeked. Scraps of paper towel clung to his stubble where he'd wiped his face. Tears still lurked, grief still lingered.

In his hands was a small plastic bottle. Blue.

'Here,' he said and placed the screen wash in her lap.

Henning Kofoed's home was a one-room flat behind the station. As squalid a bachelor place as Lund had ever seen. Books were thrown everywhere, food rotted on unwashed plates in the kitchen. Kofoed was a shifty-looking forty-year-old with a straggly brown beard and unkempt hair. He sucked on a foul-smelling pipe and regarded them with suspicion the moment they arrived.

'Why should I have this paper?'

'Because you took it,' Meyer said. 'For your . . . What is it? Linguistic study. That's about how people talk, right?'

'In a very crude fashion . . .'

'In a very crude fashion let me say this . . . Find the fucking paper, Henning.'

'I probably misplaced it. I'm sorry.'

There was a computer in the bedroom. Meyer went through and started nosing around. Kofoed followed getting edgier by the minute.

'Did you read what Nanna wrote?' Meyer asked.

'I . . . I . . . read lots of things.'

'Simple question. You don't need a degree in linguistics to comprehend it. Did you read Nanna's story?'

Silence.

'I specialize in language. I look at words. Not the sentence so much. Did you know the word ciabatta never existed . . . ?'

Meyer clutched his fists together and swore.

'Forget about ciabatta, will you? Find us the damned essay.'

'OK, OK, OK.'

He meandered into the adjoining room, started sifting through a jumble of files and papers scattered everywhere. The place looked like a record office that had been hit by a bomb.

Meyer glanced at Lund, smiled, pointed to the floor.

'Did you throw it away?'

'I'd never do that.'

He bent down over a set of collapsed drawers. Retrieved a plastic document folder.

'Ah! I knew I had it.'

He handed it over.

'Sorry. I'll show you out.'

Kofoed walked to the door, opened it. Lund stood where she was.

'I think we need to talk,' she said.

'About what?'

Meyer held up one of the magazines he found on the floor beneath the computer.

243

Hot Teenagers.

'About young girls.'

The teacher sat on the computer chair in the bedroom watching Meyer sift through the magazines, flick open the photos.

He was sweating a lot and Lund had taken away his pipe.

'Where were you on Friday?' she asked.

'At a conference in the city. About the language of youth.'

'When did it end?'

'Ten p.m.'

'And then?'

'I came home.'

Meyer leaned on the door frame, alternately scowling at the magazines and then Kofoed.

'Are there any witnesses?'

'No. I live alone. I work mostly.'

'When you're not playing with yourself,' Meyer grunted. 'Or looking at your girls.'

The teacher bristled.

'I don't like your tone.'

Meyer shook his head.

'You don't like my tone? I could arrest you for this.'

'Those magazines aren't illegal. I bought them here. Anyone can.'

'You don't mind if we take your computer then. You've got a portable hard drive down there too. What fun and games will we find on there?'

244

Kofoed went quiet. Went back to sweating.

'Oh, Henning.' Meyer came and sat in front of him. 'Do you have any idea how guys like you get treated in prison?'

'I haven't done anything. I wasn't the one they pointed the finger at . . .'

'I'm pointing the finger!'

'Meyer!' Lund looked at the shaking teacher. 'What do you mean, Henning? Who got the finger pointed at him?'

Silence.

'We're trying to help,' she said. 'If someone was under suspicion we need to know.'

'It wasn't me—'

'So you keep telling us. Who was it?'

Scared man. But he didn't want to say it.

'I can't remember—'

'I'm taking the computer,' Meyer said. 'You're going to jail. No job. No teaching. No chance to get close to the girls in the corridor—'

'It's not like that! It wasn't me. The girl retracted everything . . .' He was close to weeping. 'He was cleared. He's a nice guy.'

Meyer picked up a magazine, waved it in his face.

'Who?'

'Rama,' Kofoed said.

He looked ashamed of himself. More ashamed than when Meyer pulled out the porn.

'The girl made it up. He's a nice man. Kind to everyone.'

245

'Just like you,' Meyer said and threw the mag in his face.

Pernille sat at the table trying to smile for the teacher, Rama. The handsome, polite one from the school. He'd brought flowers, photos, messages from the shrine. Took the chair opposite looking serious and sorrowful.

'They're a bit wilted. I'm sorry.'

She took them, knowing they'd go in the bin the moment he left. And that Rama understood this too.

'Some of Nanna's class would like to come to the funeral. If that's OK.'

'That's fine.'

Rama smiled a brief, melancholy smile.

'You can come too. Please.'

He seemed surprised. Did they think she wouldn't want a foreigner?

'Thank you. We'll all be there. I won't keep you any longer—'

'Don't go.'

He wanted to, she thought. But Pernille was past worrying about what others wanted any more.

'Can you tell me something about her?'

'Like what?'

'Something she did.'

He thought about the question.

'Philosophy. Nanna always loved that. She was really into Aristotle.'

'Who?'

'He was Greek. She was in our drama group.'

'Acting?'

She never mentioned this. Not once.

'I told them what Aristotle said about acting. She was very interested in that. She thought our plays should last from dawn till dusk. Just like the ancient Greeks.'

'She was a schoolgirl,' Pernille said, cross suddenly. 'She had a life. Here. A real one. It wasn't a dream. She didn't need to make something up.'

A mistake. He looked embarrassed.

'I think it was a joke.' Checked his watch. 'I'm sorry. I have to go. I work at a youth club. There's an appointment. I can't miss it.'

Pernille looked into his calm, dark face. Liked this man. Looked at the table. Ran her fingers across the dimpled lacquered surface, stared at the photos and the faces.

'We made this together. Planed the timber. Glued it. Stuck the photos.'

The wood felt smooth now and worn. It wasn't always. There were splinters. Tears sometimes.

'You're alone,' the teacher said. 'Is that—?'

'Theis is downstairs. In the office. Doing . . .'

It was dark in there when she answered the bell. Not a single light.

Doing what?

Smoking. Hugging a bottle of beer. Weeping.

'Paperwork,' she said.

⋆   ⋆   ⋆

It wasn't paperwork.

Birk Larsen sat still and silent in the dark office. The door opened. Vagn Skærbæk walked in, turned on the dim light by the noticeboard. Keys in his hand. Checked the line of hooks on the wall. Found the right place. Kept things in order.

Didn't see the man in the black jacket hunched over the desk, cigarette in hand, bottle in fist until Birk Larsen grunted something wordless.

'Shit! You scared me.'

The figure didn't move.

'Are you OK, Theis?'

Turned on the main light. Walked forward, looked.

'I'll go and get Pernille.'

A strong hand reached out and held him.

Birk Larsen's eyes were pink and watery.

Drunk.

He said, 'A week ago I had a daughter. She walked out of here. Went to a party.'

'Theis . . .'

'I saw her again today.' The eyes beneath the black hat closed, tears squeezed between the lids. 'It wasn't really her. It was like something . . . Something . . .'

'I'm going to get Pernille. You don't drink any more either.'

'No!'

His voice was loud and fierce. Vagn Skærbæk knew not to ignore it.

'Theis. I got this friend Jannik. He heard some-thing.'

Skærbæk hesitated. Felt Birk Larsen's eyes on him.

'Heard what?'

'Maybe nothing.'

Birk Larsen waited.

'Jannik's wife works at the school. He said the police came back again.' Hands fidgeting with the silver chain. 'They started questioning the staff. All Nanna's teachers.'

Another cigarette. Another pull at the beer. He gazed at Vagn Skærbæk.

'Maybe she knows more than he told me.' Skærbæk licked his lips. 'The police are useless shits. If they weren't you and me—'

'Don't talk of that,' Birk Larsen snarled. 'Those days are gone.'

'So you don't want me to talk to Jannik's wife?'

Birk Larsen sat on the hard seat, staring into space.

'Theis . . .'

'You do that.'

Elections played on ideas. Themes. Icons. Brands. So Troels Hartmann found himself that night putting on tennis shoes then walking in his office suit, out to the sports hall, Rie Skovgaard by his side.

Basketball was a young sport. He was the young candidate. A photo opportunity. A chance to shake hands.

'Frederiksholm's a model school,' she said. 'There's

nothing on any of the teachers. I've been through every file. Lund's got them. We're in the clear.'

The smell of sweat, the sound of a ball bouncing on wood.

'You've got a photo shoot. Then we meet some of the role models. We get youth, we get recreation, we get community. One strike, three hits.'

Hartmann took off his jacket, pulled his shirt out of his trousers, rolled up his sleeves.

'When do the civil servants go home?'

'Concentrate on why we're here. These people are important for us.'

They walked into the hall. Figures playing. Black and white. Moving quickly, noisily.

'Morten told me he noticed a couple of civil servants working late. Why would they do that?'

'I don't know!'

'He says we need to watch them.'

'Morten's paid to run your campaign. Not offer you advice like that.'

'What if Bremer's got someone inside? Causing mischief? Leaking emails. Getting hold of my diary.'

'Leave me to worry about that. You're the candidate. The public face. I can handle the rest.'

Hartmann didn't move.

'I went out of my way to fix this opportunity,' Rie Skovgaard added. 'We've got every media outlet that matters out there. Try to smile for them, will you?'

Onto the floor. Strong handshakes. Friendly greetings. One by one Hartmann talked to them, Iranian and Chinese, Syrian and Iraqi. Danish now, working for his integration programme. Unpaid role models for the communities around them.

Two teams. One with a gap for him.

Hartmann tied his laces, looked at the opposition, said: 'Ready to be thrashed?'

For ten precious minutes this was all there was. Racing around the polished floor, throwing the ball. Passing it. Physical exertion. No thoughts. No strategies. No plans. Even the flash of the cameras didn't bother him. The Rådhus. The Liberal Party. Poul Bremer. Kirsten Eller. Even Rie Skovgaard. All of them were gone.

A break in play. The throw came to him. Hartmann dashed, dummied, bounced, launched.

Watched the ball turn slowly through the air, descend to the net, fall through.

A roar. He punched the air. Pure emotion. No thought in his head.

The cameras burst like lightning. Smiling he turned, high-fived the nearest player.

Captured for ever: two men grinning happily at one another. Troels Hartmann in a blue shirt, victorious. The teacher called Rama, clasping his hand.

'She walks down the corridor and finds the right hotel room. She's about to knock. She wonders if this is wrong. Should she have come? It's so different being with him. So different from everything at home. The garage she played in as a little girl with its smell of petrol. Her room and all her things. Far

251

too many things because she can't throw anything out. The kitchen where she spent hours with her mum, dad and two brothers, where they celebrated birthdays, Christmas and Easter. At home she will always be a little girl. But now . . . here in the hotel corridor . . . she's a woman. She knocks. He answers.'

Feet up on her desk in her office Lund was reading Nanna's story. Meyer walked in, arms full of food.

'For your sake there'd better be a hot dog for me.'

'No. Kebab.'

'What kind?'

A shrug.

'The meat kind. It's a kebab, Lund.'

He placed a white plastic box on her desk, then a couple of pots of sauce.

'No name,' she said. 'No description. Just a secret man she meets at various hotels.'

They flipped up the boxes and started to eat.

'All we have,' she went on, 'is a pair of boots, an old essay and some gossip among the teachers.'

'It's not just gossip.' He pulled out his notebook. 'I spoke to Rektor Koch. Rama . . . or rather Rahman Al Kemal was involved in something a few years ago. A third-year student said he groped her.'

'What happened?'

'She withdrew the complaint. Koch thinks the kid had a crush on him. Made it up when he didn't play.'

Lund emptied the entire pot of hot sauce on her kebab and took a bite. Meyer watched in horror.

'Go careful with that stuff.'

'Nothing wrong with my stomach. Why tell us about the essay if it was him?'

'We'd have found it anyway. Let's talk to him. He said he was at home with his wife. We can check that.'

Lund sifted through the personnel records.

'That incident should have been written up in his file.'

'Dead right,' he agreed.

She was rifling through the papers.

'Don't waste your time, Lund. We never got his file. Hartmann's people sent over all the rest. Not his.'

She was thinking.

'We did ask for them all, didn't we?' Meyer asked.

'Of course we did.'

Lund picked up the remains of her kebab and got her jacket.

'Well?'

Outside Rama's block in Østerbro she called home, got Mark. Spoke to him in the cobbled street, Meyer listening, not discreetly either.

There was a party. She issued instructions. Go straight home afterwards. Call if he needed her.

'We're leaving tomorrow,' Lund said. 'Saturday night. I'll book the tickets.'

She looked at the phone.

'Mark? Mark?'

Put it in her pocket.

Meyer said, 'How old's your boy?'

'Twelve.'

'Want some advice?'

'Not really.'

'You need to listen to him. A kid of that age has got a lot on his plate. What with girls and all the rest. His brain . . .' Meyer's voice took on a different tone, one she didn't recognize. 'It's at a certain stage of development. Just listen to him.'

Lund strode ahead of him, trying not to get angry.

'He says I'm only interested in dead people.'

Meyer stopped, stuttered some words she didn't hear.

'Must be his brain,' Lund said. 'Number four, isn't it?'

They found the place and rang the bell.

A blonde woman, very pregnant, very tired, answered the door and let them in without an argument.

Rama wasn't there. She said he had an appointment at the local youth club.

'You teach at the school too?' Meyer asked.

It was a nice, modern flat, only half-renovated. Stripped walls, naked doors. Barely habitable.

'Yes. Just part-time at the moment. The baby . . .'

While he talked Lund wandered round, looking. They'd fallen into this routine easily, without talking about it. The pattern seemed to work.

'Did you know Nanna Birk Larsen?' he asked.

254

The slightest hesitation.

'She wasn't a student of mine.'

Pots of paint, rolls of carpet waiting to be laid. No photos. Nothing personal at all.

'Were you at the party last Friday?'

'No. I get tired easily.'

Lund found nothing of interest, wandered back to the main room where Meyer stood with Rama's wife.

'So you were at home?' he said.

'Yes. Well, I wasn't actually at home.'

Nothing more.

Meyer took a deep breath and said, 'So you *weren't* at home?'

'We've got a little cottage on some allotments outside Dragør. We were there all weekend.'

Dragør. The other side of Kastrup. Not more than ten or fifteen minutes by car from where Nanna was found.

'This place is a mess,' she added. 'The floors were being sanded. We couldn't stay.'

'Ah.' Meyer nodded. His ears, Lund thought, looked bigger when he was curious. Which seemed impossible. 'So you were both there?'

'Rama picked me up at half past eight. We drove out there.'

'Let me get this straight . . .'

A lot bigger, Lund realized.

'You and your husband spent the weekend at your allotment?'

'Yes. Why do you ask?'

255

'No reason. I thought you might know something about the party at school.'

'Nothing, sorry.'

Lund walked towards the window. Felt her shoe stub against something. A roll of carpet. What looked like some blinds.

A black circle of plastic was curled on the floor. She bent down, picked it up. Thought of Nanna in the back of her car. Ankles tied. Wrists tied. By something like this.

Meyer said they used them in gardens. To secure building material too. For lots of things.

Lund took out an evidence bag, dropped in the tie.

'Do you want to talk to him again?' the woman asked.

'Not at the moment,' Meyer said, packing his notebook.

Lund came back and asked, 'Can I use the toilet?'

'Through there. I'll show you—'

'No need. I'll find it.'

'Your first child?' Meyer asked.

'Yes.'

Lund walked on. Still heard them.

'It's a girl.'

Meyer's voice brightened.

'A girl! Really! That's great. And you know too. Did you want to? Me, I like surprises . . .'

Plastic sheeting everywhere. A set of coat hooks. A painting.

'I could give you some good tips if you're

interested.' Meyer's voice sounded cheery. 'The first few months . . . You need to make him work.'

Lund heard her laugh.

'You don't know my husband. He'll work. I won't need to ask.'

Very quietly Lund walked into the bedroom. Clothes. Photos. Rama younger, bare-chested, smiling in what looked like a swimming team. Army insignia behind. A military pool perhaps. Good-looking man. Fit and muscular. A calendar. A school timetable.

Lund looked in the en suite bathroom. New sink, new toilet. Bare walls. There was another room. The sign on the door said 'Nursery'.

It was dark. Just enough light from the street to see. Junk in the corner. Men's toys. A sports kite. A speedboat.

By the window a pair of men's hiking boots. She picked them up, looked at the sole, felt the mud there, rubbed it between her fingers.

Thought of the canal and the woods. And Dragør close by.

There was a bottle on an upturned box. White label, brown glass. Lund picked it up, made a note.

A cross voice behind said, 'You walked past the toilet.'

The bottle went back. The bag with the tie she slid into her pocket.

'Thanks,' Lund said and went straight back to the hall. Then took Meyer outside.

★　　★　　★

Rektor Koch was in Hartmann's office, Rie Skovgaard and Morten Weber listening.

'They suspect one of our teachers,' she said. 'You need to tell me what to do.'

'What do you mean?' Hartmann asked.

'They called me just now. Asking questions. They seem to know—'

'Know what? We've an agreement with the police. They'll talk to us first.'

'They seem to know something.' She squirmed on the seat. 'I don't want any damage. We've had enough bad publicity as it is. Should I suspend him?'

'Have they taken anyone in for questioning?'

'They're going to. A particular teacher. There was an old incident.'

'What incident?' Skovgaard cut in. 'I checked the files. There was nothing there.'

'It was . . . unproven,' Koch insisted. 'But it was on the files. I wrote it myself. Nonsense on the part of a stupid girl. The teacher was innocent I'm sure. The police only started to look at him because he was Nanna's form tutor.'

Hartmann asked, 'So that's why they're interested?'

'What other reason could there be?'

No answer.

Koch looked at the two of them.

'I've explained the situation to you. I've done my duty. It's your responsibility if the police or the newspapers come looking—'

'Don't worry about that,' Hartmann said with a wave of his hand. 'Give me his name. I'll talk to the police. I'm sure this is nothing.'

He got a pen.

'His name is Rama. We call him that. His full name is Rahman Al Kemal.'

She spelled it out. Hartmann started writing. Stopped.

'And he's a teacher at Frederiksholm?'

'I just told you.'

'And they're asking about him?'

An impatient sigh.

'Yes. That's why I'm here.'

He looked at Skovgaard. She frowned, shook her head.

'Is something wrong?' Koch asked.

'No. I just wanted to be sure. Will you . . . ?' He looked at her. 'Please step outside. Help yourself to a coffee. I'll be with you in a moment.'

He closed the door. Skovgaard got up.

'What's going on here?' Morten Weber asked.

'I just shook hands with a role model called Rama,' Hartmann said. 'At the youth club.'

'What?'

Weber glared at Skovgaard.

'He met a teacher from that school? And you didn't know?'

'I didn't see a teacher's name on the list. I went through every file myself. Troels wouldn't have been in the same room if I thought there was something wrong.'

259

'But there is something wrong!' Weber cried.

'Every single file, Morten!'

Hartmann watched them, torn, not wanting to take sides.

'Who gave you the files?' Weber asked.

Skovgaard swore under her breath.

'One of the civil servants in administration.'

Weber threw up his hands in exasperation.

'I told you!'

'They gave me the files. I looked at them. What else was I supposed to do? What . . . ?'

Weber was on his feet, red-faced, screaming.

'You could come to me, Rie. You could ask a question once in a while. Instead of marching off and doing whatever comes into your vapid little head—'

'Morten,' Hartmann intervened. 'Calm down.'

'Calm down? Calm down?' He pointed to the door. 'I've spent twenty years working these corridors. She comes from selling soap powder, spends ten minutes here and thinks she knows it all—'

'Morten!' Hartmann's voice silenced him. 'That's enough.'

'Yeah, Troels. It's enough.' Weber got hold of his bag. Stuffed in his papers with a shaking hand. 'Let's face it. If this election's going to be run from between your bedsheets there's not much room for me—'

Hartmann was on him, furious, fist in his face.

'I don't care how long I've known you. I won't take that. Get out of here. Go home.'

Weber did that. No more speeches. No more hurled insults. Picked up his bag and left.

Rie Skovgaard watched.

Then when Weber had left said thanks.

'I should have listened to him though,' Hartmann said. 'Shouldn't I?'

'I guess,' she agreed.

The car back from Østerbro.

'We need to check his past,' Lund said. 'He hasn't always been a teacher. Check his allotment and his alibi.'

She pulled out the plastic evidence bag.

'This goes to the lab. He's got a bottle of ether. I wrote down the brand name. Find out if it's the same kind that was found on the girl.'

Meyer wasn't happy. For a change.

'With all that evidence why didn't we wait until he got home? Now he can get rid of everything.'

Her phone was ringing. Hartmann was in the contacts list by now. She could see it was him.

Lund passed the mobile to Meyer.

'It's Poster Boy. You talk to him. He probably wants to complain.'

'Not the only one, Lund. What time's your plane tomorrow? Do you need a lift to Kastrup?'

Bedtime stories. Pernille reading. The boys in their pyjamas, chests against the soft duvets, elbows on the bed, waggling their feet.

'Is Nanna in the coffin?' Anton asked when she closed the book.

Pernille nodded, tried to smile.

'Is she going to be an angel?'

A long wait.

'Yes. She is.'

Bright baffled faces gazed at her.

'Tomorrow we say goodbye to Nanna. Then—'

'Some of the children at school are saying things.'

Anton's feet moved a little faster.

'What sort of things?'

'Someone killed her.'

Emil added, 'And there was a man who did something bad.'

'Who said that?'

'Some children in the class.'

She took their hands, gently squeezed their small fingers, looked into their sparkling eyes. Could think of nothing to say.

Five minutes later they were tucked up and quiet. She heard Theis moving, went downstairs. The garage was filled with furniture. Rented tables and chairs. He stacked and moved some, picked up more in one hand than most men could with two.

'The boys wanted to say goodnight.'

He heaved a table across the room.

'I had to get on with this.'

'They hear things at school.'

Nothing.

Pernille's hand went to her neck.

'I said it was the bogeyman.'

262

A trellis table. More chairs.

'Theis. I'm not sure it's a good idea to take them to the funeral. I mean . . .'

He didn't listen, didn't turn to look at her.

'They should say goodbye, I know. But there'll be so many people.'

A box of plastic plates and cutlery. He wiped his brow.

'I don't know how you and I will . . .'

The table he'd moved from right to left he now moved back where it came from.

'Would you please stop doing that?'

He put it down, looked at her in silence.

In the pocket of the blue checked shirt his phone trilled.

Birk Larsen listened.

'I'll find out more from Jannik tomorrow,' Vagn Skærbæk said. 'The woman hasn't heard anything new. I'll try.'

'OK.'

'So you need any help tonight?'

'No. See you tomorrow.'

When he came off the phone the garage was empty. He watched Pernille walk up the stairs. Then went back to moving tables, stacking chairs.

Mark seemed animated. As if he saw an opportunity.

'So if we're not going—'

'We are going,' Lund insisted. 'Bengt is having a house-warming party.'

263

Her mother was ironing. She was packing clothes, throwing them into an empty suitcase, squashing them down with her palms and elbows, ready to sit on the thing if need be.

'What if—?'

'Mark! There's no what if. We leave tomorrow. Gran's coming with us for a few days. That's it—'

Her phone rang. Bengt. Sounding anxious.

'Everything's fine,' Lund told him. 'Under control. We'll see you tomorrow night. We've almost finished packing . . .'

She covered the mouthpiece, mouthed at Mark, 'Pack!'

Then listened, heard a sound at the door. Vibeke answered. Lund looked. Troels Hartmann was standing there in a black winter coat looking every inch the politician.

Bengt said something she didn't quite hear.

'Of course I'm listening,' Lund said.

She took the call into the other room, watched as Vibeke got Hartmann folding a long tablecloth for the new house.

In Sweden.

The new life.

'Bengt,' Lund said. 'I've got to go.'

When she came back into the room Vibeke was asking him, 'So are you the coroner?'

'No,' Hartmann said, holding the long white piece of cotton.

'You've never folded a good tablecloth before,'

264

Vibeke told him, shaking her head. 'I can see that. Look—'

'Mum. I don't think Troels Hartmann has time for that.'

Vibeke's mouth fell open.

'Hartmann?' She looked him up and down. 'You're different on the posters.'

In the kitchen, the two of them alone, he shook his head, like a man disappointed.

'You promised you'd keep me informed.'

'I didn't promise anything.'

She got a slice of bread, plastered on some butter and cheese, bit into it while he rambled angrily.

'You're looking at one of my teachers now. I had to hear about that from the school.'

Mouth half full, she asked him, 'Why did you tell your people not to give us Kemal's file? Where's the cooperation there?'

He shook his head, said nothing.

'We asked for all the files. On all the teachers, Hartmann. Why didn't we get his?'

'It's the first I knew about it. Believe me.'

'How come? You're the boss, aren't you?'

She finished the cheese, put the plate in the sink.

'Yes, OK, it doesn't look good. What do you want me to do?'

She raised an eyebrow, dried some dishes with a cloth.

'Cooperate.'

'I'm trying! I don't know why I didn't get his file.' Then, a tone lower, 'I don't know what's going on here. There's something, someone, in my office . . .'

Lund looked interested.

'Doing what?'

'I don't know,' Hartmann said. 'Snooping. Seeing things they shouldn't. It's an election. You expect dirt to fly. But not . . .'

He looked at her.

'If someone's broken into our system that's a crime, right?'

'If—'

'There's something going on. You could take a look—'

'I'm a homicide detective,' Lund cut in. 'Trying to find who raped and murdered a young girl. I don't do office work. And I want that file.'

'Fine.' He looked furious. Desperate too. 'I'll get it. There must be a duplicate. Somewhere.'

'Is there something special about Kemal?' she asked.

'He's one of our role models. He helps young immigrants who've got into trouble. I've got his party records for that. He's—'

'So if he did it you'll look bad? Is that it?'

Hartmann scowled at her.

'It damages your campaign.' She picked up an apple, thought about it, grabbed a bag of potato crisps instead. 'You lose votes.'

'You don't have a very high opinion of me, do you?'

Lund offered him a crisp.

'If this is your man that's all there is to it,' Hartmann said. 'No one in my office will stand in your way. I just want to know.'

'Is that all?'

He brightened a little.

'Yes. That's all. Your turn now.'

She laughed.

'What is this? A game? I've nothing to tell you. Kemal's one line of inquiry. There are questions we need answered. Where he was . . .'

'Fine. I'll have him suspended.'

'You can't do that. We don't have enough to arrest him.'

Lund got herself a bottle of milk from the fridge, sniffed it, poured herself a glass.

'You can't,' she repeated. 'I know you want a yes or no. I can't say yet.'

'When?'

Lund shrugged.

'I'm handing the case over to a colleague tomorrow.'

'Is he reliable?'

'Unlike me?'

'Unlike you.'

She toasted him.

'He's very reliable. You're going to love him.'

Eleven in the evening in Hartmann's private office. Under the blue light of the hotel sign he met Rie Skovgaard. She took one look at him and said, 'It's that bad?'

He threw his coat on the desk.

'I don't know exactly. Lund won't tell me anything she doesn't want to. They seem to think it's him. She just won't say it.'

Skovgaard checked her laptop.

'The pictures they took tonight are going out. I can't stop that. But no one knows he was a suspect, any more than you did when you shook his hand.'

'Who kept back that file?'

'I'm looking into it.'

She threw a set of dummy ads on the table. Foreign faces alongside white ones. Smiling. Together.

'The next run of the campaign was all about integration. We pushed the role model idea a lot. I'm going to pull them. We'll stop using the term. Focus on other issues till this blows over.'

'The debate tomorrow—'

'I'll get you out of it. This is a gift to Bremer. Let me make some calls.'

Skovgaard walked to her desk, picked up the phone.

'No.' Hartmann watched her. Still dialling. He walked over, put the phone back on the hook. 'I said no. The debate goes ahead.'

'Troels—'

'This is one man. A suspect. He hasn't been found guilty and even if he is that doesn't say anything about all the other role models. They've done plenty of good work. I won't let them be slandered through this.'

'Oh fine words!' she yelled at him. 'I hope they sound good when we lose.'

'This is what we're about. What I'm about. I have to stand by what I believe—'

'You have to win, Troels. If you don't it doesn't matter a shit.'

He was getting mad now. Wished he'd expended some of this on Lund, watching him all the time with those glittering eyes while she munched on a sandwich and gulped at her milk.

'We owe these people something. Day in, day out, they work with these kids. Do things you wouldn't dream of. Me neither.'

He picked up a stash of papers, threw them at her.

'We've got the statistics. The proof it works.'

'The press . . .' she began.

'To hell with the press!'

'They'll crucify us if he did it!' She got up, came to him, put her arms on his shoulders. 'They'll crucify you. Like they did your father. This is politics, Troels. Save your fine words for speeches. If I've got to go into the gutter to get you into that chair I'll do it. That's what you pay me for.'

Hartmann turned away, looked out at the night beyond the window.

Her hand came to his hair.

'Come home with me, Troels. We can talk about it there.'

A moment of silence between them. An instant of indecision, of doubt.

Then Hartmann kissed her forehead.

'There's nothing to talk about. We're going ahead as planned. Everything. The posters. The debate. Nothing changes.'

Eyes closed, fingers at her pale temple.

'The civil servant who brought you the school files . . .' Hartmann said.

'What about him?'

'Make some room in my schedule. Tomorrow. I want to see him.'

Saturday, 8th November

Lund was pinning pictures of Kemal on the board, listening to Meyer read out what he'd found. Ten officers in the room, Buchard on his feet at the head of the table.

'Born in Syria. Damascus. Fled with his family when he was twelve. His father's an imam and frequents the Copenhagen mosque.'

Meyer looked around them.

'Apparently Kemal has severed ties with his family. They think he's too Western. Danish wife. No religion. After school and national service he became a professional soldier.'

Pictures of him smiling in a blue beret.

'Then he went to university and completed his Masters. Joined the school seven years ago. Two years ago he married a colleague. The school says he's popular. Well-respected—'

Buchard cut in, shaking his head.

'This doesn't sound like the kind of man—'

'He was accused of molesting a girl,' Lund said. 'No one wanted to believe it at the time.'

The chief still looked unconvinced.

'What does the girl say?'

'We can't reach her. She's backpacking in Asia.'

Meyer held up the evidence bag with the plastic tie.

'Lund found this in Kemal's apartment. It matches the one used on the girl.'

'And you've got ether too?' Buchard asked. He scratched his pug head. 'Lots of people use those ties. Ether . . . I don't know. This isn't enough.'

'We'll run through his alibi,' Lund said. She unsealed the first of a set of envelopes. Photos of Nanna. 'I want these pictures distributed around all the city hotels. She went somewhere.'

'Put a team on Kemal,' Buchard ordered. 'So we know what he's doing. Not too close. The funeral's today. We don't want to disturb the family.'

The chief cast his beady eyes around the table.

'It's bad enough as it is. Let's not make things worse.'

Twenty minutes later Lund and Meyer sat down to interview Stefan Petersen, a podgy, retired plumber who had one of the little houses on the allotments on the edge of Dragør.

'I've got number twelve. He's got number fourteen. In a year's time I'll have been there long enough to live in it all year round,' he said proudly.

'Can't choose your neighbours. But it's a nice place all the same.'

Meyer asked, 'On Friday? Did you see Kemal and his wife arrive?'

'Oh yes.' Petersen's attention was fully on him, not Lund. He liked talking to a man. 'About eight or nine I think. I saw something else later too.'

He looked pleased with himself.

'It's because I smoke cigarillos.' Petersen pulled out a packet of small cigars. 'Mind if I—?'

'Damned right I mind,' Meyer barked at him. 'Put those things away. What did you see?'

'Smoke if you want,' Lund said, taking a lighter out of his bag, flicking it for him.

The fat plumber grinned and lit up.

'Like I was saying . . . I'm a smoker. But the missus won't let me have a cigarillo indoors. So I sit on the patio. Rain or shine. There's a roof.'

Lund smiled at him.

'The Arab came out of his house. And drove away.'

'Kemal, you mean?'

He looked at Meyer as if she was being dim.

'What time was that?' Lund asked.

He thought about this, wreathed in a cloud of stinking fumes.

'I watched the weather forecast afterwards so it must have been about half past nine.'

'Did you see the car return?'

'I don't stay out all night. But it was there the next morning.'

She got up, shook his hand, said thanks.

When the plumber was gone Meyer marched up and down the office, as if claiming it for himself.

Lund leaned on the door, watching.

'Why would Kemal's wife lie about his whereabouts?' she asked.

'Let's find out.'

'We wait until after the funeral.'

'Why? Do you want me to call Hartmann and ask his permission?'

Buchard was at the door.

'Lund,' he said, jerking his thumb towards his office.

'What about me?' Meyer asked.

'What about you?'

She went to get away from the plumber's cigarillo smoke.

'The answer's no,' Lund said before Buchard got out a word.

'Listen to me—'

'I can help you by email. Or over the phone. Maybe pop over once in a while.'

'Let me speak,' the old man pleaded. 'That's not it. Did you check out the father?'

'Of course I checked out the father!'

'What did you find out?'

She frowned, trying to remember.

'Not much. Nothing interesting. Minor offences. Stolen goods. Bar brawls. It was twenty years ago. Why?'

Buchard helped himself to some water. He looked tired and sick.

'I got a call from a retired DCI. You know the kind. Nothing better to do than read the papers.'

He passed her a note.

'He says Birk Larsen was dangerous. Really dangerous.'

'Anything sexual?'

'Not that he'd heard. But he said we didn't know the half of it.'

'So what? We checked. He's got an alibi. It can't be him.'

'You're sure?'

Sure.

There was a word. Everyone wanted to be sure. No one was really. Because people lied. To others. To themselves sometimes. She even did it herself.

'I'm sure,' she said.

In the kitchen the boys ran around, Vagn's little cars in their hands. Theis Birk Larsen in black, ironed white shirt, funeral tie. Talking on the phone. Of Thermos flasks and tables, sandwiches and what to drink.

Anton stumbled, knocked a vase to the floor. The last of Nanna's flowers. Pink roses, more stalk than petal.

Stood with his brother, both heads down. Waiting for the storm to break.

'Go and wait in the garage,' Birk Larsen said. Not severely.

'I didn't mean . . .' the child started.

'Go and wait in the garage!' Their things were on the table. 'And don't forget your coats.'

When they left he heard the radio news. The first item: Nanna's funeral at St John's Church. As if she belonged to them all now. Not the family that used to eat around the table, in the bright light of the window, thinking nothing would ever change.

'Many people have arrived to pay their respects,' the announcer went on. 'Outside there's—'

He turned it off. Tried to still his thoughts. Called, 'Sweetheart?'

An old word. One he'd used since she was a mouthy, pushy teenager looking for excitement. A glimpse of the rough world outside the middle classes where she belonged.

He remembered her clearly. Saw himself too. A thug, a thief. A villain. Getting tired of that life. Looking for a rock. Looking to be one himself.

'Sweetheart?'

It was her from the start. She saved him. In return . . .

A family. A home. A small removals firm built from nothing, their name on the side. It seemed so much. All he could hope to offer. All he had to give.

Still she didn't answer. He walked into the bedroom. Pernille sat naked and hunched on the bed. On her upper left arm, still vivid and blue as the day she got it, sat a tattooed rose. He remembered when she went down the hippie parlour in Christiania. They'd been smoking. He'd been dealing, not that she knew. It was Pernille's way of

275

saying, 'I'm yours now. Part of that life you have. Part of you.'

He hated that rose and never said so. What he wanted of her were the very things she took for granted. Her decency, her honesty, her integrity. Her infinite capacity for blind, inexplicable love.

'Are you coming?'

The black dress lay on the bed with her underwear. A black bag. Black tights.

'I can't decide what to wear.'

Birk Larsen stared at the clothes on the duvet.

'I know . . .' she began.

Voice cracked, tears starting.

He heard himself shrieking inside.

'It doesn't matter, does it, Theis? Nothing does.'

Her hands went to her brushed chestnut hair.

'I can't do this. I can't go.'

He thought, as best he could.

'Maybe Lotte can help.'

She didn't hear. Pernille's eyes were fixed on the mirror: a naked woman in middle age, body getting flabby, breasts loose. Stomach stretched by children. Marked by motherhood. How it should be.

'The flowers should be right . . .' she murmured.

'They will be. We'll get through this.'

Birk Larsen bent down, picked up the black dress, held it out.

'We'll get through this,' he said. 'OK?'

★   ★   ★

Downstairs Vagn Skærbæk sat with the boys. Out of his red overalls. Black shirt, silver chain, black jeans.

'Anton. It was just a vase. Don't worry.'

Birk Larsen heard this as he walked through the round tables and chairs, looked at the white porcelain plates they'd rented, the glasses, the food under foil at the side.

'I broke a bottle once,' Skærbæk said. 'I did lots of stupid things. We all do.'

'We need to get in the car,' Birk Larsen ordered. 'We're leaving.'

The boys moved quickly, heads down, not a word.

Skærbæk looked at him.

'What about Pernille?'

'Her sister's going to take her.'

'Isn't Mum coming?' Anton asked, climbing into the car.

'Not with us.'

Skærbæk said, 'Theis, I was thinking . . . The woman at the school. It's best I don't talk to her.'

'Why not?'

Skærbæk shrugged.

'You've got a lot on your plate. Maybe she doesn't know a thing. Just gossip.'

'That's not what you said last night.'

'I know but . . .'

Birk Larsen bristled, stared at Skærbæk, a smaller man. A weaker man. This was always their relationship. One cemented by violence, by fists in the early days.

277

Finger in Skærbæk's face he said, 'I want to know.'

The civil servant called Olav Christensen was in Hartmann's office, looking at the campaign posters. About role models. Integration. The future.

Twenty-eight but he seemed younger. Fresh-faced. Biddable.

He was sweating.

'We have a small problem,' Hartmann said. 'The files you gave us on the teachers.'

A baffled smile.

'What about them?'

'One was missing.'

A pause.

'Missing?'

'It doesn't look good, does it, Olav? I mean we ask. You deliver.' Hartmann stared at him. 'That's the way it works, doesn't it?'

Christensen said nothing.

'I'm going to be boss of you and everyone who owns you soon. How about an answer?'

'Maybe it got lost when we moved the archives.'

'Maybe?'

'That's what I said.'

'This is the Rådhus. We've got documents going back a century. All kept in locked cabinets.'

Hartmann waited.

'They are,' Christensen agreed.

'There are no cabinets missing,' Skovgaard

278

chipped in. 'Or reports of lost files. I asked your boss. He's sure of it.'

'Maybe there was an error made with the filing.'

The two of them waited.

'We have these trainees. Kids. I'm sorry. Mistakes happen.'

Hartmann got up, went to the window, looked out.

'Funny the one file they should lose is the one we wanted. The one that could embarrass us. The police needed that, Olav. They think I held it back. They think I've got something to hide.'

Christensen listened, nodded.

'I'll find out what happened and get back to you.'

'No,' Hartmann said. 'Don't trouble yourself.'

He came and stood very close to the man.

'Here's what happens,' Hartmann said. 'On Monday we order a formal inquiry. We get to the bottom of this. That's for sure.'

'An inquiry?'

Rabbit in the headlamps. Deer in the sights.

'But if the file turns up,' Hartmann added. 'It won't matter, will it?'

'I don't know anything about this.'

'Well. Then we're done.'

They watched him go.

'I remember him now,' Hartmann said. 'He applied for the job of director last year. Cocky little bastard. I didn't even put him on the short list. He's getting his own back.'

'You think he's doing favours for Bremer?'

'I don't know. He's got access to our network. Make everyone change their passwords. Let's take care.'

Hartmann looked out into the main office.

'Where the hell's Morten? I know I bit his head off but—'

'He called in sick. He's not a well man, Troels. He shouldn't be doing a job like this.'

'He's diabetic. It comes and goes. His moods are unpredictable sometimes. You learn to live with it.'

She came and sat on the edge of the sofa.

'I've been here five months. How long's Morten worked for you?'

He had to think.

'Off and on? For ever.'

'And how long have people regarded you as a serious contender to be Lord Mayor?'

Ambition. She was never short of it. Ambition was a good thing. Nothing happened without it.

Her hand fell on his cheek.

'We'll get by without Morten,' Rie Skovgaard said. 'Don't worry.'

It was bright and cold outside. A sharp winter sun. Weekend shoppers. Families out for the day.

Olav Christensen walked into the square and called.

'I want that file back,' he said.

Things were changing in City Hall. No one knew which way they'd go.

Silence on the line.

'Did you hear me?'

He was getting mad, which maybe wasn't such a good idea. But he couldn't help it. Hartmann was no fool. No naive good guy either. Christensen could see that in his eyes.

An inquiry . . .

Documents got tagged, counted in, counted out. It would take a day to discover that he'd retrieved the Kemal file along with all the others. Seen the trouble it might cause. Put it to one side just in case.

There was no way out. No excuse. No lie he could invent.

His head would be on the line in an instant. Career down the drain.

Still not a word.

'I did a big favour for you, man!' A kid walking past with a couple of red balloons stared at him for yelling. 'Don't screw me around. I want some help here. I told you before. I don't go down on my own.'

That was stupid. It sounded like a warning. Olav Christensen knew exactly who he was dealing with. Someone who issued threats, didn't take them.

'Look . . . What I'm trying to say is . . .'

He listened. Nothing there. Not even the slow rhythmic sound of his breathing.

'Hello?' he said. 'Hello?'

Brown brick spire against a pale blue sky. Bells in tumbling chimes. Cameras outside. Crowds in the street.

Lund thought of the case, of the investigations ahead.

Was he here too? The man who held Nanna hostage, raped her repeatedly, beat her, tormented the girl for hours on end? Forensics were getting somewhere. The soap on her skin was recent and unlike anything at home. There was blood beneath the mud in her nails, skin cut clumsily by scissors or clippers. How many explanations were there? Just one. He'd bathed her somewhere, washed clean her bruised, torn skin, clipped her fingernails as she fought him. Then set her running through the dark woods barefoot in her scanty slip. Until . . .

Hide and seek.

Meyer said that and Meyer was no fool.

This was a game. Not quite real. When he locked her alive in the boot of Troels Hartmann's campaign car and sent her screaming into that distant canal, he watched. The way another might enjoy a movie. Or a road accident.

Or a funeral.

A savage, unreal game.

What did he look like?

Ordinary. Criminals weren't a race apart, marked by scars or strange physical afflictions. Separate from their victims. They were one with them. A stranger on a bus. A man in a shop who says hello every morning.

Or a teacher who came to the same school day after day, impressed everyone with his honesty,

282

remarkable only for his apparent decency in a world where few cared.

Lund looked around as she always did, lustrous eyes roaming. Looked and imagined.

Monstrous deeds had no need of monsters. They were the work of the everyday and the undistinguished. Cruel tears in the fabric of a society struggling to be whole. Wounds in the city's communal body, bleeding and painful.

She observed the sea of faces around her as she walked, found a space in the darkness by a pillar, sat down.

A place from which she could watch unseen.

The organ struck up wheezing. An old hymn. Lines from a Christmas carol she could barely remember.

Lund did not sing.

Lisa Rasmussen, across the aisle, did not sing.

Birk Larsen's right-hand man from the garage, Vagn Skærbæk, face streaming with tears, black hat clutched to his chest, did not sing.

The teacher known as Rama, seated in a pew with his pupils, did not sing.

At the front, seated by the white coffin, Pernille and Theis Birk Larsen did not sing, but sat with their boys looking lost, as if everything – the church, the people, the music, but most of all the shining white coffin that sat by their side – was unreal.

The priest. A thin man, with a craggy, miserable face. In black with a white ruff round his neck, he emerged from the gloom by the altar, glanced at the casket with its rose wreath, gazed slowly round the packed and silent rows ahead.

Said in a ringing, loud, theatrical voice, 'Today we bid farewell to a young woman. She was taken from us far too young.'

Hidden in the shadows Lund looked at the parents. Pernille dabbing at her eyes. Her husband, a lion of a man, a grizzled old beast. Head down, face rigid, staring at the stone floor.

'It's most unfair,' the priest said in a tone that reminded Lund of a letter to the bank. 'Beyond comprehension.'

She shook her head. No. This was untrue. It had to be.

'So we ask ourselves – what is the meaning?'

Kemal – Rama, she still thought of him this way – was three rows back in a black suit and white shirt. Dark hair clipped close.

'We question our faith, our trust in one another.'

Lund took a deep breath, closed her eyes.

'And we ask – how are we to move on?'

She stiffened at that dread, deceptive phrase. Loathed it with a vengeance. No one moved on. They swallowed their grief. They hoped to bury it. But it lived with them. Always would. A cross they had to bear. A constant, recurring nightmare.

'Christianity is about peace. Reconciliation and forgiveness. But it's not easy to forgive.'

Lund nodded. Thought: right there.

His voice took on a high, ethereal tone.

'Yet when we forgive, the past no longer controls us. And we can live in freedom.'

Lund looked at the man, in his black robe, white ruff. Wondered: what would he say if he was there by the canal that bleak cold night? Watching Theis Birk Larsen scream and rage. Watching Nanna's dead limbs tumble from the boot with the filthy rank water, seeing the black line of snaking eels writhe down her naked legs.

Would he forgive? Could he?

The organ struck up. She noted who sang and who did not. Then Sarah Lund walked outside.

They knew the teacher would be at the funeral. So Meyer went to the apartment to talk to his wife.

Midday and she was in a bulging white nightdress and black cardigan.

Didn't take long to get her talking about the accusation from the girl a few years back.

'It's a stupid old story,' she said. 'There's nothing to tell.'

'Rektor Koch wrote a report.'

'The kid made it up. She admitted it.'

'We spoke to a man from the allotments at Dragør. The plumber.'

Kemal's wife grimaced.

'He saw your husband go out about half past nine on Friday night.'

'He hates us. Doesn't mind borrowing our hedge trimmer. I always have to ask for it back.'

Meyer asked himself: what would Lund do?

'Did your husband go out?'

'Yes. He drove to the petrol station.'

'When did he get back?'

'About fifteen minutes later, I suppose. I went to bed while he was out. I was very tired.'

'I can imagine. When did you see him again?'

'About three. I woke up. He was lying next to me.'

Meyer thought about Lund's long pauses. That relentless, glittering stare.

He took off his anorak. The woman's eyes were fixed on the gun on his hip.

'So you didn't see him between half past nine and three the next morning?'

'No. But I'm sure he was there. He likes to read or watch TV.'

She smiled at him.

'Do you have a wife?'

'Yes.'

'Do you know when she's in the house? Can't you feel . . . ?'

Meyer didn't answer. Instead he said, 'Were you there all weekend? While the floors were being sanded?'

'That's right. The workmen were being difficult.'

He got up, started walking round the room, checking out the building material.

Looking.

'In what way?'

'They didn't turn up. Rama had to sand the floors

286

himself. On Sunday he spent all day putting up new tiles in the bathroom.'

'So he was gone all day Saturday and Sunday? Did he leave first thing?'

She hugged herself inside the cardigan.

'I think you should go now.'

'Was he gone from six in the morning until eight in the evening?'

The woman got up, got angry.

'Why are you asking me these questions when you don't believe a word I tell you? Please. Leave.'

Meyer got his jacket. Said, 'OK.'

Forgive us our trespasses.

Pernille barely heard the Lord's prayer, the one she'd listened to, recited since she was a girl.

As we forgive those who trespass against us.

All she saw was the shiny white wood. The flowers, the notes. The coffin that hid the truth. Inside . . .

Lead us not into temptation but deliver us from evil.

Anton nudged her, asked in a clear, young voice, 'Why doesn't Dad have his hands together?'

Forever and ever.

'Shush,' she said, putting a finger to her lips.

'Why don't you?' asked Emil, staring at her hands.

The boys were in their best clothes, fingertips pressed together.

Her eyes filled with tears. Her mind with such memories.

Amen.

The sound came first. The low gentle fluting of

287

the organ. Then shapes slowly rose around her, one by one. Flowers in hand. Faces blank and numb. Relatives. People she half knew. Strangers . . .

Roses placed on the casket by pale, trembling fingers.

'We've got something,' Anton said. 'Mum. We've got something too.'

He was the first of the family to stand. Theis the last, brought to his feet by Anton's gentle touch. Together the four walked towards her.

Towards it.

White wood and roses. A fragrance to hide a stench.

When they got there the two boys linked hands, placed a small map on the coffin. The city. Its rivers and streets.

'What's that nonsense?' Theis asked in a low furious voice. 'What is it?'

'It's for Nanna,' Emil said. 'So when she flies past she can see where we live.'

By the casket, four of them, both bound and separated by emotions they could not name.

Anton crying, asked, 'Are you cross, Dad?'

Are you cross?

Not an angry man. Not of late. Not since the children came along and made their lives whole.

She knew that. As did he.

And the boys, mostly.

'No,' Birk Larsen said, bending down to kiss both on their heads, taking their shoulders into his wide arms, holding them to him.

Pernille barely noticed. All she saw was the coffin. Her tears running down, salt stains on white wood.

His hand, rough callused fingers, reached out, entwined themselves in hers.

'Theis . . . ?' she whispered.

Pernille bent her head, puzzled how the single word her mind was forming could contain so much meaning, so much life and hurt and grief.

Looked into his coarse and grizzled face and said, 'Now?'

A squeeze of the fingers, a nod of the head.

They walked down the aisle, past the lines of mourners. Past pupils and teachers, past neighbours and friends. Past the inquisitive policewoman who watched them at the door with glittering sad eyes.

Out into the wan daylight, leaving Nanna behind.

Hartmann was listening to the hourly newscasts now. Couldn't stop himself. The police had put out another statement, as meaningless as most of the others. They had every available resource working on the case. Buchard, the pugnacious chief inspector, came on, sounding gruff and tetchy.

'We're following a lead but that's all we can say.'

And then the weather.

Rie Skovgaard came in, said edgily, 'My dad needs to see you.'

The debate with Bremer was an hour away. He pulled a tie out of the drawer, got up, tried it on in a mirror.

'Busy?' Kim Skovgaard asked taking a seat.

'Never too busy for you.'

'So you're going to the debate? You're going to talk about integration? Foreigners? Role models?'

'That's right.'

'Rie's worried about you, Troels.'

'Yes. I know.'

'She's a very smart woman. I'm not just saying that because she's my daughter.' He got up, came and put his hand on Hartmann's arm. 'You should listen to her more. But right now you should listen to me. Don't talk about role models. Not tonight.'

'Why?'

Skovgaard's voice changed, became stern and impatient.

'It's enough that one of your cars is involved in the Birk Larsen case. Anything the papers have about you and immigrants will be dug out of the archives and thrown in your face. Save your love for dark faces till later. When it wins some votes, not loses them.'

'And tonight?'

He straightened Hartmann's tie.

'Tonight you'll focus on housing. On the environment.'

'That's not going to happen.'

Skovgaard wasn't smiling any more, and that was rare.

'But it is. You don't seem to understand. I'm telling you to do this. Not asking. There are people watching you. In this place. In Parliament. You will do what I say.'

290

Hartmann stayed silent.

'It's in your best interests. Everyone's—'

'But . . .'

'I'm only trying to help my future son-in-law.'

He patted Hartmann's arm. It was a condescending gesture. Meant that way.

'You'll get your reward, Troels. And it won't be in heaven either.'

Hartmann and Rie Skovgaard were walking to the TV studio. What started as a discussion was boiling up into an argument.

'You knew he was coming,' he said. 'You fixed that.'

She stared at him as if he were crazy.

'No. Who do you think I am? Machiavelli? Dad was in the Rådhus. He turned up in front of my desk. What was I supposed to do?'

Hartmann wondered whether he believed her.

'But you agree with him?'

'Of course I do. It's obvious. To everyone except you. When you see an iceberg you steer away from it. You don't—'

'I'm not your little puppet,' Hartmann broke in. 'Or your father's.'

She stopped, threw up her hands in despair.

'Do you want to get elected or not? There are no prizes for losers. All your fine ideals mean nothing if Poul Bremer marches back into office.'

'That's not the only issue.'

'What is then?'

The producer was walking towards them.

Skovgaard beamed at him, turned soft and charming in an instant.

'Not now, Troels,' she hissed.

Lund found Meyer in the Memorial Yard, an open space on the ground floor of the Politigården. Quiet and solitary. A statue, the Snake Killer, good fighting evil. On one wall the names of a hundred and fifty-seven Danish police officers killed by the Nazis. On another a shorter list: those killed on duty more recently.

He was eyeing that wall, smoking anxiously.

'What was he like?' Lund asked.

Meyer jumped, surprised by her presence.

'Who?'

'Schultz.'

Hurt in his eyes. An accusation too.

'You've been checking up on me?'

'I looked through the press archive for Hartmann. I just thought . . .'

Four years before. She dimly remembered the case. An undercover narcotics cop in Aarhus was murdered by one of the gangs. Meyer was his partner. Sick on the day he was killed. His career had been shaky ever since.

'He was an idiot,' Meyer said. 'Went off on his own. If he'd waited a day I'd have been back on duty.'

She nodded at the wall.

'Then maybe there'd be two names there instead.'

'Maybe.' He shrugged. 'That's not the point.'

'What is?'

'We were a team. We did things together. Looked out for each other. That was part of the deal. He broke it.'

She said nothing.

'Like me forgetting to buy you a hot dog. For which I apologize.'

'Not quite the same.'

'Yes, it is.'

He pulled a half-eaten banana from his pocket, bit at it between pulls on the cigarette.

'Buchard wants to see us,' she said.

Back in their office. An empty packet of crisps sat on the desk. Along with a sceptical Buchard.

'Kemal leaves his wife to go and meet the girl. They have an argument in the flat,' Meyer said.

Lund was on the phone.

'He ties her up and drugs her. And drives home.'

Buchard propped his chin on his fist, stared at Meyer with his round, beady eyes. Said nothing.

'On Saturday morning he claims the workman has cancelled. But really Kemal has cancelled him.'

Buchard made to say something.

'The workman confirmed that,' Meyer said quickly. 'I tracked him down.'

Lund's voice rose from the other side of the office.

'There's time, Mum. Stop panicking. I said I'd be there. Why won't you believe me? OK?'

The call ended. She pulled a pack of Nicotinell

out of her packet, eyed the cigarettes on the desk.

'So,' Meyer went on. 'He returns to the flat and the girl. He waits for it to get dark. Then he picks up the car at the school, drives back, carries the girl to the car and goes off to the woods.'

Lund came over, sat down, listened.

Meyer was warming to his idea.

'On Sunday he removes any traces, sands the floor and puts up tiles.'

'I'm going,' Lund said to Buchard. 'Talk to you soon.'

Meyer waved a hand in the air.

'Wait, wait,' he cried. 'What's wrong with it? Share the secret with dumb little Jan. Please.'

The two of them watched him.

'Please,' he repeated.

'How could he have driven Hartmann's car?' Lund asked.

Meyer struggled.

'He probably found the keys at the school on Friday night.'

Meyer watched Lund, waiting. So did Buchard.

'I don't think he's that stupid,' she said. 'In fact I think he's very clever.'

'Exactly,' Meyer agreed.

'If I were you,' she said, 'I wouldn't drag him in until you get some hard evidence.'

She smiled.

'But it's your case.' She held out her hand. 'Thanks for everything. It's been really . . .'

The word seemed to elude her.

'Really educational.'

He took her hand, shook it vigorously.

'You can say that again.'

'I've left my number. If . . .'

He stared at her.

'I'm sure you won't need it. But . . .'

Buchard sat on the desk looking miserable. Before he could say a word she shook his hand too, said goodbye.

Then walked out of the Copenhagen Police Headquarters. Career over. Job gone.

Case still open.

The cab had a dropdown TV. Mark one side, Vibeke the other, Lund watched the nightly news. A debate between Hartmann and Bremer. All the polls said the fight for City Hall was a battle between these two. One misstep might give the other the game.

'We haven't bought any beer or brandy,' Vibeke complained.

'There's plenty of time.'

'And chocolates to go with the coffee.'

'They sell chocolates in Sweden I believe.'

'Not *our* chocolates!'

Lund's phone rang. She looked at the number.

Skov. The detective she'd sent chasing information about Theis Birk Larsen after Buchard's tip-off from the retired cop.

Waited. Thought about leaving it. Answered anyway.

'What took you so long?' He sounded excited. 'I got the file from the retired DCI.'

'Oh.'

'Do you want to know what's in it?'

'Give it to Meyer.'

He hesitated.

'To Meyer?'

'That's what I said.'

The weather report. Lund picked up the remote, turned it off.

'What does it say?'

'It's a case from twenty years ago. Some kind of vendetta between dope dealers. It never went to court.'

Mark looked around the car, mumbled, 'I've forgotten my cap. Left it at Gran's . . .'

'It looks to me as if . . .'

'Mum?'

'I'll buy you a new one.'

The cop droned on, 'It's about a . . .'

'I don't want a Swedish cap.'

'We're not turning back now, Mark.'

Silence on the phone.

'I'm listening,' Lund insisted.

'Really?' Skov said. 'It involved a pusher from Christianshavn. Got beaten up. Almost killed. They never found who was responsible. Theis Birk Larsen was the main suspect. They questioned him.'

'Mark!'

He was rootling round the footwell, looking for something else.

'I forgot—'

'I don't care what you forgot,' she snapped. 'We're going.'

'Brandy and beer and cigarettes,' her mother murmured from the other side.

'Birk Larsen had a motive,' the cop said. 'The drug dealer had threatened to reveal something involving him. Was going to talk to us.'

'About what?'

'Don't know. He kept quiet after that. Real scared of Birk Larsen it seems. The man's got a reputation. Violence. Bad temper. Wait . . . I'm still reading this. There's a second file underneath.'

Then, so loud she took the phone from her ear, 'Christ!'

Mark was fidgeting, her mother still moaning.

'What is it?'

Silence.

'What is it?'

'They went back a month later to see if the pusher had changed his mind. Intelligence asked for it. They really wanted Birk Larsen.'

'And?'

'And nothing. They found him dead. I've got the pictures here. Jesus . . .'

'What?'

'This is worse than the first time. The guy looks like a piece of meat.'

'OK,' she cut in. 'You need to tell Meyer.'

'Meyer's busy.'

'Tell him to call me right away.'
'OK. Bye.'

The garage was full, the wake quiet. No speeches. No songs. Only tables covered with white cloths and flowers, portable chairs, simple food.

Theis Birk Larsen wandered among their guests, nodding, saying little. Watching the boys, Emil and Anton, grow puzzled and bored.

Pernille flitted from table to table. Listening, speaking rarely. Letting the gentle murmur of so many voices dull her pained, bruised mind.

This was a business. People still called. Customers. They had no idea.

By the door, on the extension, Vagn Skærbæk fielded them all, watching, sad-eyed in his black jumper, black jeans.

Coffee and water. Sandwiches and cake.

Birk Larsen walked like a ghost between tables, making sure cups were full, plates never empty. A waiter with nothing to say.

Then, in the office, by the hot silver urn, Skærbæk cornered him.

'Theis. I just had a call.'

'No business today, Vagn. I'm making coffee.'

'I just spoke to Jannik's wife. The woman at the school.'

Birk Larsen turned off the tap, put the half-filled cup on the table.

Walked into the shadows, away from the people outside.

'Now's not the time—'

'No,' Skærbæk insisted. 'Now is the time.'

'I told you. It can wait.'

'I've got something.'

Birk Larsen looked at him. That plain thuggish face he'd known since childhood. More lined. The hair receding. Still a little scared. A little stupid.

'I told you, Vagn. I'm making coffee.'

Skærbæk stared at him. Defiant. Angry even.

'He's here,' he said.

Birk Larsen shook his head, stroked his chin, his cheek, wondered why he couldn't shave well on a day like this.

Asked, 'Who is?'

'The man they think did it.' Skærbæk's dark, tricky eyes were shining. 'He's here.'

A name. Said with that savage distaste Skærbæk saved for the foreigners.

Through the glass Birk Larsen stared.

The room began to empty. The wake was coming to an end. After a long time he walked out of the office, crossed the room with slow, ponderous steps, trying to think of the right words to say. The proper thing to do.

Pernille was thanking the teacher for the wreath.

Rama, smart and handsome in a dark suit, prepared and presentable in a way Birk Larsen knew he could never hope to emulate, said, 'It was from the school. From all of us. Students and staff.'

The man looked at Birk Larsen, expecting something.

Words.

'We need some coffee.'

Pernille stared at him, affronted by his rudeness.

'You want me to make some coffee?'

A nod.

She left.

Words.

'Thank you for welcoming us into your home,' the teacher said.

Birk Larsen looked at the table. The cups, the glasses, the plates with half-eaten food.

Lit a cigarette.

'It means a lot to her classmates.'

His voice was slick and sweet. Just a touch of the exotic there. Not like most of them, inarticulate. Strangers. Foreign.

'It means a lot to me,' Rama said and reached out to touch his arm.

Something in Birk Larsen's eyes stopped him.

Parks and recreation. Clean technology and environmental jobs. The interview was going well. Hartmann knew it. So did the studio. He could tell from the tone of the questions, the nodding heads behind the cameras in the dark.

From Poul Bremer's stiff responses too.

'You must be happy with all these ideas, Lord Mayor?'

The interviewer was a woman Hartmann had met before. Smart and attractive.

A nod of that grey magisterial head.

'Of course. But let's talk about something different. Immigration. Role models especially.'

He looked at the camera, then at Hartmann.

'Really, Troels. They're just a gimmick.'

Hartmann stiffened.

'Try saying that in your ghettoes.'

A genial laugh.

'We built good affordable housing for people who mostly arrived here uninvited. They seem grateful. We can't tell them where to live.'

Hartmann's temper stirred.

'You can try to address social inequality—'

'Let's go back to role models,' Bremer broke in. 'You seem so fascinated by them. Your personal invention. Why is this? Why are they so important?'

'Social inequality—'

'Why treat immigrants differently? I won't tolerate discrimination against minorities. But you wish to give the minorities rights that are denied to the rest of us. To people born here. Why not treat them like everyone else?'

Troels Hartmann took a deep breath, studied the man across the table. He'd heard these sly gambits so many times . . .

'That's not the point and you know it.'

'No I don't,' Bremer retorted. 'Enlighten me. What is the point?'

Hartmann fumbled for the words. Bremer sensed something.

'You don't seem very proud of your role models right now. Why is that?'

Poul Bremer knew something. It was written in that smirk.

Hartmann's hands performed contortions. His mouth opened. Said nothing.

In the darkness he heard a faint instruction.

'Stay on him. Camera one.'

A politician's career could disappear in an instant. With a single thoughtless action. A solitary careless word.

'I'm very proud of them.'

'Are you?' Bremer asked amiably.

'These people work unpaid to make Copenhagen a better place. We should thank them. Not dismiss them as third-class citizens—'

'This is wonderful.'

'Let me answer!'

'No. No. It's wonderful.'

A glance at the camera. Then Bremer's cold eyes fell on the man across the table.

'But isn't it true some of your role models are criminals themselves?'

'That's nonsense—'

'Be honest with us. One of them's involved in a murder case.'

The interviewer broke in.

'What murder case?'

'Ask Troels Hartmann,' Bremer said. 'He knows.'

'An actual case?' the woman asked.

'As I said. A murder. But . . .' Bremer frowned as if unwilling to elaborate for reasons of taste. The point was made. The bomb was dropped. 'Hartmann's the Mayor of Education. Ask him.'

'No.' The interviewer was cross now. 'This is unacceptable, Bremer. If you won't be specific you must drop this subject.'

'Unacceptable?' He raised his hands. 'What's unacceptable is—'

'Stop this!'

Hartmann's voice was so loud a technician near the table ripped off his headphones.

'Imagine you're right. Let's say this is true.'

'Yes,' the old man agreed. 'Let's say that.'

'Then what? If one immigrant makes a mistake does that implicate all immigrants? That's absurd and you know it. If that's so then what applies to one politician must apply to all of them.'

'You're avoiding the point—'

'No.' Hartmann no longer cared how this might look. 'These role models have achieved more for integration in four years than you've managed in all your time in office. Unpaid, without thanks. While you did nothing—'

'Not true—'

'It's true!'

Hartmann heard his own furious tones echo back at him from the dark belly of the studio.

Bremer relaxed in his seat, arms folded, smug and satisfied.

'I've got plans for Copenhagen,' Hartmann began.

'We'll hear more of this,' Bremer broke in. 'We'll hear more very soon I think.'

Kastrup. Fifteen minutes to departure. Their seats were halfway along the plane. Mark by the window. Vibeke in between. Lund in the aisle, phone in hand.

Meyer'd called.

'Did you hear about Birk Larsen?' she asked, cramming her bag into the overhead locker.

'No. But we've found the girl's bike. What did you want?'

'What bike?'

'A patrol car stopped a girl on a bike for riding without lights. Turned out to be Nanna's.'

A severe-looking flight attendant came up to Lund and ordered her to turn off the phone.

'The girl said she stole the bike from outside Kemal's place. We're picking him up. Where are you?'

'On the plane.'

'Have a nice flight.'

'Meyer. Keep an eye on Birk Larsen.'

She sat down. The flight attendant was at the front of the plane, haranguing someone else.

'Why?'

'Read the old case file like I told you. Don't let him near Kemal.'

She could hear him pulling on a cigarette.

'Now you tell me. The two of them just left the wake.'

'What?'

'I sent someone to pick up Kemal. He was there after the funeral. Birk Larsen had already offered him a lift. What's wrong?'

'Has Kemal arrived home?'

'Listen.' Meyer was getting cross. 'Birk Larsen knows nothing. If he did why would they have let Kemal into their place? Why—'

'Has he arrived home?' she repeated.

'As it happens, no. I don't have time for this. Go fly away.'

'Meyer!'

The line went dead.

The attendant came back, ordered her to put on her seat belt.

They were still at the gate, door open. Not for long.

Lund punched at her phone.

'I've already told you once,' the woman said. 'Turn off that phone and put on your seat belt. We're leaving.'

Lund stared at the dial. Hit the off button. Noticed Mark was looking at her. Her mother too. Probably had been for a while.

The pilot came on. Said the usual things.

Welcome on board your flight to Stockholm. Any minute now we'll push back from the stand. The weather is fine en route. We expect an on-time arrival . . .

Lund thought about Nanna and the teacher. Meyer and Theis Birk Larsen.

The flight attendant had her hand on the door. She was talking to the man outside on the gate. Getting ready to close it. Saying goodbye.

'Fetch the luggage,' Lund said, throwing off her seat belt.

'What?' her mother roared.

Mark punched the air, cried, 'Yes!'

Then Lund marched down the plane, waving her police ID in one hand, clutching her phone to her ear with the other.

Through the dark Theis Birk Larsen gunned the van. The teacher in the passenger seat talking.

About school. About Nanna. About families and children.

Words lost on the big man at the wheel.

From Vesterbro into the city. Past Parliament and Nyhavn.

The water. The empty ground around the Kastellet fortress.

Long dark roads becoming narrow and deserted.

The teacher went silent.

Then said, 'I think we passed the turning a while back.'

Birk Larsen drove and drove, into the black night, trying to think. Wishing he could find the words.

'So we did,' he said, and carried on.

★   ★   ★

In the cab from the airport Lund read over the details to the control room. Red van number plate UE 93 682. From Birk Larsen's removals company. A general call to stop and wait for orders.

Vibeke sat in the back scolding Mark.

'Of course you're going to Sweden. You don't think some silly trick of your mother's will stop that, do you?'

When Lund came off the phone Vibeke said in a long, low voice, 'Poor Bengt. Whatever must that nice man think?'

'Bengt doesn't just think of himself. He understands me better than you do.'

Her mother scowled at her.

'I hope so. For your sake.' A long, judgemental stare. 'So shouldn't you call him? Tell him there's no point in waiting at the airport any more?'

Lund nodded.

'I was about to. Thanks.'

Svendsen was outside the teacher's home by the time Meyer got there. Kemal still hadn't arrived. His wife had heard nothing. Theis Birk Larsen was missing. Not answering his phone.

'Where's Kemal's car?'

'Still in the garage.'

'OK. Go drive the route from Birk Larsen's house to here again.'

The detective bridled.

'We did that already.'

'You know that word I just used? Again?'

307

Svendsen didn't move.

'Shall I report Kemal missing?'

'What for?' Meyer asked.

'Lund talked to Skov before she left. Birk Larsen was dangerous.'

Meyer popped some gum into his mouth, came up to the man, looked around, started calling, 'Lund! *Lund!*'

Shrugged. Looked at the cop and asked, 'Do you see Lund here?'

The man looked at him, said nothing.

'From now on we do things my way. Understand? Lund's away with the fairies. Milking cows or something.'

The radio was squawking. A message about Birk Larsen's van.

Meyer called the control room and said, 'This is 80–15. I didn't put out a search for anything. What gives?'

'Vicekriminalkommissær Lund requested the search.'

Meyer tried to laugh.

'Lund's in Sweden. Cut the jokes.'

'Lund called five minutes ago and requested a search.' A pause. 'We don't do jokes.'

Then hung up.

'This is Theis Birk Larsen. Leave your name and number and I'll get back to you.'

Pernille held out the phone while the message played. Lund listened. The cab had gone on to take

Vibeke and Mark home. She was alone with the Birk Larsen woman amidst the dirty plates, dirty cups, dirty glasses, uncleared tables of Nanna's wake.

'And you've no idea where he is?' Lund asked.

'He drove Rama home.'

Pernille looked pale, drained. And curious.

'What's so important?'

'Did anything happen before they left? Between the two of them?'

'I was talking to the teacher. Theis came over. He wanted some more coffee made.' She scanned the remains of the wake, the empty garage. 'So I went and made some. For the guests. What's this about?'

'Did your husband seem angry or upset. Or—?'

'Upset?'

Pernille Birk Larsen glowered at her. A strong woman, Lund thought. A match for her husband in some ways.

'How do you think Theis feels today? How do you think I feel? Take a look around. You've been everywhere anyway, haven't you?'

'Pernille.'

'Everywhere . . .'

There was a noise from the office. The man who seemed to be here all the time, one of the workers, was there.

She knew his name. They'd run some checks. Minor crimes. Just like Birk Larsen.

Vagn Skærbæk.

'Your husband may be about to do something

309

stupid,' she said, watching the woman very carefully. 'It's important I find him.'

'Why? What would he do that's stupid?'

There was a young voice from the stairs. One of the boys, calling for her.

'My son needs me,' Pernille said then left.

Lund walked straight into the office, showed the man her card.

'You're a friend of his?'

He was dealing with some papers. Didn't look at her directly.

'Yeah.'

'Where did he go?'

Straight out, 'I don't know.'

More papers. She walked over, took them from his hands.

'Listen to me. This is important. If you're his friend you should help him. Where did they go?'

He had a silver necklace and a young man's face growing old. Lund had dealt with a generation of people like this. Not much money. Not many prospects. She knew what to expect.

'I've no idea.'

Sound at the door. Someone chewing, clearing his throat. She recognized his presence by now.

Lund was on the phone to control by the time she turned to face Meyer.

'I need you to trace two mobiles. Theis Birk Larsen's and Rahman Al Kemal's. Here are the numbers.'

She handed the phone over to Meyer and nodded: do it.

'God, you'll pay for this, Lund.'

'We don't have time. Vagn?'

He was back in the corner, hiding.

'Where are your warehouses?'

Meyer was on the phone, handling the numbers. 'Vagn?'

Out by the waterfront, north of the city, the deserted docks in Frihavnen. Rain like tears from an endless black sky.

The red van sauntered slowly to the end of the road. A line of concrete. A path by the water. No cars. No lights. Not a sign of life.

Theis Birk Larsen bumped the front tyres against the path, pulled on the brake.

They'd sat together like this for almost an hour driving through the city. Going north. Going nowhere. Scarcely exchanging a word.

Now he killed the engine. The headlights. There was just the dim bulb above the mirror between them.

The phone in Birk Larsen's suit pocket rang again. He took it out. Turned it off without answering. Put it back. Stared ahead.

'What's going on?' the teacher said. 'What . . . ?'

Birk Larsen reached down, opened his door, climbed out.

Pulled the jacket of his funeral suit round his big frame. Walked through the blustery wind and freezing rain out to the water's edge.

Turned, stared at the van. A dark face at the glass. Worried, grey in the single light.

Birk Larsen took out a packet of cigarettes, struggled to light one in the downpour. Shielded it with his powerful shoulder. Brought the flame to life.

Alone in his office Troels Hartmann was locked on to the news again. There was a time when he craved to be the lead item. Not now. Not like this.

'The battle for the mayoral post took a dramatic turn when Bremer accused one of Hartmann's role models of being involved in a murder case.'

Rie Skovgaard walked in, chanting the standard no comment at one more reporter looking for an interview. She came off the line, handed Hartmann a sheet of paper.

'The Centre Party want a meeting. I had to promise it.'

Hartmann turned off the TV. She was walking out.

'What did the police say?' he asked.

She stopped at the door.

'I can't get through to anyone. Troels?'

She didn't even look tired. She'd grown up in the brawling world of city politics from which his own father had been excluded. It was as if this all came naturally . . .

'You realize you've got to suspend Kemal and issue a statement. Otherwise—'

'Not until I've heard from the police. When I get a reason—'

'You have to do this! It's important we show you've got nothing to hide. This is about transparency.'

312

'No it's not. It's about giving in. Letting the pressure dictate what you do. Not what's right.'

He got up from the chair, found his jacket. Felt calm. Content this was the way forward.

'Bremer stirred this up for a reason . . .'

She leaned back against the door, shifted her head left to right. Dark hair moving. What was it Morten said? The Jackie Kennedy funeral look.

'You should have stuck to the script. No mention of role models. Just because Bremer went there you didn't have to follow.'

'I did what was right.'

'You fouled up.'

'Is that Daddy speaking?'

She broke, spat at him, 'No, it's me. I want you to win. Not throw away your chances for no good reason.'

'Whose chances, Rie? Mine? Yours? Your father's?'

She shook her head, narrowed those bright, piercing eyes.

'Is that how you see it?'

'I asked—'

'You know maybe I'm not the adviser for you. What's the point? If you ignore every damned thing I say.'

A turning point.

'Maybe not,' Hartmann said.

'Here's the truth, Troels. That teacher's guilty. It doesn't matter whether they convict him or not.'

'You think so?'

'If that's what the press say. And they do . . .'

He grabbed his coat from the stand.

'Talk to the police. If they say something . . . if they arrest this man. If they tell me he's guilty . . .'

'Too late.'

'Then I act.'

She watched him get ready to leave.

'Where are you going?' Skovgaard asked. 'Troels? Where?'

'Have they traced those phones yet?'

Meyer didn't answer. He was still on a call.

Lund was going through the documents on the wall, tracing the company premises, watched by a silent, surly Skærbæk.

She read them out to the control room. A warehouse at Sydhavnen. A depot in Valby. A warehouse at Frihavnen with no address.

'Where in Frihavnen?' she asked Skærbæk.

'I've never been to that one.'

There was a cupboard full of keys. She went through those.

'What about this workshop? Could he be there?'

'I told you. I don't know a bloody thing.'

Meyer came off the phone.

'We've got a trace off a mobile phone mast. Kemal's in Frihavnen.'

Port area. Not much used at night. Easy to hide, Lund thought.

'He's in Frihavnen,' she told control. 'Send out a car.'

★   ★   ★

No rain now. Just the Øresund's black water, Sweden somewhere in the distance. Waves reflected in the lights from across the channel. Birk Larsen stood at the edge, in the headlamps of the van. Back to the world.

A sound. He turned. The teacher was out now. Not running. Which he could. Younger and fitter. Could race all the way back to the city. Avoid Birk Larsen and the van.

Instead he walked to the water. Stared at the waves. 'I'm sorry . . .'

They never lost the accent completely. Never shrugged off who they were.

'My wife's waiting for me.'

Words. Where were the words?

'She's pregnant. I don't want her to worry. Maybe I should call and tell her . . .'

Another cigarette in Birk Larsen's fist. Barely touched. But now he raised it to his lips, dragged the harsh smoke into his lungs. Wished it would spread from there, fill his big body. Make him nothing. Invisible. Gone.

Words.

They should be about her. About no one else. Always.

'Nanna was a stargazer. Did you know that?'

The teacher shook his head.

'That's what they call it when you look up when you're born. See your mother's eyes. See something else. The sky.'

So many memories. A jumble of images and

sounds. A child is a child. Its life flows like a river, never stopping, never fixed.

'We said she'd be an astronaut. Parents say . . .' He pulled on the cigarette again. 'We say such stupid things. Make stupid promises we're never going to keep.'

The teacher nodded. As if he knew.

Birk Larsen threw the cigarette into the water. Shrugged. Looked back at the van.

'She liked going to school, didn't she?'

'Very much so.'

Stamped his feet in the damp cold.

'I wasn't any good at school. Got into trouble. But Nanna was . . .'

Memories.

'Nanna was different. Better than me.'

There was a look on the teacher's dark face. The one they show parents.

'She was a very able student.'

'Able?'

'Hard working.'

'And she was fond of you, wasn't she?'

Memories. They burned like acid.

The man was silent.

'She told us about your lessons.'

Birk Larsen took a step towards him.

'People are talking about you, teacher.'

He was sweating. It wasn't rain.

'No matter what you've heard . . .' He shook his head. Didn't move. 'I can assure you. Nanna was my student. I would never . . .'

Birk Larsen waited.

'Never what, teacher?'

'I would never hurt her.'

Closer. His breath was sweet. Not mints. Something exotic.

'So why are people talking?'

Quickly, 'I don't know.'

Birk Larsen nodded.

Waited.

A long time. Then the teacher said, a touch angry, 'I didn't touch her. I never would. This is all a misunderstanding.'

'Misunder—'

'I'm going to be a father!'

Two men by the Øresund's cold expanse.

One walked to the van. Turned on the engine. Looked back at the tall hunched figure caught in the headlights by the water's edge.

Meyer hung on the phone, getting nowhere. Skærbæk was turning ugly in the corner. Pernille Birk Larsen had had enough.

'Do you get a kick out of this?' the woman stormed at them. 'You come to my daughter's funeral. I don't know what you think but . . .'

Keen, smart eyes turned on Lund.

'Theis hasn't done anything.'

Skærbæk leaned back against the office door, lit a cigarette.

'I believe he has,' Lund said.

Meyer came off the phone.

317

'There's no one at the harbour. They've looked everywhere.'

'Try the other warehouses.'

'Done what?' Pernille Birk Larsen demanded. 'You people—'

There was a sound. Lund looked, wondered about Meyer's weapon. He always had it.

The sliding door was moving upwards. Meyer was still on the phone.

Theis Birk Larsen walked in. Sharp black suit. Ironed white shirt. Black tie.

Looked at them. Cops first. Skærbæk. Then Pernille.

'Are the kids asleep?' he asked.

Lund couldn't stop staring.

'Where's Kemal?'

Birk Larsen's massive head lolled from side to side. There was something in his narrow, sly eyes she couldn't interpret, hard as she tried.

'I think he took a taxi.'

Lund glanced at Meyer. Pointed to his phone.

Birk Larsen walked for the stairs. His wife stopped him, asked, 'Where've you been, Theis? Two hours . . .?'

'It's not so late.' He nodded at the apartment. 'I'd like to read them a story.'

'Wait. Wait!' Lund called.

He walked off, out of view.

Meyer got off the line.

'Kemal just called his wife. He's on his way home.'

Pernille Birk Larsen glared at them both, shook her head, swore, stomped off. There was just

318

Skærbæk then. Silver chain at the neck. Giving them the fuck-you punk look of a teenager.

'Call off the search,' Meyer barked down the phone. 'Bring Kemal down to the station as soon as you can.'

He pocketed his mobile. Followed her outside.

'Well,' Meyer said. 'What the hell was that about?'

Lund called Sweden.

'This is Bengt Rosling. I can't take your call right now. Leave your name and number and I'll call you back.'

Best voice, trying not to sound apologetic because she wasn't. Not really.

'Hi, it's me. You must be busy welcoming the guests.'

All this she said while she was taking off her jacket, throwing it onto a chair in the corner of the office, scanning the documents on the desk.

Her desk?

Meyer's?

Didn't know. Didn't care. The documents mattered. Nothing else.

'I wish I could be there, Bengt.'

There hadn't been much new since the afternoon.

'The thing is . . . something came up in the case.'

Meyer walked in.

'I'm really, really sorry. Give everyone my best . . .'

She took a seat at the desk. It still felt hers. Rifled for her pens, her papers. Her place here.

'Tell them . . .'

He'd moved things. Her things. She felt a flicker of annoyance.

'It's a shame. But well . . .'

Meyer stood with his hands on the back of the opposite chair. Staring at her, open-mouthed.

'I'll talk to you later. Bye.'

Phone down, more sifting through the papers.

'Is he ready for questioning?' Lund asked.

'Look, look.' He seemed more amazed than angry. 'You can't do this. I don't know what you think—'

'I think you're right, Meyer.'

'I am?' he brightened. 'Oh great.'

'It isn't working. So I've decided to stay until the case is solved.'

'What?'

'Doesn't make sense going back and forth between here and Sweden. It's a mess. The Swedish police say—'

'Stop this, Lund.'

With his sticky-out ears and bright, hurt eyes Meyer suddenly looked very young.

'This is my case now. You're not staying here. End of story. We're done. The girl visited him on Friday night. Once he's admitted that I'm charging him.'

Lund took one last look at the files, picked up a couple, stood up.

'Let's hope he confesses then. Shall we go?'

'Oh no.'

Meyer stood in the way.

'I'm doing the questioning.'

'Don't make me talk to Buchard, Meyer.'

320

He bristled.

'I'm being nice here. You can sit in if you like.'

Kemal was at the table, black tie pulled down. Exhausted. Nervous.

Meyer sat on his left. Lund opposite.

'Want a coffee or a tea?' Meyer asked, throwing his files on the table.

He did all the policeman voices. Threatening. Sympathetic. Neutral now and calm.

The teacher poured himself a glass of water. Lund leaned over, shook his hand, said, 'Hi.'

'You're not under arrest,' Meyer recited from memory, 'but you have the same rights as someone who has been accused. You have the right to a lawyer.'

'I don't need a lawyer. I'll answer your questions.'

The teacher looked at Lund.

'There's something you should know.'

They watched him. Sweating. Trying to find the courage to say something. This didn't happen often, Lund thought.

'Last Friday I was supervising the Halloween party at school. My shift ended at eight thirty. I drove home to pick up my wife.'

She wondered what had happened in the van with Birk Larsen. What difference that might have made.

'We went to our house on the allotment. About nine thirty I realized we had forgotten to bring coffee. So I drove to the petrol station.'

Making it up, she thought. You are making this up.

'On the way back I remembered the workman

was coming on Saturday. I drove back to the flat to clear things out of the way.'

Meyer shuffled forward on the table.

'Just after ten the doorbell rang. It was Nanna.'

They waited.

'She wanted to return some books I'd lent her. She was only there for two minutes.'

Meyer leaned back in his chair, put his hands behind his head.

'That's it,' Kemal said and finished the glass of water.

'She came round to return some books?' Meyer asked.

'School books?' Lund wondered.

'No, my own books. Karen Blixen. She seemed to want to give them back to me right then. I don't know why. I was surprised.' He shrugged. 'I just took them.'

'On a Friday night?' Meyer asked. 'At ten o'clock?'

'She was always looking for something to read.' He closed his eyes briefly. 'I know I should have told you this before.'

'Why didn't you?' Lund demanded.

He looked at his hands, not at them.

'There was an incident with another student. A few years ago. A false accusation. I was scared you'd think—'

'Think what?' Lund asked.

'Think I'd had some kind of relationship with Nanna.'

Dark eyes met hers.

'I didn't,' he said.

'That's it?' Lund asked.

'That's it. That's all I've got to say.'

Hartmann's car roamed the bars for a while, him in the back, phone off, radio off.

'It's got to be around here somewhere,' he told the driver.

A sign he remembered. A name.

'There! There!'

It was an old pub. Noisy. Busy. Full of men who'd taken on too much beer. Bottles on the table. Clouds of cigarette smoke in the air.

Hartmann strolled through the dark bar. Found Morten Weber finally, head back on his shoulders, curly hair grubby, all over the place.

There were six men around the table. Working steadily at their drinks. Saying nothing.

Hartmann stood in front of them, held up the plastic bag. Weber groaned, got up, came over.

The insulin was delivered to the campaign office. The place where Weber seemed to live.

'I saw you on TV,' he said, taking it.

The glass in his hand was whisky. Hartmann could smell it. The last in a long line he thought.

'You don't have time to play doctor, Troels.'

'Rie thinks you're sick. She doesn't know you so well. Yet.'

Bleary-eyed, Morten Weber tried to smile.

'I'm allowed one drunk day a month. It's in my contract, isn't it?'

'Why this one?'

'Because you yelled at me.'

'You asked for it.'

'Because I needed some time out of that marble prison. To think without you or her or some damned minion getting in my face. Besides . . .'

There was an expression he didn't recognize on Weber's sad, lined face. Bitterness, Hartmann realized.

'It doesn't matter, does it? You don't listen to me any more. Does she know you're here? Your new consort?'

He knocked back the drink. Went to sit at an empty table cuddling his glass. Hartmann took the bench opposite.

'You haven't even suspended the teacher yet, have you?' Weber said. 'From what I've heard you're right. But what does Kirsten Eller think?'

Hartmann said nothing.

'Has she dumped you yet, Troels? Or is she waiting till tomorrow? What's Rie's advice there? Go running to her? Go begging? Give her what she wants? That teacher's head on a plate?'

'I need you two to work together.'

'Oh do you? Just because you brought me some insulin it doesn't . . .' His speech was slurred. His thoughts seemed clear. 'It doesn't make everything all right.'

Hartmann pulled his coat around him, ready to leave.

'I was trying to make amends. I'm sorry if I wasted your time.'

'Poor Troels. Always wants to do the right thing. But he listens to the wrong people. Poor . . .'

'I need you back in the office tomorrow. I need you to cut out these binges until this election's over. And get along with Rie.'

Weber nodded.

'Yes. I imagine you do. Now you're in the shit.'

A short, drunken laugh.

'You know it's only just started, don't you? All those hangers on who think they saw the spark of opportunity. They'll come for you, Troels. Once they think you've disappointed them. Watch out for the civil servants. Watch out for your own people. Bigum.'

Henrik Bigum, one of the senior party figures, a dour academic from the university.

'What about Bigum?'

'He loathes you and trouble's in his nature. He's the one who'll wield the dagger. But he'll get someone else to make the first move, naturally. You've no idea . . .'

He'd never seen such bleak fury in Morten Weber's face. Not directed at him anyway.

'When your wife died, Troels' – Weber banged his fist on the table – 'you were sitting here. And I was sitting there. Remember?'

Hartmann didn't move, didn't speak, didn't want to think about it.

Cheap, stupid pop music playing in the background. Loud voices. Men working through the prelude to a fight.

'You should listen to me, Troels. I deserve that. What else do I have?'

A last hateful look then Weber left the table and stumbled back to the bunch of drunks.

Hartmann had missed a call. Rie Skovgaard. He phoned her back.

'They found the girl's bike,' she said. 'It was at her teacher's flat the night she went missing.'

The music got louder. The fight was just a word, a push away.

'It's in the press already. Front page tomorrow. Pictures of you and Kemal. He's named as a suspect.'

Silence.

'Troels,' she said. 'I'm drafting the suspension papers now. I'm calling a press conference in an hour. I need you there.'

Buchard stormed into the office.

'How come our suspect's name's on television? Lund?'

'It's not a problem,' Meyer cut in. He nodded at the figure in the interview room beyond the glass. 'He's sitting right in there. We have him.'

'When the commissioner calls me it's a problem. Lund's gone from here for an hour or two and see what happens.'

'It's not Meyer's fault,' she said.

'What does the teacher say?' Buchard wanted to know.

Meyer sneered.

'Some crap about meeting the girl at his flat. She wanted to bring back some books.'

Buchard's lined face screwed up in bafflement.

'Books?'

Lund barely listened, kept running through the latest files on the PC.

'It's bullshit,' Meyer said. 'He sanded the floors. Removed everything.'

'They're renovating the flat,' Lund pointed out. 'That part's true.'

'Give me two hours with him, chief,' Meyer begged. 'I'll find out.'

Buchard looked unconvinced.

'The way you did with those boys?'

'I'll question him as a witness. I can—'

'He's lying,' Lund said and that stopped them.

Buchard folded his arms, looked at her.

'He's lying,' she said again.

'Search the flat,' Buchard ordered. 'Basement, the allotment in Dragør, everything. Locate the building waste. Tap his phone.'

Meyer didn't seem to be part of the conversation. Buchard was watching Lund scribble this down.

'Tell Hartmann what we're doing. And don't screw up with the press again.'

He was leaving. Meyer said, 'Talking about screwing up I need to talk to you in private.'

'Tomorrow,' Buchard snapped. 'Right now I want you working not whining.'

'So what do we do with him?' Meyer asked.

Buchard waited for Lund.

'We make him stay at his wife's house. Or a hotel,' she said. 'He's got to keep away from his flat and the place on the allotments. We're searching them. We need his passport. We need him watched.'

Something nagged at her and Lund couldn't begin to guess what it was.

'He says he used his own car on Friday. We need to connect him to Hartmann's vehicle. He was a role model, wasn't he?'

The press conference was fifteen minutes away. Skovgaard was laying down the line.

'The suspension's effective immediately. I've got the paperwork. I've informed the administration.'

Hartmann looked at the documents she'd placed in front of him.

'You need to distance yourself from the whole thing. Say you regret your error of judgement. You support the police's efforts.'

He scanned through the statement, the apologetic, self-serving language.

'When they ask about role models, say you can't comment. If anyone . . .'

Hartmann got up from the desk and prowled the office, hands thrust deep in his pockets, blue shirt stained with sweat.

'If you're in the public eye and make a mistake it's important to apologize immediately. Put the whole thing to bed and move on. There are some fresh clothes in the wardrobe. You need them.'

He looked at the early edition of the newspaper

on his desk. The teacher, Kemal, shaking his hand at the basketball match. Both of them smiling.

'I don't get this. He seemed a nice guy. No one has a bad word to say about him. I checked some of the records. There's a kid out there, straight and decent now. Would have been in jail if it wasn't for him.'

The first three pages were dedicated to the story.

'So I played basketball with him.'

Skovgaard was watching him with tired, worried eyes.

'And the weekend before he's supposed to have raped and murdered one of his own students.'

She looked deeply bored with this conversation.

'They're waiting for you, Troels. We need to sort out the lighting. The way you look.'

'Do you think he did it?'

'I don't know and I don't care. What I care about is saving you. I never realized it was going to be so hard.'

There was a knock on the door.

Lund stood there, waiting.

'What?' Skovgaard barked at her.

She walked in. Same old coat. Same black and white sweater. Same ponytail, long straight brown hair tied clumsily at the back.

This woman seemed to have attached herself to his life like a limpet.

'Hartmann said he wanted to be briefed,' Lund said, looking puzzled.

A shrug. Bright eyes boring into him.

'So here I am.'

'Aren't you supposed to be in Sweden?' Hartmann asked.

She smiled at that.

'Eventually. Kemal admits he met the girl at his flat. He says she left, but no one's seen her since. We're—'

'Give us the short version,' Skovgaard broke in. 'We've got a press conference.'

That smile again, a little different this time.

'The short version. He might have held her captive somewhere. We won't be charging him until we've searched his place. Maybe not then.'

'We read the papers,' Skovgaard said. 'We know all that.'

'I'll need mileage logs and documentation for any drivers using your cars over the last two years.'

'What for?'

'Kemal must have taken the car Nanna was found in. There has to be a connection . . .'

Hartmann stopped.

'He didn't drive that car.'

'It says in your records,' Lund insisted. 'The role models have access to them.'

'Not the campaign fleet. They're all brand new. Rented for a few weeks. Rie?'

She was watching him, arms folded, trying not to get drawn in.

'Rie!'

'The campaign cars are bright and shiny,' she said. 'We've got a point to make. The role models get the junk no one else wants to drive.'

'Wait a minute,' Hartmann said. 'You're going to charge him?'

'I said if we find more evidence—'

'But if Kemal never drove the car how could he even know it was one of ours?'

'Perhaps . . .' She was lost, and he'd never seen that before. 'Maybe . . . I don't know.'

Hartmann sensed something.

'We've only had those cars for two weeks or so. Maybe he's not guilty at all. We've got a press conference called about this in five minutes. What the hell are we supposed to say?'

'I don't run your press conferences, Hartmann.'

'If it wasn't for you we wouldn't need the damned things! You've been wrong before. Who's to say you're not wrong this time? You think I should suspend this man when you don't even have any evidence?'

'I just need some cooperation. You leave me to my job. I'll leave you to yours.'

She left with that. Skovgaard was watching him. He could hear the reporters assembling in the room next door.

Hartmann got the new suit, the clean shirt, started changing.

'Troels?' Skovgaard said. 'Don't even think of backing out. We've got the suspension papers. For your sake—'

'Kemal didn't do it.' He was grinning as he struggled into clean clothes. 'It's not him.'

*   *   *

331

Theis at the sink, broad back to her, pulling on a beer. Pernille at the table, watching him, pushing him to talk.

'They suspect the teacher,' she said. 'It's on the news.'

He sank some more beer and closed his eyes.

'Where did you go? What took you so long?'

'I don't know.'

Letters on the table. Bills. Late notices.

'I'll go to the house tomorrow. Do some work on it.'

She blinked.

'The house?'

'I've got to fix it up. Can't sell it till I do.'

He went to the drawer he always kept locked with a key she couldn't find. A habit from the past. Not the only place like that.

There were sheets inside. Architect's drawings.

'These were the plans. I'm sorry. I should have told you.'

'He was here,' she murmured.

Pencil projections. Dead dreams.

'We talked about Nanna.'

He folded out another sheet, smoothed it down with his elbow.

'I thanked him for the flowers in the church.'

He ran his finger over the drawings, said nothing.

'He touched her coffin.'

She looked at her fingers. The old wedding ring. The wrinkles. The marks of labour.

'I touched him.'

A rustle of papers. Nothing more.

In a calm, pleading tone she said, 'Why won't you talk to me?'

His eyes rose from the measurements and angles and drawings of beams.

'We don't know for sure.'

'You think he did it. Don't you?'

A long day. He never shaved well anyway. Now he looked like a miserable bear who'd strayed from the woods.

'Let's leave this to the police.'

Her hands flew across the table, swept away the papers of the home they'd never see.

'The police?'

Tears in her eyes. Fury in her face.

'Yes. The police.'

Bengt was still on voicemail. Vibeke was back at her sewing machine, running up another perfect dress for another perfect wedding.

An expression on her face that said: I knew it all along.

'Hi,' Lund said and threw her bag on the nearest chair.

Her mother turned off the machine, rolled back the white billowing fabric. Pushed the glasses down to the end of her long sharp nose.

'If you want a family, Sarah, you have to work for it.'

'I tried calling Bengt. He's not answering. I tried.'

Her mother said, 'Huh!'

'It's because of the party. He can't hear the phone.'

Vibeke came and sat next to her. An unexpected, almost apologetic expression on her face.

'I know you think I chased your father away before he died.'

'No.'

'I know you think that. I may not have been the best example for you . . .'

'We haven't broken up, Mum.'

'No. But you never let him close, do you? He's like the rest of us. Outside your life.'

'That's not true. You don't know us.'

Vibeke took the half-made dress off the stand, examined the seams.

'I just want you to be happy. I don't want you to be lonely in your old age.'

'You're not lonely, are you?'

Vibeke looked thrown by the question.

'I wasn't talking about myself.'

'I won't be lonely. I wasn't lonely before Bengt. Why should I . . . ?'

Now there was an expression she did recognize. Summed up in one word: *exactly*.

Lund turned on the TV and watched the news headlines. One story only. Troels Hartmann at his press conference, saying he wasn't suspending the teacher Kemal.

'Why in God's name not?' she whispered.

On the TV Hartmann answered.

'Rahman Al Kemal has been neither charged nor convicted. I won't take part in an act of character assassination. Bremer may be hell-bent on that. Let him square it with what passes as his conscience.'

His right hand rose, a gesture of politicians everywhere.

'Only if there's concrete evidence will there be a suspension.'

He leaned forward, an earnest face for the camera.

'It's the job of the police to convict criminals. Not politicians. We should stay out of their way except to offer every possible assistance we can. And that I will do. Thank you.'

A crowd of bodies rose, flinging questions. Lund watched, wished she'd got this on the recorder, could play back every word, catch every inflection, every expression on Hartmann's face.

'What if he murdered the girl?' yelled a reporter.

'As far as I know,' Hartmann replied, 'in this country a man is innocent until he's proven guilty. That's all . . .'

'That's all?' Lund murmured.

Then it was over. On to other news. The Middle East. The economy. She turned off the TV. Realized the room was dark and empty. Vibeke had gone off to bed without a word.

She was alone.

Sunday, 9th November

Dull morning. Lund walked into headquarters and was briefed by the leader of the overnight team. A security camera at the petrol station showed Kemal buying coffee at twenty to ten on the Friday night Nanna disappeared. He received a call from a launderette payphone around the same time. A place near his flat in the city. Twenty minutes before Nanna visited.

There was still nothing of use from the home. But if they could prove he'd arranged to meet her that broke his story. A lie.

The only other call he made was to the workman cancelling him.

Lund was thinking about this when she glanced into her office. Bengt was sitting there.

A quick smile. She closed the door, got some coffee from the flask.

'How'd you get here?' Lund asked.

'I drove last night.'

She handed him a cup, still wondering about the phone calls. Why would Nanna be in a launderette? Why wouldn't she use her own mobile?

'How did the house-warming party go?'

'Fine.' He looked tired and a little grubby from the drive. For once there was a touch of anger in his calm grey eyes. 'I sent people home at nine.'

She was wearing the black and white Faroese jumper from the day before. If she'd known Bengt was going to be there . . . She ran a hand through her untidy hair and thought: I'd still have worn it.

He came and put his hands on her shoulders. Professional face. Very serious. Fatherly.

'Listen, Sarah. It's not hard. Just walk out of that

door, get in the car and we'll go home. You don't know those people. What about your family? What about Mark? He's supposed to be starting school.'

Lund walked to her desk, grabbed a folder.

'I want you to read the case. Here's the coroner's report. Here's what we found by the canal—'

'No!'

It was as close to a shout as she'd ever heard.

'I need your help,' she said calmly.

'You need? What about everyone else?'

She wasn't listening.

'He bathed her and clipped her nails. What kind of person does that? He removed every trace, carefully. Or there's some other reason I haven't guessed yet. Look . . .'

She got some of the morgue shots. Injuries. Bruises. Blood.

'The coroner thinks he's probably done this before. But I can't find anything similar.'

'I'm not interested in your case. I'm interested in you.'

He pointed to the door.

'The car's out there.'

There was a knock. Meyer came in. Sailor shirt, open-necked jerkin. Looking brighter and tidier than usual.

'I'm going to see Birk Larsen,' he said. 'But you don't need to—'

'I'll be right there.'

She grabbed her coat.

Bengt Rosling was a handsome man. That wasn't

why she liked him. Loved him. He was placid, intelligent, patient.

'Please stay, Bengt.' She came and took his hand, smiled, looked into his eyes. 'It would mean a lot to me.'

He was wavering.

She picked up the folders, thrust them at him.

Then she quickly kissed him and went out to meet Meyer.

Rie Skovgaard had been through the vehicle files. The role models didn't use the cars.

'That's good news,' Hartmann said.

'We need a new campaign manager. If Morten isn't coming back.'

'He won't be.'

'I'll find someone. Knud Padde's here. He wants to talk to you. Alone. He's in your office.'

Padde held the assembly group chair, a mid-ranking party hack. Influential, important even at times. Tedious.

'Can't you—?'

'No. Go and talk to him.'

A trade union official, Padde was a bear-like shambling man with a bad suit, big spectacles and wild, uncombed hair.

'Have you seen the papers?' he complained the moment Hartmann walked in.

'Of course I've seen them.'

'The constituency's worried, Troels. The group wants a meeting. Today. One o'clock.'

338

'Knud. Not now. Kirsten Eller will be here in two minutes.'

'Why didn't you suspend the teacher? It looks as if you're covering for him.'

Hartmann looked him in the eye.

'According to the police the teacher's probably innocent.'

'That's not what the papers say.'

Padde was feeling unusually brave, Hartmann thought.

'I'm not sure we can take this pressure, Troels.'

Hartmann thought of his conversation the previous night with Weber.

'I'll deal with this. We don't need a meeting at one . . .'

'But there is a meeting. It's fixed,' Padde said. 'Best you be there.'

'You never told me he was a nut doctor,' Meyer said.

She was letting him drive again. It stopped him stuffing crisps and sweets and hot dogs into his mouth. Most of the time.

Lund didn't answer.

'Not that there's anything wrong in going out with your therapist.'

She sighed.

'He's a criminal psychologist.'

Meyer raised an eyebrow as if to say: does that matter?

'He's the cleverest man I know.'

'Met him through work, eh?'

Silence.

'Am I right in thinking your ex-husband was a cop too?'

Silence.

'You're not the only one who can run background checks, Lund.'

Meyer shook his head. Stared at her as he took the corner.

'Watch the road,' she ordered.

'Do you know anyone outside the police?'

'Of course I do! Bengt—'

'Is a criminal psychologist.'

'I know lots of people.'

'Of course you do. I've asked Buchard for a meeting. About us.'

She looked at him. Big ears. Bulbous eyes. Stubble and that cocky haircut.

Meyer started to whistle. Then he turned the corner into Birk Larsen's street.

'Where's your husband?' Lund asked.

Pernille Birk Larsen was wiping down the kitchen table. The place looked too clean. As if the woman was trying to scrub away the memory of her lost child.

The tablecloth was unusual. Photographs and school reports were lacquered into the surface. Faces and words. A young Nanna, on her own, in the box of the red Christiania trike with a tiny Indian boy. The sons as toddlers.

A sweep of the tablecloth which was spotless already.

'He works weekends too.'

'We need information,' Lund said. 'We need to understand whether Nanna knew her murderer or not. Would you mind . . . ?'

The obsessive sweep of the hand, the cloth that removed nothing because there was nothing to remove.

'Would you mind doing that later please?' Lund said.

Pernille Birk Larsen didn't look at her. Just kept rubbing at the table.

Meyer rolled his eyes.

'It could be something she said,' Lund went on. 'Times she wasn't at home. Anything. Presents, books she borrowed . . .'

Pernille Birk Larsen stopped working with the cloth, leaned on both hands, glowered at both of them.

'You knew that teacher was a suspect. And you let him come to the funeral. Let me welcome him into my home.'

Meyer was shaking his head.

'He held my hand. And you said nothing!'

Lund shrugged, got up, looked around.

'And now you come asking questions!' Pernille shouted at them. 'It's too late.'

They didn't say a word.

'What are you doing about him?'

'We're searching his home,' Meyer broke in. 'As soon as we know something I'll call you.'

341

A look of bewilderment in the woman's intelligent, searching eyes. A connection she'd never made.

'Nanna was there?'

No answer.

'She was at his home that night?'

Lund shook her head, started to say, 'We can't go into details . . .'

'Yes,' Meyer broke in. 'She was there that night.'

Lund closed her eyes, furious.

'No one's seen her since,' he added.

Still livid, Lund said, 'This doesn't prove anything. We need information that links the two of them. We need . . .'

What? She wasn't sure either.

'We need a reason,' Lund said half to herself.

Pernille Birk Larsen picked up the cloth, wiped the clean table again.

'All I know is Nanna liked him as a teacher.' She waved at the girl's bedroom. 'Go round the place. Help yourself. There's nowhere you haven't poked your noses already.'

She glared at them.

'But keep me informed. You hear that?'

'Sure,' Meyer said.

Theis Birk Larsen and Vagn Skærbæk had picked up some fresh timber beams from the yard. They were in the garage stacking them in the van. There were jobs to be done. But the house in Humleby came first.

'I'll help you with the work, Theis,' Skærbæk promised. 'Just tell me what you want.'

Birk Larsen heaved some more timber into the truck, said nothing.

Skærbæk dodged a beam.

'Just as well you didn't touch him with all those police about.' He picked up some more planks, threw them in the van. 'How can an ape like that be a teacher? It's a sick world.'

Birk Larsen took off his black hat, looked at the wood. Fetched some more.

'Know what?' Skærbæk checked around, made sure no one was listening. 'He's finished. I promise you. Listen . . .'

He put a hand on Birk Larsen's black coat. Stopped him.

'We wait,' Skærbæk said. 'We've done this before. We know how.'

A sudden fury gripped Birk Larsen's stony face. He picked up the smaller man by his overall, threw him towards the back of the van. Grabbed him by the throat.

'Don't ever talk like that again. Ever.'

Skærbæk stood still, defiant, almost squared up to him.

'Theis. It's me. Remember?'

A shape at the edge of his vision. The lean, gruff cop came into view, phone ringing. Birk Larsen let go.

'Meyer speaking,' the cop said.

The Lund woman was with him, walking round

the place the way she always did. Eyeing up everything as if she could record it with those unblinking eyes.

Birk Larsen loaded the van and closed the door. Vagn had made himself scarce without a sound. A talent he'd had since the two of them were kids on the street.

Lund came up to Birk Larsen.

'If there's anything I can do . . .'

'You know what you can do,' he said.

Kirsten Eller arrived, a look of mild outrage on her pasty face.

'This role model of yours is the prime suspect. In a murder case.'

'He may be innocent.'

'Not suspending him is madness.'

'That may be your opinion but it's not mine. Don't let this ruin our agreement.'

'Our agreement?'

He waited. Rie Skovgaard studied her nails.

'Words on paper,' Eller said. 'That's all they are. Nothing more.'

There was coffee on the table and croissants. Barely touched.

'You mean you want out?'

'It's a question of credibility.'

'It's a question of principle.'

'Your principles. Not ours. I won't go down with you. I won't be held accountable. I won't—'

'What,' he cut in, 'are you saying?'

344

'If you don't make this go away I'll distance myself from you. We have to—'

A knock on the door. Morten Weber walked in. He looked as if he'd been shopping. Smart new jacket, red sweater, white shirt.

Hartmann and Skovgaard stared at him.

'Here's the document you asked me to find,' Weber said, coming over to Hartmann, a sheet of paper in his hand.

No one spoke.

Weber asked, 'More coffee?'

When there was no answer he smiled and left.

Hartmann looked at the colour printout. It was a page from Kirsten Eller's own website.

'What's it to be, Troels?'

He read the sheet carefully.

'OK,' she went on. 'I won't be seen with you. All joint arrangements are cancelled, including tonight's.'

Eller tidied her papers, dropped them into her briefcase with her pen. Got ready to go.

'What about your credibility?'

'What do you mean?'

Hartmann passed the paper across the table.

'You've been taking credit for my role models. It's here. On your home page.'

She snatched the page, read it.

'You liked our joint initiative so much you wrote about it.' Hartmann leaned back in his chair, put his hands behind his head. 'I'm happy to share the credit, Kirsten. But the trouble is . . . if there's blame to be apportioned you have to share that too.'

345

He leaned forward, smiled at her, added, 'That's what being accountable means.'

'This is blackmail.'

'No it's not. It's your website, not mine. Your responsibility. A matter of public record. Hang me out to dry and you'll find yourself swinging from the same line. But—'

'Thank you for the coffee,' Eller snarled.

'It was a pleasure. I'll see you tonight. As arranged.'

They watched her go then went back into the main office.

'She didn't like that,' Skovgaard said.

'I don't give a damn whether she liked it or not. I won't take lectures on accountability from some carpetbagging hack who'll climb into bed with anyone who'll have her.'

Morten Weber was at his desk. Hartmann walked over. Weber didn't take his eyes off his computer screen.

'I thought you'd deserted us.'

Weber scanned his inbox. Line after line of messages.

'I get bored on my own.'

Hartmann placed the page from Eller's website in front of him.

'How did you know?'

Weber stared at him as if it were obvious.

'I'd have grabbed the credit if I was running her campaign. You need to think like other people sometimes. It helps.'

'I'm glad you're back, Morten,' Skovgaard said.

He laughed, looked at her.

'Me too.'

Kemal's flat in Østerbro. The forensic team had pored over every inch of every room. All they had were two prints from Nanna Birk Larsen by the front door.

Meyer wanted more.

'Look,' the head forensic guy said. 'We've done everything. That's all there is.'

Lund read through the preliminary reports.

'What about the boots?' Meyer demanded.

'We analysed the mud. It's not from the crime scene.'

'What about the ether? Who the hell keeps ether in the house?'

'People with helicopters.'

One of the team pulled out a model helicopter.

'Boys' toys,' the forensic guy said. 'He likes them. This thing flies on a mixture of oil, paraffin and ether.'

'The neighbours?' Lund asked. 'What do they say?'

'There was a party on the third floor. A tenant saw him take out some rubbish at one thirty in the morning. That's all.'

Lund stared at him. The man wilted.

'Rubbish? At one thirty?'

'That's what he said.'

Twenty minutes later Kemal arrived for the reconstruction. He didn't look like a man expecting to

347

be arrested. Smart jacket, grey scarf. Schoolteacher even on a Sunday.

'She never got much beyond the door?' Lund asked. 'That's what you're saying?'

'I buzzed her in. She rang the bell.'

'And then?'

'She felt guilty about some books I'd lent her.'

'You didn't go inside?'

'No. We talked here. At the door.'

'So why are her prints on a photo in the living room?'

'I was going to sand the floor. All the things were out here. It was the class photo. She looked at it before she left.'

'Why?'

'I don't know. She wanted to for some reason.'

'Then?'

'Then she left.'

'Did you see her out of the building?'

'No. I just closed the door. It's safe here. No reason . . .' He fell silent. 'I thought it was safe.'

'Why did you cancel the floor people?' Meyer asked.

'It was going to be too expensive. I thought I'd do it myself.'

'So you phoned him? At one thirty in the morning?'

'He had an answering machine. Why not?'

Lund checked the door, went in and out again. 'You took a call minutes before Nanna arrived.'

The man's dark eyes flickered between the two of them.

'It was a wrong number. That was when I was at the petrol station.'

Meyer said, 'What? You talk for ninety seconds on a wrong number?'

'Yes . . .' The two of them watched him struggling. 'He wanted to talk to the person who had the number before me.'

'The call came from a launderette just round the corner. Quite a coincidence, huh?'

'I don't know.'

Lund said, 'You threw out some rubbish.'

'On Saturday,' he agreed.

'On Saturday at one thirty in the morning. What was in the black bag?'

'An old rug.'

'A rug?'

'I took it to the bins on my way back to the allotment.'

Silence.

'If that's all . . .'

Silence.

'My wife's coming here soon. I'd like you gone by then.'

'Don't run away,' Meyer told him.

Back at headquarters Buchard listened to their briefing.

'So you don't have a bloody thing?'

'Kemal's lying,' Lund said.

'You found nothing at the flat.'

'He cleaned up. He took her somewhere else.'

The chief was stomping round the office like an angry dog.

'Where? You've checked everything. Flat, car, basement, allotment, youth club—'

'If you feel pressured by Troels Hartmann's campaign, chief,' Lund cut in. 'Do let us know. Only polite.'

Buchard looked ready to explode.

'I don't give a shit about politics. There's nothing here that makes the man a rapist and a murderer.'

'Kemal's lying,' Lund said again. 'He's got to have a place—'

'Then find it,' Buchard ordered.

Kemal's wife was walking round their apartment, looking at the walls covered in crimson fingerprint dust. There were markers everywhere.

He stood in the hall, not following her as she went round turning on the lights in each room, clutching at her big belly, face angry and confused.

'What were they looking for?'

No answer.

'What do they think you did to her?'

'They'll soon see they're wrong.'

'I don't understand why you didn't tell them before.'

He leaned against the wall, didn't meet her eyes.

'I didn't want you to worry.'

He wrapped his arms around her, persisted even when she tried to fight him off.

'I told you I'm sorry. I can't undo what's been done. We—'

She pulled away. Still furious. His phone rang.

'Rama speaking.'

He strode off, out into freshly sanded living room with its bare floorboards and the marks of the police forensic team everywhere.

She hated it when he spoke Arabic. A language she couldn't begin to understand.

Hated it when he got angry too. This was so rare. He was a placid, decent man. Yet as she listened to him, voice rising to a fury in that foreign tongue, she wondered how much she really knew him. How much there was still hidden in his life.

The tap on Kemal's phone caught the loud and angry exchange. Forty minutes later a woman in a cream chador was sitting in front of a computer listening to the phone tap.

Duty translator. She scribbled down the original, looked at it.

'What did he say?' Meyer asked.

'"Keep quiet. Don't go to the police or you'll regret it for the rest of your life."'

'Have you traced it?' Lund asked.

'Landline. Somewhere in the north-west.'

They listened to the tape again. There was a sound in the background. A long cry. He replayed it, slowed down but at the same fidelity. Full volume.

The translator listened, nodding.

'It's Isha,' she said. 'It's the evening prayer.'

Meyer was working on the computer.

'The phone belongs to Mustafa Akkad. No criminal records. Runs a small business renting lock-up garages near Nørreport Station.'

'Tell Svendsen to get Akkad in here,' Lund said as she went for her jacket.

The lock-ups were underneath a flyover. It was a grubby, desolate place. Metal doors covered in graffiti. Rubbish strewn in the lane. Bad drains.

Jansen was outside, blue plastic shoes on his big feet, ginger hair wet in the rain. A team of three technicians were working on the door.

'Only one of the garages isn't rented,' Jansen said. 'We thought we'd start there.'

They pulled on gloves and blue plastic shoe covers. Then the technicians got the padlocks off the door and slid it open.

Meyer was in first, Lund second, torches high in their hands.

In the wandering, searching beams the place looked like nothing but a junk store. Tables, half-dismantled engines, office storage racks, tents, fishing rods, furniture . . .

Lund walked through to the back. Lines of paintings in frames stood along both sides with some model ships and plaster statues.

At the rear of the garage, against the wall that ran parallel with the street, stood several large canvases. Cheap paintings, the kind a restaurant might use for decoration. They were stored oddly. Propped against each other, two frames high. Set at an angle of thirty degrees or so against the brickwork.

Lund looked and thought.

She went up close, removed all four frames. There was a door behind.

Her gloved hands fell on the handle. Unlocked, it opened easily. Lund stayed on the threshold for a moment, checking the interior carefully, looking for a figure trying to hide in the dark.

This place was smaller. More organized too. A couple of metal chairs stood together, nothing on the seats as if they'd been used recently. A lamp stand was next to them, the cable running to a socket in the corner.

Lund's torch checked the walls once more then she stepped inside, ran the beam down to the floor.

A worn, stained double mattress lay there, with a crumpled blue and orange sleeping bag on it next to an ashtray.

Closer. There was a child's teddy bear next to the makeshift bed. She got down, started looking more closely.

'Lund?'

Meyer had walked in and she'd barely noticed.

'Lund?'

She looked. He'd found a girl's yellow zipped top. There was a bloodstain on the front.

It was old and dark and big.

Yellow, she thought. The kind of thing a schoolgirl might wear. Childish even.

★　★　★

One o'clock. Hartmann watched the committee members assembling in the meeting room.

'The vultures are circling, Troels,' Weber said. 'Watch your back.'

'Anything from the police?' Hartmann asked.

'Not a thing.'

'Let's get this done with.'

When he entered they were scattered round the room, talking in fragmented groups.

Cabals and cliques. Every party had them.

Two women, the rest men, mainly middle-aged, in business suits. Long-term party workers.

'This meeting was called with insufficient notice,' Hartmann said, taking a chair at the head of the table. 'So let's keep it short.'

Knud Padde ruffled his curly hair nervously, glanced across the table, said, 'It's short notice, Troels. On the other hand. The situation with the press. The publicity . . .'

'Fine, Knud. Could we get to the point, please?'

'You're the point.'

Morten Weber's prediction was accurate as usual. It was Henrik Bigum who spoke. A lean, unsmiling economics lecturer at the university, bald with the severe, ascetic face of a judgemental priest. Bigum had put himself forward for election to the city council and the Parliament on several occasions. Never got past the short list. An intelligent, committed man, but caustic in private and addicted to scheming.

'Henrik. How nice to hear from you.'

The room was silent, tense.

Hartmann put down his pen, sat back in his chair.

'OK. Let's hear it.'

'We're all very fond of you,' Bigum went on, as if pronouncing a death sentence. 'Appreciative of the work you've done.'

'I hear a but, Henrik.'

'But lately your judgement and your honesty have been called into question.'

'Bullshit. By whom? You?'

'By events. The evidence suggests the teacher's guilty. By not suspending him you give the impression you're protecting the innocent when in fact you're protecting yourself.'

Morten Weber asked, 'Where's this on the agenda?'

'We're beyond agendas. Secondly, Kemal's file wasn't handed over to the police at the outset.'

Bigum looked round the table, addressing the meeting now, not Troels Hartmann.

'Why not? Does Troels have something to hide? Thirdly, confidential information has been leaked from this office. Very private information. Handed to people who can do us harm. We're losing votes. We're losing credibility. Our support in Parliament is fragmented and waning. Does it look as if you have the situation in hand, Troels? Not to me. Not to anyone.'

Hartmann stared at him across the gleaming table, laughed and asked, 'Is that it?'

'What do you mean?'

'I don't expect you to possess the assassin's skills

of Poul Bremer, Henrik. But really . . . You abandoned your students for this?'

'Isn't it true? Everything, about the file, the police, the leaks from this place?'

'No. Everything you say has been taken out of context. These problems are dealt with. You don't need to worry—'

'If Troels doesn't withdraw his candidacy of his own accord,' Bigum interrupted, 'I propose a meeting be called for a vote of confidence.'

'Are you serious?' Hartmann.

'I am.'

'And who would stand in my place?' Hartmann gazed at him, waiting for an answer. 'Do you have any suggestions? I wonder—'

'That we deal with when the need arises. You're destroying what we've worked for—'

'This is not your decision, Henrik!' a lone female voice cried. 'It's not up to you.'

Elisabet Hedegaard, a nursery school teacher from Østebro.

Bigum took a moment to answer. This was an opportunistic stab in the back. Based on hope and the moment.

'It's in the constitution,' he said. 'Knud?'

'According to the regulations,' Padde said, pulling a copy out of his pocket, 'a majority of votes allows it.'

'What about the constituency?' Hedegaard asked. 'They chose Troels in the first place. They have a say.'

An old man Hartmann barely recognized snarled at her, 'We're looking for a solution to the problem, here. Some of us have been working for the party for decades. Not since yesterday . . .'

Hartmann sat back, stayed silent.

'The constituency has a voice,' the woman went on. 'What you suggest will only make matters worse.'

'They can be worse?' Bigum asked. 'We've got a candidate for Lord Mayor who's embroiled in a murder investigation. With leaks from his office. Numerous highly questionable decisions—'

'The constituency—' Hedegaard went on.

'The constituency decides whether Troels is fit to stand as a councillor,' Padde broke in. 'It's up to us to say who leads the campaign.'

'I propose . . .' Henrik Bigum began.

Theis and Pernille Birk Larsen turned up at headquarters just after two. Lund pulled out photos of some of the items from the lock-up. Meyer stood behind her, watching closely.

'I need you to tell me if you recognize any of these things,' she said.

A khaki rucksack.

Nothing.

A red notebook with a distinctive leaf pattern on the cover and a felt-tip pen.

'No,' the mother said.

The mattress with the teddy bear and the blue sleeping bag.

Theis Birk Larsen stared at the items.

Lund looked at him, looked at the photograph. Next to the mattress was a cup half full with orange juice. An uneaten biscuit on a plate. A bowl with the remains of what looked like curry. An ashtray with several stubbed-out cigarettes.

'Nanna didn't smoke,' he said. 'She always nagged me about it.'

Lund passed over a close-up of the teddy bear and a key ring. Two keys, and a plastic design of clover leaves and flowers.

'You've already got her keys, haven't you?' Pernille said.

'We thought there might be a second set.'

'I've never seen any of this.'

Then the yellow top with the bloodstain and a brand logo.

Pernille Birk Larsen's eyes opened wide, never left the photo.

'I think she's got one like that,' she said, still staring at the yellow fabric and the bloodstain on the left side, close to the zip at the waist.

'You're sure?' Lund asked quickly. 'You're absolutely sure?'

'Like it,' Pernille said, nodding.

'Thanks.'

Lund took the photos away.

'Where's he now?' Birk Larsen asked. 'The teacher?'

'He's in custody,' Lund said. 'He's under arrest until we've finished our investigation.'

He got up. Black jacket, red boiler suit.

'What do you know?' Pernille persisted.

'We can't go into details—' Meyer began.

'I'm her mother,' the woman cried. 'I have the right—'

'We can't go into—'

Lund interrupted.

'Apparently she went to his flat after the party. Maybe they had a relationship. We're not sure. She was taken somewhere. Perhaps this place. Then driven out to the woods.'

Meyer was grumbling wordlessly behind her.

'Thanks,' Birk Larsen said.

'Thanks,' the woman echoed.

There was nothing more. They left. Meyer sat in the corner of the office, smoking.

After a while he said, 'Lund?'

She was looking at the photos again. They had a potential ID of an item of clothing. It was the hardest piece of information they possessed.

'Lund?'

She met his gaze. Two days' stubble, big ears, glassy round eyes.

'That,' Meyer said, shaking his miserable head, 'was wrong.'

Buchard listened to Lund's report and shook his head.

'The mother identified the shirt,' Lund said.

'It's a kid's top,' Buchard complained. 'Millions like it. Forensics found nothing to suggest it was Nanna's.'

359

'The blood—'

'We haven't got the results yet.'

'There's enough evidence.'

Meyer watched in silence.

'Like what?' Buchard asked.

'Like a witness who saw Kemal carry something to his car.'

'No,' Buchard said. 'The only evidence you have is an inconclusive phone call.'

'And the fact that he lied!'

'If we charged everyone who lied to us half of Denmark would be in jail. Any judge with half a spine's going to tear us to pieces with this shit. Find Mustafa Akkad. Clear this up one way or the other. Or I'll get someone who can.'

Theis Birk Larsen went out to cost a job for the week ahead. Pernille hung round in the arcades outside police headquarters then, when he'd driven off, talked her way back inside.

She confronted Lund in her office.

'Why haven't you arrested him?'

'We don't have enough evidence.'

'How much do you need?' she yelled. 'You said she was at his flat. At the party. In the garage.'

'We're still looking.'

'And if you don't find more? After everything—'

'I told you,' Lund said. 'We're still working on the case. We're making progress. I understand—'

'Don't tell me you understand.' She stood there rigid, determined, right hand raised, finger wagging, like a teacher, like a mother. 'Don't do that. Do not tell me you understand.'

Back home. Back at the sink, manically washing dishes that didn't need washing, wiping surfaces that were already clean.

He'd returned, sat at the table, saying nothing. In their small quarter of Vesterbro he was a king of a kind. The man the neighbours asked for help when there were problems with tearaways. Even the immigrants would knock on the door sometimes and beg Theis Birk Larsen for advice. When Nanna was tiny, five or six or seven, she'd seized an Indian kid and made the bright-eyed little waif her first boyfriend.

Amir.

Pernille remembered the two of them together, hand in hand, giggling as she rode them down the street in the box of the Christiania trike. Remembered the way Theis dealt with a couple of local thugs who picked on Amir too. Not gently. It wasn't his way. But it worked.

Amir he defended. The boy was still in a picture on the table, in the scarlet box of the Christiania trike.

Nanna . . .

'They'll get him,' he said finally. 'In the end.'

'You know about these things?'

She glared at him as she stacked the plates.

'They never found enough evidence for you, did they? Not for everything . . .'

His face fell, became fierce.

Birk Larsen got up from the table, confronted her.

'Did I fail you? Am I a poor husband?' His eyes were sly again, but full of pain. 'A bad father?'

'I didn't say that. I said you of all people know the police don't find everything they ought to. Don't ask me to believe in them.'

He put his hands on her waist. She wriggled from him.

Birk Larsen cursed, got his leather jacket, put it on.

'I'm going over to the house.'

'Do that.'

She started washing the boys' dishes again.

'Go back to your stupid house and hide.'

'What?'

'It's what you do when things get difficult. Isn't it? Run away.'

She put down the dishes, pulled off her gloves, faced him, discovered a savage thrill in her own courage, found words she'd never dared speak before.

'That's what you did with Nanna.'

'What the hell does that mean?'

'When she wanted to talk. You never had time. Then you'd go. Down into the garage. Down to talk to Vagn. Isn't that right?'

'No.' He took a step towards her. 'It isn't.'

Pernille picked up the plates from the table, tidied them away. The boys were out with Lotte. She was glad of that.

'Why did she have so many secrets? Why didn't we know about her life?'

'Because she was nineteen years old! Did you want your parents knowing what you did then? Besides . . . You two stuck together like glue . . .'

'Because you weren't around.'

A roar like a lion, fury and pain.

'I was working. Paying for her school. Paying for all this. You were the one who let her do what she wanted. Go out at night, come back God knows when, never say who with or why.'

'Not me, not me.'

'Yes you. It didn't bother you at all.'

Tears in her eyes. Anger in her face.

'How can you say that? How *dare* you say that? I couldn't sleep until she was home.'

'That helped.'

'At least I didn't take it out on her.'

'And look where we are now.'

He waved a hand around the empty kitchen.

'Look at this,' Theis Birk Larsen said. 'This . . .'

But she was gone, back into their bedroom, slamming the door behind her.

He ate his sandwiches at his desk. Didn't want to leave the garage. Didn't want to work.

Vagn Skærbæk came in. Black cap, scarlet overalls, usual jaunty walk, silver chain round his neck.

'Rudi and I are going to the house. Are you coming?'

Birk Larsen huddled over the desk and the uneaten food, a cigarette in his fist. He shook his head. 'Is there something I can do, Theis?'

Birk Larsen stubbed out his cigarette in the bread. Skærbæk pulled up a chair, put his elbows on the table.

'You know how much she meant to me, don't you?' he said. 'You and Pernille. The boys. Nanna. You've been my family. I hate seeing all this.'

Birk Larsen watched him.

'It isn't fair, Theis.'

'I don't want to talk about it.'

Skærbæk said, 'OK.'

He didn't leave. Sat there. Waiting.

'What am I supposed to do?' Birk Larsen said eventually.

'I don't know.'

Birk Larsen stood up. A head taller than Skærbæk. A year older. Stronger by far. King of the quarter. Once anyway.

'It never lets you go,' Birk Larsen said.

'What?'

'What you've done. Who you are.'

Birk Larsen nodded at the van keys on the wall.

'Don't go to the house, Vagn,' he said. 'Send Rudi on his own.'

'OK.'

'I've got a better idea,' the big man said.

Svendsen's men found Mustafa Akkad when he walked back to the garages at Nørreport, straight into the arms of the team working there. By five that Sunday he was in an interview room with the woman interpreter. Lund was watching through the door, talking on the phone to Mark, telling him to get something to eat. Meyer came out and she ended the call.

'He won't say a word,' Meyer told her.

'We'll see about that,' she muttered and walked towards the room.

He didn't follow.

She stopped.

'What is it?' Lund asked.

'Are we sure he's involved?'

'Yes. Why?'

'He's got a clean record. He works. He's got four children. He prays five times a day.'

'So what?'

'So something doesn't fit.'

'Oh for Christ's sake. Where did you come from? Are they meant to wear badges or something?'

'There's something wrong! He could have removed all that stuff from the garage if he'd wanted.'

'But he didn't.'

'And he came back. To a murder scene. Please . . .'

'Watch me,' she said and marched into the room.

Akkad was a swarthy man of thirty-five. Leather bomber jacket. Scruffy gleaming black hair. Scared face that looked too young for his age.

Lund sat down, threw some papers on the table, said, 'Here's the thing. If you don't talk I throw you in a cell. With a couple of bikers we picked up pushing dope in Christiania. They're not into integration, Mustafa. Or didn't you know that?'

He suddenly looked worried.

'No language problems then.' She pointed to the door. 'So what is it? The cell? Or you talk? You tell me.'

The interpreter was still translating.

'He doesn't need this,' Lund said. 'Don't translate another word. He talks to me in Danish. Or he goes to meet his new biker friends. Listen.'

Akkad's eyes were on the table.

'Listen!' Lund shrieked in his face. 'The court doesn't care what you promised Kemal. Any more than I do. I can get you served with a deportation order in three days flat. You won't see daylight. We'll bundle you on a plane straight back to the place you came from.'

Finger in his face. That got some attention.

'Straight back, Mustafa. We'll make sure the police meet you at the airport.' She waited a moment. 'How are the police back home? Do they smile at you like we do? Are they nice?'

The translator was interpreting anyway. Lund let her chant on. It helped with the atmosphere.

'After that,' Lund said, speaking over the woman in the burka, 'I visit your wife and kids. Check their papers. See if I can send them after you.'

His face went down into his hands.

'Can you support them from a jail back home? Can they go to school? Go to hospital for free? Pick up benefits when they feel like it while everyone else goes out to work? Or maybe they'll be begging on the streets like everyone else—'

'I work!' he roared.

The armed uniformed cop at the door took a step towards the table.

'I work every hour I can.'

'You speak good Danish too,' Lund said, and folded her arms, sat back as if to listen. 'So why the silence?'

'It's not what you think.'

Meyer pulled up a chair.

'What is it then?' he asked.

Mustafa Akkad shook his head.

'Rama's a good man. You've got to believe me.' He stared at Lund. 'He wouldn't hurt anyone.'

He leaned back in his chair, closed his eyes.

'He just did something stupid.'

'What?' Lund asked.

'I went to his place that Friday night. He knew the girl would be coming by. I said I didn't want anything to do with it.' A shrug. 'But he needed somewhere. When I arrived the girl was hurt. She'd been beaten up. She could hardly walk. We carried her to the car and drove her to my garage. So she could hide from her family. Then I left . . .'

'Her family?' Lund asked. 'What are you talking about?'

'The girl. You keep asking me about the girl. I'm telling you . . . the girl Rama helped.'

'What girl?'

Mustafa Akkad said, very slowly, 'The girl from

his father's congregation. The one you keep asking about. Abu Jamal's daughter. Leyla. They wanted her to marry some guy from home so he could come in here. So she tried to run away.'

'Shit,' Meyer muttered.

'If they found her I don't know what they'd do.' He glared at them. 'Not that you'd be much help. So Rama got her away from them. He hid her in my garage. Then somewhere else on Sunday. I don't know where.'

Meyer swore again then got up and walked out of the room. Lit a cigarette in the dim corridor. Looked down towards the end.

Kemal's wife was there. Big in an old khaki anorak. Phone in hand.

She said, 'Rama didn't come home. Where is he?'

'I don't know. I'm not his babysitter.'

'He went to pick up some shopping. He doesn't answer his phone.'

Lund came to the door, listened.

'I left lots of messages. He never got back to me.' She showed Meyer the phone. 'He always calls.'

Lund walked into Svendsen's office. He was there looking relaxed over a mug of coffee.

'Where's Theis Birk Larsen?' she asked.

'Last I heard he was at home.'

'I told you to keep him under surveillance.'

'Give me a million men and maybe I can do a quarter of what you ask.'

'Find out where he is,' she ordered.

He picked up the coffee mug, toasted her.

At quarter past six the scarlet van drew up by the front door of the deserted warehouse. Skærbæk got out first, looked around.

No one came to this part of the city much on a Sunday night.

Checked right, checked left. Remembered the old days when he and Theis worked the streets. A good team. Good partners too, most of the time.

'Clear,' he said and banged the driver's side. Then he took out the security card, opened the locks, rolled up the folding door, guided him in. Stood back and watched as Birk Larsen edged the vehicle into the half-empty interior.

A train went past. A shriek of a klaxon. Pigeons scattered round the inside of the building, flapped anxiously as they flew to the door.

Skærbæk popped on the lights then rolled the outside door back down.

The old days.

Birk Larsen had brought a sledgehammer with him. Skærbæk a pickaxe handle. Both men stood at the back of the van, swinging them idly, remembering.

'Theis—'

'Keep quiet.'

Skærbæk fell silent. Watched. Wondered.

It was Birk Larsen who walked up to the back, unlocked the doors, threw them open.

The teacher crouched by the racks still pretending to be white.

Smart black jacket. Preppy scarf. Shiny shoes.

Skærbæk had a torch. He shone it in the man's eyes.

Kemal got up, climbed out, opened his arms, looked at both of them.

Half angry, half terrified.

'Listen to me,' the teacher pleaded. 'I haven't done anything. I told you everything I know. I told the police—'

Birk Larsen upturned the sledgehammer, held it by the iron head, swung the shaft round, landed it in his gut.

Kemal went down, shrieking. Birk Larsen got a kick into his head, watched as he rolled round once on the floor, dragged him up by the leather jacket, threw him against the van.

Stood there, next to Skærbæk, waited.

'Your daughter was in my flat for a minute,' Kemal said, wiping the blood from his mouth. 'She brought some books back. Then she left.'

Birk Larsen upturned the sledgehammer, let the iron head hang down to the ground, swinging it like a pendulum.

'There was another girl there that night. Someone I was helping. I couldn't tell you. I couldn't tell the police.'

Skærbæk wiped his nose with his sleeve, banged his pickaxe handle against the van wall.

'I know I should have told you but I couldn't,' Kemal yelled. 'It's the truth.'

Birk Larsen nodded. Looked at Skærbæk.

'Gimme his phone,' he said.

'Theis . . .' Skærbæk began.

'Ring her,' Birk Larsen ordered, handing over the mobile.

The teacher stood by the back of the van, hunched over, rigid, hurting and scared.

'Go on,' Birk Larsen ordered. 'Ring the girl.'

Trembling fingers stabbed at the buttons. Rahman Al Kemal made the call.

As soon as she knew Lund left in her own car. Now she was out on the road, listening to the radio.

Control said, 'We have a possible kidnapping. We're looking for number plate PM 92 010. It's a red van from Birk Larsen's Removals. It left the garage around 6 p.m.'

Meyer was working up a team. She liked being on her own, trying to think.

'Theis Birk Larsen is six foot four tall. About forty-five years old. Exercise caution when approaching him. He may be violent. Apprehend immediately and . . .'

She put her phone headset on, called Meyer.

'What do you know?'

'Where the hell are you? You can't just walk out on me like that.'

'I did.'

'We've got the kidnap negotiators on standby.'

'It's not a kidnap, Meyer. He's going to kill him. What do you know?'

'We found Kemal's car near his house. Looks like there's been a struggle. Birk Larsen took a van.'

She was heading towards Vesterbro. This was Birk Larsen's territory. Surely . . .

'Places,' she demanded. 'Give me places.'

'Where the hell are you?'

'Places!'

He sighed.

'We've checked the garage and the warehouse next door. Trouble is Birk Larsen's got little cubby-holes all round the city.'

'Isn't there a warehouse at Teglholmen?'

There was a big industrial park south of Vesterbro. The closest deserted area in the city to Birk Larsen's home.

She heard the sound of papers being shuffled.

'Yeah but he hasn't used it in six months.'

'What does Pernille say?'

'I brought her in. She won't even speak to me.'

'Ask his best friend Skærbæk. If Theis is going to use anyone he'd pick him.'

'Yeah,' Meyer said. 'I notice things too. Skærbæk's not at home. Both of them have got their mobiles turned off.'

'Shit.'

'He used his credit card at a petrol station on Enghavevej about an hour and a half ago. That's in Vesterbro, three streets from where he lives.'

Lund pulled in to the side of the road. She was near the turning for Vesterbro, by the Fisketorvet shopping centre. Several roads converged here. She could head anywhere in the city.

'Wait,' he ordered. 'OK. We have a call from Kemal's mobile registered in P Knudsens Gade. Let me look at a map.'

She knew where that was.

'He's going south-east to Valby,' Meyer said.

'No,' she said. 'He isn't. I checked the Valby address.'

'For Christ's sake, Lund. Maybe he's taking the motorway. What about Avedore? They've got a depot there.'

She pulled out into the traffic.

'Would he use his own place?'

'My psychic powers fail me. You got any better ideas?'

'Birk Larsen isn't stupid. He knows we have a list of his depots.'

'Yeah!' Meyer yelled. 'They're all we have. Think of something, will you? Damned if I can.'

'Where did you say the call came from?'

'P Knudsens Gade.'

'I'll take a look. Tell the wife she'd better talk to you if she wants to see her husband again.'

'Yeah.'

The street was five minutes away, a broad, double carriageway lined with bare trees, running parallel with the motorway.

Houses and offices. Brightly lit.

Not the place for a killing.

★ ★ ★

Birk Larsen looked at his watch.

Kemal had tried the number repeatedly. Never got through. Now he sat on the ledge of the van door, pressing the buttons, getting nowhere.

'I couldn't give the girl away,' the teacher said, getting more desperate by the minute. 'It was an arranged marriage. You understand? You know what I mean?'

Vagn Skærbæk leaned against the wall, eyes closed, looking bored.

'I couldn't tell anyone. If her parents find her they'll hurt her again.' Kemal hesitated. 'Kill her maybe.'

'And?' Birk Larsen asked, swinging the sledge-hammer from side to side like the pendulum on a clock slowing down to nothing.

'I was afraid they'd come after her. She'd run away from home.'

Skærbæk opened his eyes, looked at him, said, 'You sound like a man digging his own grave.'

'Why hasn't she rung back?' Birk Larsen asked.

'I don't know! How can I know? Nanna came round to return some books. That's the last I saw of her—'

'I said shut up,' Skærbæk yelled, then slapped him round the head.

'There is no girl,' Birk Larsen said. 'You're lying.'

'No! I left her a message. She'll ring back in a minute.'

'Long minute,' Skærbæk moaned.

374

Then the phone rang. Kemal glanced anxiously at the screen. A name: *Leyla*. A number.

He answered, stood up, showed it them.

Birk Larsen came over, took the phone off him. Answered.

A voice.

Gave the phone to Kemal. He tapped the speakerphone. The three of them listened.

'Leyla? This is Rama.'

'Rama?' She sounded sleepy. 'Is that you?'

'Don't be afraid,' he said. 'Everything will be OK.' He cleared his throat. 'I really need your help now, Leyla. I need you to say what happened on the Friday you came to see me.'

Silence.

'Hello?' he said.

'Where are you calling from?'

'Doesn't matter. Do you remember the girl you met? The girl from my school? Her father's with me. It's important you tell him what happened. Tell him she brought me some books—'

'Don't tell her what to say, you idiot!' Skærbæk shouted.

The girl began speaking in Arabic. Kemal answered in the same.

'Hey! Hey! Bin Laden!' Skærbæk screamed. 'This is Denmark. Speak Danish. Don't you understand?'

Birk Larsen snatched the phone, put it to his ear. Said, 'Hello? Hello?'

Looked at the dead phone. Looked at Kemal, eyes bright in the gloom.

One moment.

One decision.

The teacher ran behind the door. Skærbæk screamed and went for him. Hand on the scarlet metal, Kemal rammed it back into his face, grabbed his pickaxe handle, punched it hard into Birk Larsen's chest as the big man came for him.

Ran for his life.

Panting.

Pigeons flapping frightened overhead.

Felt something take his legs from under him.

Down on the ground, chest heaving. Above him in the pale fluorescent light Birk Larsen raised the sledgehammer, swinging the head in a slow and certain arc.

She sat opposite Meyer in the low light of the office.

'Pernille,' he said. 'You have to help us. Kemal didn't kill your daughter. He had nothing to do with it. Theis has kidnapped him. Do you understand—?'

'No,' she cried. 'I don't! First it was that kid Scharndorff. Then the teacher. I don't!'

'If Theis hurts Kemal he'll go to prison. Do you understand that?'

She was quiet for a moment.

'Theis wouldn't hurt him.'

'Really?' Meyer asked.

He picked up the file photos on the desk. The bloodied corpse in Christiania.

'Twenty years ago a drug dealer was murdered.'

She looked at the grim pictures, didn't flinch.

'They thought Theis did it.' Meyer looked at her. 'I guess that was around the time the two of you got together. Did you not suspect—?'

'We're all different when we're young. Then we leave it behind.'

She stared at him.

'Didn't you?'

'Maybe. But this is now and he's making a big mistake.'

She picked up the photos, looked at them, turned them over.

'I told you. He'd never do that.'

'I always thought it was Vagn who came up with the alibis.'

'Screw you.'

'Vagn's with him too. They won't run from this.' He leaned forward in the dim light. 'Help me. Help Theis.'

Slowly, 'He wouldn't do it.'

Sirens outside. Cars setting off into the night.

'I know you lost your daughter. But Kemal's innocent. His wife's about to have a baby. He's a good man. Don't make it worse. You have to help me. I need to know where Theis is.'

Meyer watched her.

Silence.

'We can stay here all night,' he said. 'I've got all the time in the world. Have you?'

She glowered at him. They hated you even when you tried to help, he thought.

'Pern—'

'There's a place he uses sometimes. I don't know why. An abandoned warehouse.'

'What's the address?'

'I can't remember. It's out on Teglholmen. Somewhere.'

Lund drove up and down, looking, looking.

Finally, in the darkness close to the end of the road, she saw a red sign half-hidden behind a wire fence.

Birk Larsen Removals.

The phone rang.

'We're on our way to Teglholmen,' Meyer said. 'He's there somewhere. I've got an armed response unit on the way.'

'There already,' she said.

'What?'

'Birk Larsen's got a lock-up on the industrial estate. The lights are on.'

She gave him the number and a street cross reference.

'I've got Pernille with me,' Meyer said. 'We'll be there in two minutes. Wait for us. Lund? Lund?'

She put the phone in her pocket, got out of the car, shone her torch on the security gates.

Open.

Walked in.

Cold dark night. Thin clouds. Half moon. No wind. No sound or sign of life.

Except for the lights all round the building.

There was a side door covered in graffiti. Open. She went through, shining the torch ahead.

A short corridor. Lights at the end.

A man screamed, the cry loud and liquid, full of agony and fear.

Lund began to run.

He didn't want to kill him. Yet. He wanted to hear. The sledgehammer was gone. Now he had Skærbæk's pickaxe handle, kept swinging it into Kemal's guts and chest and limbs.

There was blood on the floor. One of the man's arms hung crazily broken at the elbow. Birk Larsen swung again, caught him in that dark and handsome face.

Another scream and not a word.

'Theis,' Skærbæk said.

He stood there shuffling from foot to foot, hadn't done a thing except watch and grumble.

Birk Larsen walked around the bloody heap on the floor, thinking of somewhere new to hurt. Kicked Kemal in the head.

'OK, Theis,' Skærbæk said.

Another thrashing blow with the wooden stick, another scream.

'Theis, for God's sake! He's had enough. Maybe . . .'

Birk Larsen glared at him, a fierce and frightening animal expression.

'Maybe what?'

'Maybe he's telling the truth.'

Birk Larsen cursed, swung the handle again, struck Kemal on the ribs.

Went for the sledgehammer.

'Theis!' Skærbæk pleaded.

A voice from the darkness.

'Theis Birk Larsen. This is Sarah Lund.'

Skærbæk found his spine, got between Birk Larsen and the man, said, 'Come on. We're done here.'

'You go running, Vagn,' the big man roared, and with one huge hand tossed him aside like a rag doll, sending him crashing against the van.

The sledgehammer came up, caressed Skærbæk's neck, drew back for a moment.

And then Vagn Skærbæk was gone.

A hand around a bloody neck, dragging Kemal from the ground.

'Sit up,' Birk Larsen ordered. 'Sit up! On your knees.'

The way they were on TV. In the videos of executions. Blindfolded men in faraway places. Waiting for death.

'Theis!' The voice was louder, nearer, higher. 'Stop. Stop now.'

But the heat was in him and the rage. They never abated easily.

He could hear her running across the concrete floor. Looked. In the harsh fluorescent light blue jeans and that black and white jumper.

'Kemal's innocent!' she yelled at him. 'Listen to me. He's nothing to do with it.'

The teacher was on all fours, bloody mouth

dripping gore on the ground. Birk Larsen kicked him hard in the ribs, grabbed his hair.

'I said get up,' he barked, and looked into the bruised and bleeding face.

The head of the hammer stroked Kemal's neck. A single blow. To a kneeling man. Justice.

'Sit up!' he screamed.

In the van's headlights, shadows silhouetted against the wall. This was the right place, the right position. This was the point where the pain came to an end.

Another figure racing from the door.

'Theis! Put down the weapon. He didn't do it.'

The mouthy bug-eyed cop with the big ears.

The hammer. One long, strong swing.

He heard a gun cock, saw out of the corner of his eye the cop called Meyer had a weapon on him now, pointed, ready to go.

A shot. The sound echoed round the empty warehouse like a burst balloon. Birk Larsen blinked, hesitated. Was lost.

Then a third shape. A fawn raincoat. Long hair. A face, the precious face.

Pernille stood next to them, staring at him openmouthed.

This is me, Birk Larsen thought. The me you knew existed even if you never dared ask.

This is me.

The hammer came back one more time.

'Theis!' Meyer yelled, gun out, barrel at him. 'Listen to me. Put the weapon down. I'll shoot you before you touch him. I swear to God.'

Pernille walked past them, straight towards Birk Larsen and the bloody heap on the grimy floor.

'Put it down!' the cop screamed. 'Don't do anything stupid.'

He hesitated and that was time enough. When he was ready again there were three more of them, black pistols pointed at his face.

As if that was enough . . .

But there was Pernille too, a stride away, her pale, pained face caught in the hard light of the bright strips. Pernille gazing at him as if to say: I knew but I never wanted to.

'Theis,' she said. 'Put it down.'

And so he did.

Rie Skovgaard and Morten Weber finished working the phones. Hartmann called a few more people himself. Spoke to police headquarters then, at eight exactly, walked into the meeting.

Knud Padde began.

'It's undesirable but necessary that we take a vote of no confidence against Troels Hartmann. May I—?'

'We're wasting time,' Henrik Bigum said wearily. He looked as if the result had already been declared. 'We all know where this is going.'

'Don't worry, Henrik,' Hartmann said. 'A vote won't be necessary.'

'I'm sorry, Troels. It will. We've decided to do this.'

'If you want I'll withdraw. You don't need to vote.

Except for . . .' He smiled at Bigum. 'Whoever takes my place.'

'No, Troels!' Elisabet Hedegaard protested. 'Why? Why do this? Henrik speaks for himself, always . . .'

'Withdrawal's also an option,' Bigum agreed. 'If that's your choice.'

He took a pen out of his jacket. Offered it to Hartmann.

'You haven't checked your phone, Henrik? No private messages? No tips from Bremer's office? Not even the news?'

Bigum laughed, shook his head.

'I thought you might have done this with a little dignity. Resign and have done with it.'

'I just spoke to the police chief in charge of the Birk Larsen case,' Hartmann said. 'There's new evidence that proves beyond any doubt the teacher's innocent. He's going on TV in a few minutes. If you want to ditch me for defending an innocent man that's your prerogative. What it's going to do for the prospects of my successor—'

'Over to you, Knud,' Bigum bellowed.

Padde sat open-mouthed, unable to decide which way to turn.

'Maybe we should think about this,' he said eventually. 'Not vote now after all. If what Troels says is true we need to know the facts.'

'The facts!' Bigum was furious. 'The facts are Hartmann screwed this up from beginning to end. If you fall for a trick like this . . .'

Hartmann was nursing a cup of coffee. He looked at it. Made them wait.

'I think,' he said, 'we should all sleep on it and talk again in the morning. What's a few hours? Agreed?'

A long silence. Broken only when Henrik Bigum swore, got up, stormed out of the room. Then Elisabet Hedegaard squeezed Hartmann's hand, beamed at him, leaned over, whispered, 'Well done.'

Ten minutes later, alone in his office, in front of the TV.

'It's now evident that Hartmann's role model has been cleared of all suspicion,' the newscaster said.

A reporter was chasing Poul Bremer down a City Hall corridor, shoving a microphone in the mayor's face.

'I'm pleased the case has turned out this way for Hartmann's sake,' Bremer said with no conviction. 'But you saw the way he behaved. He was paralysed by indecision. Troels Hartmann isn't fit to be Lord Mayor. Not up to the job.'

Weber walked in, all smiles for once.

'Lots of people calling, Troels. The press would love to talk to you. Everyone's happy with the outcome.'

Skovgaard was behind him.

'Even in Parliament,' she added. 'People like a winner.'

Kirsten Eller came on the screen, smug outside her office.

'This is a happy moment,' she said. 'It proves

384

Troels Hartmann is a trustworthy alternative to Bremer. That's why we placed our faith in him from the very beginning.'

Hartmann rolled back his head and laughed at the ceiling.

Then he turned off the TV.

'The press,' Skovgaard said.

'I don't want to talk to them till tomorrow. Put out a statement saying I'm glad justice has been done. Morten?'

Weber got out his notepad.

'Step up the poster campaign. Let's focus on our integration policy. Make a point of mentioning the role models. What a success they've been. Oh . . .'

He got his coat, put it on.

'I want another group meeting tomorrow. Don't call anyone till the morning. Tell them then. Say everyone who was here today needs to be there.'

'Short notice,' Weber said.

'Same as they gave me.'

Weber wandered off.

Troels Hartmann got Rie Skovgaard's coat, brought it to her. She looked happier than she had in days. Beautiful too, though exhausted. He worked everyone too hard.

'I'm hungry,' he said. 'And we need to talk.'

Theis Birk Larsen sat in a room with two uniformed officers going through the paperwork. Lund watched from outside with Pernille.

'What happens now?'

'We charge him,' Lund said.

'Where will he go?'

'A holding cell.'

The uniformed men nodded at the big man in the black jacket. He got up, walked out with them.

'When can he come home?'

Lund didn't answer.

'We've got two boys. When can he come home?'

'That depends on the charge.'

'Is he going to jail?'

Lund shrugged.

'This is all your fault, Lund. If it wasn't for you—'

'I'm sorry.'

'Sorry?'

'I'll have a car drive you home. Someone will be in touch after the hearing.'

'That's it?'

'Pernille . . .' She wondered if this was worth saying. Whether it might make a difference. 'We're not special. We're just like you. If people lie to us we think ill of it. We don't know whether their reasons are good or bad. All we know is . . . they're lying.'

Pernille Birk Larsen stood in the Politigården office, rigid with fury.

'You think I'm lying now?'

'I think there's a lot we still don't know.'

She waited.

'Fine,' Pernille said and walked off.

Meyer was at his desk, going through the latest papers.

'The Muslim girl's made a statement.' He looked like a tired schoolboy in his zip-up jerkin and striped T-shirt. 'She confirmed Kemal's alibi. She said it was her top we found. I've spoken to Kemal.'

She was listening, just. Mostly Lund was staring at the photographs on the wall. The car. The canal. The Pentecost Forest.

'The doctors say he'll recover,' Meyer added. 'He doesn't want to press charges.'

'It's not up to him.'

'Can you not do that again, Lund?'

'Do what?'

'Disappear on your own without telling me.'

'Birk Larsen is going to be charged with false imprisonment and grievous bodily harm. For starters.'

Meyer lit a cigarette, blew smoke at the ceiling.

'We did the right thing,' Lund insisted.

'We did nothing. The father's going to prison. Kemal's in hospital. Jesus . . .'

Knock on the door. Svendsen. He looked pleased with himself.

'Buchard wants a meeting with you two in the morning.'

'Thanks for keeping an eye on Birk Larsen,' Lund shot at him. 'Like I asked.'

Svendsen glared at her.

'If you ask for too much, Lund, you get it in alphabetical order. I talked to the chief about that already. He's straight on things.'

'A meeting about what?' Meyer asked.

Svendsen laughed.

'The commissioner's going to rip him apart tonight. I guess he wants to pass on some of the pain. Goodnight. Sleep tight.'

He closed the door behind him.

Meyer sat there looking shocked and worried, his big ears moving backwards and forwards as he chewed on some gum. Any other time it would have looked comical.

Lund kept peering at the photos on the wall.

'I'm not taking the fall for this,' Meyer said. He got up, got his jacket. 'I refuse.'

She was glad when he was gone. It was easier being alone.

Back to the photos. Nanna Birk Larsen. Nineteen years old though she could easily pass for twenty-two or -three. Curly blonde hair. Good with her make-up. Smiling at the camera easily, confidently. Not like a teenager at all.

They still didn't know this girl. Something was missing.

Lund went for her things, mumbled goodnight, walked off into the corridor.

Footsteps behind her. Meyer running, panting, wild-eyed.

'Lund,' he said. 'I'm sorry.'

'About what?'

'There's been an accident.'

CHAPTER 6

Monday, 10th November

She slept in a chair by the bed in his hospital room. Bengt had a bandage round his head, a drip in his right arm, a cast on his left.

He didn't wake up. Not even when she came close to his face and whispered his name.

When the morning light began to filter through the dusty windows Lund looked around. They'd brought some of the things he'd had with him in the car when he crashed on the way to the bridge to Malmo͏̈.

A coat. A scarf and sweater.

A black leather briefcase. Some papers were sticking out of the top. They had the police stamp on them.

Lund checked him. Still sleeping. Then she began to look through the documents.

The file was thick, full of official reports. Autopsies and crime details. Photos and forensic material.

She sat down, spread them out on the floor in front of her, began to go through them one by one.

A voice broke her concentration.

'You're right,' Bengt said in a pained, croaky voice. 'He's done it before.'

Lund put the papers to one side, came and stood over him.

'How are you feeling?'

He didn't answer.

'They said you had concussion and a broken arm. The car's a write-off. You were lucky.'

'Lucky?'

'Yes. Lucky. You hadn't slept in a day . . .'

'I was so pissed off with you.'

She didn't say anything.

'I decided to drive home. I'd had enough. Jesus . . .'

Lund wondered if she was about to cry. Her eyes pricked. Her mind was wandering.

'I don't know why I'm like this,' she said softly. 'I'm sorry. I can't help myself. Sometimes . . .'

Bengt's hand came out and took hers. Fingers entwined. Warmth. Closeness.

'I read the file. It wasn't a crime of passion. It wasn't the usual.'

'We can talk about this later,' she said, and wondered if she meant it.

'Maybe he has a kind of method,' Bengt went on, eyes closed, thinking.

'We looked at that. We can't find any links to anything earlier.'

'That doesn't mean they're not there. He dumped Nanna in the water. You saw what it was like. Wild.

Remote. There are probably more you don't know about.'

'Later, Bengt.'

'No.' His voice sounded cross, his eyes were open and flashing. 'Not later. You don't know what that word means. I'm telling you. It turns him on that only he and the girl know how and where it ends. To him that's intimacy. Like a love affair.'

'Later,' she said and turned on the TV.

They watched the news together. Buchard had put out a statement clearing Kemal. He'd been a suspect through a tragic coincidence, the chief said. Nothing about how the police had been misled.

That was the way of things. You were either right and a hero or wrong and a villain. There was no halfway house, no grey area. Not in the eyes of the media. Black and white. Nowhere else.

Same in politics, she thought, watching the rerun of Hartmann and Bremer bickering in a clip from their earlier debate on TV.

Nothing was different in their words, their gestures, their expressions. But before it was Bremer who seemed to have the upper hand, his sense of superiority obvious, the hint of victory in his eyes. Now that identical interview had a different, opposing tone. Bremer's statesmanship seemed smug and superficial. Hartmann's incautious and seemingly unwise defence of the teacher appeared brave and farsighted.

It was the context that made the difference. But

to understand the context one needed facts, waypoints, fixed positions from which to judge perspectives.

All of which the Birk Larsen case lacked.

'They said I can leave later today,' he said, switching off the news.

'I'll talk to my mother. We can move in with her.'

'You don't need to go to the trouble. I'm going home to Sweden.'

A flicker of something that might have been panic.

'Why?' Lund asked.

'You're busy. We've got workmen in the house. Your mother would find it odd.'

He closed his eyes for a moment. She looked at the bruising on his face. Wondered how long it would take to disappear.

'There's no shame in being wrong,' he said.

'Do you want some water?'

She got up. His hand reached out to stop her.

Bengt looked at her and said, 'Don't worry. You'll find him. Be patient.'

Lund sat on the edge of the bed.

'What if we don't?'

'You will.'

'We're at a dead end. I don't have any more ideas.'

'They're there. Keep going. What do you know for certain?'

'Nothing.'

'Stop this, Sarah. You know that's not true.'

'OK. On Friday the thirty-first of October Nanna Birk Larsen goes to a party at her high school. Earlier the same day a driver delivers campaign material for Troels Hartmann there.'

Lund got up, walked round the room, trying to think this through.

'The driver feels unwell. He loses the car keys and goes to hospital. About nine thirty Nanna leaves the party on her bicycle. Someone found the car keys and followed her.'

'Wait, wait,' Bengt interrupted. 'Stop there. This can't be spontaneous. He didn't just happen upon the keys and commit a crime.'

She shook her head.

'He must have.'

'He's not impulsive. He plans his actions and then he covers them up.'

'Bengt! The car was outside the school. That's what happened. No one could have known the driver was going to be taken ill.'

'It doesn't fit the profile I came up with.'

'What if your profile's wrong? I know you're trying to help but . . . what if everything's wrong? The way we're trying to see this. The idea there's a pattern. Some kind of logic.'

Lund got herself some water.

'A nineteen-year-old girl is snatched and held and raped repeatedly. Horribly. There's a kind of logic usually. But this . . .'

'Forget what you know. Forget everything I told you. Go back to the beginning. Then go back further. There's a method here, Sarah. A way of working he's established in his own mind.'

She waited.

'The scissors, the soap, the ritual . . .' He shook his head. 'I can't believe Nanna was the first. Go back further. Until you find something.'

'Further,' Lund whispered.

Out in the Kalvebod Fælled by the Pentecost Forest. A black shape emerging from the water. An eel slithering over a dead girl's naked limbs.

Events had shaped everything that came after. Events had stolen her head.

She kissed him carefully on the cheek, avoiding the bruises, then with a brief word of thanks she left.

The black Ford was stored in a garage used by the forensic department. It was in the basement of the headquarters, reached by a ramp that led to the yard by the prison where Theis Birk Larsen was now in custody.

The vehicle looked grubbier now it was dry. Mud-stained and covered in leaves. All the doors open and up on a ramp.

The forensic technician got her the current reports as Lund turned on the huge vertical fluorescent tubes that surrounded the car. Numbered markers were stuck everywhere, on the windows, on the doors, on the floorpan.

She looked at the paperwork. Nothing new.

Lund took off her jacket, walked round with the duty officer.

There was a sad chalk outline in the boot where Nanna was found. She felt she'd looked at it a million times. Lund pulled on some throwaway plastic gloves, sat in the driver's seat, the passenger's. Checked the mirrors, the glovebox, the door compartments. Sat in the back, did the same.

The man stayed on a bench outside watching her, bored.

She got him to raise the thing, checked underneath. Mud and sticks from the canal. Nothing else.

'Like I said,' he told her. 'There's not a thing on it. He got everything out from the inside. The water did the rest.'

He finished his coffee, threw the plastic mug into a bin.

'I've been here all night looking. You're wasting your time. There's nothing new.'

She went back to the paperwork.

'I promised my wife I'd remind her what I looked like,' the man said, pulling on his jacket. 'Is that OK?'

Lund had the tech report in front of her.

'It says here there were fifty-two litres of petrol in the tank when the car was found. Are you sure of that?'

He sighed.

'Yes. It was five or six litres short of a full tank.'

'You're sure?'

'I'm sure. Turn the lights off when you're done. Bye.'

'You're sure?' she shouted as he left.

'How many times—?'

'This is important. Could you have made a mistake? It was in the water—'

'No, no mistake. We checked that car over a thousand times. Five or six litres short of a full tank. Where's the problem? What did we do wrong?'

'I didn't say you did anything wrong.' She waved a document from City Hall at him. 'According to the logs the tank was last filled a week earlier. If that's the case it should be almost empty.'

He came over, looked at the log.

'Oh. I'm sorry. We should have . . .'

'So who filled it up?' Lund wondered.

It was sunny though grey clouds were gathering. Meyer was waiting for her in the yard outside forensics. He wore a shiny leather jacket she'd never seen before and fashionable shades.

Cool, she thought. He belonged in narcotics or robbery or the gang squad. Not murder. He took it personally. That was always a mistake.

'How's Bengt?' Meyer asked as he handed her a cup of coffee.

'What?'

'How . . . ?'

'Yes.'

'And you?'

'We need to check for young women who've disappeared in the last ten years.'

'Because?'

'In the city. All over the country. See if anything links to the Kalvebod Fælled. Or anywhere in Vestamager.'

Meyer took off his sunglasses and looked at her.

'How's Bengt? How are you?'

'I told you.'

'No you didn't.'

'He's fine. Can we get to work now?'

They had a room for lawyers' meetings in the main block of the Politigården, near the court. The woman was called Lis Gamborg. Birk Larsen looked at her smart business suit, her pearl necklace, her immaculate hair and wondered how he was going to pay for this.

He was in a prisoner's blue suit, unshaven, dirty, hungry.

'Take a seat,' she said.

A guard stood and watched, a handgun on his belt.

It looked bright outside the barred window.

'I'm your court-appointed lawyer. It's very busy today. We won't get a hearing for a few hours.'

He sat twiddling his thumbs, barely listening. Two decades ago, when he married Pernille, Birk Larsen had promised himself he'd never be in this situation again. Not that he mentioned this to Pernille. It was part of an unspoken pact between them. He would be a different man. No more tangles with the law. No more skipping dates for reasons he'd never reveal to her. He was young then. Angry and determined to mark his place in the world, with his strength, with his fists if need be.

Then along came family and he tried to forget what he once was. Buried young Theis. Tough Theis. Theis the thug who would never be needed again.

'Still,' she went on, 'that gives us time to talk about your case.'

'What's there to talk about?'

'The prosecution are going to charge you with attempted manslaughter, false imprisonment and grievous bodily harm.'

Birk Larsen closed his eyes.

He had to say something. Had to ask.

'How's the teacher?'

She kept looking at him as if he were a specimen. A zoo animal trapped in a cage.

'He'll recover. He says he won't press charges.'

Birk Larsen watched her.

'That's not enough. It won't get you acquitted. Not on charges like this.'

'The police told us it was him. The papers said it was him. No one did a damned thing.'

She took a deep breath.

'The judge may think there are some mitigating circumstances.'

'I'll plead guilty. Just tell me what to say.'

He didn't want to utter the words for fear of the answer that was coming.

'I just want to go home to my family.'

She said nothing.

'I need to go home.'

'I understand. In the circumstances we should hope for leniency.'

She put her slender hands together, leaned over the table, looked into his face.

'I'll try to convince the judge that you don't need to stay in custody. You've confessed. You came in willingly. You're not going to flee. You've got a family. A business to run—'

'I'd like to talk to my wife.'

The lawyer shook her head.

'You have to wait until after the hearing.'

His head went down.

'I'm sorry,' she added. 'Your friend? Vagn?'

'Vagn had nothing to do with this. He tried to stop me. Don't involve him.'

'He is involved. He's charged as an accessory.'

'That's not right!'

'It's a minor charge. He's free. I don't think . . .'

He waited.

'Don't think what?'

'He won't go to jail. I wish I could promise the same for you.'

Silence.

'Any questions?' she asked.

When he didn't answer she looked at the guard.

Part of the process. Part of a system that almost swallowed him once before. Theis Birk Larsen was back in the belly of a beast he hated, and that hated him. With no one to blame but himself.

Pernille was manning the phones. Lotte had arrived to help. Their usual luck. Every minute a customer was on the line demanding something straight away.

'I can't do that right now,' Pernille said to the latest. 'Let me get back to you. I will. I promise.'

Lotte waited until she put down the phone then asked, 'What's he going to be charged with?'

Another call.

'Birk Larsen's Removals. Please wait a moment.'

Hand over the mouthpiece.

'I don't know. Can you look after the boys for a while?'

'Sure. What did Theis do?'

Pernille went back to the phone and made excuses.

Lotte was still there, getting cross.

'He did something to that teacher, didn't he?'

'It's all my fault. I pushed him.'

Her hand ran through her straggly hair. She looked a mess and didn't care.

She looked at the appointments, wondered how all this was done.

One of the men came in asking for instructions. Pernille did her best. The phone went. Lotte answered.

'Do the job in Østerbro first,' she told him. 'Do it the way Theis would do it. Ask Vagn.'

He stared at her.

'Where's Vagn?' she asked.

'I dunno.'

'Just . . .' She waved a hand at him. 'Just do what you think. I'm sorry . . .'

'Pernille?'

Lotte had waited till he was gone.

'What?'

'The bank called when you were out. They said they need to talk to you.'

Buchard wore his best shirt, freshly pressed. Best suit. The uniform for a lecture from the commissioner.

He was straight from that and hurting.

Bent over that morning's papers, reading them in the grey light streaming through the window of Lund's office. Downturned mouth, shaking head.

Saying plenty without speaking a word.

Lund and Meyer sat next to one another, fidgeting like naughty children brought before the teacher.

Meyer broke the silence.

'We realize things haven't gone as well as they should.'

Buchard said nothing, just showed them another headline: 'Hartmann's Role Model Cleared'.

'If Kemal had told us the truth . . .' Lund started.

Buchard shut her up with a single caustic glance.

'I told you our working relationship wasn't the

best,' Meyer added. 'Not that I'm kind of blaming anyone.'

'Kemal lied!' Lund said again. 'He had every opportunity to clear himself and didn't. If he'd—'

Buchard waved the paper at her again.

'All people see is this,' he snarled. 'Not your excuses.' A pause. 'The commissioner wants you off the case. We don't need this kind of coverage. Getting caught up in an election campaign . . . it's embarrassing. And now the father's charged with manslaughter.'

'Kemal doesn't want him prosecuted!' Meyer cried. 'Doesn't that mean anything?'

'It's up to the lawyers, not him. You screwed up, both of you.'

They stared at the carpet.

'Give me one good reason why I shouldn't kick you out of here right now?'

'Just the one?' Lund said straight off. 'I could give you . . .'

'Start then.'

'We know more about this than anyone. Bring in a new team and they'll take a week to go through the papers.'

'I'd rather wait a week and get it straight than have you two bringing the commissioner down on my head again.'

'We know more than we did yesterday.'

'I've got an appointment at the school,' Meyer added. 'I can clear things there. We'll bring this under control. Lund's right. Get someone else and they'll be starting from scratch.'

Buchard thought for a long moment.

'If this case is still going nowhere tomorrow you're off it. Both of you.'

He stood up, headed for the door.

'Stay well away from the Rådhus. And Troels Hartmann. I don't want any more shit from that direction. Understood?'

'Sure,' Meyer said.

Buchard left. Lund sat silent, thinking, arms tightly folded over her black and white sweater.

Meyer went out into the corridor, talked to the day team.

'We need to get this back on track,' he ordered. 'Go back to the school. Talk to everyone. Workmen, cleaners. Everyone.'

Lund got up and started going through the evidence bags, found the one she wanted.

'Get Nanna's picture out to all the taxi drivers,' Meyer said.

'We did that already,' Svendsen moaned.

Meyer turned on him.

'Every driver? Every last one in Copenhagen? No. I didn't think so. See who was working near Kemal's flat. Find out if she took a taxi from there. Anything!'

He came back into the office, grumbling.

'Jesus. How hard can it be?'

She had the City Hall vehicle logbook open.

'Send a photo of the car to all the petrol stations

403

in the city,' Lund said. 'Ask if they saw it on the evening of October the thirty-first.'

'Why?'

'We missed something.'

She passed him the logbook.

'According to this there shouldn't have been much petrol left in the car. The tank's almost full. If he went to a petrol station—'

'He'll be on a surveillance tape. Yes. I know. I'm not stupid.'

'Good! Let's start with the petrol stations near Nanna's school.'

'Lund. If you were driving a stolen car with a kidnapped girl in the boot would you fill the car up yourself? The log might be inaccurate.'

She nodded.

'You could be right. Check it out with the security people at the Rådhus.'

Meyer laughed.

'Oh! Good joke! You heard what Buchard said. He'll have my balls if I go near that place.'

She stared at him. Hands on hips. Bright wide eyes. Expectant. Dogged.

'Don't look at me like that,' Meyer complained. 'I don't like it.'

She didn't move an inch.

'I'm not going to City Hall, Lund. That's that. You do what you want. I am *not* going.'

He went back towards the corridor.

'You told the father you'd find whoever did this, Meyer.'

He stopped, turned, scowled at her.

'Was that just something to say?'

'I also told my wife I'd hold down a job for more than three weeks. Which do you think matters most?'

She started saying something.

'No,' Meyer cut in. 'Not a word. I know the answer. Really. No need.'

Same people, same room. Yet everything now was different. The group meeting was beginning and the tension of the night before had vanished. Smiling, joking, acting as if nothing had happened at all they sat waiting, Knud Padde beaming more broadly than the rest.

He'd been on the phone to Rie Skovgaard already. Wondering what the available committee places were. Angling for promotion.

Troels Hartmann sat at the head of the table next to Elisabet Hedegaard. The rest picked at croissants and pastries. He stuck to a single cup of coffee.

'Good morning,' Hartmann said and went through all the polite preliminaries. Thanks for their attendance. Apologies for the short notice.

Bigum sat at the far end of the table, slumped in his chair, trying to smile.

'There's no need for this to be long,' Hartmann began.

'Troels.'

It was Bigum. The smile looked ever more forced.

'Please. I would like to speak for a moment.'

Hartmann acted surprised.

'Of course, Henrik. If you wish.'

Bigum took a deep breath.

'I owe you all an apology. For the unfortunate course of events.'

No one spoke.

'It's been difficult for all of us.'

Padde had seated himself next to Elisabet Hedegaard who stared at Bigum, hand on her chin.

'I hope we all realize our disagreements only came about because of a mutual concern for the welfare of the party.' Henrik Bigum glanced at Hartmann. 'Nothing else, Troels. Nothing personal. So . . .'

An attempt at laughter. A deferential pass of the right hand.

'I'd like us all to bury the hatchet and move forward.'

'Thank you, Henrik,' Hartmann said with good grace.

'It's a pleas—'

'But you were right. This can't go on.'

Bigum squirmed on his seat.

'Troels. There's really no reason for you to withdraw now. The constituency and the group are behind you. Your stand on the role model—'

'Yes, yes, yes.' Hartmann waved him down. 'Don't worry. I'm not withdrawing.' He looked at each of them in turn, smile set to modest and

406

self-effacing. 'Don't panic. Our common goal is to change the system here at City Hall. Right?'

They nodded, Bigum more vigorously than anyone else.

Hartmann rapped a finger on the table.

'We can't do this if we're fighting amongst ourselves.'

An approving murmur.

Hartmann played the crowd.

'I can't hear you!' He laughed. 'Am I right?'

Louder this time, and Henrik Bigum laughed too, said, 'You're right, Troels. You were right all along.'

Hartmann gazed at him the length of the shiny committee table.

'I know, Henrik. So I'm giving you the same choice you gave me yesterday.'

Bigum's smile froze.

'I'm sorry?'

Hartmann's face had changed again. Serious. The expression he used when facing Bremer.

'Either you step down . . .' He paused. 'Or we take a vote on it.'

Bigum shook his head.

'What?'

The room was silent. Hartmann had kept Weber out of this. He never liked conflict. Rie Skovgaard, standing close to the table, smiling, expectant, had worked the phones from six that morning. They knew precisely where he stood.

Bigum was getting angry.

'This is absurd. I've worked for this party for twenty years. As long as you, Troels. I was only acting in our best interest.'

'You went to Bremer, Henrik. You offered him a pact.'

The lecturer's bony, ascetic face flushed.

'I wanted to gauge opinion. Nothing more. We won't win outright. There are compromises to be made—'

'What's it to be, Henrik? Your resignation or a vote?'

Bigum looked at each of them. No one met his eyes. Not even Padde.

'I see.'

He got up, leaned across the table, glowered at Hartmann, said, 'Fuck you, Troels. You'll never be Lord Mayor. You haven't got the . . . the . . .'

'Stomach?' Hartmann asked.

Rie Skovgaard opened the door, smiling brightly.

'Fuck you all,' Bigum muttered and left.

Hartmann folded his arms and sat back in his chair.

Finally, Knud Padde said, 'Well. That's that. As chairman I will now give the floor to Troels.'

Hartmann got the coffee pot and poured himself another cup.

'That goes for you too, Knud. On your way.'

Padde laughed like a nervous child.

'Oh come on, Troels. I know I screwed up. But I worked hard for the party. I'm a loyal . . .'

Hartmann took a sip of his coffee.

408

'You're out,' he said, nothing more.

No one looked at him. No one uttered a word.

Skovgaard had the door open again, still smiling.

'That's why you dragged me here?' Padde said. 'To humiliate me?'

'Knud,' Skovgaard called, knocking on the door with her knuckles. 'We've a meeting to start. Please . . .'

He mumbled the first curse Hartmann had ever heard him utter then shambled out.

'Good,' Hartmann declared brightly. 'Let's get on with it.'

He beamed at the faces around the table. They were his now. No one else's.

'Elisabet. You'll take over from Knud as chair. Is that OK?'

She nodded, smiled.

'Now I'd like you to meet two new people.'

Skovgaard called out into the corridor.

'Sanjay? Deepika? Will you come this way?'

A young man and a young woman. Asian. Smartly dressed, professional. Straight from the role model programme.

'You may know Sanjay and Deepika from our youth organization,' Hartmann announced. 'Have a seat. Welcome. They're our two new group committee members.'

He waited. Then asked, 'Are there any questions?'

There were none.

★　★　★

Halfway through the meeting Hartmann came out to ask for some photocopies. Morten Weber and Rie Skovgaard were bickering over the machine.

'You never told me the knives were coming out,' Weber complained.

'You wouldn't have liked it.'

'This isn't a good time to start sacking people.'

'They asked for it, Morten,' Skovgaard said. 'How can we have a snake like Bigum sitting amongst us?'

'And Knud?' Weber asked. 'What did he do except behave the way he always did? Bending with the wind?'

'Knud's an example,' Hartmann answered.

Weber opened his mouth, in mock amazement.

'An example? Am I really hearing this from Saint Troels? Since when did you learn to wield daggers in the night?'

'Since I wanted to bring down Poul Bremer. They're gone. That's it.'

He slapped some papers on the machine.

'I want copies of these and some more coffee.'

'Get your own damned coffee! Bigum won't take this lying down. He'll cause shit for you in the party.'

'Listen, Morten,' Hartmann told him. 'We've been the nice guys too long. On the defensive. I had to act. I had to show I could be strong.'

'You did that. I hope you talked it over with Kirsten Eller. Bigum was close to her in case you didn't know.'

Nothing.

'Oh,' Weber snapped. 'You didn't. If you'd asked . . .'

Hartmann fought to keep his temper.

'I'll deal with Kirsten. You don't need to worry about that.'

'The problem,' said the bank manager, 'is you're paying for two places.'

He'd come to the depot to see her. Sat in the office, face a mix of shame and anger. She wanted to ask him: why now? Didn't he read the papers? Couldn't he see this wasn't the time?

But he was a bank manager. A man in a smart suit. Doubtless with a big house in one of the fancier suburbs. It was his job to chase small, struggling businesses in Vesterbro. Circumstances didn't matter. Only kroner in the bank.

'It won't go on for long.'

'It can't. You don't have the finances to sustain it. So . . .'

'So what?'

'When will you be able to sell the house?'

One of the men came through the door and said, 'The tail lift on the big truck's stuck.'

What would Theis do? What would Vagn say?

'Make two trips with the little one. We can't cancel.'

'If we do that the next job's late.'

She looked at him, said nothing. He left.

'I can put your loan on hold,' the bank manager

411

said. 'That means you skip this month's payment. But . . .'

She was thinking about trucks and jobs and appointments. Work hard enough and the money came in. That was what Theis always said.

'Pernille? You've got a big overdraft. There's the cost of the funeral. We need some kind of—'

'Money?' she asked. 'Collateral?' She looked around at the office, the depot, the men outside. 'All this is yours anyway. What else can I offer?'

'You need a plan. Otherwise . . .'

'Theis will be home soon,' she said firmly. 'He'll find a solution. He always does.'

'Pernille . . .'

'You can wait till Theis comes, can't you? Or do you want to serve papers at the cemetery when I put Nanna's urn in the earth?'

He didn't like that. It was, she thought, a cruel thing to say.

'I'm trying to help.'

Her phone was ringing.

'You'll get your money. Excuse me. I have to take this.'

It was Theis, calling from the jail.

She went out into a quiet corner of the garage to talk.

'Hi.'

'Are you OK, Theis?'

'Yeah.'

She tried to picture him there. Had they put

412

him in uniform? Did he get enough to eat? Would there be an argument? His temper . . .

'How are the boys?'

He sounded old and broken.

'They're fine. Waiting for you to come home.'

There was a long, asthmatic breath on the line, then he said, 'I won't be coming home today.'

'When will they let you out?'

'They want to keep me in custody.'

A couple of the workers were staring at one of the trucks. There was a problem there as well.

'For how long?'

'A week today I go back to court. Maybe then.'

She couldn't think of a thing to say.

'I'm sorry about . . .'

She'd never seen him cry. Not even when his mother died. Everything about Theis happened inside, hidden, trapped in silence. The emotions were there. She'd learned to feel them, to sense them. Never expected to see them made plain.

'I have to go now, love,' he said.

She was choking back the tears, for him, for her, for Nanna and the boys. For all the sad grey world.

Pernille had no words either and this seemed the worst thing, the greatest sin of all.

'Bye,' he said and then was gone.

Lund went to the brown-brick fortress that was the Rådhus, found the place in the basement that dealt with the cars. Stood there in her black coat, jeans and woollen sweater dealing with a tetchy old man in uniform who thought he had better things to do.

The parking garage was dealt with by a security office situated near the exit. There was a glass screen between the man and her, for reasons she couldn't begin to fathom. CCTV screens covered the building, the prison-like halls of the council quarters, the civil servants' offices, the basement, the garage.

'We're busy,' the security man said.

'This won't take long. I need to understand how your system works.'

He looked as if he'd worked here since the place was built a century or so ago. An unsmiling man of about sixty-five, half-moon spectacles he liked to fiddle with, bald with a fringe of silver hair. Self-important in his official blue jumper as if the city crest, three gold towers rising from the water, were a badge of office. More interested in his keys and cameras and pigeonholes than looking at the people around him.

'It's a garage,' he said. 'What do you expect? They hand in the keys once they've parked. They pick them up when they leave.'

There was a board behind him. Full of key rings. A driver came and asked for a car. The man got up, stretched out the half-moon glasses with his left hand so he could read the numbers. A long way. To the end of his sharp nose.

'You need to see an optician,' she said trying to be friendly.

He handed the driver a set, glared at her, sat down, said nothing.

'So the key to the stolen car should have been hanging there?'

'If it hadn't been stolen.'

'Who's responsible for filling up the cars?'

'Whoever's driving them, I guess. I don't deal with that side of things.'

'And is that always entered in the log?'

He didn't like that question.

'I can't speak for the electoral candidates. Talk to them.'

Lund hesitated, looked at him. Stood where she was.

'I'm talking to you.'

Then she walked into his office, placed the vehicle log in front of him.

'This is the log we took from here. Explain it to me. Does it mean no one filled the car?'

'You're supposed to stay outside the glass.'

'You're a city employee. You're supposed to help the police. Tell me about the log.'

'Doesn't mean a thing,' the man said. 'Drivers don't fill them in straight away. They wait till they've got time. Sometimes they don't fill them in at all.'

He peered at the entries.

'This driver never came back here. So he never filled in the log. Where's the surprise? Can I go back to my work now?'

He messed with his glasses again, peered at her.

'Unless you have some more questions?'

She walked out of the office, went to the door. Looked outside at the monochrome winter day.

No one helped the police much. They were an enemy of a kind. Even in the bowels of City Hall.

Lund went back and stood outside the glass as she was supposed to. He was still fidgeting with his spectacles, nervously it seemed to her.

'How do the drivers pay for petrol?'

He pressed the button for his mike.

'What?'

'How do the drivers pay for petrol?'

He thought about this.

'There's a charge card in the car. Look. This isn't anything to do with us—'

'We didn't find any charge card. What kind is it?'

'I don't know. We're security. We don't handle money. Now if you'll excuse—'

'I understand that. But you can look it up. See which petrol stations they usually use.'

'You want me to look it up?'

'Yes.' She smiled. 'And then I'll let you get back to work.'

He sat on his little seat, miserable pale face, fingers playing with his glasses.

'I promise,' she said.

The details were in a book in front of him. He scribbled on a piece of paper and passed them under the glass.

'Anything else?' he asked.

'Not right now, thanks.'

★　★　★

416

Meyer and his men were at the school wearing hard hats, looking at the building site that was to become the new wing.

'Talk to all the workers,' he ordered. 'Find out what time they arrived. When they left. Anything they saw. When you've done that talk to the cleaners. After that—'

His phone rang.

Lund.

'Are you coming to the school or what? We've got plenty to do here.'

'There was a charge card for the car. I don't have the card but I've got the number.'

A pause. The sound of traffic. He could see her juggling the phone, some papers, trying to drive, all at the same time.

'That Friday it was used at seven twenty-one in the evening. Petrol station on Nyropsgade.'

'Where?'

'Two minutes from City Hall.'

Meyer said nothing.

'We'll get hold of the surveillance tapes,' Lund said.

'We should do what Buchard tells us.'

She didn't answer.

'Can't you do this on your own?' he asked, and felt bad the moment he'd said it.

'Sure,' she replied in that lilting sing-song tone she could turn on and off at will. 'If you like.'

Then she was gone.

The men were looking at him.

Meyer threw the nearest his hard hat.

'You know what you need to do,' he said.

'Going somewhere?' the man asked.

'I'll be back at headquarters if you need me.'

The days were shortening. It was dark just after four.

Pernille Birk Larsen found herself alone in the office, fending off phone calls from irate customers, the media, strangers with odd offers of help.

The bank manager had been on the phone asking for financial information. So she'd been forced to find the key to Theis's private files to look for some missing bank statements. There was a picture in there: Theis and Nanna. Probably taken just a few weeks before, she guessed. He wore his black woollen hat and the guileless smile she loved. Nanna was beautiful, arm round her father's shoulders as if protecting him. Not the other way round. The way it was supposed to be.

She turned it over. A scribble on the back in Nanna's handwriting: *Love you!*

Pernille had never seen this photo. One more secret of Nanna's. And her father's. Nanna was always messing around in places she wasn't allowed. She took Pernille's clothes sometimes without asking. Hunted in other people's drawers for things she might want. It caused an argument from time to time. Never a serious one. They didn't have those. In some ways she wondered if they ever really connected with Nanna at all. Perhaps

418

that was the inevitable distance brought about by her death. Perhaps . . .

Nanna was a curious kid, always looking for something new. Maybe she looked down here at Theis's private things too.

He wouldn't like that, Pernille thought. There was a side to him he wanted to keep to himself. She'd seen it the previous night. A huge, savage figure holding a sledgehammer over a bleeding figure on the floor of that distant warehouse. A man she loved, one she scarcely recognized at that moment.

A noise in the darkness of the garage made her jump. Vagn Skærbæk came out of the shadows. He looked guilty, furtive. There was a cut on his face and some bruising.

'Hi,' he said.

She put the photo away, looked up at him. Could think of nothing to say.

He stood hunched in his scarlet overalls, black woollen hat. The little brother. They'd known each other before she met Theis. Before she took the risk, felt the thrill of being with a man like him. The silver chain glittered at Skærbæk's neck.

'It was my idea,' Skærbæk said. 'Blame me. Not him.'

Pernille closed her eyes briefly, went back to the papers.

'Is he still inside?'

There was a pile of invoices. Some statements

in red. She opened a drawer and brushed them inside with her hand.

'I can manage this, Pernille. Let me help you with the business. With the boys. I'll do whatever I can. I just . . .'

More papers. More bills. They seemed to be growing in front of her.

'I just want to help.'

Pernille strode up and slapped him on his cut, bruised face. As hard as she could.

He didn't flinch. Just put a hand up to his cheek. The wound had reopened with the blow. He wiped the blood away.

'How could you do that?' she asked. 'How could you?'

He swept away more blood with his hand, looked at her oddly.

'Theis thought he was doing it for you.'

'For me?'

'If it had been him, Pernille. If it was the teacher. What would he be now? Your hero? Or an idiot?'

She drew back her hand again. He didn't move.

'I shouldn't have told him,' Skærbæk said. 'I did my best to stop it. When I saw. Kemal would have been dead if I hadn't.'

'No. No more.'

He nodded. Went to the desk. Looked at the jobs for the following day.

She had to ask.

'Vagn. Back then. Twenty years ago. Before I knew him.'

'Yeah.'

'What was he like?'

He thought about this.

'Unfinished. Waiting. A kid. The way we all were.'

'The police showed me some pictures.'

'What pictures?'

'Someone murdered. A man. A drug dealer.'

'Oh.'

'What happened? Tell me the truth.'

'We all get stupid sometimes. Your parents thought that when you took up with Theis. Didn't they?'

'The police—'

'The police are trying to trick you.'

He came and peered at her. These two were close before she knew him. Thick as thieves.

'Theis didn't do anything, Pernille. Not a thing. OK?'

Kirsten Eller stuck out a flabby, sweaty hand.

'I'm so glad everything turned out well for you. All this unpleasantness was quite unwelcome.'

'Yes. Sit down.'

She planted her full frame on the sofa in his office.

'And you've sorted out your group. This is good.'

Hartmann took the chair opposite.

'I didn't have any choice, Kirsten. I had to do something.'

She had an image of a kind. Long coat to cover the weighty body. Permasmile. Owlish spectacles pushed back on a head of dyed brown hair as if she'd just come from a busy board meeting. Eller had been around City Hall for as long as he had. In a way she'd achieved more. By means he was beginning to appreciate.

'At least it's all over now,' she said. 'The polls are looking good. The media are starting to see which horse to back. So now we reap the benefits.'

'My thoughts exactly.'

She took a folder out of her briefcase and opened it.

'We have some suggestions for winning any floating voters out there. It's the undecided who'll put us in, Troels. Let's not forget it.'

He grinned at her, shook his head. Genuinely amused.

'What is it?' she asked.

'You're a wonderful actor. Quite a talent.'

The smile stayed. No response.

'Bigum would never have tried a trick like that without talking to you first. He went to Bremer. He came to you. And you gave him the nod.'

The smile went.

'Troels—'

'No. Please. Don't insult my intelligence by trying to deny it.'

'This is—'

'The truth,' he cut in. 'I know my people,

Kirsten. I know Bigum. He's not big enough or brave enough to do this on his own. Maybe you went to him. I don't care.'

This was clear in his head now. He wondered why it had taken so long to see it.

'They were acting out of fear. Not strength. Not courage. Fear. I guess you could smell it.'

She held up her hands.

'Troels. Before you say another word . . . under-stand this.'

'I'm giving you two choices.'

Kirsten Eller fell quiet.

'Either I inform the press and they paint you for the untrustworthy, disloyal, conniving bitch you are.'

He waited, head to one side, listening.

'And the alternative?'

'You step down. Let your deputy take over.'

Kirsten Eller turned to look at Rie Skovgaard happily making notes.

'You need me, Troels. You all need me. Think of—'

'No, Kirsten. I don't need you at all.'

She waited. Not another word. Then Eller angrily gathered up her things, stormed to the door. There she turned and looked at him.

'This was about winning. Not you. Don't flatter yourself.'

'I won't,' he promised.

She bustled into Morten Weber on the way out. He watched her go.

423

'What happened there?' Weber asked. 'I thought we were having a meeting.'

Hartmann got to his feet.

'Rie!' Hartmann called. 'Line up some press interviews for me. Pick friends.'

'What the hell's going on?' Weber cried.

'I was going to tell you. There wasn't time. Kirsten's resigning.'

'Jesus, Troels! We've fought for this alliance—'

'She put Bigum up to it. She wanted me out all along.'

'You can't keep rocking the boat like this.'

'Morten.' Hartmann took him by his frail shoulders. 'Bremer's been one step ahead of us every inch of this campaign. It's time we set the agenda. It's time we moved more boldly than him.'

'By firing everyone in sight?'

Hartmann's temper broke.

'She went behind my back. She tried to cut deals with Bremer. Then with Bigum. You need to change your thinking. We can knock Bremer off his perch without those mealy-mouthed sons of bitches in the Centre Party.'

'No, Troels! We can't. On our own we don't have the votes.'

Hartmann shook his head. Rie Skovgaard stayed silent, smiling.

'How long have we played these games, Morten? Twenty years? Always the same rules. Theirs. From now on we play by mine. Call the minority leaders

to a meeting tonight. Tell them I have an important proposition.'

'Half of them hate you,' Weber said.

'No more than they hate each other.'

'They're with Bremer!'

'Not if they've seen the polls. They're with
whoever's going to win.'

He looked around the campaign office. There
were posters everywhere, his own face. Modest
smile. Blue eyes wide open. The new broom
looking to sweep out the old.

Hartmann pointed to his portrait.

'That's me.'

'He filled the car the night Nanna died, ten days
ago,' Meyer said.

They were in the office looking at the CCTV
tapes. Black and white, split into four windows.
Date and time in the corner of each grainy
frame.

'The tapes run twenty-four hours a day. The
chances of finding it after all this time are pretty
slim, Lund.'

She was closest to the screen, looking. The
numbers. The shadowy figures moving between
the pumps.

Everything.

'Also,' Meyer added, 'all these people reuse the
tapes. So if it's that old—'

'It's not this one,' Lund cut in, popping out the
cassette.

'We've only got one left.'

'It's always the last.'

He took a deep breath.

'It's rarely the last, Lund.'

'Look at the screen. See something I can't. Please.'

He picked up a banana in one hand, a cigarette in the other. Lit the cigarette.

The video started. The date in the corner of the frames said 7th November.

'Shit,' Meyer muttered. 'It's from last Friday. Like I said. They reuse the tapes. That's why they're so scratchy.'

She took a sip of tepid coffee. Everyone else had gone home. A cleaner was sweeping along the corridor outside.

'Doesn't mean the rest of it's from the seventh, does it?' she said. 'When we had videotapes at home . . .'

Mark as a baby, back when she was married. They were all jumbled up together. Different months, different years. It was hard to keep track when you used the same cassettes over and over again.

'Fast forward,' she said.

Meyer worked the remote.

Black and white cars, hazy figures running around.

'Stop there,' Meyer said.

He clapped his hands and let out a whoop of joy. She looked at him. Big ears, big eyes. Big kid.

426

Meyer's face fell.

'I was trying to cheer you up.'

'It's the thirty-first,' Lund said.

'I know. That's what I was saying.'

Around eight p.m. He rewound, went too far, started moving forward more slowly.

They came to seven seventeen p.m. Four frames. Only one car.

It was a white Beetle.

'Shit,' Meyer muttered again.

'The clock's wrong. Why would you keep it accurate to the minute? Keep going forward.'

The Beetle left. No cars at all. Just empty concrete and the lights above the pumps.

Then at twenty minutes and thirty-seven seconds past seven a black car pulled onto the forecourt, to the pump in the right-hand upper frame, arriving with the jerky motion of a kid's stop-frame film.

Meyer squinted at the plate.

'That's the car,' he said.

It was raining. She hadn't seen that till now. Knew what it meant. Had to mean. It was that kind of case.

The door opened. The driver got out. He was dressed in a long dark winter anorak. The hood was pulled up over his head. He walked to the boot and the fuel cap.

His face didn't show for a moment.

'Sh . . .' Meyer began.

She put her hand on his.

'Patience.'

Round the boot to the pump. Face down every step.

'Come on, for Christ's sake,' Meyer whispered then took an anxious pull on the cigarette.

It was a pump with a card slot by the handle. They saw his hand go out, insert something, take it out.

No face.

He finished, went round the back to the fuel cap, then made for the door.

'Come on. Smile for the birdie. Just look at something, will you?'

Straight behind the wheel. Features hidden by the angle. The Ford drove off.

'Shit, shit, shit,' Meyer groaned.

'Wait a minute.'

She pressed the back button. Looked at the man working the pump.

Looked at his left hand. The way it stretched out and up to his head then took hold of something when he went to read the card numbers.

'I know who that is,' Lund said.

Meyer looked nervous.

'Don't tell me.'

'I'm going to City Hall. Want to come?'

Five minutes through the rain and the sparse night traffic. The security man was about to come off duty. He began squawking the moment Meyer waved the cuffs at him.

428

'I didn't do anything. I didn't do anything.'

'Good God,' Meyer said. 'I never heard that one before. You're coming with us, mate.'

'All I did was fill up the car.'

Lund followed as Meyer marched him to the door, thinking, listening.

'Before or after you snatched Nanna Birk Larsen?' Meyer asked.

The man in the blue city sweater looked at him aghast.

'I'm sixty-four years old. What the hell are you talking about? I didn't touch anyone.'

'Sit him on that bench over there,' Lund ordered.

'We need to take him in.'

Lund looked the old man up and down. Bent back. Lousy eyesight. He didn't seem to breathe too well.

'Tell us the truth,' Lund said. 'Tell us what really happened. Then maybe you'll keep your job.'

'My job? *My job?* It's because I was doing my job I've got you baboons in my face.'

Meyer shoved him onto the stone bench by the bike rack.

'They're never going to put you front of house are they, chum? Tell us what happened or you won't see daylight for sixteen years.'

The security man stared at him with a mixture of fear and outrage.

'Do I need to turn up your hearing aid, Grandad?' Meyer yelled.

'Where's the charge card?' Lund asked more gently.

He didn't say a thing.

'I'm trying to help,' she told him. 'If you don't talk now we're taking you in.'

'I took the card with me. I was going to put it back when I came in to work on the Monday. But then . . .'

'Then what?' Meyer asked.

'You people were here. Everywhere.'

'Why did you go to the school?'

'Why wouldn't I? My flat's round the corner. I walked home and saw the car there. One of our cars. Just left. I didn't understand. I knew the schedules. They were all supposed to be back.'

'And you had the keys?' Meyer said.

'No. They were still in the ignition. I guess the driver forgot them or something.'

He shook his head.

'I couldn't leave it there, could I? Keys in the ignition. Some thug would have had it before midnight.'

Lund was getting impatient.

'No. This isn't good enough. You could have called the campaign office. It was their car.'

'I tried,' he said very deliberately. 'They said the secretary was in Oslo. It's the city's car, you know. Not theirs. We own it. Our taxes—'

'You could drive me nuts,' Meyer spat at him. 'The girl—'

430

'I didn't know that girl. I didn't do anything. Except a favour.'

'What did you do with the car?' Lund asked.

'It belongs to Hartmann's pool. He's a flashy prick but that's not my business. Maybe he needed it. So I drove it to the petrol station, filled it up, and drove it back. Put the keys back.'

'Back? Back where?'

'Back here. Where else? There's a car park opposite. We keep the pool over there. So that's where I left it.'

She waited.

'I never gave it a second thought,' he said. 'Not until I read about the dead girl. And then . . .'

She sat down next to him.

'Then you kept quiet.'

He was fiddling with his glasses again. Licking his lips nervously.

Meyer sat down on his other side, gave him an evil smile, asked, 'Why?'

'A city official needs to stay out of politics. It's very important. We don't take sides. We don't get involved.'

'You're involved now,' Lund said. 'Very.'

'I thought I'd check the tapes to see who'd taken the keys. It was only right.'

'And?'

'It wasn't there.' He looked baffled. 'All I can think is whoever took the keys must have taken the tape too. How else—?'

'Oh for God's sake,' Meyer hissed.

'It's the truth. I'm telling you the truth. I'm sixty-four years old. Why would I lie? If they knew the tape was gone we'd all be in trouble. Those bastards upstairs can't wait to kick our arses. I've got one year left. Why should I carry the can for someone else? I brought that car back when I wasn't even on duty. And here you are treating me like I'm some criminal—'

'You are a criminal,' Meyer said. 'We've wasted a week chasing ghosts. There's a decent man in hospital and that kid's father in jail. If we'd known this from the beginning . . . Lund? Lund?'

She was on her feet, staring back into the Rådhus. The elegant tiled corridors. The shining wooden staircases. Crests and chandeliers. Plaques and memorials. All the trappings of power.

Someone had walked down here, taken the keys to the car in which Nanna Birk Larsen died. Taken the tape that would have shown who he was.

They'd been looking in the wrong place all the time.

'Show me. Show me where the car was.'

Meyer hesitated.

'The chief told us to call if—'

'Buchard can wait,' she said.

The council used a multi-storey garage across the road. Bare floors of grey concrete. The old security guy was getting scared.

'I parked the car here at half past seven that Friday.'

Third floor. Not a vehicle there any more.

'You're sure of the time?' Meyer wanted to know.

'Yes! Then I hung up the keys on the board behind our desk. Then I went home.'

Lund was looking at the ceilings, the walls, the layout of the place.

'Who's got access to your room?' Meyer said.

'Not many people. We're security, aren't we? But there was a party that night.'

'In City Hall?'

'Yes.' He scowled. 'One of their parties. Not what you'd call a party.'

He tried to smile at Meyer.

'Me neither. All piss and wind and cheap champagne. They always launch an election campaign with a party. A poster party they call it. Once the posters are ready they come and stand around and kid themselves they've won.'

'So what if there's a party?' Lund asked.

'You've got people coming and going. You can't keep track of everything. They leave their keys, they want their keys. You've got to show people where to find the room, take them for a piss.'

She waited.

'I wasn't there,' he said. 'If I was I'd try to keep control of things. But it's not easy. We don't man the place all the time. We can't.'

'So anyone could walk in and get the keys?'

'And the tape,' he added.

Meyer slapped his forehead and grunted, 'Wonderful.'

433

'Let's get hold of what's still there,' she said.

She turned to the security man.

'Whose party was it?'

He looked as if she ought to know.

'Hartmann. The one who keeps strutting round thinking he can boot old man Bremer out into the street. The ladies love him, I know. He makes a pretty picture. But honestly . . .'

A brief, grim laugh.

'Boys against men.'

Half past eight. Back at headquarters. Lund and Meyer in front of the PC, watching the security tapes. Buchard next to them, hands in pockets.

'We can't know who picked up the keys,' Lund said. 'Someone took that tape. But . . .'

She sat happy and comfortable in front of the screen, working the forward and back buttons, edging the video to the right place.

'At seven fifty-five this happened.'

Two cars left on the third floor of the garage. The black Ford on the far side of the image, a silver Volvo close to the camera.

At the right of the screen, two spaces along from the car in which Nanna died, a door opened from the staircase.

People started coming through. A family. Fresh from the party.

'Balloons,' Buchard said. 'You brought me here to see balloons?'

'Forget the balloons,' Lund said. 'Watch the background.'

A man. Two little kids with balloons. The Volvo was theirs. As they walked towards it a figure was just visible going through the shadows to the other vehicle. Little more than a shadow. A blur on the screen.

'How the hell do you see these things?' Meyer asked.

'I look. He's a man, about six foot two I'd say. At this point Nanna is still at the school party.'

The black Ford reversed just as Volvo man and his kids were getting into the car. Blocking the view.

'Later she stops by her teacher's. And then . . .'

The Ford headed for the exit, left of the screen, behind the car in front.

'Then I think she meets this man.' Lund watched the screen, caught by it, unaware she was smiling. 'Somewhere.'

She switched to another camera. The black Ford cruising along the garage. Then another on a corner. Turning towards the down ramp. The registration number was clear on the monochrome screen.

'That's him,' she said. 'XU 24 919. That's the car Nanna was found in.'

Cigarette in mouth, eyes shiny and tired, Meyer gave her a little salute.

'Thank you,' Lund said with a note of dry sarcasm.

'No, Lund. I mean it. Jesus . . .'

'We were wasting our time with the school. Nothing happened there. The car was back at the Rådhus garage all the time.'

'Someone's been taking the piss . . .' Meyer grumbled.

'We can rule out Hartmann and his staff,' she went on. 'We looked into them. The thing is . . .'

The two men waited.

'Nanna was going somewhere. The way she was acting at the party. Kemal said she picked up a school photo at his place for some reason. It's as if . . .'

'She was saying goodbye?' Meyer said.

'Maybe.' Lund shrugged, and tugged at the sleeves of her sweater. 'I think she was having an affair with someone. The parents suspect it too. They don't want to tell us. Perhaps they don't want to face it.'

'Birk Larsen's got history, chief. That teacher would have been dead.'

'Forget the parents,' Buchard ordered. 'They're stuck out in Vesterbro. What's going to get people like that into City Hall?'

Lund couldn't take her eyes off the screen.

'It's someone who cultivated her. Nanna was beautiful. Old for her years. Someone told her she was special. Gave her expensive gifts. Told her to keep quiet. To wait.'

She thought of the cramped bedroom above the garage in Vesterbro, full of books and souvenirs and mementoes. The clothes in the cupboard. The faint smell of a perfume that should have been beyond a teenager.

'Nanna had another life that no one knew about.'

'Doesn't work like that, Lund,' Meyer said. 'Someone had a clue.'

'Not Pernille. Or Theis maybe.'

'Someone,' Meyer insisted.

'Who've you told about this?' Buchard asked. 'The car being back in the City Hall garage?'

The question surprised her.

'No one except you. I'll get things started right now. Maybe there are some cameras in the street.'

Buchard strode out of the room.

'Maybe . . .' Lund said watching him.

The chief was in the corridor, visible through the glass. On his mobile.

'Is he calling his wife, do you think?' Meyer asked. 'Ordering a celebration pizza?'

Lund was back at the screen.

'What?'

'I was just wondering. You show him something like this. He doesn't say a word. Walks off. Calls someone.'

She waved away his smoke.

'I wish you'd stop that.'

'I worked in a little town down south before all this shit. No one ever complained about the smoke there.'

'Maybe you should go back.'

He looked a little down in the mouth.

437

'Can't,' Meyer said, nothing more.

Buchard marched back in.

'Check the guards' schedules and records. Pull in this old man who had the keys—'

'He didn't do it,' Meyer snapped.

'Bring me everything you can find on the staff.'

'It's not someone on the staff,' Lund said. 'They're not the kind of people to groom a pretty young kid like Nanna. Give her things she couldn't dream of. Pull tapes, fix keys, find places God knows where—'

'Look at the staff. Bring me what you find,' Buchard repeated.

She was thinking as she spoke. Couldn't stop even if she wanted.

'It has to be someone higher up. Someone who thinks they can get away with all this. Because we're beneath them. We're—'

'That's already been checked,' Buchard broke in.

'What?' Meyer asked.

Lund wanted to laugh.

'Checked? Who checked it? We're working this case. If we didn't check it—'

Buchard exploded.

'If I tell you it's been done it's been done. Now get going on the guards.'

Lund flew at him as he went for the door. Meyer wasn't far behind.

'No. This isn't good enough, Buchard. Who did you call?'

438

He was scuttling towards his office, back turned to them.

'Never mind who I call,' Buchard said and didn't even bother to turn.

'Wait, wait.' Meyer was mad too. 'This doesn't make sense.'

Buchard stopped, looked over his burly shoulder.

'Then I guess you must feel at home.'

'I want to know what's going on,' Lund demanded.

He turned. Big barrel chest pushed out. Face a picture of misery.

'Come with me,' Buchard said.

The two of them moved.

'Lund!' he barked at Meyer. 'Not you.'

She looked at the man next to her. Tried to smile.

Then followed Buchard, ignoring Meyer's bleats behind in the corridor.

The chief closed the door. She did smile then. She'd known this man all her working life. Had learned from him. Fought with him sometimes. Eaten dinner round his house. Even made up a foursome when she was married.

'You can tell me,' Lund said. 'It won't go any further. You know that.'

Buchard looked at her.

'You can tell that cretin too if you want. I don't mind.'

'Meyer's good,' Lund said. 'Better than he knows.'

The chief raised his hands. Took on that

arrogant, scholarly pose he used when delivering a lecture.

'If I say they're not involved,' he told her, 'they're not involved.'

She cocked her head, looked at him in disbelief.

'Listen, Sarah. I want this solved just as much as you do.'

'So why are you tying my hands behind my back?'

He didn't like that.

'I'm your boss. I decide what you do. I've made myself clear.'

Then he left.

Meyer marched up, wanting to know what the chief said.

'Nothing,' Lund told him. 'When we checked Nanna's mobile how far did we go back with the calls?'

'I don't know. A week or so. There was no one from City Hall showing there. Just kids and home.'

'Can you check it again? Go back further?'

The phone was ringing back in the office. She marched off to get it. Meyer followed, whining all the way.

'What did Buchard say? Lund? Lund!'

The call was from a radio journalist asking for a comment on the case and Hartmann's campaign.

'We heard the focus is now back on City Hall,' the reporter said. 'Why is that? Is Hartmann a suspect?'

'Who told you that?' Lund asked.

'Sources.'

'Well, ask your sources what's going on,' she said.

She passed the phone to Meyer.

'What did Buchard say, Lund?'

Her phone beeped. A text message. She looked at it. Got her jacket and her bag. Didn't know what to think.

'I have to go.'

'Where?'

'Keep me informed,' Lund said and heard him bawling out the reporter as she left.

She left the car on the pavement outside the station, lights on, unlocked. Left her jacket in the driver's seat. Raced down the stairs in her black and white sweater and jeans.

Raining again. No moon. A few people fleeing the weather and a couple of drunks spoiling for a fight.

The train to Stockholm was close to leaving. That long journey over the water by the Øresund Bridge. One she could have made herself. Any time. If only . . .

Five hours later Stockholm. The new life. Bengt and Mark. A quieter job. A different world.

He stood by the platform, coffee cup in hand, left arm in a sling, face still bruised and swollen.

Lund stopped for a moment. Wondered what to say. What to do.

He hadn't seen her. Had turned towards the train. She could walk away now and she wondered whether that might be for the best.

Instead she strode up to him, said to his back, 'Bengt.'

Saw the pain, physical and inward, in his familiar, craggy face as he turned.

The first thing you did was make excuses. Always.

'Something came up again. I'm sorry. There was a . . .'

Her eyes were welling up. The words didn't come right.

'Things happening.'

She jerked a thumb over her shoulder.

'Can we talk about it in the car?'

Something different in his eyes. An expression she'd never seen before. A distance. A look that almost seemed like pity.

'Really,' Lund said. 'I understand why you don't want to stay at my mother's. I didn't think we'd be there long.'

A hope. A plan.

'Let's find a hotel,' she said. 'We can get a family room. It won't take long.'

He was shaking his head and she wanted to find the words that would stop him.

'We rushed into things, Sarah,' he said in a voice that seemed remote and impersonal. 'Maybe it's for the best. Moving to Sweden . . .'

That sharp stinging pain was back in her eyes.

'No! We didn't rush anything. What do you mean?' A single tear escaped and ran down her right cheek. 'I want to do this.'

Her sleeve went to her face, as if she were one

more distraught kid at Nanna Birk Larsen's school.

'I want to be with you, Bengt. Please stay.'

'I can't watch this any more,' he said, then coffee cup in hand, embraced her once.

A short hug. The kind a friend gave. It didn't even feel like goodbye.

'Take care,' he said casually. Then climbed on the train.

Lund saw the station lights go blurry as she stood on the platform, watching the train pull out. Sobbing in a way she hadn't for years.

Words were never easy.

Not saying them anyway. What they signified, what the world meant in all its strange and impenetrable faces . . . these were matters that fascinated her in an obsessive, constant fashion.

She'd told Bengt she loved him. Not often. Not repeatedly. It seemed unnecessary. Importunate.

And it made no difference anyway. She was what she was and happy with it. The cost . . .

That rough wool sleeve fell across her face again, harsh against her eyes and skin.

For a moment the lights around her dimmed. She was back in the Pentecost Forest, amidst the dead trees with their shedding silver skin. Back chasing the man who chased Nanna Birk Larsen. Lost again, as Nanna must have been in those last few savage moments.

The dark wood . . .

Nanna fighting for her life amid the birch trunks.

Her own struggle through the shadows of the girl's violent death, Meyer fighting to keep up by her side. They had all disappeared into the woods too. Faced with a choice of forks in the road. Left or right. Up or down. The straightforward pathway hidden from view.

Alone.

In a way she had been from the very beginning.

Perhaps that was what Bengt recognized. That when he was out of sight he was out of her thoughts. That nothing mattered except what she saw ahead of her with those gleaming, searching eyes.

And even that now seemed a lie, a joke, a phantom flitting, laughing through the shadows.

For her there was no pathway. No right direction, no correct course. Only the search for it. The chase not the conclusion.

The train pulled out towards the straight and certain track that led to the Øresund Bridge.

A turning not taken. A path that soon would be lost and overgrown.

They were all in the darkness, hunting the quarry within them and without. Meyer grappling to keep his job. The Birk Larsens fighting over how to bury their grief. Even Troels Hartmann, the poster boy of politics. A striking, intelligent man haunted by a demon beneath the surface. Of that she was sure.

So perhaps, Lund thought, she wasn't alone at all.

★ ★ ★

444

Meyer called when she was back in the car.

'Hello? Cat got your tongue?'

'What is it?'

'I went to forensics and made them take another look at her phone. There were fifty-three numbers on her contacts list.' He paused. 'We were only given fifty-two.'

She couldn't face talking to him.

'Can this wait till the morning?'

'I found a list of the calls she made going back a couple of months. I compared it to the data on the phone. Someone's screwing us around here, Lund. The list wasn't complete. She made calls we were never told about.'

'Where are you speaking from?'

'Outside. You think I'm stupid, don't you?'

'No. I don't. Do I have to keep saying this?'

'Here's the worst part. The first person to see those lists and take a look at the phone was Buchard.'

Lund kept driving.

'That can't be right.'

'It's right, Lund. I don't like this. If Buchard is covering for someone it's got to be Hartmann. Everything points there.'

'Not now,' she whispered.

'If we can't talk to Buchard who can we talk to? Huh? Who pulls his strings? Jesus . . .'

She took the phone from her ear.

'Lund? Lund!'

The headquarters building loomed ahead in the

445

darkness, a pale grey palace, with so many curving corridors, offices and hidden corners, she could still lose herself there if she tried.

Sarah Lund kept going. Right past. On the way to what was, for now at least, home.

There were four minority parties on the Copenhagen City Council, right and left and somewhere in between, all bickering constantly, then pandering to Bremer to win a few prize committee chairs and paid appointments.

At a quarter to ten Hartmann had their leaders in his office.

He'd got a new shirt from the wardrobe, shaved, had Rie Skovgaard check him over. Combed his hair.

These people didn't get the smile. They were part of the game. They didn't need it.

'We represent five parties and five very different kinds of politics,' he said in a calm, practised tone. 'If we took the last election and added your votes to ours we would have had a clear majority.'

He paused.

'A clear majority. From what we've seen of the polls it's the same this time around. Maybe even better in our favour.'

Jens Holck, the leader of the Moderate Group, the biggest, the toughest nut to crack, sighed, took out a handkerchief and began to polish his glasses.

'Don't act bored, Jens,' Hartmann said. 'We're looking at the difference between victory and

446

defeat. Bremer knows it. Why do you think he's playing these games with me on TV?'

'Because you keep inviting it, Troels.'

'No,' Hartmann insisted. 'I didn't. What happened to me could happen to any of us if he felt you threatened him. That's the state the Rådhus is in. That's why we need a broad alliance that gets Bremer out for good.'

Mai Juhl was a small, intense woman who'd created the Environment Party out of nothing. She carried plenty of respect and little goodwill. Politics was everything for her, which seemed odd to Hartmann since she'd achieved precious little in her time in office.

'That's all very well but what do we have in common?' she asked. 'How could we—?'

'We've plenty, Mai. Education, housing, integration. The environment too. You're not the only one to care, you know. We've more common ground among us than you think.'

'And the role models?' On most conventional issues Juhl swung to the right. 'You'd do anything to keep them.'

'Yes,' he agreed. 'I would.'

'We're a million miles apart there.'

Someone else agreed.

He looked at each of them, picking the subject carefully from the research Morten Weber had provided.

'Leif. Last time round Bremer promised you he'd reduce CO_2 levels? Never happened. What's he

447

done for the elderly? Isn't that a key issue for you too? Bistrup? Did he create jobs like he promised? Jens? You used to say the city needed to attract families with children. What happened to all that?'

They didn't answer.

'Bremer took your well-meant commitments when he needed your support then threw them in the bin afterwards.'

He pushed their own election material across the table.

'If we were sitting round a TV studio now I'd tear you apart for this. You're asking for votes yet you never deliver on your promises. Because Bremer never delivers to you. It doesn't have to be that way. We can work together. We can compromise.'

He raised his shoulders in a gesture of indifference.

'We've all got issues we'll sacrifice. Me too.' Hartmann held up his own manifesto. 'This is a piece of paper, not the Bible. What matters is we win something. With Bremer you'll come away empty-handed and you know it.'

Hartmann got up, distributed Morten Weber's document around the table.

'I've drafted a collaboration between the five of us. Obviously it's only a beginning. Everything's up for discussion. You'll want changes. I welcome that.'

He went back to his seat, watched as they picked up the paper.

448

'I know it's a big step. But between us we have the talent and the energy and the ideas to make this city better. If we don't do something now he's back again. An administration stuck in the doldrums. No imagination. No fresh blood—'

'I think Bremer's done a good job,' Jens Holck broke in.

'So do I!' Hartmann said. 'Twelve years ago he was the right man. Now—'

'This is Copenhagen. Not paradise. I haven't seen anything from you that suggests you can be as good a Lord Mayor. Lately, more the opposite.'

'Fair enough. We should talk frankly. Let's see what the voters think.'

'And,' Holck added, 'you're on bad terms with Parliament. The Lord Mayor's there to negotiate the city's budget. If Parliament hates you they starve us. I really don't see this—'

'The way we deal with Parliament is through strength. If we have a broad alliance . . .' His hand swept the table. 'Then we can do better than Bremer. If they piss us off they piss off everyone. Don't you see?'

Jens Holck got to his feet.

'No. I don't. I'm sorry, Troels. I don't believe in you.'

'Won't you even look at the proposal?'

'I already did. Goodnight.'

Mai Juhl was leaving too.

'We couldn't do this without Jens,' she said.

The other three followed.

Alone in the office, in the blue light of the Palace Hotel's neon sign, Hartmann wondered whether he'd jumped the gun.

There'd never been a broad coalition like this before. Maybe it was madness. But madness had its place in politics sometimes. When the old order gave way a little chaos was only to be expected. That was when the bold would strike.

And he wasn't the only bold one around.

Morten Weber predicted Holck would reject the offer outright and the others follow. He rarely read the situation poorly. He also said they'd think about it offline. That before long someone would call.

Hartmann poured himself a brandy.

It took exactly seven minutes.

He looked at the name flashing on the phone and laughed.

Jens Holck was in the garden courtyard hidden in the heart of City Hall, smoking among the Russian vines and ivy next to the fountain.

'You're back in bad habits,' Hartmann said, looking at the cigarette. 'That's a shame.'

'Yes. It is.'

Holck was a couple of years short of Hartmann's age, about the same height and build, a one-time student leader, young-looking at first glance but worn down by underachievement. He had dark hair and black fashionable glasses, a bleak schoolmasterly face. He hadn't smiled

450

much of late. Or shaved either. He looked a mess.

'Didn't I make myself clear?' Holck asked.

'Very. So why did you call?'

Holck's head went from side to side.

'In case I could make myself a little clearer.'

'Jens. We've got to do something. The city's drifting. Bremer's administration is disorganized. The finances are a mess. He only listens to himself.'

Holck took a draw on the cigarette, blew smoke over the fountain.

'He's like a dying king,' Hartmann added. 'We all know he's not long for this world. But no one wants to mention it. Or say a word in case the old man hears.'

'Then maybe we should wait for the funeral. And pick up the pieces from there.'

Hartmann looked around the courtyard. They were alone.

'Did you hear about his trip to Latvia?' he asked.

Holck's head bobbed up. He was on the audit committee. Rie Skovgaard had been fishing there too.

'What about it?'

'Officially it was a visit to a company. Inward investment. But the expense account—'

'Been snooping have we, Troels? I thought you were the good guy.'

'I don't mess with public money.'

'We see the expenses. There wasn't a thing wrong with them.'

451

'What you saw was tampered with. Thousands—'

'Oh for God's sake. Is this your new politics? I don't give a damn if Bremer creams a little here and there. He's an old man and he's worked like a dog here. Always has. In spite of the miserable salaries and the godawful hours.'

'So we just carry on as we are?'

'Someone has to be Lord Mayor. Do you really think you're different?'

'Give me the chance.'

'And you *are* on terrible terms with Parliament. That's the heart of it. They don't like you, Troels. They don't like the way you preen yourself for the cameras. The women swooning. Your sanctimonious smugness. The way you think you're better than everyone else.'

Holck laughed, a short, harsh sound.

'Not me. I don't have that problem. I've known you long enough to see through the performance. Tell me. Are you running for the sake of Copenhagen? Or the benefit of Troels Hartmann? Which matters most?'

'You called to tell me this?'

'Pretty much,' Holck said, then threw the cigarette into the fountain and walked off.

Ten minutes later.

'You're wasting your time on Jens Holck,' Morten Weber said. 'He's Bremer's lapdog.'

'Then let's throw him the right bone. They were interested, Morten. They were wavering. If I'd got

452

Holck on side they'd all fall in line behind him. In a heartbeat. Do we have any food?'

Weber bowed, said, 'At your service.'

Then went off to find something.

'So if we don't placate Jens Holck we're sunk?' Skovgaard said.

She sat on the desk, feet on his chair, chin propped on her hands. She didn't look unhappy with the idea.

'No,' Hartmann insisted. 'We know who we are. We're strong.'

Skovgaard held out her arm, flexed her bicep.

'I'm strong too. Feel.'

Hartmann laughed, came to her, tested her arm with his fingers.

'Not bad. One more thing.'

He bent down. Her arms went round his neck. They kissed. Fingers though hair. Grey business suit against black business dress.

She stayed in his embrace, said dreamily, 'It seems a long time since that happened.'

'When this is over I will take you somewhere with the biggest, softest, warmest bed . . .'

'When it's over?'

'Or sooner.'

'Is that a politician's promise?'

Hartmann pulled away from her, smiling.

'No. It's mine. Call your father and get him to talk to the Interior Minister. Tell me what I have to do. Just a word from Parliament. Holck will hear it.'

Morten Weber walked back in with a dinner plate full of sandwiches.

'The car park's crawling with policemen,' he said.

'Why?' Skovgaard asked.

Weber frowned.

'Search me.'

Lotte Holst was eleven years younger than her sister Pernille, pretty enough to hold down a job behind the bar of the Heartbreak Club for five long and eventful years. The place catered to businessmen, young executives, anyone with enough money to pay two hundred kroner for a weak cocktail. It was near Nyhavn, close to the hordes of tourists heading for the canal boats and the restaurants.

She had her hair up, glossy lipstick, a revealing halter dress open at the midriff, and a permanently bored smile as she served up bottles of Krug and vodka to the deafening music.

The money was good. The tips better. And sometimes there were surprises.

Around eleven one of the barmen came over and said she had a visitor.

Lotte walked to reception, saw Pernille there in her fawn raincoat, hair a mess. Put a hand to her own head, felt embarrassed, the way she always did as a kid.

Pernille was pretty. But she was the beautiful one. Everyone said that. No one knew why it was

Pernille who got married, even to a rough and inarticulate man like Theis, not her.

Her sister was rocking to and fro. She looked terrible. There was a small storeroom next to the cloakroom. They went there, sat on beer crates. Lotte listened.

'I didn't want to bother you,' Pernille said.

'Then why . . . I mean. It doesn't matter. The boys are round with Mum. They're OK.'

'I know. I asked.'

'I have to work, Pernille.'

'I know that too.'

'Have you heard from Theis? When he's coming home?'

'No. The lawyer's doing her best.'

She hugged herself in the stained raincoat even though the little room was stifling.

'Did Nanna say anything to you about . . .'

The words died.

'About what?'

'I don't know. You were so close. Like sisters.' There was something accusing in her eyes. 'Closer than I got.'

'You were her mum.'

Pernille was starting to cry.

'She told you everything! She told me nothing.'

The door was open. One of the security men was watching them.

'She didn't . . .'

'Nanna had a life I didn't know about! I'm sure of it.'

'I don't know what you mean, Pernille.'

'What did she say? Were there problems at home? With me? With Theis?'

'No . . .'

'Sometimes we argued. She never stopped. Always coming and going. Taking things. Wearing my clothes.'

'She wore my clothes too,' Lotte said. 'Never asked.'

'Did she . . . ?' The tears again, closed eyes. An agony Lotte Holst didn't want to see. 'Did she hate us?'

Lotte put a hand on her sister's arm.

'Of course not. She loved you. Both of you. And the boys. She never said anything.'

'No?'

'No.'

'So it's just me?'

The security man was making signs. She wasn't supposed to take breaks from work. Not more than five minutes an hour.

'Something happened last summer,' Pernille said. 'Between her and Theis.'

She nodded, as if trying to recall a specific incident.

'When I look back I can see it. She was always Daddy's girl. She could wind Theis round her little finger. Then they suddenly stopped doing things together. She didn't tell me.'

'Theis thought it was too early for her to move out. She was a bit upset.' Lotte shrugged. 'That's all. She was nineteen. She wasn't a kid. It was nothing.'

456

'You're sure?'

'You have to stop thinking about it so much. Theis was a good father. He still is. Even if he did something stupid.'

The barman was at the door, beckoning her.

'I've got to go. I don't want to get fired. Listen.'

She squeezed her hands.

'I'll come round tomorrow and do what I can. Come on. You can get through this.'

She got Pernille to her feet, embraced her, took her to the exit.

Went back, made drinks for rich businessmen, smiled when they leered.

Then waited an hour till the break came again, walked into the toilet, took out the coke, snorted a long, expensive line, trying not to cry.

Tuesday, 11th November

Eight in the morning. Lund was watching the security tapes from the garage. Again. The family, the kids with the balloons getting into the silver Volvo. The black Ford pulling away.

Meyer came in with news. There was no sign of any connection between Nanna Birk Larsen and City Hall. She never worked there as staff or volunteer. Didn't even seem to have visited on a school trip.

'I've been through her things again,' he added. 'That key ring we found.'

He showed her an evidence bag.

457

'What about it?'

'They're not hers. Not for home.'

Lund had pushed those to the back of her mind.

She took the bag off him. They were Ruko keys. Used everywhere.

'They don't look like anything they use at City Hall,' he said. 'They have all these old fancy locks. I don't know . . .'

'Later,' she said. 'Can we enhance the picture? Zoom in on the driver and see what he looks like?'

'In theory.'

'Then let's do it.'

Meyer hesitated.

'Buchard says this has all been checked.'

She pointed at the reports.

'I can't see anything about it in here.'

'You heard him. I don't want any part in this.'

He came and sat down next to her. Looked almost humble.

'I really don't want to spell this out. But this . . .' He looked round the office. 'This is my last chance. Things didn't go too well in a couple of other places.'

'A couple?'

'I use that in a broad sense. I've got to keep this job. I have to.'

'Is that why he didn't kick us off the case?' she wondered. 'Because he's got us where he wants?'

Meyer stared at her with his big, sad eyes.

'If I was Buchard I would have fired us by now,' Lund added.

'The next time you're going to say something like that will you please warn me. So I can put my hands over my ears.'

'They're big ears. It won't work.'

'Thank you. If Buchard says it's been looked at—'

'No one's looked at this. You don't believe that either.'

He had his hands over his ears.

Quickly he took them away and said, 'He's coming.'

The chief marched in.

'You wanted to talk to me?'

Lund smiled.

'I wanted to say sorry about yesterday. We were both tired.'

Meyer nodded.

'Tired,' he agreed.

'No problem,' Buchard said. 'So long as we're making progress.'

'Progress.' She nodded. 'We are.'

'Good.'

He was ready to go.

'Who checked the contacts and the list of calls on Nanna's mobile?' Lund asked.

Buchard froze in the door.

'I don't know,' he said.

'Something might point to one of the guards. Maybe. I don't know.'

'Look into it.'

Another smile.

'I will,' she said.

They watched him go.

'What would you have been?' Lund asked. 'If you weren't a cop?'

'A DJ,' Meyer said. 'Did it when I was a student. I was very good. Except the face.'

He ran his hand over his bristle and cheeks.

'I don't know if I've got the looks.'

She laughed.

'And you?'

'Nothing,' Lund said. 'I'd have been nothing.'

'I did consider running a hot dog cart once,' Meyer added. 'You're your own boss there. Maybe one day soon. The way we're going. Lund?'

She was somewhere else.

'Nothing at all,' Lund said.

There was nothing to look at in the phone records. But twenty minutes later a detective stuck his head through the door with news. A taxi driver had appeared in the office after one more run by the night team pushing out pictures of Nanna. He said he thought he might have picked her up the night she died.

'I don't believe it,' Meyer said.

'Believe what?'

'This is the first time anyone's volunteered a damned thing about that poor kid. Didn't you notice, Lund? Everyone else expects us to be mind-readers.'

He rubbed his stubbly chin.

460

'They do want us to find this bastard, don't they?'

The taxi driver was called Leon Frevert, a tall, skinny man in his mid-forties. He had a long grey face that matched his cheap suit and smelled of cigarettes and sweat. Straight from a night driving a cab round the city.

'I'm not positive it's her,' Frevert said, looking at the photos they'd given her.

'Forget whether it was her or not,' Meyer ordered. 'Tell us what happened.'

He worked weekends driving a cab for one of the city firms.

'I picked her up on Friday. If it was her. We talked a bit. She wanted to go into town. I dropped her off on Grønningen, near the junction with Store Kongensgade.'

Long straight street at the edge of the city. Next to the Kastellet fortress. Nowhere near any of the addresses they'd looked at.

'You've got a receipt?'

'Sure. You're in trouble if you haven't.'

Frevert pulled a bunch of papers out of the pocket of his threadbare suit.

'I think it was this one. I picked her up near Ryparken. See.' He pointed to the receipt. 'The ride started at ten twenty-seven p.m. Finished at ten forty-five.'

Lund asked, 'What happened when you got to Grønningen?'

'She got out. I found a new customer straight

461

away. Didn't even have to drive off. Plenty of work on Fridays.'

He scratched his thinning fair hair.

'The thing is we didn't go direct. We stopped. You don't get that so much with kids. They don't have the money.'

'Stopped where?'

'On Vester Voldgade. At the back of City Hall.'

Meyer closed his eyes and groaned.

'What happened there?' Lund asked.

'She got out and asked me to wait. I wouldn't do that normally. They just run off. But she seemed a nice girl. She wasn't drunk or anything.'

'What did she want at City Hall?'

'She didn't say. She went inside for a couple of minutes.'

'Did you see anyone with her?'

'No. She came out. And then we went to Grønningen. I don't want to waste your time. I can't promise it was her.' He glanced at the photos again. 'Maybe, but . . .'

'Thanks.'

She shook his hand, waved at Svendsen who was wandering down the corridor outside, asked him to take a statement.

Then the two of them sat in the office alone.

'There are lots of hotels around there,' Lund said.

'We've been round the hotels.'

'Then go round again. Ask them if they've seen

a politician. If anyone from City Hall lives nearby. Are you working on the guards?'

He was getting tense and angry. Wouldn't look at her.

'Yes. I certainly am.'

'The taxi took her from Kemal's house to City Hall,' Lund went on.

'He said he wasn't sure if it was her.'

She didn't want an argument. Meyer was scared for his job. Torn, she guessed. Between what he thought was right and what he thought was smart. For himself.

'I've an appointment,' she said getting up, grabbing her jacket. 'Call me when you hear something.'

Rie Skovgaard had been putting out feelers to Parliament overnight. Hartmann's relations with the Interior Minister remained good.

'The problem's the Prime Minister. He thinks you're ambitious. You steal the limelight. He thinks you'll come for him if you unseat Bremer.'

Hartmann listened, shook his head.

'I'm not coming for him. Not for four years anyway.'

Morten Weber was reading the morning papers.

'At least the polls are staying with us. No one believed that nonsense about the girl.'

'If we've got the Interior Minister on board that's enough.'

'Only if the Prime Minister allows it,' Skovgaard said. 'He could still sink you.'

'This is ridiculous. We're in the same party. And they're backing Bremer?'

She was smiling at him.

'Out with it,' he said.

'There's one possibility. The Prime Minister's not doing well at the moment. He could use some of your limelight.'

Hartmann felt out of his depth for a moment. Skovgaard and Weber swam so easily in these muddy waters.

'What are you getting at?'

'He's never caught on to the integration issue properly. If we said his office helped put together our programme. Helped with role models. Some of the school projects . . .'

Hartmann laughed.

'Not a chance. We came up with that. They hated the idea.'

'Forget the past, Troels. If we give them credit—'

'For what?'

'For anything. So long as we get their backing.'

'It's a lie!'

Weber's head went from side to side.

'Lie's a very strong word. This is politics. What's true . . . what's untrue. After a while it doesn't matter so much.'

'Then what does matter?'

'What works,' Weber said, looking at him as if he were a simpleton.

'No. It's out of the question.'

464

'OK,' Skovgaard said and stared at the sheets in front of her.

'OK,' Weber agreed and read the paper.

A long minute's silence.

'I'm glad to see you're working well together,' Hartmann noted.

'We usually do,' Skovgaard replied.

'The answer's still no.'

Another long minute.

Then Hartmann took a long deep breath, looked around at the wooden walls, the leaded windows, the crests and gilt, up at the fancy artichoke lamp.

All the trappings of office. None of the power.

'What would we get in return?'

'We could invite him to your campaign meetings,' Skovgaard said.

'The most important thing is to get Holck into the deal,' Weber added. 'I hate this shit as much as you do.'

He shrugged.

'But if it can bring us the alliance . . .'

'Find out exactly what we can expect in return. I don't want any escape routes.'

'If we ask that question we've already said yes,' Weber told him. 'No going back.'

'No going back,' Skovgaard repeated.

'Cut the deal then make me an appointment. With the Prime Minister. If it gets us into office I don't give a shit who gets the credit.'

He got up from the table, walked out.

The two of them sat there, uneasy allies.

'Any news on why the police were in the car park?' Skovgaard asked.

'What?'

'You heard, Morten. You hear everything, even if you pretend you don't.'

'No news that I know of. I'll call Parliament.'

'I can do that. This is policy. You leave it to me.'

There was a new man round from the bank. Younger. Friendlier. Pernille had called the jail, tried to talk to Theis, failed. He was going to be kept in for another day at least. No phone calls but at least she might be able to see him later.

'Sorry,' she told the bank man. 'I can't talk to my husband.'

'No problem.' He spread out the papers in front of her. 'So let's assume the house will go on the market while you continue the renovations.'

'OK.'

'We'll extend your credit so you don't have to pay the instalments. Let's hope the house sells quickly so we can break even.'

'That's fine by me.'

'Then there's the account your daughter opened.'

She stared at him.

'In Anton and Emil's names. Where should that money go?'

Pernille brushed back her hair.

'What account?'

He pushed forward a statement.

'It's got eleven thousand kroner in it. She was a steady saver. It's a lot of money . . .'

'What kind of account?' she asked.

'It's a savings account for the boys.'

'Can I see?'

She snatched the statement before he could answer. Stared at the figures. Regular deposits. Hundreds of kroner a time. Never a withdrawal.

'Where did she get the money?'

'From a job?' the man suggested. He was blushing, embarrassed.

'She didn't have a job. She worked for us from time to time. But that was pocket money. Not this . . .'

He shrugged, said nothing.

The account was opened the previous January. Regular deposits every fortnight. They stopped in the summer.

'There's no rush,' he said. 'You don't have to make a decision right now. Well . . .'

A brief smile. He stood up.

'Unless there's something else.'

Pernille couldn't take her eyes off the bank statement. It sat on the table, above the family pictures captured in the surface. Taunting her. Laughing.

When he was gone she called the prison again. Found someone amiable.

'I'll come now,' she said.

The guard let Pernille into the tiny prison interview room then stood by the door. Theis sat

467

hunched at a scratched wooden table in a bright-blue prison suit, eyes on the floor.

A moment of indecision. Then Pernille walked over, threw her arms round him, felt him clasp her, felt the tears rise in her face.

The two stayed locked together, rocking gently, his huge hand moving through her long chestnut hair as if looking for something that was lost.

Then they sat down opposite each other, Pernille's eyes swimming as she cried.

Finally he asked, 'How are the boys?'

'The boys are fine.'

He wouldn't look at her as he spoke.

'I talked to the lawyer. She's doing everything she can. When I get out I'll take care of the bank and the house.'

She turned away, wiped the tears. Felt a stiff hot flicker of anger and couldn't work out why.

'I'll fix everything,' he said. 'It'll be OK.'

Looking out of the window at the monochrome day beyond she asked, 'What happened between you and Nanna last summer?'

His head went up. His eyes – they were the part of him she liked the least – caught her. Unreadable. Aggressive sometimes.

'What?'

'You used to . . .'

The tears were coming again and she couldn't stop them, however hard she tried.

'Did you have an argument? Did you say some-thing to her?'

468

Her voice was breaking and it was full of unintended blame.

'What do you mean?'

Two decades she'd been with this man. There were always secrets between people. Perhaps there had to be.

'Nanna opened a bank account in the boys' names,' Pernille said. 'She made regular deposits. She had a job. The account . . .' She said this very slowly. 'It had eleven thousand kroner in it.'

'You know she had a job! With us.'

'She didn't earn that kind of money with us.'

'Maybe I paid her extra. Or she saved it up.'

'Then why keep it a secret?'

'I don't know.'

She'd no idea whether she believed him or not.

'Nanna never said anything to you?'

'No.' He rubbed his bearded chin, closed his eyes. 'She was angry with me. I know that. I thought it was too early for her to move out.'

He reached over and took her hands across the table.

'I used to give her money to cheer her up sometimes. What she did with it . . .'

'Yes,' Pernille said.

'That's all I can think of.'

She watched him trying to smile. Trying to say what he always said.

I will fix this. Things will get better.

So she smiled back, squeezed his hands in return,

came forward over the old wooden table and kissed him.

'Everything's going to be OK,' he said again.

Lund drove to the TV station to see a reporter who was making a documentary about the election campaign. The woman was following Hartmann and Bremer from beginning to end.

'I'm just interested in what happened on the night of the poster party,' Lund said.

They were seated in front of a screen, the woman flicking through unedited video.

'What do I get out of this?'

'Nothing.'

The TV woman blinked.

'It's only fair—'

'No it isn't. I could get a warrant in five minutes. If I do that you won't work again today. We'll take everything.' Lund smiled at her. 'If I think there's evidence here I can stop you using this.'

'So why should I show it you?'

'Because you don't have a choice.'

'I still want something.'

'If there's a story you'll get it first. If there's a story . . .'

Lund sat on the edge of the desk, not moving an inch.

'All I need is footage from seven p.m. to eight p.m.'

'The poster party was October the thirty-first?'

'That's right.'

'OK. I remember that. They were in Hartmann's office.'

Her fingers flashed across the keyboard. Then she scrolled through the footage. Poul Bremer came on the screen, laughing and joking, glass in hand.

'I love the way they pretend they respect each other. You should hear what they say in private.'

'Like what?'

'They smile and smile and hate each other's guts. And they'd climb into bed with anyone if it'd get a few votes.'

Lund was watching the screen, barely listening.

'Hartmann invited everyone into his office for a drink.'

Skovgaard, the leaders of the minority parties, Morten Weber, Bremer, all together, laughing and joking over glasses of wine.

'Does anything interesting happen?' Lund asked.

'Hartmann gives a short speech. Nothing special. No point in wasting effort on this bunch, is there? Either they're voting for him or they're not.'

Lund leaned forward, looked more closely. There was a figure in black at the back of the crowd. Talking to no one. Looking uncomfortable.

'Who's that?'

'Jens Holck. Leader of the Moderates. He's behind Bremer.'

'Was he there all evening?'

'Yep.'

Hartmann clinked a glass against a bottle. Poul Bremer came and stood next to him beaming, genial.

Lund wasn't watching them. Her eyes were on the figure at the back.

'So why's Holck putting on his coat?'

She didn't answer.

'Is there any more footage of him?'

'Why do you ask?'

'Curiosity.'

Lund nodded at the keyboard. The woman worked it, set the video to run more quickly.

The camera scanned the room. She went forwards, back, looking round the sea of bodies.

'I can't see him. I thought he was there. Sorry.'

'What's he like?' Lund asked.

'Holck? Been in politics for years. Serious. Bit of a loser. Nothing without Poul Bremer.'

She sat back in her chair, put her hands behind her head.

'Not exactly oozing charm if I'm honest with you. There was some gossip about him having an affair and getting found out. It never made the papers. His wife's divorced him though.'

'He had an affair? Is that true?'

The woman laughed at her.

'You don't know politics, do you?'

'Enlighten me.'

'They feed off gossip. Off one another. They live in this little world of their own and nothing else matters. I'll tell you something . . .'

Lund waited.

'Anybody who had an affair with Jens Holck must have been pretty desperate. Or they had a high boredom threshold.'

Lund called Meyer as she left the TV station.

'The car left at seven fifty-five. Jens Holck slunk out of the poster party fifteen minutes earlier and wasn't seen again.'

'Buchard's been asking for you,' Meyer said.

'Does Holck live near Grønningen? It might even be a hotel room.'

'I couldn't care less, Lund.'

'The talk in City Hall is that he's been having an affair.'

'We're not making inquiries at City Hall. Not with the politicians. Leave it. Didn't I mention Buchard was asking for you?'

'You did.'

'Were you listening by any chance?'

She looked at the phone. Tried to imagine Jan Meyer's face at that moment.

'Lund?' said a tinny, uncertain voice from the speaker. 'Lund?'

She found Troels Hartmann as he was leaving his office.

'I need two minutes of your time,' she said.

'Does your boss know you're here?'

'It'll only take a moment. I just wanted to apologize.'

473

'You need to leave,' Rie Skovgaard said. 'You've caused us no end of problems.'

'I know, I know. I'm sorry. This is a difficult case. Two minutes . . .'

Hartmann waved her into the office and closed the door.

'I need your help,' she said.

'I have a citizens' surgery on Mondays. You can make an appointment like anyone else.'

'What if I said your car wasn't at the school?'

'Then I'd say you'd screwed up again.'

'What if I said it was driven back here? To the City Hall car park?'

He was silent.

'That Friday night. When you held your poster party. All the group leaders. All your campaign workers.'

'What the hell is this about, Lund?'

'I need to know if anyone left the party early.'

'Wait, wait. I don't understand. You're saying the car was brought back here?'

'Did anyone leave early?'

Skovgaard walked in. She was on the phone. Saying, 'Can I speak to Buchard now?'

'Did Jens Holck leave early?' Lund asked.

'Holck?'

Skovgaard was through, whining to Buchard.

'Do you remember seeing him later in the evening?'

Hartmann shook his head.

'Your boss wants to talk to you,' Skovgaard cut in, offering the phone to Lund.

474

She stared at this woman. Attractive in a hard, unemotional way. It never seemed to touch these people that a young girl had died. No one except Hartmann, and that still interested her.

'Yes?' Lund said, taking the phone, not really listening.

When it was done she passed the handset back to Hartmann's smiling campaign manager.

'Get out of here,' Skovgaard said.

Lund looked around her. At the wooden walls, the panelling, the beautiful lamps, the expensive furniture.

'This place must feel like a castle,' she said.

'Go,' Skovgaard repeated.

Lund glanced at her, then, lingering more, at Hartmann.

'It's not a castle,' she said.

Back in her empty office Lund took a cigarette from Meyer's pack, rolled it in her fingers. Did all the bad things. Turned it round, tip to end, juggled it, smelled it. Lifted it to her lips, felt the dryness as she put it in her mouth, lit the thing and breathed in the choking smoke.

It didn't taste good. It didn't make anything better. It just was.

Outside Buchard was briefing the team, in a voice pitched loud enough for her to hear.

'Lund starts her new job in Sweden tomorrow,' the chief told them. 'Meyer takes over. Svendsen, you're Meyer's assistant.'

He'd taken her name off the door already. Now it simply said: Vicekriminalkommissær Jan Meyer.

Buchard came in to see her straight after. He looked at the cigarette.

'I've informed the Swedish police you're ready to start there. I refrained from telling them about your activities.'

'My gratitude knows no bounds.'

She took a suck on the cigarette and looked at him. Buchard wasn't good at shifty.

'I'm sorry things had to end this way,' he added.

'You're the only one in this place who rates Svendsen.'

A flicker of anger in his pug eyes.

'That's the last thing you have to say to me?'

'No. There's more.' The cigarette was starting to feel good now. 'But you've probably got calls to make.'

When he'd gone Meyer came in, stood by the sign with his name on it. He didn't seem happy.

'We couldn't find anything around Grønningen. Anything that links in Holck.'

Svendsen stuck his head around the door. He was smiling.

'There's a delivery from Sweden, Lund,' he said. 'You need to sign for it. Before you go.'

Emphasis on the last word then a big grin.

'I will,' Lund said. She pointed at the cigarette. 'When I'm done.'

Lund watched him wander off, turned to Meyer,

pointed at the retreating Svendsen and said, 'He's theirs, Meyer. Not yours. Remember.'

Then she went to the window. A yellow removals van stood below, the driver waiting by the door.

'I've got some guy waiting in forensics,' Meyer said. 'So . . .'

She blew smoke out of the window, remembered how many times she'd scolded him for doing the same.

'You can keep the packet.'

One more pull, one more lungful out into the damp November air.

'Lund?'

'Thanks,' she said and didn't look at him.

When he was gone she went to the desk, went through the plastic evidence bags, found Nanna's keys, the Rukos on a red plastic ring, and pocketed them.

It was starting to rain. Bengt had sent back what things she had in Sweden. She opened up the first case. Clothes and bedding, nothing she could use.

So she signed for them, made a call to the company, ordered storage, then watched the yellow van drive off with a part of her life still inside. Gone until she reached some point in the future she still couldn't begin to imagine.

The lawyer, Lis Gamborg, saw Birk Larsen in his cell.

'Vagn's been questioned. He confirmed he encouraged you to take revenge against the teacher.'

'He didn't do that. He tried to stop me.'

'That's what he says. It's to your advantage. Let's leave it there. Vagn will be charged as an accessory. He's not looking at jail.' She paused. 'You are.'

Birk Larsen took a deep breath, stared at the grey concrete floor, said nothing.

'I argued that you wouldn't try to abscond. That you'd suffered enough. You wouldn't interfere with witnesses, since you've already pleaded guilty.'

'And?'

She shrugged.

'And you're free to go.'

In his blue prison suit Birk Larsen felt like a child being gulled by a performer on stage. He didn't like tricks and maybe she realized that.

'Provided,' she added quickly, 'you don't leave Copenhagen. And under no circumstances must you interfere with the investigation again. I mean that, Theis. If you do anything else . . .'

'I won't do anything. I just want to go home.'

'Good. For your sake and your family's it's important you keep a low profile. Don't talk to the media. Don't get involved. Go back to the way you were.'

He stared at her.

'As much as you can. I'm sorry. That was thoughtless of me. You can get your things now. Theis . . .'

She hesitated over something.

'What?' he asked.

'People have got such sympathy for you. For

478

Pernille. But sympathy's like a dripping tap. One little turn . . .'

The lawyer made a twisting gesture with her hand.

'Then it's off. What replaces it may not be so nice. Be invisible. Be patient. I'll see you when we come back to court. If no one's heard a word of you in the meantime then maybe I can keep you out of jail.'

He nodded.

She smiled then left him alone, in his blue prison suit and black boots. Unshaven, unwashed. Thinking about the strange world beyond the door.

Pernille took the call, shrieked with a sudden burst of joy. Called Lotte round to look after the boys, shuffled on her coat before getting the car.

Her sister came straight away with a bagful of shopping, ready for the night. Sweets ready, and a book.

Families ran on these daily rituals, all taken for granted, all so painful when the reason for them was gone.

Lotte started running the bath, got the boys in. Pernille went for her keys.

One packet of sweets only, she thought, and looked in Lotte's shopping bag.

Plenty of crisps and snacks. Some shampoo. The kind of things a woman on her own bought in such small quantities it seemed ridiculous.

A pile of letters. Lotte must have picked them

up on the way out, brought them round to read while she was babysitting.

The top one was square and formal, a card in an envelope.

It bore Nanna's name and Lotte's address.

Squeals from the bathroom, the noise of Lotte scolding them.

'I want the duck,' Emil cried.

'Not until you stop splashing,' Lotte said.

Without a thought Pernille reached in, took out the square envelope, ripped it open.

The card was silver with an ornate Christmas tree. An invitation to a staff Christmas party for a nightclub in the centre. Four weeks away.

She stared at it feeling cold and stupid and betrayed.

'Where's the duck?' Lotte asked by the bathroom door. 'Oh. Right.'

She'd found it. Then looked. Saw.

'Nanna worked with you all along,' Pernille said, the card in her hands. 'She gave them your address. That's why we never knew.'

Lotte came over, stared at the card, retreated, guilty.

'When did she start there?'

Little sister, little sister, Pernille thought. I never did trust you really.

'In January.'

Lotte had the evasive, shifty look of the naughty child she once was.

'She only started as a temp. She left last summer.'

480

Pernille held the card and waited.

Lotte licked her lips, tried to get hold of herself. Look convincing.

'She didn't plan it. She came to visit me and thought it seemed . . .' Lotte shrugged. 'Exciting.'

Pernille looked around their little apartment. The cramped rooms. The photos on the walls. The table they made. The books. The TV. The kids. The close and intimate thing called family.

'Exciting?'

'It just happened. I didn't see any harm in it.'

She didn't know whether to cry or scream. To fly at Lotte or run away.

Instead she asked, 'What happened last summer?'

Lotte folded her arms. Confident in herself now. Afforded an escape route.

'Maybe you should talk to Theis.'

'Charlotte. You're my sister. Tell me what happened.'

Sounds from the bathroom. The boys giggling, splashing.

'She liked the job. Then she started seeing someone. A man.'

'Who?'

'Someone she met there. I don't know who. She wouldn't tell me.'

'Did he give her money?'

Lotte looked sly again.

'Why do you ask?'

'Just tell me. Did he give her money?'

481

'I don't think so. It wasn't like that. She started to turn up late for her shifts. Then one day she didn't turn up at all. I was worried.'

Pernille knew what was coming, had to hear it.

'I called Theis,' Lotte said. 'I'm sorry. We found her in a hotel room. She was dead drunk. It was when you were away with the boys on the school trip. Nanna promised she'd stop seeing him. She promised Theis.'

Pernille laughed at the idea, laughed and held back her head, let the tears begin to flood her bright eyes.

'I'm sorry,' Lotte said again.

Pernille walked over, took the towels off her and the rubber duck.

'I want you to go now,' she said.

'Pernille—'

'I want you to go.'

The debate was in the Black Diamond, the angular glass building by the water that housed the Royal Danish Library.

Still the Nanna Birk Larsen case haunted Troels Hartmann. Rie Skovgaard and Morten Weber had bickered about little else in the car.

'Lund thinks the car was driven to City Hall,' Hartmann said as they walked into the library. 'Why? Why would anyone drive it back?'

'If any of this was important,' Skovgaard cut in, 'we would have heard of it. Lund's off the case. I told you.'

'So that's why the police were in the car park?' Weber asked.

'Doing what?' said Hartmann.

Weber shrugged.

'I don't know. Whatever police do.'

They got out, walked through the doors.

'This is a public event, Troels,' Skovgaard said. 'Time to smile.'

He wasn't in the mood.

'Why did she ask me about Holck?'

On the escalator, rising towards the busy crowds above.

'The only thing that matters about Holck is whether he's with us or not.'

'No,' Hartmann insisted. 'We need to know what's going on. I don't want all that shit again.'

'The shit came from Lund!' she barked at him. 'Lund's gone. Focus on the meeting. This is important.'

'I need to know!'

'Jesus, Troels . . .' Skovgaard muttered and wandered away.

Weber watched her, looked at Hartmann.

'For once I'm with her. Think about the meeting. We can deal with the rest later.'

Then they wandered off into the audience while Hartmann lugged his briefcase to the podium.

Bremer was there already. Immaculately dressed. Smiling as always. A little flushed under the lights.

'Welcome, Troels,' he said, shaking Hartmann's hand. 'You've been fishing in troubled waters, I hear. Did you catch anything?'

A laugh. A hard slap on Hartmann's shoulder. Then a wave to the crowd, some private gestures to people he maybe knew and maybe didn't.

All the politician's tricks and habits. Troels Hartmann had learned them, from Bremer mostly. Could summon them up too. But then . . .

A figure in a crumpled black suit entered from the right. Bremer leapt up, took Jens Holck by the hand, made a point of saying, 'Good evening, old friend. Sit by me, Jens . . . . Sit.'

He pulled up a chair. Holck looked at it.

'No thanks.'

Walked on, looked at the empty seat next to Hartmann.

'Is this free? I've been thinking . . .'

'If you want it, Jens.'

'I believe I do,' Holck said and sat down.

Grønningen ran straight along the side of the Kastellet grounds for half a kilometre. There were buildings, apartment blocks, on one side only. Nanna's Ruko keys didn't work in any of the front doors.

After Lund wasted half an hour testing every lock there she checked the short road at the south, Esplanaden. Nothing.

She called Meyer.

'I need your help,' Lund said.

'You were wrong about Holck. He drove off in his own car that night.'

'Did you check if any party members owned flats around Grønningen?'

'We did. No one does. And there are no politicians living nearby. The Liberals own a flat on Store Kongensgade.'

'Whereabouts?'

'What are you up to?'

'Where?'

'Number hundred and thirty.'

Lund walked the short way into the street, checked the numbers. It was back to the north, closer to Grønningen. Store Kongensgade was a long and busy road that ran all the way from close to Østerport Station into the city itself. The taxi driver, Leon Frevert, said he dropped Nanna near to the junction between the two streets. She should have worked this out earlier.

On the left ran lines and lines of low, old ochre-coloured houses. The naval cottages of Nyboder, laid out in low rows in the dark like soldiers frozen to attention.

'It's on the fourth floor,' Meyer said. 'Where are you?'

A massive building. Red brick, white facings gleaming in the street lights. Grand communal entrance. Lots of bells. A Ruko lock.

'It's irrelevant,' he added. 'We've checked out Hartmann already. Lund?'

485

'What?'

'Where are you? What's going on?'

'Nothing,' she said, then put the phone in her pocket.

Two keys. One for the outside. One for the apartment.

Lund walked up to the double door, put the first key in the lock, turned.

Nothing.

Tried the second.

The door opened.

The lift was gleaming and ancient, double folding doors, room for no more than four inside.

She got in, pressed the button for the fourth floor. Listened to the mechanism whirr and hum.

The place seemed empty. She rose past offices and dentists' surgeries, past private apartments and places that bore no name.

Then the lift stopped. Lund got out and started to look around.

Meyer was back in forensics, going through the video from the car park again. The black car pulling away. The driver just out of sight.

'Stop it there,' he told the technician. 'What was that? It looked like a flash of light.'

'It's the fluorescent tube. On the way out. Flickering.'

'Go back, back. Take it step by step.'

Seven frames. Just visible in the driver's window,

illuminated by a single brief flash of light, was the face of a man.

'Who the hell is that?' Meyer asked, trying to stifle his impatience. 'Can you enhance it?'

'I can try.'

His phone rang.

'It's Lund.'

'Good timing. We're about to find out who was in the car.'

'It was Troels Hartmann,' Lund said.

'What are you talking about?'

Silence.

'Lund? Lund? Where are you? What's going on? Talk to me. Please.'

'I'm in the Liberals' flat in Store Kongensgade. Nanna's keys open the door to the block and the door to the flat. Call forensics. Meet me here.'

'Hartmann?'

'That's what I said.'

The screen was rendering the enhanced image. A face was emerging out of the grey murk. Angular and handsome. Grim-set and familiar.

Meyer thought: Poster Boy. You're mine.

'We're on our way,' he said.

A full team were in place within the hour. Ten men in the blue uniforms of forensics, white bunny suits, white gloves at the ready. Floodlights. Cameras. Chemicals.

Lund had a second unit outside, in the courtyard behind the block, was walking among them, checking their work, offering advice and opinions, some of them well received, others plainly ignored.

Meyer brought her coffee. Buchard didn't say a word.

She took the two of them through the front door, into the noisy old lift.

'The taxi driver dropped her off on Grønningen at quarter to eleven. I imagine she didn't want anyone to know she was coming here. Nanna could have been in the flat four or five minutes later. It belongs to the Liberals. A donation from a supporter. They use it for work lunches, meetings, putting up guests.'

'Who lives in this place?' Meyer asked.

'Most of the units are offices or corporate accommodation. It was pretty much empty all weekend.'

They got to the fourth floor. Lund walked to the flat, showed them how Nanna's key worked.

'She had one for the front door too?' Buchard asked.

'Yes.'

Six technicians in bunny suits and blue plastic mob caps were working in the interior. The place was decorated like a luxury hotel suite. Red velvet wallpaper, old, stylish furniture.

'We've found her fingerprints already,' Lund said, handing them forensic gloves and shoe covers to wear.

When they were ready she led them in.

Posters of Troels Hartmann were scattered round the room. There was a broken glass table and splinters from what looked like a tumbler on the floor.

Lund walked to the table, showed them the marks on the carpet.

'The blood's Nanna's type. I've sent away for confirmation it's hers. There was some kind of fight.'

There was a heavy walnut desk by the window.

'We've got prints on the paperweight there. Nanna threw it at the mirror for some reason.'

Lund turned three hundred and sixty degrees on her heels, looking at the room. The broken glass. The disorder.

'She didn't just fight him. She got mad. Lost her temper I think. This wasn't random. Unexpected. She knew him. It was an argument. A lovers' tiff gone wrong.'

'We've got lots to send to forensics,' Meyer broke in. 'With a bit of luck we'll have a DNA result by tomorrow afternoon.'

Lund walked into the bedroom. The door was open, covered in forensic marks and stickers.

'Nanna ran in here and tried to block the door. He kicked it open.'

The bed sheets were ruffled as if someone had sat on them, nothing more.

'I don't think he raped her here. Or beat her up. That was to come. Somewhere else.'

Lund tried to imagine what had happened. An argument. A fight. But Nanna didn't die for another two days. A big piece of the jigsaw was still missing.

She walked outside onto the terrace.

Meyer and Buchard followed.

Buchard stood still, Lund eyeing him.

'If you went down to forensics and checked the video you know perfectly well Hartmann was on the surveillance tape,' Meyer added. 'I got that in two minutes, Buchard. You're no fool.'

'I want to talk to Lund alone,' the chief said.

'Enough of that shit!' Meyer shouted. 'I'm sick of it.'

He slammed his hands on the iron railings.

'Buchard! Buchard! Look at me! I want to know what's going on. You owe us that. Both of us.'

The old man looked downcast, lost, defeated somehow.

'It's not what you two think.'

'What is it then?' Lund asked. 'You erased a name from her mobile. You deleted a call from the list.'

'No I didn't.' It was a weak, pathetic whine. 'It wasn't me.'

'Who was it then?'

He didn't answer.

'We're bringing in Hartmann for questioning,' Lund announced.

'And we want that information,' Meyer added.

He stood on the cold terrace, panting. Someone's servant. Not a happy one.

'Well?' Lund asked.

'I'll get it for you.'

'Good,' she said and then they left him there, pop-eyed and breathless in the dark.

The three of them were back in Hartmann's office feeling satisfied. The debate had gone well. Morten Weber said the minority leaders were meeting in the morning to discuss the alliance.

'If we've got Holck,' Skovgaard said, running to her computer, 'the rest of them will come too. What changed his mind?'

Hartmann was the only one who looked unhappy.

'I don't know. He didn't say. Why was Lund asking about him? What's all this about the car?'

Skovgaard waved him away.

'If Holck's involved I need to know.'

'I left Meyer a message.'

'That's not good enough.'

Weber was getting wine from the cupboard, putting out sandwiches he'd brought.

'No surprises, Morten,' he said. 'That's what you want too.'

'No surprises.' Weber uncorked the wine, poured three glasses, toasted them both. 'Jens Holck's just following his nose, Troels. He knows you're going to win. Don't complicate things unnecessarily.'

Skovgaard's phone rang.

'Bremer looked worried as hell,' Weber added. 'He can feel the ground disappearing beneath him.'

Skovgaard spoke quietly into the phone, ended the call. Looked at Hartmann.

'That was the police,' she said.

'And?'

'They want to talk to you.'

'Oh for God's sake—'

'Troels. They want you to go to police headquarters. Now.'

'Is this about Holck and the car?'

'It didn't sound like it.'

'Then what could it be?'

'I don't know. They said straight away. Either that or they come here for you. I really don't want that.'

Hartmann's glass stopped halfway to his mouth. He slammed his hand on the table. Dark burgundy spilled over the walnut veneer.

Then he got his coat. So did Skovgaard. So, after she stared at him stuffing his face, did Morten Weber.

Ten minutes later they were crossing the open courtyard, heading for the spiral staircase that led to homicide.

Lund waited with Meyer and Svendsen outside the interview room.

'I only asked for you, Hartmann,' she said, looking at Skovgaard and Weber.

'I really don't have time for this.'

'We want to talk to you alone.'

'What's this about?'

Lund indicated the door.

'Just take a seat.'

Skovgaard was getting mad.

'If this is an interrogation say so. We've taken so much shit from you, Lund.'

Meyer smiled at her.

'It's just a few questions. A politician ought to help the police, surely.'

'If he wants a lawyer you can call one,' Lund added.

Hartmann glared at her.

'Why in God's name would I want a lawyer?'

They didn't answer.

Hartmann swore, walked into the room, indicated for Skovgaard and Weber to stay outside.

Lund and Meyer sat opposite him, showed him the video of the car leaving the parking garage.

'Looks like one of ours,' Hartmann said. 'But there are a lot of black cars out there.'

'Any idea who's driving?' Lund asked.

He shrugged.

'No. Why should I? If it's important I can ask one of our people to check.'

'You don't need to,' Meyer said. 'We're police remember.'

He hit some keys on the computer. Zoomed in. Face on the screen. Just to rub in the point he passed over a printout.

Hartmann stared at her.

'Right,' he said. 'It was after the poster party. I gave my driver the night off. So I borrowed a campaign car.'

Lund smiled. Svendsen came in with some coffee. Hartmann relaxed a little.

'You left the poster party early?' she said.

'I had a headache. And a speech to write.'

Lund poured him a cup.

'Where did you go?'

'We've got a flat on Store Kongensgade. I thought I'd go there to finish the speech. Why?'

'Who has a key to the flat?' Meyer asked.

'I do. There's a spare key in the office. Some other officers too, I think. I don't really know.'

'But you use the flat?'

'I told you. What is this?'

Lund shuffled some photos on the table, let him see them.

'The car you drove is the car Nanna was found in. It was driven back to City Hall that night. You drove it away.'

He shook his head, said nothing.

'What happened in the flat?' Meyer asked.

'It can't be the same car,' Hartmann said.

'What happened in the flat?' Meyer asked again.

'Nothing. I was there for a couple of hours.'

'So was Nanna Birk Larsen,' Lund said, fetching some new photos. 'She had a key. She was attacked there. Then driven away in the car you took.'

Lund pushed the photos from Store Kongensgade across the desk. Broken table, shattered mirror. Glass on the floor. Fingerprint markers.

'In our flat?' Hartmann asked finally.

'How long did you know her?' Meyer asked.

494

Hartmann couldn't take his eyes off the pictures. Slowly he flicked through them, mouth open, face frozen.

'I didn't know her. I never met the girl.'

Meyer snorted.

'The car. The flat. The fact you never mentioned any of this.'

'There was nothing to mention! I took the car. I went to the flat. I had a couple of beers. Then I decided to walk home.'

They said nothing.

'On Monday morning I came to pick up the car but it was gone. I assumed someone from the campaign office had gone in and found the keys. I left them on the table. Someone must have taken them.'

Meyer sighed.

'Why did you take the surveillance tape? So we couldn't see it was you in the car?'

'What? I didn't take any tape.'

'Your number was deleted from Nanna's mobile,' Lund added.

'That's not possible. I didn't even know the girl.'

'What did you do with the rest of the weekend?' Meyer asked.

Hartmann swore and got up.

Lund strode to the door, blocked it, looked at him. He was agitated and angry.

'Are you going to tell us or not, Hartmann?'

'Why the hell should I? My private life's my own business. None of yours.'

'This isn't about your private life . . .' Meyer began.

The door got pushed open. In walked Lennart Brix.

Brix.

Buchard's new number two. Fresh from one of the regional forces. A tall and striking man with an angular unsmiling face. He'd arrived two weeks before, kept himself scarce. Now he looked as if he owned the department.

'I'm the deputy chief here,' Brix said. 'Good evening.'

He walked straight over, shook Hartmann's hand. Stood next to him, turned to Lund and Meyer and Svendsen.

'I understand there's a problem,' Brix said.

Five minutes later. Lund lit her second cigarette of the month as she watched Hartmann leave with Skovgaard and Bremer by his side. Jan Meyer stood next to her chewing gum.

Brix saw the three of them out then came back to the office.

Black shirt. Black suit. Shiny black Italian shoes. He looked like a politician himself.

'Hartmann told me he took the car in good faith. He clearly left the flat before the girl arrived. He's willing to talk about the flat. You can question his employees as much as you need. You don't even have evidence she was raped there, Lund. She might have just had an argument with someone.'

496

'We don't want to talk to his employees,' Lund said.

Brix leaned against the door, watching her. A fixed, determined man.

'If you'd asked nicely you'd have discovered he had an alibi. You're looking for someone who had Nanna Birk Larsen all weekend. Hartmann left the flat around ten thirty and went to Rie Skovgaard's.'

'He said he went home.'

'His relationship with Skovgaard is a private matter. He wishes to keep it that way.'

'If these damned people told us the truth . . .' Meyer began.

'The next morning they went to a conference centre where they had meetings all day.'

'Can we check that?' Meyer asked.

'You don't need to.' He pointed at the pair of them. 'The next time you pull in someone like Hartmann I suggest you do your homework first.'

They watched him go. Lund passed the half-smoked cigarette to Meyer.

'Let's check the alibi. See if anyone else from City Hall uses the flat. Everyone in Hartmann's office comes in for questioning.'

She looked at Meyer.

'Are you OK with that?'

'Oh yes,' he said.

Svendsen came back in with a message. Pernille Birk Larsen was coming in. She wanted to see Lund urgently.

'We don't have time. If it's about her husband being in custody . . .'

'It can't be that. He got let out.' Svendsen shook his head, laughed. 'She didn't even come to meet him, Lund. You should feel flattered.'

Theis Birk Larsen walked home to Vesterbro. Twenty minutes in the rain through deserted streets.

Pernille wasn't there. Nor were the boys. In the kitchen, by the pot plants and the photographs, he phoned her, got nothing more than voicemail, waited five minutes, phoned again.

Just after eleven a door slammed downstairs. He ran down into the garage. Lights on. Vagn in his red overalls and black woollen hat, looking at the diary in the office.

Skærbæk looked surprised to see him.

'Have you seen Pernille, Vagn?'

'When did you get out?'

'Just now.'

'That's good. What happened with the teacher—'

'Have you seen her?'

Skærbæk looked baffled.

'Lotte came round to babysit. She wasn't here long and then they left.'

Birk Larsen stood by the office, hands in pockets, trying to make sense of this.

'Why?'

'I don't know.'

'Where to?'

'Christ, Theis! I don't know.'

498

Birk Larsen glared at him.

'You did talk to her?'

'I thought she went to pick you up.' Skærbæk hesitated. 'Didn't she?'

Birk Larsen went back upstairs. Called again. Got nowhere.

Pernille Birk Larsen brought her sister Lotte to headquarters. Dragged her there by the looks of it.

Lund listened then asked, 'Tell me about this club, Lotte. The Heartbreak.'

'It's for members. Private. Invitation only.'

Meyer sat silent, scribbling notes.

'What did Nanna do?'

'She waited on tables. I always kept an eye on her.'

'Nanna liked the place?'

'Sure. It was exciting. Different.'

'Different?' Meyer asked.

'Different from taking calls for a removals company.'

Pernille sat in the corridor beyond the glass. She'd refused to leave.

'How did you know she was seeing someone?'

'She missed some shifts and kept asking for time off. It seemed . . .'

She was a pretty woman, but with a sad and pasty face that spoke of late nights and maybe something else.

'It seemed innocent.'

'Then something happened?'

'One night she didn't turn up. I called Theis and told him about it. We drove around looking for her. I got a call from a hotel near the station. She gave them my number.'

Lund watched her, wondering.

'Why did she get a room?'

'She'd had too much to drink. She was upset. I think the guy had dumped her. He wasn't there. It was just Nanna.'

'Did she do drugs?' Meyer asked.

'I don't think so.'

'Did she talk about the man?'

'I think he was married or something. She was really secretive. She wouldn't tell me his name. Nanna . . .'

A long pause.

'It was kind of a time when a kid falls in love with someone different every week.'

'But she didn't,' Lund said. 'This went on for months.'

'That time. She always called him Faust.'

'Faust?' Lund checked, writing this down.

'It's not his real name.'

'It wouldn't be. Why did she call him that?'

'I don't know.'

Meyer chipped in.

'This was spring and summer. She didn't talk about him after that?'

'No.' Her eyes strayed to the figure in the corridor. 'Pernille thought this might be important.'

500

'She was right,' Meyer said and left it at that.

'Did she tell you where she and Faust used to meet?' Lund asked.

'Hotels, I think.'

'Do you know which ones?'

Lotte Holst was trying to remember something.

'It was hotels in the beginning. Later on I think they went to a flat.'

'A flat?'

'Yeah. I remember she said it was really cool. Old furniture. Very expensive.'

Lund waited. When there was nothing else she said, 'Whereabouts?'

'I don't know.' One more memory. 'All she said was it was near the old navy houses. The yellow ones they take you to on a school trip.'

'Nyboder?' Lund asked, staring at Meyer.

'I think so.'

'How about Store Kongensgade?'

Lotte blinked.

'Yes. That was it.' She looked at them both. 'How did you know?'

Lund got back to her mother's flat just after ten. Meyer called as she was walking up the stairs.

'There's no one called Faust on the Heartbreak Club's membership list. Hartmann's people have been on to say we can only talk to him through a lawyer from now on.'

'Is anyone from his office a member?'

'Not that I can see.'

501

The flat was dark and silent. And empty.

'It's an alias, Meyer. Remember Faust? The good man who was tempted by the Devil? Go to the club and ask around.'

'Can't you hear the music? Where the hell do you think I am?'

There was something in the background. Tinny disco and a million voices.

Lund kicked off her boots and turned on the kitchen light then opened the fridge.

Nothing.

There was a saucepan of stew on the hob.

'I can't see a politician prancing round this place,' Meyer said. 'People would know. But maybe he doesn't come here.'

She put the phone on speaker, placed it on a kitchen top and lit a low flame beneath the pan.

'What do you mean?'

'The club has a dating chat room on its website. People meet up online. Maybe that's it.'

The stew didn't look as if it would improve with cooking. Lund got it to tepid then picked up a spoon and took a taste from the pan.

'I'll have a specialist take a look,' Meyer said.

There was a Carlsberg in the fridge. She cracked the crown top and took a swig from the neck.

'OK,' she said, starting on her second spoonful. 'Let me know if something turns up.'

'Oh, lucky you,' Meyer moaned. 'Getting something to eat. I haven't had a bite since lunch.'

Lund looked at the pan.

'Yes. Lucky me.'

She went to the sofa with the stew, realized she was still in her coat, shrugged it off, threw it on the floor.

Then she turned on her laptop, sat there going from the pan to the beer to the computer.

Meyer was right. The Heartbreak had a dating section. Open to anyone, not just members of the nightclub.

She clicked for a new profile. Filled in the form as Janne Meyer. Female. Heterosexual. Password: bananas.

Her mother came back as she was waiting for the confirmation email.

'Where's Mark?' Lund asked.

'We went to see a film with Magnus. I bought them pizza afterwards. He wanted to spend the night at Magnus's. I said it was all right.'

Vibeke smiled sourly at her.

'You weren't around to ask.'

The confirmation message came through. Lund clicked on the acceptance link and found herself in the Heartbreak's dating forum.

'It's fine for him to stay there,' she said.

Her mother busied round the room doing nothing.

'How are you?' she asked.

'I've just eaten. It's been busy.'

'Are you getting anywhere?'

'Yes. I'm still doing things. Sorry.'

There was a search box at the bottom of the page. She typed in 'Faust'.

'Mark talked to his father today.'

The site was slow to load. Lund took another swig of beer.

'About what?'

'He's coming to Copenhagen. He'd like to see Mark. Mark didn't know if you'd be in Sweden or not.'

'This is dragging on. He can see Mark.'

'Yes. We noticed that.'

Vibeke came and stood at the door, staring at her with that mix of anger, sympathy and bafflement she'd made her own.

'The storage company called about the things Bengt sent back from Sweden. They wouldn't take your boxes into storage without an account. So I said they could leave them here. They're in the basement.'

Then she went to the bathroom without another word.

Lund was glad. She didn't know what to say.

Bengt.

That odd farewell on the station seemed an age away.

She looked at the laptop. There was one result called 'Faust'.

Lund clicked on it.

No photo. Just a silhouette. Next to it a quotation. It read: 'Ruling the heart is the most difficult thing.'